Praise for #1 *New York Times* bestselling author Sandra Brown

"When it comes to telling stories that are suspenseful, complex and romantic, no one does it better than Brown... Looking for excitement, thrills and passion? Then this is just the book for you!"
—*RT Book Reviews* (4½ stars, Top Pick) on *Seeing Red*

"Brown is an excellent and almost effortless writer.... The chemistry is undeniable."
—*Kirkus Reviews* on *Sting*

"Brown crafts facets and depths of characters in a taut novel full of surprises."
—*Booklist* on *Sting*

"[An] exceptional romantic thriller... Brown handles the romance with her usual panache and adds some nifty plot twists that will keep readers guessing."
—*Publishers Weekly*, starred review, on *Sting*

"Deft characterizations and eye for detail make this a winner.... Satisfying, vintage Brown storytelling."
—*Kirkus Reviews* on *Deadline*

"Pulse-pounding...a relentless pace and clever plot."
—*Publishers Weekly*, starred review, on *Lethal*

D0965047

**Also available from
Sandra Brown**

Previously published under the pseudonym
Erin St. Claire

THE THRILL OF VICTORY
HONOR BOUND
THE DEVIL'S OWN
TWO ALONE
A SECRET SPLENDOR
LED ASTRAY
TIGER PRINCE

SANDRA BROWN

TWO ALONE

&

A SECRET SPLENDOR

PREVIOUSLY PUBLISHED UNDER THE PSEUDONYM ERIN ST. CLAIRE

HQN™

HQN™

Recycling programs
for this product may
not exist in your area.

ISBN-13: 978-1-335-00806-0

Two Alone and A Secret Splendor

Copyright © 1987 by Harlequin Books S.A.

The publisher acknowledges the copyright holder
of the additional works as follows:

Two Alone
Copyright © 1987 by Sandra Brown

A Secret Splendor
Copyright © 1983 by Sandra Brown

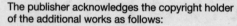

Printed in U.S.A.

CONTENTS

ISBN-13: 978-1-335-00806-0

Two Alone and A Secret Splendor

Copyright © 1997 by Harlequin Books S.A.

The publisher acknowledges the copyright holder
of the individual works as follows:

Two Alone
Copyright © 1987 by Sandra Brown

A Secret Splendor
Copyright © 1983 by Sandra Brown

All rights reserved. For use in any manner, the reproduction or
utilization of this work in whole or in part in any form by any
electronic, mechanical or other means, now known or hereafter
invented, including xerography, photocopying and recording, or in any
information storage or retrieval system, is forbidden without the
written permission of the publisher, Harlequin Enterprises Limited,
225 Duncan Mill Road, Don Mills, Ontario, Canada M3B 3K9.

This is a work of fiction. Names, characters, places and incidents are
either the product of the author's imagination or are used fictitiously,
and any resemblance to actual persons, living or dead, businesses,
establishments, events or locales is entirely coincidental.

This edition published by arrangement with Harlequin Books S.A.

For questions and comments about the quality of this book,
please contact us at CustomerService@Harlequin.com.

® and ™ are trademarks of Harlequin Enterprises Limited or its
corporate affiliates. Trademarks indicated with ® are registered in the
United States Patent and Trademark Office, the Canadian Intellectual
Property Office and/or other countries.

www.Harlequin.com

Printed in U.S.A.

TWO ALONE

CHAPTER ONE

THEY WERE ALL DEAD.

All except her.

She was sure of that.

She didn't know how long it had been since the impact or how long she'd remained bent over with her head in her lap. It could have been seconds, minutes, light-years. Time *could* stand still.

Endlessly, it seemed, torn metal had shifted before settling with a groan. The dismembered trees—innocent victims of the crash—had ceased to quiver. Hardly a leaf was stirring now. Everything was frightfully still. There was no sound.

Absurdly she thought of the question about a tree falling in the woods. Would it make a sound? It did. She'd heard it. So she must be alive.

She raised her head. Her hair and shoulders and back were littered with chips of shattered plastic—what had previously been the window next to her seat. She shook her head slightly and the chips rained off her, making tinkling, pinging little noises in the quiet. Slowly she forced herself to open her eyes.

A scream rose in her throat, but she couldn't utter it. Her vocal cords froze. She was too terrified to scream. The carnage was worse than an air-traffic controller's nightmare.

The two men sitting in the seats directly in front of hers—good friends, judging by their loud and rambunctious bantering with each other—were now dead, their joking and laughter forever silenced. One's head had gone through the window. That fact registered with her, but she didn't look too closely. There was a sea of blood. She slammed her eyes shut and didn't open them until after she'd averted her head.

Across the aisle, another man lay dead, his head thrown back against the cushion as though he'd been sleeping when the plane went down. The Loner. She had mentally tagged him with that name before takeoff. Because the plane was small, there were strict regulations about weight. While the passengers and their luggage were being weighed before boarding, the Loner had stood apart from the group, his attitude superior and hostile. His unfriendliness hadn't invited conversation with any of the other passengers, who were all boisterously bragging about their kills. His aloofness had segregated him—just as her sex had isolated her. She was the only woman on board.

Now, the only survivor.

Looking toward the front of the cabin, she could see that the cockpit had been severed from the fuselage like a bottle cap that had been twisted off. It had come to rest several feet away. The pilot and copilot, both jovial and joking young men, were obviously, bloodily, dead.

She swallowed the bile that filled the back of her throat. The robust, bearded copilot had helped her on board, flirting, saying he rarely had women passengers on his airplane and when he did, they didn't look like fashion models.

The other two passengers, middle-aged brothers,

were still strapped into their seats in the front row. They'd been killed by the jagged tree trunk that had cut into the cabin like a can opener. Their families would feel the tragedy with double intensity.

She began to cry. Hopelessness and fear overwhelmed her. She was afraid she would faint. She was afraid she would die. And she was afraid she wouldn't.

The deaths of her fellow passengers had been swift and painless. They had probably been killed on impact. They were better off. Her death would be long in coming because as far as she could tell, she was miraculously uninjured. She would die slowly of thirst, starvation, exposure.

She wondered why she was still alive. The only explanation was that she was sitting in the last row. Unlike the rest of the passengers, she had left someone behind at the lodge on Great Bear Lake. Her goodbye had been drawn out, so she was the last one to board the aircraft. All the seats had been taken except that one in the last row.

When the copilot assisted her aboard, the rowdy dialogues had ceased abruptly. Bent at an angle because of the low ceiling, she had moved to the only available seat. She had felt distinctly uncomfortable, being the only woman on board. It was like walking into a smoke-filled room where a heated poker game was in progress. Some things were innately, exclusively male, and no amount of sexual equality was ever going to change that. Just as some things were innately, exclusively female.

An airplane leaving a hunting and fishing lodge in the Northwest Territories was one of those masculine things. She had tried to make herself as inconspicuous

as possible, saying nothing, settling in her seat and staring out the window. Once, just after takeoff, she had
turned her head and inadvertently made eye contact
with the man sitting across the aisle. He had looked at
her with such apparent disfavor that she had returned
her gaze to the window and kept it there.

Besides the pilots, she was probably the first one
to notice the storm. Accompanied by dense fog, the
torrential rain had made her nervous. Soon the others
began to notice the jouncy flight. Their braggadocio
was replaced with uneasy quips about riding this one
out and being glad the pilot was "driving" instead of
one of them.

But the pilots were having a difficult time. That
soon became apparent to all of them. Eventually they
fell silent and kept their eyes trained on the men in
the cockpit. Tension inside the aircraft increased when
the two-man crew lost radio contact with the ground.
The plane's instruments could no longer be depended
upon because the readings they were giving out were
apparently inaccurate. Because of the impenetrable
cloud cover, they hadn't seen the ground since takeoff.

When the plane went into a spiraling nosedive and
the pilot shouted back to his passengers, "We're going
in. God be with us," they all took the news resignedly
and with an amazing calm.

She had bent double and pressed her head between
her knees, covering it with her arms, praying all the
way down. It seemed to take an eternity.

She would never forget the shock of that first jarring
impact. Even braced for it, she hadn't been adequately
prepared. She didn't know why she had been spared instantaneous death, unless her smaller size had allowed

her to wedge herself between the two seats more securely and better cushion the impact.

However, under the circumstances, she wasn't sure that being spared was a favorable alternative. One could only reach the lodge on the northwestern tip of Great Bear Lake by airplane. Miles of virgin wilderness lay between it and Yellowknife, their destination. God only knew how far off the flight plan the plane had been when it went down. The authorities could search for months without finding her. Until they did— if ever—she was utterly alone and dependent solely on herself for survival.

That thought galvanized her into action. With near-hysterical frenzy she struggled to release her seat belt. It snapped apart and she fell forward, bumping her head on the seat in front of her. She eased herself into the narrow aisle and, on hands and knees, crawled toward the gaping tear in the airplane.

Avoiding any direct contact with the bodies, she looked up through the ripped metal seam. The rain had stopped, but the low, heavy, dark gray clouds looked so laden with menace they seemed ready to burst. Frequently they belched deep rolls of thunder. The sky looked cold and wet and threatening. She clutched the collar of her red fox coat high about her neck. There was virtually no wind. She supposed she should be grateful for that. The wind could get very cold. But wait! If there was no wind, where was that keening sound coming from?

Holding her breath, she waited.

There it was again!

She whipped her head around, listening. It wasn't

easy to hear anything over the pounding of her own heart.

A stir.

She looked toward the man who was sitting in the seat across the aisle from hers. Was it just her wishful imagination or did the Loner's eyelids flicker? She scrambled back up the aisle, brushing past the dangling, bleeding arm of one of the crash victims. She had studiously avoided touching it only moments ago.

"Oh, please, God, let him be alive," she prayed fervently. Reaching his seat, she stared down into his face. He still seemed to be in peaceful repose. His eyelids were still. No flicker. No moaning sound coming from his lips, which were all but obscured by a thick, wide mustache. She looked at his chest, but he was wearing a quilted coat, so it was impossible to tell if he were breathing or not.

She laid her index finger along the top curve of his mustache, just beneath his nostrils. She uttered a wordless exclamation when she felt the humid passage of air. Faint, but definitely there.

"Thank God, thank God." She began laughing and crying at the same time. Lifting her hands to his cheeks, she slapped them lightly. "Wake up, mister. Please wake up."

He moaned, but he didn't open his eyes. Intuition told her that the sooner he regained consciousness the better. Besides, she needed the reassurance that he wasn't dead or going to die—at least not immediately. She desperately needed to know that she wasn't alone.

Reasoning that the cold air might help revive him, she resolved to get him outside the plane. It wasn't going to be easy; he probably outweighed her by a hundred pounds or more.

She felt every ounce of it as she opened his seat belt and his dead weight slumped against her like a sack of concrete mix. She caught most of it with her right shoulder and supported him there while she backed down the aisle toward the opening, half lifting him, half dragging him with her.

That seven-foot journey took her over half an hour. The bloody arm hanging over the armrest snagged them. She had to overcome her repulsion and touch it, moving it aside. She got blood on her hands. It was sticky. She whimpered with horror, but clamped her trembling lower lip between her teeth and continued tugging the man down the aisle—one struggling, agonizing inch at a time.

It struck her suddenly that whatever his injury, she might be doing it more harm than good by moving him. But she'd come this far; she wouldn't stop now. Setting a goal and achieving it seemed very important, if for no other reason than to prove she wasn't helpless. She had decided to get him outside, and that's what she was going to do if it killed her.

Which it very well might, she thought several minutes later. She had moved him as far forward as possible. Occasionally he groaned, but otherwise he showed no signs of coming around. Leaving him momentarily, she climbed through the branches of the pine tree. The entire left side of the fuselage had been virtually ripped off, so it would be a matter of dragging him through the branches of the tree. Using her bare hands, she broke off as many of the smaller branches as she could before returning to the man.

It took her five minutes just to turn him around so she could clasp him beneath the arms. Then, backing through the narrow, spiky tunnel she had cleared, she pulled him along with her. Pine needles pricked her face. The rough bark scraped her hands. But thankfully her heavy clothing protected most of her skin.

Her breathing became labored as she struggled. She considered pausing to rest, but was afraid that she would never build up enough momentum to start again. Her burden was moaning almost constantly, now. She knew he must be in agony, but she couldn't stop or he might lapse into deeper unconsciousness.

At last she felt cold air on her cheeks. She pulled her head free of the last branch and stepped out into the open. Taking a few stumbling steps backward, she pulled the man the remainder of the way, until he, too, was clear. Exhausted beyond belief, the muscles of her arms and back and legs burning from exertion, she plopped down hard on her bottom. The man's head fell into her lap.

Bracing herself on her hands and tilting her head toward the sky, she stayed that way until she had regained her breath. For the first time, while drawing the bitingly cold air into her lungs, she thought that it might be good to still be alive. She thanked God that she was. And thanked Him, too, for the other life He'd spared.

She looked down at the man and saw the bump for the first time. He was sporting a classic goose egg on the side of his temple. No doubt it had caused his unconsciousness. Heaving his shoulders up high enough to get her legs out from under him, she crawled around to his side and began unbuttoning his bulky coat. She prayed that she wouldn't uncover a mortal wound. She didn't. Only the plaid flannel shirt that no game hunter would be without. There were no traces of blood on it. From the turtleneck collar of his undershirt to the tops of his laced boots, she could find no sign of serious bleeding.

Expelling a gusty breath of relief, she bent over him and lightly slapped his cheeks again. She guessed him to be around forty, but the years hadn't been easy ones. His longish, wavy hair was saddle brown. So was his mustache. But it and his heavy eyebrows had strands of blond. His skin was sunburned, but not recently; it was a baked on, year-round sunburn. There was a tracery of fine lines at the corners of his eyes. His mouth was wide and thin, the lower lip only slightly fuller than the upper.

This rugged face didn't belong in an office; he spent a good deal of time outdoors. It was an agreeable face, if not a classically handsome one. There was a hardness to it, an uncompromising unapproachability that she had also sensed in his personality.

She wondered uneasily what he would think when he regained consciousness and found himself alone in the wilderness with her. She didn't have long to wait to find out. Moments later, his eyelids flickered, then opened.

Eyes as flinty gray as the sky overhead focused on her. They closed, then opened again. She wanted to speak, but trepidation held her back. The first word to cross his lips was unspeakably vulgar. She flinched, but attributed the foul language to his pain. Again he closed his eyes and waited several seconds before opening them.

Then he said, "We crashed." She nodded. "How long ago?"

"I'm not sure." Her teeth were chattering. It wasn't that cold, so it must have been from fear. Of him? Why? "An hour, maybe."

Grunting with pain, he covered the lump on the side of his head with one hand and levered himself up, using the other hand as a prop. She moved aside so he could sit up straight. "What about everybody else?"

"They're all dead."

He tried to come up on one knee and swayed dizzily. She reflexively extended a helping hand, but he shrugged it off. "Are you sure?"

"Sure they're dead? Yes. I mean, I think so."

He turned his head and stared at her balefully. "Did you check their pulses?"

She changed her mind about his eyes. They weren't like the sky at all. They were colder and much more foreboding. "No, I didn't check," she admitted contritely.

He nailed her with that judgmental stare for several seconds, then, with a great deal of difficulty, pulled himself to his feet. Using the tree behind him for support, he struggled to stand up and regain his equilibrium.

"How…how do you feel?"

"Like I'm going to puke."

One thing about him, he didn't mince words. "Maybe you should lie back down."

"No doubt I should."

"Well?"

Still holding his head in one hand, he raised it and looked at her. "Are you volunteering to go in there and check their pulses?" He watched the faint color in her cheeks fade and gave her a twisted smile of ridicule. "That's what I thought."

"I got *you* out, didn't I?"

"Yeah," he said dryly, "you got me out."

She didn't expect him to kiss her hands for saving his life, but a simple thank-you would have been nice. "You're an ungrateful—"

"Save it," he said.

She watched him lever himself away from the tree and stagger toward the demolished aircraft, pushing aside the branches of the tree with much more strength than she could have garnered in a month.

Sinking down onto the marshy ground, she rested her head on her raised knees, tempted to cry. She could hear him moving about in the cabin. When she raised her head and looked, she saw him through the missing windshield of the detached cockpit. He was emotionlessly moving his hands over the bodies of the pilots.

Minutes later, he thrashed his way through the fallen tree. "You were right. They're all dead."

How did he expect her to respond? Nah-nah-nah? He dropped a white first-aid box onto the ground and knelt beside it. He took out a bottle of aspirin and tossed three of them down his throat, swallowing them dry. "Come here," he ordered her rudely. She scooted forward and he handed her a flashlight. "Shine that directly into my eyes, one at a time, and tell me what happens."

She switched on the flashlight. The glass over the bulb was cracked, but it still worked. She shone the light directly into his right eye, then the left. "The pupils contract."

He took the flashlight away from her and clicked it off. "Good. No concussion. Just a rotten headache. You okay?"

"I think so."

He looked at her skeptically, but nodded.

"My name's Rusty Carlson," she said politely.

He barked a short laugh. His eyes moved up to take in her hair. "Rusty, huh?"

"Yes, Rusty," she replied testily.

"Figures."

The man had the manners of a pig. "Do you have a name?"

"Yeah, I've got a name. Cooper Landry. But this isn't a garden party so forgive me if I don't tip my hat and say, 'Pleased to meet you.'"

For two lone survivors of a disastrous plane crash, they were off to a bad beginning. Right now Rusty wanted to be comforted, reassured that she was alive and would go on living. All she'd gotten from him was scorn, which was unwarranted.

"What's with you?" she demanded angrily. "You act as though the crash was my fault."

"Maybe it was."

She gasped with incredulity. "What? I was hardly responsible for the storm."

"No, but if you hadn't dragged out that emotional, tearful goodbye to your sugar daddy, we might have beat it. What made you decide to leave ahead of him— the two of you have a lovers' spat?"

"None of your damned business," she said through teeth that had been straightened to perfection by an expensive orthodontist.

His expression didn't alter. "And you had no business being in a place like that—" his eyes roved over her "—being the kind of woman you are."

"What kind of woman is that?"

"Drop it. Let's just say that I'd be better off without you."

Having said that, he slid a lethal-looking hunting knife from the leather scabbard attached to his belt. Rusty wondered if he was going to cut her throat with it and rid himself of the inconvenience she posed. Instead, he turned and began hacking at the smaller branches of the tree, cutting a cleaner path to make the fuselage more accessible.

"What are you going to do?"

"I have to get them out."

"The…the others? Why?"

"Unless you want to be roommates with them."

"You're going to bury them?"

"That's the idea. Got a better one?"

No, of course she didn't, so she said nothing.

Cooper Landry hacked his way through the tree until only the major branches were left. They were easier to step around and over.

Rusty, making herself useful by dragging aside the branches as he cut them, asked, "We're staying here then?"

"For the time being, yeah." Having cleared a path of sorts, he stepped into the fuselage and signaled her forward. "Grab his boots, will ya?"

She stared down at the dead man's boots. She couldn't do this. Nothing in her life had prepared her for this. He couldn't expect her to do something so grotesque.

But glancing up at him and meeting those implacable gray eyes, she knew that he did expect it of her and expected it of her without an argument.

One by one they removed the bodies from the aircraft. He did most of the work; Rusty lent him a hand when he asked for it. The only way she could do it was to detach her mind from the grisly task. She'd lost her mother when she was a teenager. Two years ago her brother had died. But in both instances, she'd seen them when they were laid out in a satin-lined casket surrounded by soft lighting, organ music, and flowers. Death had seemed unreal. Even the bodies of her mother and brother weren't real to her, but identical replicas of the people she had loved, mannequins created in their images by the mortician.

These bodies were real.

She mechanically obeyed the terse commands this Cooper Landry issued in a voice without feeling or inflection. He must be a robot, she decided. He revealed no emotion whatsoever as he dragged the bodies to the common grave that he'd been able to dig using his knife and the small hatchet he found in a toolbox beneath the pilot's seat. He piled stones over the shallow grave when he was finished.

"Shouldn't we say something?" Rusty stared down at the barbaric pile of colorless stones, put there to protect the bodies of the five men from scavenging animals.

"Say something? Like what?"

"Like a scripture. A prayer."

He shrugged negligently as he cleaned the blade of his knife. "I don't know any scriptures. And my prayers ran out a long time ago." Turning his back on the grave, he stamped back toward the airplane.

Rusty mouthed a hasty prayer before turning to follow him. More than anything, she feared being left alone again. If she let the man out of her sight, he might desert her.

That was unlikely, however. At least not right away. He was reeling with fatigue and on the verge of fainting. "Why don't you lie down and rest?" she suggested. Her strength had deserted her long ago. She was running only on adrenaline now.

"Because night's coming on fast," he said. "We've got to remove the seats of the plane so we'll have room to stretch out in there. Otherwise you might have to spend a night in the great outdoors for the first time in your life." He sarcastically added the last as an afterthought before reentering the airplane. Moments later, Rusty heard him cursing viciously. He came out, his brows drawn together in a fierce scowl.

"What's the matter?"

He held his hand up in front of her face. It was wet. "Fuel."

"Fuel?"

"*Flammable* fuel," he said, impatient with her ignorance. "We can't stay in there. One spark and we'll be blown to China."

"Then don't build a fire."

He glared at her. "Once it gets dark, you'll want a fire," he said scornfully. "Besides, all it would take is a spark from anything. One piece of metal could scrape against another and we'd be history."

"What do we do?"

"We take what we can and move."

"I thought it was always best to stay with the airplane. I heard or read that once. Search parties will be looking for a downed plane. How will they find us if we leave the crash site?"

He cocked his head arrogantly. "You want to stay? Fine, stay. I'm going. But I'd better warn you that I don't think there's any water near here. The first thing I'm going to do in the morning is look for water."

His know-it-all attitude was insufferable. "How do you know there's no water?"

"No animal tracks around. I suppose you could exist on rainwater for as long as it held out, but who knows how long that will be."

When and how had he noticed that there were no animal tracks around? She hadn't even thought to look. In fact, having no water was almost as frightening as having to cope with wild animals to get it. Search for water? How did one go about that? Wild animals? How would she defend herself if one attacked?

She'd die without him. After several moments of deliberation, that was the grim conclusion she reached. She had no choice but to go along with whatever survival tactics he knew and be grateful that he was there to implement them.

Swallowing her pride, she said, "All right, I'll go with you." He didn't even glance up or otherwise acknowledge her. She had no way of knowing whether he was glad or sorry over her decision. By all appearances, he was indifferent. He was already making a pile of things he'd salvaged from the wreckage. Determined not to be ignored, Rusty knelt down beside him. "What can I do to help?"

He nodded toward the luggage compartment of the aircraft. "Go through the luggage. Everybody's. Take whatever might come in handy later." He handed her several tiny suitcase keys, which he had obviously taken off the bodies before he buried them.

She glanced warily at the suitcases. Some had already popped open as a result of the crash. The victims' personal belongings lay strewn on the damp ground. "Isn't that...violating their privacy? Their families might resent—"

He spun around so suddenly that she nearly toppled over backward. "Will you grow up and face facts?" He grabbed her by the shoulders and shook her. "Look around. Do you know what our chances are of coming out of this alive? I'll tell you: Nil. But before I go down, I'm going to fight like hell to stay alive. It's a habit I have."

His face moved closer to hers. "This isn't a Girl Scout outing gone awry; this is survival, lady. Etiquette and propriety be damned. If you tag along with me, you'll do what I tell you to, when I tell you to. Got that? And there won't be any time to spend on sentiment. Don't waste tears on those who didn't make it. They're gone and there's not a damn thing we can do about it. Now, move your butt and get busy doing what I told you to do."

He shoved her away from him and began collecting pelts that the hunters had been taking home as trophies. There was mostly caribou, but also white wolf, beaver, and one small mink.

Holding back bitter tears of mortification and accumulated distress, Rusty bent over the suitcases and began sorting through their contents as she'd been instructed. She wanted to strike out at him. She wanted to collapse in a heap and bawl her eyes out. But she wouldn't give him the satisfaction of seeing her do either. Nor would she provide him with an excuse to leave her behind; he would probably grab at the flimsiest.

A half-hour later she carried her findings and added them to the pile of articles he had gathered. Apparently he approved of her selection, which included two flasks of liquor. She couldn't identify it by the smell, but Cooper wasn't particular. He seemed to enjoy the healthy drink he took from one of the flasks. She watched his Adam's apple bob up and down as he swallowed. He had a strong neck, and a solid, square jaw. Typical, she thought peevishly, of all stubborn mules.

He recapped the flask and tossed it down along with the books of matches, a travel sewing kit, and the extra clothing she had accumulated. He didn't remark on how well she'd done. Instead he nodded down at the small suitcase she was carrying. "What's that?"

"That's mine."

"That's not what I asked."

He yanked the suitcase from her hand and opened it. His large hands violated her neat stacks of pastel silk thermal underwear, nightgowns, and assorted lingerie. He pulled one set of leggings through the circle he made of his index finger and thumb. His gray eyes met hers. "Silk?" Coldly, she stared back at him without answering. His grin was downright dirty. It insinuated things she didn't even want to guess at. "Very nice."

Then his grin disappeared beneath his mustache and he tossed the garment at her. "Take two sets of long johns. A couple pairs of socks. A cap. Gloves. This coat," he added, piling a ski jacket atop the other garments he'd selected. "One extra pair of britches. A couple of sweaters." He opened the zippered, plastic-lined travel bag she'd packed her cosmetics and toiletries in.

"I need all of that," she said quickly.

"Not where we're going you don't." He rifled through her cosmetics, heedlessly tossing a fortune's worth of beauty-enhancing creams and makeup into the rotting, wet leaves. "A hairbrush, toothpaste and toothbrush, soap. That's it. And, just because I'm merciful, these." He handed her a box of tampons.

She snatched it out of his hands and crammed it back into the cosmetic bag along with the other few items he had allowed her.

Again he grinned. The juxtaposition of his white teeth and wide mustache made him look positively wicked. "You think I'm a real son of a bitch, don't you? You're just too nice to say so."

"No, I'm not." Her russet brown eyes flashed hotly. "I think you're a real son of a bitch."

His smile merely deepened. "It's only gonna get worse before it gets better." He stood up, glancing worriedly at the darkening sky. "Come on. We'd better get going."

As soon as he turned his back, Rusty slipped a colorless lip gloss, a bottle of shampoo and a razor into the bag. He might not need to shave before they reached civilization, but she was sure she would.

She jumped guiltily when he turned back and asked her, "Do you know how to shoot one of these?" He held up a hunting rifle.

Rusty shook her head no. Only yesterday she'd seen a beautiful Dall ram being brought down with a rifle just like that. It was a distasteful memory. Rather than celebrating the kill, her sympathies had been with the slain animal.

"I was afraid of that," Cooper muttered. "But you can carry it anyway." He hooked the heavy rifle over her shoulder by its leather strap and placed another, presumably his own, over his shoulder. He shoved a fearsome-looking pistol into his waistband. Catching her wary glance he said, "It's a flare gun. I found it in the cockpit. Keep your ears open for search planes."

By seaming up the neck of a sweater with a shoe-lace, he had fashioned a backpack out of it. He tied it around her neck by the sleeves. "Okay," he said, giving her a cursory inspection, "let's go."

Rusty cast one last sad, apprehensive look at the wreckage of the airplane, then struck out after him. His broad back made an easy target to follow. She found that by keeping her eyes trained on a spot directly between his shoulder blades, she was able to put herself into a semitrance and ward off her memory of the bodies they had left behind. She wanted to lapse into forgetfulness.

She plodded on, losing energy with each step. Her strength seemed to be seeping out of her with alarming rapidity. She didn't know how far they had gone, but it couldn't have been very far before it seemed impossible for her to put one foot in front of the other. Her legs were trembling with fatigue. She no longer swatted aside the branches that backlashed, but indifferently let them slap into her.

Cooper's image grew blurry, then began wavering in front of her like a ghost. The trees all seemed to have tentacles that tried to catch her clothes, tear at her hair, ensnare her ankles, impede her in any way possible. Stumbling, she glanced down at the ground and was amazed to see that it was rushing up to meet her. How extraordinary, she thought.

Instinctively, she grasped the nearest branch to break her fall and called out weakly, "Coo...Cooper."

She landed hard, but it was a blessed relief to lie on the cool ground, damp and soggy as it was. The leaf mold seemed like a compress against her cheek. It was a luxury to let her eyes close.

Cooper murmured a curse as he shrugged off his backpack and let the strap of the rifle slide down his arm. Roughly, he rolled her over onto her back and pried her eyelids open with his thumbs. She gazed up at him, having no idea that her face was as pale as death. Even her lips were as gray as the clouds overhead.

"I'm sorry to hold you back." She was vaguely surprised that her voice sounded so faint. She could feel her lips moving, but she wasn't sure she had actually spoken aloud. It seemed imperative to apologize for detaining him and being a nuisance in general. "I've got to rest for just a minute."

"Yeah, yeah, that's fine, uh, Rusty. You rest." He was working at the hook and eye buried deep in the fox-fur collar of her coat. "Do you hurt anywhere?"

"Hurt? No. Why?"

"Nothing." He shoved open her coat and plunged his hands inside. He slipped them beneath her sweater and began carefully pressing his fingers against her abdomen. Was this proper? she thought fuzzily. "You might be bleeding somewhere and don't know it."

His words served to clarify everything. "Internally?" Panicked, she struggled to sit up.

"I don't know. I don't— Hold it!" With a sudden flick of his hands, he flipped back the front panels of her full-length coat. His breath whistled through his teeth. Rusty levered herself up on her elbows to see what had caused him to frown so ferociously.

The right leg of her trousers was soaked with bright red blood. It had also made a sponge of her wool sock and run over her leather hiking boot.

"When did you do this?" His eyes, razor sharp, moved up to hers. "What happened?"

Dismayed, she looked at Cooper and wordlessly shook her head.

"Why didn't you tell me you were hurt?"

"I didn't know," she said weakly.

He slipped his knife from its scabbard. Pinching up the blood-soaked hem of her trousers, he slid the knife into the crease and jerked it upward. With one heart-stopping stroke, it cut straight up her pants leg, neatly slicing the fabric all the way from her hem to the elastic leg of her underpants. Shocked and fearful, she sucked in her breath.

Cooper, gazing down at her leg, expelled a long, defeated breath. "Hell."

CHAPTER TWO

RUSTY'S HEAD BEGAN to buzz. She felt nauseous. Her earlobes were throbbing and her throat was on fire. Each individual hair follicle on her head felt like a pinprick. The pads of her fingers and toes were tingling. She'd fainted once after having a root canal. She knew the symptoms.

But, damn, did they have to afflict her here? In front of him?

"Easy, easy." He grasped her shoulders and lowered her to the ground. "You don't remember hurting yourself?" She shook her head dumbly. "Must have happened when we crashed."

"I didn't feel any pain."

"You were too shocked. How does it feel now?"

Only then did she become aware of the pain. "Not bad." His eyes probed hers for the truth. "Really, it's not that bad. I've bled a lot, though, haven't I?"

"Yeah." Grim-faced, he rummaged through the first-aid kit. "I've got to sponge up the blood so I can see where it's coming from."

He tore into the backpack she'd been carrying and selected a soft cotton undershirt to swab up the blood. She felt the pressure of his hands, but little else as she gazed up through the branches of the trees overhead. Maybe she'd been premature to thank God for being alive. She might bleed to death lying here on the ground. And there wouldn't be anything Cooper or she could do about it. In fact, he would probably be glad to get rid of her.

His soft curse roused her from her macabre musings. She tilted her head up and looked down at her injured leg. Along her shinbone a gash ran from just below her knee to just above her sock. She could see flesh, muscle. It was sickening. She whimpered.

"Lie down, dammit."

Weakly, Rusty obeyed the emphatic order. "How could that happen without my feeling it?"

"Probably split like a tomato skin the moment of impact."

"Can you do anything?"

"Clean it with peroxide." He opened the brown opaque plastic bottle he'd found in the first-aid kit and soaked the sleeve of the T-shirt with the peroxide.

"Is it going to hurt?"

"Probably."

Ignoring her tearful, frightened eyes, he dabbed at the wound with the peroxide. Rusty clamped her lower lip with her teeth to keep from crying out, but her face twisted with anguish. Actually, the thought of the peroxide bubbling in the gash was as bad as the pain.

"Breathe through your mouth if you feel like vomiting," he told her tonelessly. "I'm almost finished."

She squeezed her eyes shut and didn't open them until she heard the sound of ripping cloth. He was tearing another T-shirt into strips. One by one he wrapped them around her calf, binding her lower leg tightly.

"That'll have to do for now," he said, more to himself than to her. Picking up his knife again, he said,

"Raise your hips." She did, avoiding his eyes. He cut the leg of her trousers from around her upper thigh. His hands worked beneath her thighs and between them. His callused knuckles brushed against her smooth, warm skin, but she needn't have felt any embarrassment. He could have been cutting up a steak for all the emotion he showed.

"You damn sure can't walk."

"I can!" Rusty insisted frantically.

She was afraid that he would go off without her. He was standing over her, feet widespread, looking around. His brow was beetled and beneath his mustache she could tell that he was gnawing on the inside of his cheek as though giving something careful consideration.

Was he weighing his options? Deciding whether or not to desert her? Or maybe he was thinking of killing her quickly and mercifully instead of letting her die of her wound.

Finally he bent down and, cupping her armpits in his palms, lifted her into a sitting position. "Take off your coat and put on that ski jacket."

Without an argument, she let the fur coat slide from her shoulders. Using the hatchet he'd brought along, Cooper hacked down three saplings and stripped them of their branches. Silently, Rusty watched as he fashioned them into an H, only placing the crossbar higher than normal. He bound the intersections with rawhide tongs, which he'd taken from the boots of the men they'd buried. Then he took her fur coat and ran a sleeve over each of the tops of the two longer poles. Rusty flinched when he stabbed through the fur and satin lining, gouging out a hole in the bottom of her precious fox coat.

He glanced up at her. "What's the matter?"

She swallowed, realizing that he was testing her. "Nothing. The coat was a gift, that's all."

He watched her for a few seconds more before making a similar hole in the other side. He then ran the poles through the holes. The finished product was a crude travois. No self-respecting American Indian would have claimed it, but Rusty was impressed with his ingenuity and skill. And vastly relieved that he obviously didn't plan to leave her behind or otherwise dispose of her.

He laid the rough contraption on the ground. Turning to her, he caught her under the knees and behind the back and lifted her. He laid her on the soft fur, then piled several pelts on top of her.

"I didn't see any animal up there with a hide that looked like this," she said, running her hand over a skin of short, fine wool.

"Umingmak."

"Pardon?"

"That's what the Inuit called the musk-ox. Means 'the bearded one.' It wasn't my kill; I just bought the pelt. It's very warm." He tucked the wool around her and threw another pelt on top of that. "It's up to you to stay on and keep covered."

Standing, he wiped perspiration off his brow with the back of his hand. He winced when he grazed the bump on his temple. Rusty would have gone to bed for a week if she had sustained a blow like that; it must be killing him.

"Thank you, Cooper," she said softly.

He froze, glanced down at her, nodded quickly, then turned and began gathering up their paraphernalia. He tossed both backpacks onto her lap, along with both rifles. "Hang on to those, too, will you?"

"Where are we going?"

"Southeast," was his succinct reply.

"Why?"

"Sooner or later, we'll bump into an outpost of civilization."

"Oh." She dreaded moving, anticipating that the journey wasn't going to be a joyride. "May I have an aspirin please?"

He unpocketed the plastic bottle and shook two aspirin tablets into her hands.

"I can't take them without water."

He made an impatient scoffing sound. "It's either dry or with brandy."

"Brandy, please."

He passed her one of the flasks, watching her closely. She bravely put the spout to her mouth and took a hefty swallow to wash down the aspirin tablets. She choked and sputtered. Tears filled her eyes, but with dignity and poise she returned the flask to him. "Thank you."

His narrow lips twitched with the need to smile. "You might not have any common sense, but you've got guts, lady."

And that, she thought, was as close to a compliment as she was ever likely to get from Cooper Landry. He secured the trunks of the saplings beneath his arms and moved forward, dragging the travois behind him. After having gone only a few teeth-jarring, butt-bruising yards, Rusty realized that she wasn't going to be much better off in the travois than she would have been walking. It required all her concentration just to keep from sliding off. Her bottom would be black and blue with bruises—legacies of the rocks it encountered every grueling step of the way. She dared not even think of the satin lining of her coat being ripped to shreds by the forest debris as it was hauled over the rough ground.

It grew progressively darker and colder. A light precipitation began—snow grains she thought the meteorologists called the stuff, pellets of ice no larger than grains of salt. Her injured leg began to ache, but she would have bitten her tongue in two before she complained. She could hear Cooper's labored breathing. He wasn't having an easy time of it either. If it weren't for her, he could cover three times the distance in the same amount of time.

Darkness closed in suddenly, making it perilous for them to continue over the unfamiliar terrain. He stopped in the next clearing he came to and dropped the poles of the travois. "How're you doing?"

She didn't think about how hungry, thirsty, and uncomfortable she was. She said, "Fine."

"Yeah, sure. How are you really?" He knelt down and whipped off the covering of furs. Her bandage was soaked with fresh blood. He quickly replaced the furs. "We'd better stop for the night. Now that the sun has set, I can't tell which direction I'm going in."

He was lying, only saying that to make her feel better. Rusty knew that he would keep going if it weren't for her. It was doubtful that he was afraid of the dark or that inclement weather would faze him. Even though he'd been dragging her for hours, he appeared to have enough stamina to go at least another two.

He circled the clearing and began shoveling pine needles into a pile. He spread the pelts over them and came back for Rusty.

"Cooper?"

"Hmm?" He grunted with the effort of lifting her off the travois.

"I have to go to the bathroom."

She couldn't see him clearly in the darkness, but she could feel his shocked stare. Embarrassed beyond belief, she kept her head down. "Okay," he replied after a moment. "Will your leg support you while—"

"Yes, I think so," she said in a rush.

He carried her to the edge of the clearing and gently lowered her to stand on her left leg. "Brace yourself against the tree," he instructed gruffly. "Call me when you're done."

It was much more difficult than she had expected it to be. By the time she had refastened what was left of her trousers, she was shaking with weakness and her teeth were chattering with cold. "All right, I'm finished."

Cooper materialized out of the darkness and lifted her into his arms again. She would never have thought a bed of pine needles and animal pelts could have felt so good, but she sighed with relief when he laid her on it and she was able to relax.

Cooper packed the furs around her. "I'll build a fire. It won't be much of one. There's not enough dry wood. But it'll be better than nothing and might help ward off visitors."

Rusty shivered and pulled the furs over her head, as much to protect her from the thought of wild animals as the icy precipitation that continued to dust the ground. But the increasing pain in her leg wouldn't let her doze. She grew restless and finally peeped out from beneath the covering. Cooper had succeeded in building a sputtering, smoky fire. He'd lined the shallow bowl he'd scooped out of the ground with rocks to keep it from igniting her bed.

He glanced over at her and, unzipping one of the many pockets in his coat, took something out and tossed it to her. She caught it one-handed. "What is it?"

"Granola bar."

At the thought of food, her stomach rumbled noisily. She ripped open the foil wrapper, ready to stuff the whole bar into her mouth. Before she did, she got hold of herself and paused. "You…you don't have to share with me," she said in a small voice. "It's yours and you might need it later."

His gray eyes looked as hard and cold as gunmetal when he turned his head. "It isn't mine. I found it in a coat pocket that belonged to one of the others."

He seemed to take brutal delight in telling her that, implying that if the granola bar were his, he'd think twice before sharing it with her.

Whatever his intention, he had spoiled it for her. The bar tasted like sawdust in her mouth; she chewed and swallowed it mechanically. The tastelessness was partially due to her thirst. As though reading her mind, Cooper said, "If we don't find water tomorrow, we're in trouble."

"Do you think we will?"

"I don't know."

She lay amid the furs contemplatively. "Why do you think the plane crashed?"

"I don't know. A combination of things, I guess."

"Do you have any idea where we are?"

"No. I might have a general idea if it hadn't been for the storm."

"You think we were off course?"

"Yes. But I don't know how far."

She rested her cheek against her hand and stared into the feeble flame that was struggling for life. "Had you ever been to Great Bear Lake before?"

"Once."

"When?"

"Several years ago."

"Do you do a lot of hunting?"

"Some."

He wasn't exactly an orator, was he? She wanted to draw him into conversation to keep her mind off the pain in her leg. "Do you think they'll find us?"

"Maybe."

"When?"

"What do you think I am, a damned encyclopedia?" His shout bounced around the ring of trees surrounding them. He came to his feet abruptly. "Stop asking me so many questions. I don't have the answers."

"I just want to know," she cried tearfully.

"Well, so do I. But I don't. I'd say the chances of them finding us are extremely good if the plane was still on the flight plan and extremely remote if it was too far off, okay? Now, shut up about it."

Rusty lapsed into wounded silence. Cooper prowled the clearing in search of dry tinder. He added a few sticks to the fire before moving toward her. "Better let me tend to your leg."

He brusquely threw the covers back. The fire shed meager light onto the bloody bandage. Expertly wielding the hunting knife, he cut through the knots he'd tied earlier and began unwinding the stained cloth. "Does it hurt?"

"Yes."

"Well, it has every right to," he said grimly as he gazed down at the wound. His expression wasn't very encouraging.

While she held the flashlight for him, he soaked the gash with peroxide again and wrapped it in fresh bandaging. By the time he had finished, tears were stinging her eyes and her lips were blotchy from biting them, but she hadn't cried out once. "Where'd you learn to bandage so well?"

"Nam." His answer was curt, indicating that the subject was closed. "Here, take two more aspirin." He passed her the bottle after shaking out two for himself. He hadn't complained, but his head must have felt as though it were splitting in two. "And drink some more brandy. At least two swallows. I think that by morning, you're going to need it."

"Why?"

"Your leg. Tomorrow will probably be the worst day. After that, maybe it'll start to get better."

"What if it doesn't?"

He said nothing; he didn't have to.

With trembling hands, Rusty held the flask of brandy to her lips and took an occasional sip from it. Now that the dry kindling had caught, Cooper stacked more wood on the fire. But it wasn't burning hot enough for him to take off his coat, which he surprised her by doing. He took off his boots, too, and told her to do the same. Then, making a bundle of the coats and boots, he stuffed them down between the furs.

"What's that for?" Her feet were already getting cold.

"If we sweat in our boots and it turns colder, we'll get frostbite. Scoot over."

She stared up at him apprehensively. "Huh?"

Sighing impatiently, he crawled in with her, forcing her to move over and allow him room beneath the pile of furs. Alarmed, Rusty exclaimed, "What are you doing?"

"Going to sleep. If you'll shut up, that is."

"Here?"

"Accommodations with separate beds were unavailable."

"You can't—"

"Relax, Miss... What was it again?"

"Carlson."

"Yeah, Miss Carlson. Our combined body heat will help keep us warm." He snuggled close to her and pulled the furs up over their heads, effectively cocooning them inside. "Turn on your side, away from me."

"Go to hell."

She could almost hear him mentally counting to ten. "Look, I don't want to freeze. And I don't look forward to digging another grave to bury you in, either, so just do as I say. Now."

He must have been an officer in Vietnam, she thought petulantly as she rolled on to her side. He put his arm around her waist and drew her back against him, until they were lying together spoon fashion. She could scarcely breathe. "Is this really necessary?"

"Yes."

"I won't move away. There's nowhere to go. You don't have to keep your arm there."

"You surprise me. I thought you'd like this." He

pressed against her stomach with the palm of his hand. "You're a real looker. Don't you expect men to get all hot and bothered when they're around you?"

"Let go of me."

"All that long hair, its unusual color."

"Shut up!"

"You're proud of your round little butt and perky tits, aren't you? I'm sure most men find you irresistible. That copilot sure did. He was salivating after you like a Doberman over a bitch in heat, almost stumbling over his tongue."

"I don't know what you're talking about."

He stroked her stomach. "Oh, yes, you do. You must have enjoyed stunning all those men on the plane into speechlessness when you climbed aboard with your fur collar pulled up, brushing against your flushed cheeks and sexy mouth."

"Why are you doing this?" she sobbed.

He cursed and when he spoke again, his voice wasn't lilting and teasing. It was weary. "So you'll rest assured that I'm not going to take advantage of you during the night. Redheads have never been my preference. Besides, your body is still warm from your sugar daddy's bed. All things considered, your virtue is safe with me."

She sniffed back tears of humiliation. "You're cruel and vulgar."

He laughed. "Now you sound offended that I'm not tempted to rape you. Make up your mind. If you have a hankering for sex tonight, I can oblige you. My body isn't as particular as my head. After all, it's awfully dark in here. And you know what they say about cats in the dark. But personally, I prefer safer, more comfortable surroundings to screw in. So just go to sleep, will you?"

Rusty grit her teeth in outrage. She held her body rigid and put a barrier between them, if not physically, then mentally. She tried to ignore his body heat, which permeated her clothing, and his breath that drifted over her neck each time he exhaled, and the latent power in the thighs that conformed to the backs of hers. Gradually, and with the help of the brandy she'd drunk, she relaxed. Eventually she dozed.

IT WAS HER own moan that woke her up. Her leg was throbbing painfully.

"What is it?"

Cooper's voice was gruff, but Rusty didn't think it was because he'd been roused from a deep sleep. Intuitively she knew that he had been lying there awake. "Nothing."

"Tell me. What's the matter? Your leg?"

"Yes."

"Is it bleeding again?"

"I don't think so. It's doesn't feel wet. It just hurts."

"Drink some more brandy." He angled himself away from her and reached for the flask of brandy, which he'd brought into the fur cocoon with them.

"I'm already woozy."

"Good. It's working." He poked her lips with the uncapped flask and tipped it forward. She either had to drink or drown.

The potent liquor burned a fiery path down her middle. At the very least, it took her mind off her painful wound for a few seconds. "Thanks."

"Open your legs."

"Pardon?"

"Open your legs."

"How much brandy have you had, Mr. Landry?"

"Do it."

"Why?"

"So I can get mine between them."

Without giving her another chance to argue, he slid his hand between her thighs and raised her injured leg. He wedged his knees between hers, then gently lowered her right leg to rest on top of his. "There. Keeping it elevated will help relieve the pressure. It'll also keep me from jostling it in the night."

She was too flabbergasted to fall back to sleep immediately; too uncomfortably aware of his nearness. And there was something else keeping her awake: a nagging guilt.

"Cooper, did you know any of the other men?"

"Those on board the plane? No."

"The men in the front two seats were brothers. While we were weighing our luggage, I heard them talking about getting their families together for Thanksgiving in a few weeks. They were going to show them the slides they'd taken this week."

"Don't think about it."

"I can't help it."

"Yes, you can."

"No, I can't. I keep asking myself why I'm alive. Why was I allowed to live? It doesn't make any sense."

"It doesn't have to make sense," he said bitterly. "That's just the way it *is*. It was their time, that's all. It's over, forgotten."

"Not forgotten."

"Force it out of your mind."

"Is that what you did?"

"Yes."

She shuddered. "How can you be so unfeeling about another human life?"

"Practice."

The word affected her like a hard slap on the cheek. It had been cruelly delivered to shut her up, and it did. But it didn't stop her from thinking. She wondered how many of his buddies Cooper had seen killed in Vietnam. Dozens? Scores? Hundreds? Still, she couldn't imagine ever becoming inured to death.

She'd had practice dealing with it, but not to the extent that he apparently had. It wasn't something she could block out, dismiss, by an act of will. When she thought about her losses, she still ached.

"My mother died of a stroke," she told him quietly. "Her death was almost a relief. She would have been severely incapacitated. I had a week to prepare myself for it. But my brother's death was sudden." Cooper wouldn't care to hear about any of this, but she wanted to talk about it.

"Brother?"

"Jeff. He was killed in a car wreck two years ago."

"No other family?"

"Only my father." She drew a gentle breath. "He was the man I was with at the lodge. The one I said goodbye to. Not a sugar daddy. Not a lover. My father."

She waited for an apology, but it never came. If his body hadn't been so tense, she might have thought he'd fallen asleep.

Finally he broke the silence by asking, "What is your father going to think when he's notified about the crash?"

"Oh, my God!" Reflexively she clutched Cooper's hand where it still rested against her stomach. "I hadn't thought of that."

She could imagine her father's despair when he heard the news. He'd lost his wife. Then his son. Now his daughter. He would be disconsolate. Rusty couldn't bear to think of the suffering he would go through, the hell of uncertainty, of not knowing what had happened to her. Hopefully, as much for her father's sake as her own, they would be rescued soon.

"The guy looked like a real mover and shaker to me," Cooper said. "He'll ride the authorities until we're found."

"You're right. Father won't give up until he knows what happened to me."

Rusty was certain of that. Her father was a powerful man. He was dynamic and had both the talent and the means to get things done. His reputation and money could cut through miles of red tape. Knowing that he'd leave no stone unturned until she was rescued gave her an optimistic thread to cling to.

She was also surprised to discover that Cooper hadn't been as withdrawn and impervious as he had appeared to be. Before they boarded the plane, he had kept to himself. He hadn't mingled with the other passengers. But he'd noticed everything. Apparently her companion was an observant student of human nature.

Nature was having its way with him right now. While she'd been talking, Rusty became nervously aware of his sex snuggled solidly against her bottom. She blurted, "Are you married?"

"No."

"Ever?"

"No."

"Involved?"

"Look, I get my share of sex, okay? And I know why you're suddenly so curious. Believe me, I feel it too. But I can't do anything to help it. Well, actually I can, but as we discussed earlier, that isn't a very workable solution under the circumstances. The alternatives that come readily to mind would embarrass us both I'm afraid."

Rusty's cheeks grew hot and rosy. "I wish you wouldn't."

"What?"

"Talk like that."

"How?"

"You know. Dirty."

"You just left a big game hunting lodge. Didn't you intercept a few dirty jokes? Overhear some lewd comments? I thought you'd be used to bawdy language by now."

"Well, I'm not. And for your information, I went on that hunting trip for my father's sake. I didn't particularly enjoy myself."

"He forced you to go?"

"Of course not."

"Coerced you to? In exchange for that fur coat, maybe?"

"No," she grated with irritation. "The trip was my idea. I suggested that we take it together."

"And you randomly chose the Northwest Territories? Why not Hawaii? Or St. Moritz? I can think of a thousand other places on the globe where you would have fit in better."

Her sigh was an admission that he had her correctly pegged. On a big game hunt she was as out of place as a rusty nail in an operating room. "My father and brother always went hunting together. Four weeks every year. It was a family tradition." Filled with remorse, she closed her eyes. "Father hadn't been hunting since Jeff was killed. I thought the trip would be good for him. I insisted that he go. When he hesitated, I offered to go with him."

She expected murmurs of sympathy and understanding—perhaps even whispered praise for her unselfish and noble gesture. Instead all she heard from him was a grumpy "Be quiet, will you? I'm trying to get some sleep."

"Stop it, Rusty."

Her brother's voice echoed through her dream. They were wrestling, as only brothers and sisters who either hate each other intensely or love each other intensely can. With Jeff and her, the latter had been true. They were barely a year apart in age. From the time Rusty took her first steps, they had been bosom buddies and playmates. Much to their father's delight and their mother's aggravation, they had often engaged in rowdy hand-to-hand combat and always came up laughing.

But there was no levity in Jeff's voice now as he clasped her wrists and anchored them to the floor on either side of her head. "Stop it, now." He shook her slightly. "You're going to hurt yourself if you don't stop flailing around."

She came awake and opened her eyes. It wasn't Jeff's well-remembered, well-loved face she stared into, but the man's. The Loner's. She was glad he was alive, but she didn't like him very much. What was his name? Oh, yes, Cooper. Cooper...? Cooper something. Or something Cooper.

"Lie still," he commanded her.

She stopped thrashing. The air was cold on her exposed skin, and she realized that she'd kicked off all the furs he'd piled over them for the night. On his knees, he was straddling her chest and bending over her. Her wrists were stapled behind her head by his hard fingers.

"Get off me."

"Are you all right now?"

She nodded. She was as all right as a woman could be upon waking up to find a man the size and shape of Cooper Landry—that was it, Landry—straddling her with thighs that rose like columns above her, coming together... She averted her eyes from that mouth-drying juncture. "Please," she gasped. "I'm fine."

He eased himself off her. She sucked in frigidly cold air that hurt her lungs. But God, it felt good against her hot face. It felt good for only a second. Then she shivered with a chill and her teeth started clicking together. Cooper's brows were drawn together worriedly. Or crossly. She couldn't tell. He was either concerned or annoyed.

"You're burning up with fever," he told her bluntly. "I left the bed to build up the fire. You were delirious and started shouting for somebody called Jeff."

"My brother." Her shudders were convulsive. She pulled one of the furs around her.

It hadn't rained or drizzled anymore during the night. She could actually see flames and glowing coals beneath the sticks Cooper had added to the fire. The flames were so hot they burned her eyeballs until they hurt.

No, impossible. That must be the fever.

Leaving the fur covering her upper body alone, Cooper lifted the lower half of it off her leg. Once again he painstakingly unwrapped the bandage and stared down at the open wound. Rusty stared at him.

Finally he looked at her, his mouth set in a bleak line. "I won't try to fool you. It's bad. Infected. There's a bottle of antibiotics in the first-aid kit. I was saving them in case this happened, but I'm not sure they'll be adequate to take care of it."

She swallowed with difficulty. Even her feverish brain could assimilate what he was telling her. Raising herself to her elbows, she looked down at her leg. She wanted to gag. On either side of the deep gash, the skin was raised and puckered with infection. Flopping back down, she drew in shallow, rapid breaths. She wet her lips, ineffectually because the fever was making her mouth drier than it had been before. "I could get gangrene and die, couldn't I?"

He forced a half smile. "Not yet. We've got to do what we can to prevent that."

"Like cut it off?"

"God, you're morbid. What I had in mind was lancing out the pus and then closing the gash with stitches."

Her face turned ashen. "That sounds morbid enough."

"Not as bad as cauterizing it. Which it might come to." Her face went as colorless as chalk. "But, for right now, let's put some stitches in. Don't look relieved," he said, frowning deeply, "it's gonna hurt like hell."

She stared into the depths of his eyes. Strange as it was, rocky as their beginning had been, she trusted him. "Do whatever you have to do."

He nodded brusquely, then went to work. First he withdrew a pair of her silk long johns from the sweater cum backpack. "I'm glad you wear silk undies." She smiled waveringly at his mild joke as he began to unravel the casing of the waistband.

"We'll use these threads for the sutures." He nodded down toward the silver flask. "Better start on that brandy. Use it to swallow one of those penicillin tablets. You're not allergic to it, are you? Good," he said when she shook her head. "Sip the brandy steadily. Don't stop until you're good and drunk. But don't drink all of it. I'll have to sterilize the threads and bathe the gash with it."

She wasn't anesthetized nearly enough when he bent over her leg. The hunting knife, which he'd sterilized in the fire, was held poised in readiness over the infected wound. "Ready?" She nodded. "Try to keep still." She nodded again. "And don't fight unconsciousness. We'd both be better off if you passed out."

The first tiny puncture he made into the red, puffy skin caused her to cry out and yank her leg back. "No, Rusty! You've got to lie still."

It was an agonizing process and seemed to go on forever. He meticulously lanced the areas that needed it. When he doused the entire wound with brandy, Rusty screamed. After that, the stitches didn't seem so bad. He used the sewing needle from the matchbook kit they'd brought with them. After soaking individual threads in brandy, he drew them through her skin and tied them, firmly pulling the edges of the wound together.

Rusty stared at the spot where his tawny eyebrows grew together above the bridge of his nose. His forehead was sweating in spite of the cold. He never took his eyes off his work except to occasionally glance down at her face. He was sensitive to her pain. Even sympathetic toward it. His hands were amazingly tender for a man so large, and for one who had a cold, unfeeling stone where his heart should have been.

Eventually that spot between his eyebrows began to swim in and out of focus. Although she was lying still, her head was spinning, reeling with pain and trauma and the anesthetizing effects of the brandy. Despite Cooper's advice, she struggled to stay awake, afraid that if she went to sleep she might never wake up. Finally she gave up the fight and let her eyes drift closed.

Her last conscious thought was that it was a shame her father would never know how brave she'd been right up to the moment of her death.

"Well," Cooper said, sitting back on his heels and wiping his perspiring forehead, "it's not pretty, but I think it will work."

He looked down at her with a satisfied and optimistic smile. But she didn't see his smile. She was unconscious.

CHAPTER THREE

SHE CAME TO, actually surprised that she was alive. At first she thought that darkness had fallen, but she inched her head upward. The small mink pelt slid off her head. It was still daylight—exactly what time was impossible to pinpoint. The sky was gloomily overcast.

With a sense of dread, she waited for the pain from her leg to penetrate her consciousness, but miraculously it didn't. Dizzy from the brandy she'd consumed, she eased herself into a sitting position. It took every ounce of strength she had left to lift the furs off her leg. For one horrid moment she thought it might not be hurting because Cooper had amputated it after all.

But when she moved aside the largest caribou pelt, she found that her leg was still intact and bandaged in strips of white cotton. No signs of fresh blood. She was by no means ready to run a marathon, but it felt much better.

Sitting up had exhausted her and she fell back amid the furs, pulling them to her chin. Her skin was hot and dry, but she was chilled. She still had a fever. Maybe she should take more aspirin. But where were they? Cooper would know. He—

Where was Cooper?

Her lethargy vanished and she sprang into a sitting position. Frantically her eyes scanned the clearing. Not a trace. He was gone. His rifle was missing, too. The other one lay on the ground within her reach. The fire still had glowing coals and was giving off heat.

But her protector had deserted her.

Forcibly tamping down hysteria, she reasoned that she was jumping to conclusions. He wouldn't do that. He wouldn't have nursed her so meticulously only to leave her stranded and helpless in the wilderness.

Would he?

Not unless he was an unfeeling bastard.

Hadn't she decided that was exactly what Cooper Landry was?

No. He was hard. Tough. Cynical, certainly. But not completely lacking in feelings. If he were, he'd have deserted her yesterday.

So where was he?

He'd left a rifle behind. Why? Maybe that was the extent of his human kindness. He'd tended to her wound, done all he could on that score. He'd provided her with the means to protect herself. Maybe now it was every man for himself. Survival of the fittest.

Well, she would die. If not of fever, then of thirst. She had no water. She had no food. She had no shelter to speak of. In just a little while the supply of firewood, which he'd cut and stacked nearby, would be used up. She'd die of exposure if the weather turned even marginally colder.

Like hell she would!

Suddenly she was furious with him for going off and leaving her. She'd show him; she'd show her father. Rusty Carlson was not an easily expendable, spineless wimp.

She threw off the covers and pulled on her ski jacket.

For the time being she'd leave off her left boot because
the pair of them were still stashed farther down in the
pile of furs, too far for her to reach. Besides, if one foot
was bare, the other might just as well be, too. And on
top of that, putting on her coat had sapped her energy.

Food and water.

Those essentials were necessary. That's what she
had to find first. But where? At best, her surroundings were intimidating. At worst, terrifying. For three
hundred and sixty degrees, all she could see was virgin forest. Beyond the nearby trees—some so tall she
couldn't even see the tops of them—there stretched
endless miles of more just like them.

Before she could go in search of water, she had to
get to her feet. It seemed like an impossible task, but
she gritted her teeth with the determination to do it.

*When they discovered her body, it wouldn't be hun-
kered under a pile of furs!*

Reaching out as far as she could, she closed her
hand around a stick of firewood and pulled it toward
her. Using it as a prop, she came up on her good knee,
keeping the injured one straight out in front of her.
Then she paused to catch her breath, which was forming clouds of white vapor in front of her face.

Repeatedly she tried to stand up, but failed. She was
as weak as a newborn kitten. And light-headed. Damn
Cooper Landry! No wonder he'd urged her to drink
so much brandy. He'd wanted her to pass out so she
wouldn't know when he sneaked away like the miserable skunk that he was.

Making a Herculean final effort, she put all her
weight on her left foot and stood up on it. The earth
tilted precariously. Closing her eyes, she clasped her

supporting stick of firewood and held on for dear life. When she felt it was safe to reopen her eyes, she did— and let out a thin squeak of astonishment. Cooper was standing on the other side of the clearing.

"Just what the hell do you think you're doing?" he bellowed.

Dropping what he was carrying, including his rifle, he bore down on her like a sorely provoked angel. Catching her under her arms, he kicked the stick of wood out from under her and lowered her back into her sickbed. He packed the covers around her shivering body.

"What the hell were you trying to do?"

"F...find water," she stuttered through chattering teeth.

His muttered expletive was so vivid it was almost tangible. He laid his open hand on her forehead to gauge her temperature. "You're so cold, you're blue. Don't try another damn stupid stunt like that again, understand? It's *my* job to find water. *Yours* is to stay put. Got that?"

Swearwords continued to pour out of him like the payoff of a slot machine. He turned toward the fire and began stoking it, angrily throwing firewood onto the smoldering coals and fanning them to life. When the fire was blazing, he crossed the clearing and picked up the limp rabbit carcass he'd dropped on the ground. He was also carrying a thermos, one of the things he'd brought with them from the wreckage. Uncapping it, he poured water into the lid/cup and knelt on one knee beside Rusty.

"Here. I'm sure your throat is dry and sore. But don't drink too much too fast."

She cupped her hands around his and raised the cup to her parched lips. The water was so cold it hurt her teeth, but she didn't mind. She took three deep swallows before Cooper withdrew the cup.

"Easy, I said. There's plenty."

"You found a source?" She licked drops of water off her lips.

Watching that motion closely, Cooper said, "Yeah. A stream about three hundred yards that way." He indicated the direction with his head. "Must be a tributary of the Mackenzie."

She looked at the lifeless carcass lying next to his boot. "Did you shoot the rabbit?"

"Killed it with a rock. I didn't want to waste any ammo unless I had to. I'll dress it and put it on to cook. We can… Oh, hell. What's the matter?"

Rusty, much to her dismay, burst into tears. The sobs racked her entire body. She covered her face with her hands, but even as dehydrated as she was, tears leaked through her fingers.

"Look, it was either him or us," Cooper said with agitation. "We've got to eat. You can't be so—"

"It's not the rabbit," she blubbered.

"Then what? Does your leg hurt?"

"I thought you had de…deserted me. Left me behind beca…cause of my leg. And maybe you should. I'm holding you up. You probably could have wa…walked to safety by now if it weren't for me and my leg."

She hiccuped around several attempts to go on. "But my leg really doesn't make much difference because I'm a washout in situations like this anyway. I loathe the great outdoors and think it's anything but great. I hate it. Even summer camp never appealed to me. I'm cold. And scared. And guilty for complaining when I'm alive and everybody else is dead."

She dissolved into another torrent, her shoulders shaking. Cooper let out a long-suffering sigh, several florid curses, and then walked forward on his knees to take her into his arms. He pressed her shoulders between his large hands. Rusty's initial reaction was to tense up and try to pull away. But he kept his hands there and drew her against him. The promise of comfort was too much for her to resist. She slumped against his broad chest, clutching handfuls of his thick hunting coat.

The clean, fresh essence of pine clung to his clothes and hair—and that appealing, musty smell of damp leaves and fog. In Rusty's weakened, woozy state, he seemed unnaturally large, as fantastic as the hero in a children's tale. Powerful. Strong. Fierce but benevolent. Able to slay any dragon.

When one of his capable hands cupped the back of her head, she burrowed her face deeper into the quilted cloth of his coat and luxuriated in the first feeling of security she'd known since the plane went down—even before that, since leaving the hunting lodge and her disappointed father.

Finally the tumult passed. Her tears dried up. There was no excuse for Cooper to go on holding her, so she eased away from him. Embarrassed now, she kept her head down. He seemed reluctant to let her go, but at last his hands slid away.

"Okay now?" he asked gruffly.

"Yes, fine, thank you." She wiped her moist nose on the back of her hand, as though she did that all the time.

"I'd better get that rabbit ready to cook. Lie back down."

"I'm tired of lying down."

"Then turn your head. I want you to be able to eat this and I'm afraid you won't if you watch me gut it."

Carrying the rabbit to the edge of the clearing, he laid it on a flat rock and proceeded to dress it. Rusty wisely kept her eyes averted. "That's what we had our argument over," she said quietly.

Cooper looked at her over his shoulder. "You and who?"

"My father. He had brought down a ram." She laughed without humor. "It was a beautiful animal. I felt sorry for it, but I pretended to be ecstatic over the kill. Father hired one of the guides to field-dress it. He wanted to supervise, to make sure the guide didn't damage the hide." Blinking tears out of her eyes, she continued. "I couldn't watch. It made me physically ill. Father—" she paused to draw in a deep breath "—I think I disgusted and disappointed him."

Cooper was cleaning his hands on a handkerchief he'd soaked with water from the thermos. "Because you couldn't stomach a field-dressing?"

"Not just that. That capped it off. I proved to be a terrible marksman, but I couldn't have shot anything if it had walked up and put its nose against the barrel of my rifle. I didn't like anything about that whole scene." Softly, she added almost to herself, "I wasn't as good an outdoorsman as my brother Jeff."

"Did your father expect you to be?" He had skewered the rabbit on a green twig and was now suspending it over the coals.

"I think he was hoping I would be."

"Then he's a fool. You're not physically equipped to be a hunter."

His eyes dropped to her chest. And lingered. Heat rushed into her breasts, filling them like mother's milk, making them heavy and achy. Her nipples drew tight.

The reaction startled Rusty enormously. Instinctively, she wanted to cover and press her breasts back to normalcy, but he was still looking at her, so she couldn't. She didn't dare move at all. She was afraid that if she did, something terribly fragile would be broken—something that couldn't be replaced or repaired. Any reckless move would be disastrous and irrevocable. Something dreadful might happen as a result.

It was the first time he had made any sexual reference besides the vulgarities he'd spouted last night. He'd done that only to rile her. She realized that now. But this was something altogether different. This time, he was as much the victim as the perpetrator.

He yanked his eyes back toward the fire and the moment passed. But they didn't speak to each other for a long time. Rusty closed her eyes and pretended to doze, but she watched him as he busied himself around what was gradually coming to look like a bonafide camp. He sharpened the hatchet on a stone. He checked the roasting rabbit, turning it several times.

He moved with surprising agility for a man his size. She was sure that some women would consider him handsome, particularly now that his chin and jaw were deeply shadowed by a twenty-four-hour beard. The wide, curving mustache was sexy…if one liked facial hair. It sat directly on top of his lower lip, completely obscuring his upper one, making the thought of going in search of it intriguing.

She found herself staring at his mouth as he leaned down and spoke to her. "I... I beg your pardon?"

He looked at her strangely. "Your eyes are glassy. You're not going delirious again, are you?" He pressed his palm to her forehead.

Impatient with him and herself for her adolescent fantasies, she swatted his hand aside. "No, I feel fine. What did you say?"

"I asked if you were ready to eat."

"That's an understatement."

He assisted her into a sitting position. "This has been cooling for a minute or two. It should be about ready." He slid the rabbit off the spit and tore off a leg at the joint. He passed it to Rusty. Hesitantly she took it, staring at it dubiously.

"You're going to eat it if I have to force it down your throat." He tore off a bite of meat with his strong white teeth. "It's not half bad. Honest."

She pinched some of the meat off the bone and put it into her mouth, making herself chew and swallow it quickly. "Not so fast," he cautioned. "It'll make you sick."

She nodded and took another bite. With a little salt, it wouldn't have been bad at all. "There are some very nice restaurants in Los Angeles that have rabbit on the menu," she said conversationally. She instinctively reached for a napkin, remembered that she didn't have one, shrugged, and licked her fingers.

"Is that where you live, Los Angeles?"

"Beverly Hills, actually."

He studied her in the firelight. "Are you a movie star or something?"

Rusty got the impression that he wouldn't be impressed if she told him she was a three-time Oscar winner. She doubted if Cooper Landry put much stock in fame. "No, I'm not a movie star. My father owns a real-estate company. It has branches all over southern California. I work for him."

"Are you any good at it?"

"I've been very successful."

He chewed a mouthful and tossed the cleaned bone into the fire. "Being the boss's daughter, how could you miss?"

"I work hard, Mr. Landry." She took umbrage at his sly implication that her father was responsible for the success she had achieved. "I had the highest sales record of the agency last year."

"Bravo."

Miffed that he was so obviously unimpressed, she asked snidely, "What do you do?"

He silently offered her another piece of the meat, which she tore into as though she'd been eating fresh, unseasoned roasted rabbit cooked over an open fire every day of her life.

"I ranch," Cooper replied.

"Cattle?"

"Some. Horses mostly."

"Where?"

"Rogers Gap."

"Where's that?"

"In the Sierra Nevada."

"Never heard of it."

"I'm not surprised."

"Can you make a living at just ranching?"

"I do all right."

"Is Rogers Gap close to Bishop? Do people ski there?"

"We have a few runs. Serious skiers consider them a real challenge. Personally I think they're some of the most spectacular on the continent."

"Then why haven't I ever heard of this place?"

"We're a carefully guarded secret and want to remain that way. We don't advertise."

"Why?" Her interest was piqued. She never passed up an opportunity to locate new and interesting property for her clients to invest in. "With the right developer handling it, you could make something out of Rogers Gap. If it's as good for skiing as you say, it could become the next Aspen."

"God forbid," he said under his breath. "That's the point. We don't want to be put on the map. We don't want our mountains to be littered with concrete condos or the peaceful community to be overrun by a bunch of pushing, shoving, rude skiers from Beverly Hills who are more interested in modeling their Rodeo Drive duds than preserving our landscape."

"Does everyone in town hold to this philosophy?"

"Fortunately, yes, or they wouldn't be living there. We don't have much going for us except the scenery and the tranquillity."

She tossed her denuded bones into the fire. "You sound like a holdover from the sixties."

"I am."

Her eyes were teasing. "Were you a flower child, advocating universal harmony? Did you march for peace and participate in war protests?"

"No," he replied sharply. Rusty's goading grin collapsed. "I couldn't wait to join up. I wanted to go to war. I was too ignorant to realize that I would have to kill people or get killed myself. I hadn't bargained on getting captured and imprisoned. But I did. After seven months in that stinking hole, I escaped and came home a hero."

He practically snarled the last sentence. "The guys in that POW camp would have killed each other for a meal like the one you just ate." His gray eyes looked like glittering knife-blades as they sliced toward her. "So I'm not overwhelmed by your Beverly Hills glitz and glamour, Miss Carlson."

He stood up abruptly. "I'm going for more water. Don't wander off."

Don't wander off, she silently mimicked. All right, he had put her in her place, but she wasn't going to wear sackcloth and ashes for the rest of her life. Lots of men had fought in Vietnam and returned to lead happy, productive lives. It was Cooper's own fault if he was maladjusted. He thrived on his own bitterness. That's what fueled him. He nursed it. He cultivated his quarrel with society because he felt it owed him something.

Maybe it did. But it wasn't her fault. She wasn't responsible for whatever misfortune had befallen him. Just because he walked around with a chip on his shoulder the size of Mount Everest didn't make him a worthier human being than she was.

He returned, but they maintained a hostile silence while she drank her fill of water from the thermos. Just as wordlessly, he assisted her as she hobbled out of the clearing for a few minutes of privacy. When he eased her back down onto the thick pallet, which had become the nucleus of their world, he said, "I need to check your leg. Hold the flashlight for me."

She watched as he unbound the bandages and pulled them back to reveal a jagged, uneven row of stitches. She stared at it in horror, but he seemed pleased with his handiwork. With his hands around her calf muscles, he raised her leg to inspect it closer. "No signs of new infection. Swelling's gone down."

"The scar," she whispered roughly.

He looked up at her. "There wasn't much I could do about that." His lower lip thinned until it was hardly visible beneath his mustache. "Just be glad I didn't have to cauterize it."

"I am."

He sneered. "I'm sure a high-ticket plastic surgeon in Beverly Hills can fix the scar."

"Do you have to be so obnoxious?"

"Do you have to be so superficial?" He aimed a finger in the direction of the crashed plane. "I'm sure any of those guys we left up there would settle for a scar on their shin."

He was right, of course; but that didn't make his criticism any easier for her to swallow. She lapsed into sullen silence. He bathed her leg in peroxide and re-bandaged it, then gave her one of the penicillin tablets and two aspirins. She washed them down with water. No more brandy for her, thank you.

Drunkenness, she had discovered, aroused her emotionally and sexually. She didn't want to think of Cooper Landry as anything but a wretched grouch. He was a short-tempered, surly ogre harboring a grudge against the world. If she didn't have to rely on him for her survival, she would have nothing to do with him.

She had already settled beneath the pile of furs when he slid in and embraced her as he had the night before.

"How much longer do we have to stay here?" she asked crossly.

"I'm not clairvoyant."

"I'm not asking you to predict when we'll be rescued; I was referring to this bed. Can't you rig up a shelter of some kind? Something we can move around in?"

"The accommodations aren't to m'lady's liking?"

She sighed her annoyance. "Oh, never mind."

After a moment, he said, "There's a group of boulders near the stream. One side of the largest of them has been eroded out. I think with a little ingenuity and some elbow grease, I could make a lean-to out of it. It won't be much, but it will be better than this. And closer to the water."

"I'll help," she offered eagerly.

It wasn't that she didn't appreciate this shelter. It had saved her life last night. But it was disconcerting to sleep this close to him. Since he had taken off his coat as he had the night before, Rusty was keenly aware of his muscled chest against her back. She could therefore assume that he was keenly aware of her body because she wasn't wearing her coat, either.

She could think of little else as his hand found a comfortable spot midway between her breasts and her waist. He even wedged his knees between hers, elevating her injured leg again. She started to ask him if that was necessary, but since it felt so much better that way, she let it pass without comment.

"Rusty?"

"Hmm?" His warm breath drifted into her ear and caused goose bumps to break out over her arms. She snuggled closer to him.

"Wake up. We've got to get up."

"Get up?" she groaned. "Why? Pull the covers back up. I'm freezing."

"That's the point. We're soaking wet. Your fever broke and you sweated all over both of us. If we don't get up and dry off, we stand a good chance of getting frostbite."

She came fully awake and rolled to her back. He was serious. Already he was tossing off the furs. "What do you mean, dry off?"

"Strip and dry off." He began unbuttoning his flannel shirt.

"Are you crazy? It's freezing!" Recalcitrantly, she pulled the pelt back over herself. Cooper jerked it off her.

"Take off all your clothes. Now!"

He shrugged off his flannel shirt and draped it over the nearest bush. With one fluid motion, he crossed his arms at his waist and peeled the turtleneck T-shirt over his head. It made his hair stick up funnily, but Rusty didn't feel like laughing. Laughter—in fact any sound at all—got trapped inside her closed throat. Her first glimpse of the finest chest she'd ever seen rendered her speechless.

Hard as rocks those muscles were. Beautifully sculpted, too, beneath taut skin. His nipples were dark and pebbly from the cold, their areolae shriveled around them. It was all tantalizingly covered with a blanket of crisp hair that swirled and whorled, tipped and tapered beguilingly.

He was so trim she could count every single rib. His stomach was as flat and tight as a drum. She couldn't see his navel very well. It was deeply nestled in a sexy tuft of hair.

"Get started, Rusty, or I'll do it for you."

His threat plucked her out of her trance. Mechanically, she peeled off her sweater. Beneath it she was wearing a cotton turtleneck much like his. She fiddled with the hem while she watched him stand up and work his jeans down his legs. The long johns weren't the most alluring sight she'd ever seen.

But Cooper Landry unclothed had to be.

In seconds he was standing there, silhouetted against the dim glow of the fire, stark naked. He was beautifully shaped and generously endowed—so marvelously made that she couldn't help her gaping stare. He quite literally took her breath away.

He draped the articles of discarded clothing on the bush, then pulled a pair of socks over his hands and ran them over his body, drying it thoroughly—everything—before removing the socks from his hands.

Kneeling, he tore into one of the backpacks looking for underwear. He pulled on a pair of briefs, all with a supreme lack of self-consciousness, much less modesty.

When he turned toward her and noticed that she hadn't moved, he frowned with irritation. "Come on, Rusty. Hurry up. It's damn cold out here."

He reached for her sweater, which, so far, was the only thing she'd taken off. She handed it to him and he hung it up to dry. Holding out his hand for more clothes, he snapped his fingers quickly and repeatedly to hurry her along. "Come on, come on." Casting one anxious glance up at him, she pulled the T-shirt over her head and passed it to him.

The cold air was a breathtaking shock to her system. Immediately she was chilled and started trembling so violently she couldn't handle the button on her one-legged trousers.

"Here, let me do that, dammit. Or I'll be standing out here all night." Cooper dropped to his knees and straddled her thighs. Impatiently he pushed her hands out of the way so he could unfasten the button and pull down the zipper. With a detached air he eased the trousers down her legs and tossed them haphazardly toward the nearest bush.

But he was brought up short by what he obviously hadn't expected. A pair of extremely feminine, extremely scanty bikini panties. He'd seen the lace-edged leg, but that was all. For what seemed like an eternity, he stared at them before saying gruffly, "Take them off."

Rusty shook her head. "No."

His face became fierce. "Take them off." Rusty shook her head emphatically. Before she could brace herself for it, he pressed his open hand directly over the triangular scrap of silk and lace. "They're wet. Take them off."

Their eyes, like their wills, clashed. It was as much the chill in his stare as the chill in the air that prompted Rusty to slide the damp garment down her legs.

"Now dry off."

He handed her a cotton sock like the ones he'd used. She ran it over her lower body and her legs. Keeping her head bowed, she groped blindly for the underwear Cooper handed her. He hadn't chosen long johns because they would chafe her injury. She pulled on a pair of panties similar to the ones she'd just taken off and which were now dangling from the lower branches of the bush, fluttering like a victory banner the morning after a fraternity beer bust.

"Now the top."

Her brassiere was just as frivolous as the panties that matched them. The morning she left the lodge, she had dressed in clothes befitting her return to civilization. After having to wear thermal underwear for several days, she had been good and sick of it.

Leaning forward, she grappled with the hook at her back, but her fingers were so numb from the cold she couldn't get it to open. Muttering curses, Cooper reached around her and all but ripped the hook from its mooring. The brassiere fell forward. She peeled the straps down her arms, flung it away and faced him defiantly.

Beneath his mustache, his mouth was set in a hard, unyielding line. He paused for only a heartbeat before he began roughly rubbing the cotton sock over her throat, chest, breasts, and stomach. Then, reaching around her again, he blotted the sweat off her back. They were so close that her breath stirred his chest hair. Her lips came perilously close to touching one of his distended nipples. Hers, hard and peaked from the cold, grazed his skin.

He pulled back quickly and angrily dragged a thermal top over her head. While she was working her arms into the sleeves, he ripped the damp fur they'd been lying on off the pallet and replaced it with another one. "It's not as soft, but it's dry."

"It'll be fine," Rusty said hoarsely.

Finally they were cocooned again. She didn't resist when he pulled her close to him. She was shivering uncontrollably and her teeth were chattering. But it wasn't long before they began to warm up. Their bodies were in chaos because of what their eyes had seen. Erotic impressions lingered in their minds.

Lying in his embrace fully dressed had been unnerving enough. Lying there with him wearing only underwear wreaked havoc on Rusty's senses. Her fever had broken, but her body was burning like a furnace now.

His bare thighs felt delicious against hers. She liked their hair-smattered texture. Because she was braless, she was sharply aware of his hand resting just beneath her breasts, almost but not quite touching them.

He wasn't immune to the enforced intimacy. He'd exerted himself by switching out the pelts and changing clothes so quickly, but that wasn't the only reason he was breathing heavily. His chest swelled and receded against her back rhythmically but rapidly.

And then there was that other inexorable evidence of his arousal.

It prompted her to whisper, "I don't think I need to…uh…prop my leg on top of yours."

A low moan vibrated through his chest. "Don't even talk about it. And for God's sake, don't move." His distress was obvious.

"I'm sorry."

"For what? You can't help being beautiful any more than I can help being a man. I guess we'll just have to tolerate that from each other."

She honored his request and didn't move so much as a muscle. She didn't even reopen her eyes once they were closed. But she did fall asleep with a tiny smile on her lips. Inadvertently, perhaps, but he had told her that he thought she was beautiful.

CHAPTER FOUR

IT MADE A difference in their relationship.

The forced intimacy of the night before didn't draw them closer together. Rather, it created a schism of uneasiness between them. Their conversation the following morning was stilted. They avoided making eye contact. They dressed with their backs to each other. They moved awkwardly. Their motions were jerky and unsure, like those of invalids who had just regained the use of their limbs.

Taciturn and withdrawn, Cooper whittled her a pair of crutches out of two stout tree branches. Aesthetically, they weren't much to rave about, but Rusty was immensely grateful for them. They allowed her mobility. She would no longer be confined to the bed.

When she thanked him, he only grunted an acknowledgement and stamped off through the underbrush toward the stream to get water. By the time he returned, she was accustomed to the crutches and was hobbling around the clearing on them.

"How does your leg feel?"

"Okay. I cleaned it with peroxide myself and took another pill. I think it's going to be okay." She had even managed to dress in her one remaining pair of slacks and put her boots on. Enough of the soreness was gone that the additional pressure of clothing didn't irritate the wound.

They drank from the thermos in turn. That passed for breakfast. Cooper said, "I'd better start building that shelter today."

They had awakened to find their cocoon dusted with snow. This time the flakes weren't merely grains; they were real and ominous, harbingers of the first winter storm. Both knew how harsh the winters in this area could be. It was imperative that they have a shelter to use until they were rescued. If they weren't rescued, a temporary shelter would be of little consequence, but neither wanted to think about that.

"What can I do to help?" she asked.

"You can cut up that suede jacket into strips." He nodded toward a jacket that had belonged to one of the crash victims and handed her an extra knife. "I'll need plenty of thongs to tie the poles together. While you're doing that, I'd better see if we've got food for dinner." She looked at him quizzically. "I set some snares yesterday."

She glanced around her apprehensively. "You won't go far, will you?"

"Not too far." He shouldered his rifle and checked to see that he had pocketed a box of ammunition. "I'll be back before the fire needs to be refueled. Keep the knife and rifle handy, though. I haven't seen any bear tracks, but you never know."

Without another word he turned and dissolved into the dense screen of trees. Rusty stood leaning on her crutches, her heart thumping fearfully.

Bears?

After several moments, she shook off her paralyzing

fright. "This is silly," she muttered to herself. "Nothing's going to get me."

She wished she had a radio, a television set, anything to relieve the oppressive silence. It was only occasionally broken by the cracking of twigs and the rustling of leaves as unseen forest animals scurried about on their daily forages. Rusty's eyes searched out these silence-breakers, but they remained hidden and thereby more intimidating. She couldn't put Cooper's mention of bears out of her mind.

"He probably said that on purpose just to frighten me," she said out loud as she viciously sliced through the tough suede with the knife he'd left behind for her use. It was smaller than the one that constantly rode in the scabbard attached to his belt.

Her stomach growled. She thought about fresh, hot and buttery breakfast croissants, toasted bagels and cream cheese, warmed glazed donuts, pancakes and bacon, ham and eggs. That only made her hungrier. The only thing she could do was to fill her empty stomach with water.

Soon, however, drinking so much water created another problem. She put it off as long as possible, but finally had no choice but to set aside her handiwork. Painstakingly, and without a smidgen of grace or coordination, she stood up and propped her arms on her crutches. Going in the direction opposite to that Cooper had taken, she found a spot in which to relieve herself.

As she struggled with her crutches and her clothes, at the same time checking for creepy crawlies on the ground, she marveled that this was really Rusty Carlson, real-estate princess of Beverly Hills, seeking a place in the woods to pee!

Her friends would never have guessed she could come this far without going stark, staring mad. Her father would never believe it. But if she lived to tell about it, he would be so proud of her.

She was in the process of refastening her pants when she heard the nearby movement. Swiveling her head in that direction, she listened. Nothing.

"Probably just the wind." Her voice sounded unnaturally loud and cheerful. "Or a bird. Or Cooper coming back. If he's creeping up on me as a joke, I'll never forgive him."

She ignored the next rustling noise, which was louder and nearer than the last one, and moved as fast as she could back toward the camp. Determined not to do anything so cowardly as to whimper or cry out, she clenched her jaw in fear as she stumbled along over the uneven ground.

All her bravery deserted her when the form materialized from between the trunks of two pines and loomed directly in her path. Her head snapped up, she looked into the beady eyes, the hairy, leering face, and let out a bloodcurdling scream.

COOPER WAS IN a hurry to get back, but he decided to dress the two rabbits before he returned. He had told himself that he wasn't testing her fortitude when he'd gutted the rabbit where she could see it.

But he knew deep down inside that's exactly what he'd been doing. Perversely, he had wanted her to cringe, to retch, to get hysterical, to demonstrate some feminine weakness.

She hadn't. She'd borne up well. Far better than he'd expected her to.

He tossed away the entrails and began scraping the insides of the pelts. They would come in handy later. The fur was warm and he could always use it to make Rusty—Rusty. Her again. Couldn't he think of anything else? Did his every single thought have to come full circle back to her? At what point had they become a pair as inseparable as Adam and Eve? Couldn't he think of one without thinking immediately of the other?

He remembered the first thought that had registered when he regained consciousness. Her face, alluringly framed in that tumble of russet curls, had been bending over him, and he'd thought of the vilest obscenity the marine corps had ever coined and came just short of saying it out loud.

He'd been glad to be alive—but barely. He had thought he'd be better off dead rather than having to put up with this airhead swathed in expensive fur and sexy perfume. In the wilderness she wouldn't stand a marshmallow's chance at a bonfire. He'd figured that before it was over, he'd probably have to kill her to put them both out of their misery.

That was an unsettling and unappetizing thought, but he had been forced to do worse in order to save his own life in Nam. The plane crash had caused him to automatically revert to the law of the jungle, to slip back into the role of survivor.

Rule number one: You either killed or got killed. You stayed alive no matter what it cost. The survival tactics taught to the army's special services knew no conscience. You did whatever was necessary to live one more day, one more hour, one more minute. He had been steeped in that doctrine and had practiced it more times than he wanted to remember—but too many times to let him forget.

But the woman had surprised him. That leg injury had caused her a great deal of pain, but she hadn't whined about it. She hadn't nagged him about being hungry and thirsty and cold and scared, although God knew she must have been. She'd been a tough little nut and she hadn't cracked yet. Unless things got drastically worse, he doubted now that she would.

Of course that left him with a whole new set of problems. Few people had ever won his admiration. He didn't want to admire Rusty Carlson, but found himself doing so.

He was also coming to acknowledge that he was stranded in the middle of nowhere with a tempting piece of womanhood, and that they might be alone and dependent on each other for a long time.

The demons who had guided his fate were having a huge laugh at his expense this time. They'd run amok many times in the past, but this was the clincher. This was the big punch line that had made his whole life a joke.

Traditionally, he despised women like Rusty Carlson. He had no use for wealthy, silly, superficial society broads who'd been born with silver spoons in their mouths. They didn't know, or want to know, about anything outside their gilded cages. Wasn't it just his luck to draw one who had earned his grudging respect by bearing up under the worst of circumstances?

But even that wasn't enough for the malicious gods. She could have been a silly society broad who wouldn't have given a warthog any competition in the looks department. She could have had a voice that would shatter glass.

Instead, the fates had forced on him a woman who looked like a dream. Surely the devil had designed her. Temptation incarnate. With cinnamon-colored hair a man could wrap himself in and nipples that looked so sweet they must taste like candy. Her voice would melt butter. That's what he thought about every time she spoke.

What a cruel joke. Because he would not touch her. Never. He'd been down that road. Women like her followed vogue. Not only in clothes; in everything. When he'd met Melody it had been fashionable to love a veteran. She had, until it became convenient not to.

Scratch the silky surface of Rusty Carlson and you'd find another Melody. Rusty was only sucking up to him now because she depended on him for her survival. She looked like a tasty morsel, but inside she was probably as rotten and devious as Melody had been.

Slinging the rabbit pelts over his shoulder and folding the meat in a cloth, he headed back toward their camp. She wasn't going to get to him. He couldn't afford to start feeling soft toward her. Last night he'd let her cry because he felt that she deserved one good, cleansing cry. But no more. He'd held her during the night because it was necessary for them to keep warm. But he would keep his distance from now on. Once the shelter was built, they wouldn't have to sleep together like that. He wouldn't have to endure any more nights with her curled against his front and her bottom cushioning his involuntary reaction to her.

Stop thinking about it, he told himself. Forget how smooth her belly felt beneath your hand. Forget the shape of her breasts and the color of the hair between her thighs.

Groaning, he thrashed through the woods, viciously determined to keep his thoughts on track. As soon as he built the shelter, such close proximity wouldn't be necessary. He would keep his eyes and his hands—

The piercing scream brought him up short.

If he'd walked into an invisible wall, he couldn't have stopped more abruptly. When Rusty's next scream rent the stillness, he instinctively slipped into the role of jungle fighter as easily as well-greased gears fitting into their notches. Silently, he slithered through the trees in the direction of her scream, knife drawn and teeth bared.

"WHO...WHO ARE YOU?" Rusty's hand was gripping her own throat, where her pulse was beating wildly.

The man's bearded face split into a wide grin. He turned his head and said, "Hey, Pa, *she* wants to know who *I* am."

Chuckling, another man, an older version of the first, stepped out from between the trees. The two gaped at Rusty. Both had small, dark eyes embedded in deep sockets.

"We could ask you the same question," the older one said. "Who are you, little girl?"

"I... I... I survived the airplane crash." They gazed back at her with perplexity. "You didn't know about the crash?"

"Can't say that we did."

She pointed with a shaking finger. "Back there. Two days ago. Five men were killed. My leg was injured." She indicated the crutches.

"Any more women?"

Before she could answer, Cooper lunged up behind the older of the two men and laid the gleaming blade of his knife against the whiskered throat. He grasped the man's arm, twisted it behind him and shoved his hand up between his shoulder blades. The man's hunting rifle clattered to the ground at his feet.

"Move away from her or I'll kill him," he said to the stunned younger man.

He was staring at Cooper as though he were Satan himself, who had sprung up out of the ground straight from hell. Even Rusty was quelled by the evil threat in Cooper's eyes. But she was trembling with relief to see him.

"I said to move away from her." Cooper's voice seemed as deadly as his knife. It was void of inflection, emotionless. The younger man took two exaggerated steps away from Rusty. "Now, drop the rifle," Cooper told him.

Since it appeared that the attacker was human after all, the younger man's face puckered with rebellion. He whined, "Pa, do I have to do—"

"Do as he says, Reuben."

Reluctantly the younger man tossed down his hunting rifle. Cooper kicked the two rifles now on the ground out of reach and gradually released his stranglehold on the man. He stepped around him and stood beside Rusty, facing the two. "Rusty?" She jumped. "Are you okay?"

"Fine."

"Did they hurt you?"

"They scared me, that's all. I don't think they meant to."

Cooper didn't take his eyes off the two men, but regarded them warily. "Who are you?"

His bark carried more authority than Rusty's feeble question. The older man answered him at once. "Quinn Gawrylow and my son, Reuben. We live here." Cooper didn't even blink. The man went on. "Across the deep ravine." He hitched his chin in that direction.

Cooper had discovered the ravine the day before. The stream where he'd been getting water lay at the bottom of it. He hadn't crossed it to explore because he hadn't wanted to leave Rusty alone that long. He thanked God now that he hadn't. These men might be perfectly harmless. Then again, they might not be. His suspicious nature had served him well on more than one occasion. Until they proved to be otherwise, he'd consider this duo the enemy. They hadn't done anything harmful so far, but he didn't like the way the younger one was staring at Rusty as though she were a celestial vision.

"What brought you across the ravine?" Cooper asked.

"We smelled your wood smoke last night and this morning came to investigate. We don't usually see other people in our woods."

"Our plane crashed."

"That's what the young lady said."

She'd been elevated from a little girl to a young lady. Rusty silently thanked Cooper for that. She, too, was unnerved by the younger man's stare and inched closer to Cooper, taking shelter behind his arm. "How far are we from the nearest town?" she asked.

"A hundred miles." Her hopes plummeted. The man obviously noticed. "But the river isn't too far."

"The Mackenzie?"

"Right. If you reach that before it freezes closed, you'll catch a boat on its way down to Yellowknife."

"How far to the river?" Cooper asked.

The man scratched his head beneath his wool stocking cap. "Ten, fifteen miles, wouldn't you say, Reuben?"

The younger man bobbed his head, never taking his lustful eyes off Rusty. Cooper squinted at him, his stare malevolent and dangerous. "Could you direct us to the river?"

"Yes," the elder Gawrylow said. "Tomorrow. Today we'll feed you. Let you rest up." He glanced down at the fresh meat Cooper had dropped. "Would you like to follow us to our cabin?"

Rusty glanced up at Cooper expectantly. His face remained a mask as he studied the two men cautiously. At last he said, "Thanks. Rusty could use the food and rest before we strike out. You go on ahead." Using his rifle, he pointed them toward their camp.

The two men bent to pick up their rifles. Rusty felt Cooper's muscles tense with precaution. But the father and son shouldered their rifles and turned in the direction Cooper had indicated. Cooper glanced down at her and spoke from the side of his mouth. "Stay close. Where's the knife I gave you?"

"I left it behind when I went—"

"Keep it with you."

"What's the matter with you?"

"Nothing."

"You don't act very glad to see them. I'm delighted. They can lead us out of here."

His only comment was a thin-lipped "Yeah."

The Gawrylows were impressed with Cooper's improvisations. They helped gather up the pelts and the belongings Cooper and Rusty had salvaged from the crash. Nothing in the wilderness was ever wasted. Reuben kicked stones into the fire to make certain it was out.

The band, under Quinn's guidance, with his son following closely, set out for their cabin. Cooper brought up the rear so he could keep an eye on both Gawrylows and on Rusty, who was making admirable if awkward progress on her crutches.

The men seemed to be well-meaning, but Cooper had learned the hard way never to trust anyone. He'd seen too many soldiers blown to bits by hand grenades handed to them by smiling children.

At the stream they paused to rest. Rusty's lungs felt as though collapse were imminent; her heart was beating double time; and the crutches were chafing her armpits, even though Cooper had tried to prevent that by padding the tops of them with articles of extra clothing.

"How are you doing?" he asked her, uncapping the thermos and passing it to her.

"Fine." She forced a smile.

"Does your leg hurt?"

"No, it just feels like it weighs a ton."

"It can't be much farther. Then you can lie down for the rest of the day."

The Gawrylows waited patiently nearby until she had regained her breath and was ready to start again. "We'll cross at the easiest point," the elder one informed Cooper.

They walked along the streambed for several hundred yards. At any other time, Rusty would have been entranced with the landscape. The stream was crystal clear. It gurgled over rocks that had been polished as smooth as mirrors by the gallons of water that had rushed across them. Towering trees interlaced and formed canopies overhead. The evergreens were so deeply green that they appeared blue. The leaves of the deciduous trees ranged from vivid red to vibrant yellow. Encroaching winter had already caused many leaves to fall. They provided a crunchy carpet beneath their feet.

Rusty's chest was burning with exertion by the time the Gawrylows drew to a halt. She laid her crutches on the ground and gratefully sank down onto a rock beside the stream, which ran shallow at this point. The side of the ravine rising up on the other side of the brook looked as high as the Himalayas.

"This is it," Quinn said. "I'll lead the way. Reuben can carry the woman. You can bring your gear."

"Reuben can bring the gear. I'll carry the woman," Cooper amended in a steely voice.

The older man shrugged and ordered his son to take the bundles from Cooper. Reuben did so, but not without shooting Cooper a sour look. Cooper stared back at him unmoved. He didn't care whether Reuben liked it or not; he wasn't going to let those grubby hands get anywhere near Rusty.

When the father and son had moved out of earshot, he bent over her and whispered, "Don't be shy of using that knife." She looked up at him with alarm. "Just in case these Good Samaritans turn on us." He laid the crutches across her lap and picked her up in his arms.

The Gawrylows were already well up the side of

the ravine. He started after them, keeping one eye on them and the other on the treacherously steep incline. If he fell, Rusty would go with him. She had put up a brave front, but he knew her leg must be causing her considerable discomfort.

"Do you really think we'll be rescued tomorrow, Cooper?"

"Looks like there's a good chance. If we make it to the river and if a boat of some kind happens by." He was breathing with difficulty. Sweat had popped out on his forehead. His jaw was set with determination.

"You need a shave." The remark came from nowhere, but it indicated to them both how carefully she'd been studying his face. Without moving his head, he cast his eyes down toward her. Embarrassed, she looked away and murmured, "Sorry I'm so heavy."

"Hardly. Your clothes weigh more than you do."

That comment reminded them that he knew just how much of her was clothing and how much was flesh and bone. He'd seen her without any clothes, hadn't he? Rusty decided that if all their conversations were going to result in awkwardness, it was safer not to engage in conversation at all.

Besides, by this time they had reached the top of the ravine. Quinn was biting off a chaw of tobacco. Reuben had removed his stocking cap and was fanning himself with it. His dark hair was greasily plastered to his head.

Cooper set Rusty down. Wordlessly Quinn offered him the brick of tobacco. Rusty was grateful when, with a shake of his head, Cooper turned it down.

"We'll wait until you're rested," Quinn said.

Cooper looked down at Rusty. Her face was pale with fatigue. Her leg was probably hurting. The moist wind had picked up, making the temperature noticeably colder. No doubt she needed to take it slow and easy, but all things considered, the sooner he got her under a roof, fed, and lying down, the better.

"No need to wait. Let's go," he said tersely.

He pulled Rusty to her feet and propped her up on her crutches. He noticed her wince with pain, but steeled himself against compassion and indicated to their hosts that they were ready to proceed.

At least the remaining distance to the cabin was level ground. By the time they reached it, however, Rusty's strength was totally spent. She collapsed on the sagging porch like a rag doll.

"Let's get the woman inside," Quinn said as he pushed open the door.

The rickety door was attached to its frame by leather hinges. The interior of the cabin looked as uninviting as an animal's lair. Rusty eyed the opening with trepidation and a sense of dread. Then and there she decided that there were worse things than being exposed to the outdoors.

Cooper remained expressionless as he scooped her into his arms and carried her into the gloomy interior. The small windows were so blackened by grime that they let in little light. A dim, smoky fire gave off meager illumination, but what Rusty and Cooper saw would have been better left hidden in darkness.

The cabin was filthy. It stank of wet wool, rancid grease, and unwashed men. The only merit it had was that it was warm. Cooper carried Rusty toward the stone hearth and set her down in a cushionless, straight-backed chair. He upended an aluminum bucket and propped the foot of her injured leg on it. He stirred the fire with an iron poker. The desultory flames showed new life when he added sticks of firewood from the wooden box on the hearth.

The Gawrylows stamped in. Reuben closed the door behind them, deepening the darkness inside. In spite of the warmth the fire was now giving off, Rusty shivered and shrank deeper into her coat.

"You must be hungry." Quinn went to the wood-burning stove in one corner. He lifted the lid on a simmering pot and peered inside. "Stew smells done. Want some?"

Rusty was on the verge of refusing but Cooper answered for both of them. "Yes, please. Got any coffee?"

"Sure. Reuben, start a pot of coffee to boiling."

The younger man hadn't stopped staring at Rusty since he'd slunk in and dropped Cooper's and her belongings just inside the door.

Cooper followed Reuben's gawking stare back to Rusty. He wished to hell the firelight didn't shine through her hair, making it shimmer. Pale and drawn as her face was, her eyes looked huge, vulnerable, female. To the young man, who apparently lived alone in this wilderness with his father, a woman wouldn't even have to be pretty to be enticing. Rusty must have embodied his wildest fantasies.

With his bare hand, Reuben reached into a metal canister of coffee and tossed a handful into an enamel pot. He filled the pot with water from the pump in the dry sink and set it on the stove to boil. Within a few minutes Rusty and Cooper were handed plates filled with an unidentifiable stew. She was sure she was better off not knowing what meat was in it, so she refrained from asking. She chewed and swallowed quickly. It was at least hot and filling. The coffee was so strong that she grimaced as she swallowed, but she drank most of it.

While they ate, Cooper and she had a captivated audience. The older man's stare was more subtle than his son's, but possibly more observant. His deep-set eyes didn't miss a single move they made.

He broke a long silence by asking, "You married?"

"Yes," Cooper lied easily. "Five years."

Rusty swallowed the last bite she'd taken, hoping that the Gawrylows didn't notice how difficult it was to get down. She was glad Cooper had taken the initiative to answer. She didn't think she could have uttered a word.

"Kids?"

This time Cooper got tongue-tied, so it was left to Rusty to say "No," hoping that that answer was satisfactory to her "husband." She planned on asking him later why he had lied, but for now she would play along. His wariness was out of proportion, she thought; but she would still rather ally herself with him than with the Gawrylows.

Cooper finished eating and set his plate and cup aside. He glanced around the cabin. "You don't have a transmitter, do you? A ham radio?"

"No."

"Have you heard any airplanes flying over lately?"

"I haven't. Reuben?" Gawrylow nudged his gawking son in the knee. The younger man dragged his eyes away from Rusty.

"Planes?" he asked stupidly.

"We crashed two days ago," Cooper explained. "They're bound to have figured that out by now. I

thought there might have been search planes out looking for survivors."

"I haven't heard any planes," Reuben said abruptly
and returned his unwavering attention to Rusty.

"How can you stand to live so far away from everything?" she asked. Such self-imposed isolation dismayed her. She couldn't imagine doing without the
amenities a city had to offer, particularly by choice.
Even rural living would be tolerable if one could get
to a city every now and then. But to deliberately sever
all contact with civilization—

"We walk to the river and hitch a ride to Yellowknife twice a year," Quinn told them. "Once in April
and once in October. We stay for a few days, sell a
few pelts, buy what supplies we'll need, and hitch a
ride back. That's all the dealings we want with the
outside world."

"But why?" Rusty asked.

"I got a bellyful of towns and people. I lived in Ed-
monton, worked on a freight dock. One day the boss
accused me of stealing."

"Were you?"

Rusty was amazed at Cooper's audacity, but the old
man didn't seem to take offense at the blunt question.
He merely cackled and spat a stringy wad of tobacco
juice into the fireplace.

"It was easier to disappear than to go to court and
prove my innocence," he said evasively. "Reuben's
mother was dead. He and I just up and left. Took nothing with us but what money we had and the clothes on
our backs."

"How long ago was this?"

"Ten years. We drifted for a while, then gradually

migrated here. We liked it. We stayed." He shrugged. "We've never felt the urge to go back."

He concluded his story. Rusty had finished eating, but the Gawrylows seemed content to continue staring at Cooper and her.

"If you'll excuse us," Cooper said after an awkward silence, "I'd like to check my wife's injury."

Those two words, *my wife's*, seemed to come easily to his lips, but they jangled with falsehood in Rusty's ears. She wondered if the Gawrylows were convinced that they were a couple.

Quinn carried their plates to the sink where he pumped water over them. "Reuben, do your chores."

The young man seemed inclined to argue, but his father shot him a baleful, challenging glance. He shuffled toward the door, pulling on his coat and cap as he went. Quinn went out onto the porch and began stacking firewood against the wall of the cabin.

Rusty leaned close to Cooper where he knelt in front of her. "What do you think?"

"About what?"

"About them," she replied with asperity. He pinched the hem of her slacks between his fingers and sliced a knee-high tear in them with his knife. She reacted angrily. "Why'd you do that? This is my last pair of slacks. I won't have any clothes left by the time you get through cutting them to shreds."

He raised his head. His eyes were hard. "Would you rather take them off and give Reuben an eyeful of those nothing-to-them panties you wear?"

She opened her mouth, but discovered that she had no proper comeback, so she fell silent while he unwrapped her bandages and checked her stitched wound.

It seemed to have suffered no ill effects as a result of her hike. But it was sore again. Lying to him about it was useless since she was grimacing by the time he finished rewrapping it.

"Hurt?"

"A little, yes," she admitted.

"Stay off it for the rest of the day. Either sit here or lie on the pallet I'm about to make."

"Pallet? What about the beds?" She glanced across the room to where two beds stood against adjacent walls. "Don't you think they'll offer me one?"

He laughed. "I'm sure Reuben would love for you to join him in his. But unless you want lice, I'd advise you to stay out of it."

She jerked her leg back. Cooper just couldn't be nice, could he? They were comrades because they had to be, but they were not—no, definitely not—friends.

CHAPTER FIVE

IT SEEMED TO take forever for bedtime to arrive. Early in the evening they shared another meal with the Gawrylows. Their discussion about the extensive hike to the Mackenzie River carried over long after they were finished eating.

"There's no path to follow. It's rugged terrain, so it's a full day's walk," Quinn told them.

"We'll leave as soon as it's light enough." Cooper hadn't let Rusty out of his sight. He'd kept an eagle eye on her all afternoon. Now, as she sat in the straight-backed chair, he sat beside her on the floor, a proprietary arm draped over her thigh. "We won't need to pack much. I don't plan to take everything—only what's absolutely necessary."

Quinn asked, "What about the woman?"

Rusty felt Cooper's biceps contract against her leg. "What about her?"

"She'll slow us down."

"I'll stay here with her, Pa," Reuben offered gallantly.

"No." Cooper's response was as sharp as a jab made with a hat pin. "She goes. I don't care how slow we have to travel."

"It's all the same to us," Quinn said with his characteristic shrug, "but I thought you were in a hurry to contact your friends and family. They must be worried about you."

Rusty glanced down at the top of Cooper's head. "Cooper?" He looked up at her. "I don't mind staying here alone. If you can cover more ground without me hobbling along, it only makes sense, doesn't it? You could call my father as soon as you get to a telephone. He'll send someone to pick me up. This could all be over by tomorrow night."

He regarded her wistful expression. She'd go along and bear up under the hardships stoically if he insisted. But it wouldn't be easy for her to cover fifteen miles of forested ground even if she weren't injured. Through no fault of her own, she would cause them endless delays that might necessitate making camp for a night.

Still, he didn't like the idea of being separated from her. No matter how feisty she was, she couldn't effectively defend herself. In this environment she was as helpless as a butterfly. He wasn't being sentimental, he assured himself. It was just that she had survived this long against incredible odds; he would hate for something to happen to her now that rescue was a probability instead of a pipe dream.

His hand folded around her knee protectively. "Let's wait and see how you feel in the morning."

The next several hours crawled by. Rusty didn't know how the Gawrylows maintained their sanity. There was nothing to do, nothing to read, nothing to listen to or to look at—except each other. And when that became boring, they all stared at the sputtering kerosene lamp that put out more smelly black smoke than light.

One would expect these hermits to ply them with

a million questions about the outside world, but the Gawrylows showed a marked absence of interest in anything that was going on beyond their boundaries.

Feeling grimy and unwashed, Rusty timidly asked for a bowl of water. Reuben stumbled over his own long feet while fetching it for her and slopped some of it in her lap before successfully setting it down.

She pushed the sleeves of her sweater up to her elbows and washed her face and hands with the bar of soap Cooper had permitted her to bring along. She would have liked to savor the luxurious feeling of cupping handful after handful of water over her face, but three pairs of eyes were focused on her. When Cooper thrust one of his own T-shirts into her wet hands, she accepted it regretfully and dried her face.

Picking up her hairbrush, she began pulling it through her hair, which was not only dirtier than it had been in her life, but also matted and tangled. She was just beginning to work all the snarls out when Cooper jerked the brush out of her hands and said bossily, "That's enough."

She rounded on him, ready to protest, but his stony face stopped her. He'd been behaving strangely all day—more so than usual. She wanted to ask what the hell was wrong with him, why he was so edgy, but wisely decided that now wasn't an opportune time for an argument.

She did, however, show her irritation by angrily snatching her hairbrush back and repacking it in her precious bag of toiletries. They were her only reminders that somewhere in the world hot water, cream rinse, perfume, bubble bath and hand lotion were still realities.

At last, they all settled down for the night. She slept with Cooper as she had the past two nights. Lying curled on her side, her injured leg the uppermost, she faced the fire. Beneath her was the pallet Cooper had made using the pelts they'd carried with them. He had tactfully declined to use the bedding Quinn had offered them.

Cooper didn't curve his body around hers as he had been doing. He lay on his back tensely, never completely relaxed, and ever watchful.

"Stop twitching," she whispered after about half an hour. "What's your problem?"

"Shut up and go to sleep."

"Why don't you?"

"I can't."

"Why?"

"When we get out of here I'll explain it to you."

"Explain it to me now."

"I shouldn't have to. Read the signs."

"Does it have anything to do with why you told them we were married?"

"It has everything to do with that."

She pondered that for a moment. "I'll admit that they're kinda spooky, the way they keep staring at us. But I'm sure they're only curious. Besides, they're sound asleep now." The chorus of loud snores should have been his assurance that the Gawrylows were harmlessly asleep.

"Right," he said dryly, "and so should you be. Nighty-night."

Exasperated with him, she rolled back onto her side. Eventually she sank into a deep sleep. It was mercilessly short-lived. It seemed only minutes after her eyes closed that Cooper was nudging her awake. She groaned in protest, but remembering that today was the day her ordeal would come to an end, she sat up.

The cabin was still in total darkness, although she could see the shadowy outlines of Cooper and the Gawrylows moving about. Quinn was at the stove brewing coffee and stirring the pot of stew. It must never run out but be continually added to, she thought, hoping that she didn't return home with a case of ptomaine poisoning.

Cooper knelt beside her. "How do you feel?"

"Cold," she replied, rubbing her hands up and down her arms. Even though she hadn't slept in his embrace, his body heat had kept her warm throughout the night. He was better than any electric blanket she'd ever slept with.

"I meant health-wise. How does your leg feel?"

"Stiff, but not as sore as yesterday."

"You sure?"

"Positive."

"Get up and move around on it. Let's give it a test run."

He helped her to her feet. Once she had slipped her coat on and propped herself on her crutches, they went outside so she could have some privacy; the Gawrylows cabin didn't have indoor plumbing.

When she emerged from the outhouse, the rising sun had turned the overcast sky a watery gray. That light only emphasized her wanness. Cooper could tell that the effort of leaving the cabin to go to the bathroom had taxed her. Her hard breathing created clouds of vapor around her head.

He cursed beneath his breath. "What?" she asked him anxiously.

"You'll never make it, Rusty. Not in days." Hands on hips, he expelled his frustration in a gust of ghostly white breath and said, "What the hell am I going to do with you?"

He didn't soften the question with any degree of tenderness or compassion. His inflection intimated that he'd far rather not be bothered with her at all.

"Well, I'm sorry to inconvenience you further, Mr. Landry. Why don't you bait a bear trap with me? Then you can jog all the way to that damn river."

He stepped forward and put his face close to hers. "Look, Pollyanna, you're apparently too naive to see it, but there's a lot more at stake here than just getting to the river."

"Not as far as I'm concerned," she shot back. "If you sprouted wings and flew there, it couldn't be fast enough for me. I want to get out of here, away from you, and back home where I belong."

His stern lip all but disappeared beneath his mustache. "All right, then." He spun around and stamped back toward the cabin. "I'll get there much faster without having you tagging along. You'll stay here."

"Fine," she called after him.

Then, setting her own chin as stubbornly as his, she made her halting progress up the incline toward the cabin. The men were in the midst of an argument by the time she reached the door, which Cooper, in his haste or anger, had left ajar. Turning sideways and using her elbows, she maneuvered her way inside.

"Be reasonable, Gawrylow," Cooper was saying. "Reuben is twenty or so years younger than you. I want to move fast. He goes with me. You stay with my...my wife. I can't leave her here alone."

"But, Pa—" Reuben whined.

"He's right, Reuben. You'll move much faster than

I could. If you're lucky, you might reach the river by midafternoon."

The plan wasn't to Reuben's liking at all. He gave Rusty one last, hungry glance, then ambled out, muttering under his breath. Cooper didn't appear much happier. He drew Rusty aside and handed her the flare gun, curtly instructing her on how to use it.

"Think you can manage that?"

"I'm not an idiot."

He seemed prone to argue, but changed his mind. "If you hear an airplane, get outside as fast as you can and fire the flare straight up."

"Why aren't you taking it with you?"

The flare gun had been within Cooper's reach since they left the wreckage. "Because the roof of the cabin would be easier to spot than two men on foot. Keep this with you, too." Before she knew what he was about, he pulled the waistband of her slacks away from her body and slid the sheathed skinning knife inside. The smooth leather was cold against the naked skin of her abdomen. She gasped and sucked in her breath. He smiled at her startled reaction. "That should keep you mindful of where it is at all times."

"Why should I be mindful of that?"

He stared into her eyes for a long moment. "Hopefully you'll never have to know why."

She returned his stare. Up until that moment, she hadn't realized how much she hated the thought of his leaving her behind. She had put up a courageous front, but the idea of covering miles of wilderness on crutches had been overwhelming. In a way she was glad he had opted to go without her. But now that he was actually leaving, she wanted to cling to him and beg him not to.

She didn't, of course. He had little enough respect for her as it was. He thought she was a petted, pampered, city girl. Obviously he was right, because at that moment, she was sorely dreading the hours she would have to spend until he came back for her.

Cooper broke the telling stare and, with an impatient curse, turned away.

"Cooper!"

He spun back around. "What?"

"Be…be careful."

Within a heartbeat, she was anchored against his chest and his mouth was above hers, taking from it a scorching kiss that burned her soul. It surprised her so that she slumped against him. His arms tightened around her waist and drew her up so close and high that her toes dangled inches above his boots. She sought to regain her balance by clutching handfuls of his coat.

His lips ground against hers. They were possessive and hard. But his tongue was soft and warm and wet. It filled her mouth, explored, stroked. A desire that had been building for forty-eight hours overcame his iron control. His self-discipline snapped, but he was still masterful. This was a no-nonsense kiss that had nothing to do with romance. It was a kiss of passion. Raw. Carnal. Selfish.

Dizzily Rusty threw one of her arms around his neck and tilted her head back to give him deeper access, which he took. His stubbled jaw scraped her skin, but she didn't care. His mustache was surprisingly silky. It tickled and tantalized.

All too soon for her, he broke the kiss, pulling his head back abruptly and leaving her lips parted and damp and wanting more. "I'll be back as soon as possible. Goodbye, honey."

Honey? *Honey?*

He released her and turned toward the door. That's when she noticed Quinn Gawrylow sitting at the table, mindlessly chewing his perpetual wad of tobacco and watching them with the still, silent concentration of a cougar.

Rusty's heart sank like lead. Cooper had kissed her for the old man's benefit—not for his own. And certainly not for hers.

She shot his broad back a venomous look as he went through the door. It slapped closed behind him. Good riddance, she thought. How dare he—

Then, realizing that the old man's eyes were still on her, she looked at him with a vapid good-little-wife smile. "Do you think he'll be all right?"

"Reuben knows what he's doing. He'll take care of Mr. Landry." He waved down at the pallet still spread out in front of the hearth. "It's early yet. Why don't you go back to sleep?"

"No, I, uh—" she cleared her throat noisily "—I'm too keyed up to sleep. I think I'll just sit here for a while."

"Coffee?" He moved toward the stove.

"Please."

She didn't want any, but it would give her something to do and help pass the time. She set her crutches and the flare gun on the hearth within easy reach and lowered herself into the chair. The knife's scabbard poked her lower abdomen. Why it hadn't plunged right into her when Cooper had pulled her against his—

Her heart fluttered with the memory. It hadn't been only the knife's hardness she'd felt against her middle.

He'd probably derived a lot of joy out of humiliating her like that.

Feeling rebellious, she defiantly took the knife out of her waistband and laid it on the hearth. Accepting the cup of steaming coffee from Quinn, she settled down to wait through what would probably be the longest day of her life.

COOPER CALCULATED THAT they'd gone no farther than a mile when Reuben commenced to talk. Cooper could have gone the whole fifteen miles without a conversation, but maybe talking would make the time pass more quickly and help take his mind off Rusty.

"How come you don't have any kids?" Reuben asked him.

Cooper's instincts slipped into overdrive. Each of his senses was on the alert. That prickle at the back of his neck, which could always be relied upon to warn him that something wasn't quite right, hadn't gone away. Ever since he'd heard Rusty's scream and found her in a standoff with the Gawrylows, he had been suspicious of the two men. He might be doing them a grave injustice. They were probably on the level. But probabilities weren't worth a damn. Until he had Rusty safely turned over to the authorities, he wasn't giving either of the recluses the benefit of the doubt. If they proved to be reliable, then they would have earned his undying gratitude. Until then—

"Huh?" Reuben probed. "How come you—"

"I heard you." Cooper was following Reuben's lead. He didn't let the man get too far ahead of him, nor did he crowd up too close behind him. "Rusty has a career. We're both busy. We'll get around to having kids one of these days."

He hoped that would end the discussion. Children and families were topics Cooper always avoided talking about. Now, he didn't want to talk at all. He wanted to pour every ounce of energy into reaching that river as soon as possible.

"If I'd been married to her for five years, we'd have five kids by now," Reuben bragged rashly.

"But you're not."

"Maybe you ain't doing it right."

"What?"

Reuben gave him a sly wink over his shoulder. "You know, screwing."

The word crawled over Cooper like a loathsome insect. It wasn't that he was offended by the word. He used far worse on a daily basis. It was that he was offended by the word in connection with Rusty. It didn't occur to him that only the night before last he'd used it himself. He was too busy hoping that before the day was out, he wouldn't have to pound Reuben's face to mush; but if he made many more references to Rusty in that context, he just might.

"If she was my woman—"

"But she isn't." Cooper's voice cracked like a bullwhip.

"She will be, though."

With that, Reuben, wearing the grin of a madman, spun around and aimed his rifle at Cooper's chest. Cooper had subconsciously been bracing himself all morning for such an attack. He raised his rifle a split second after Reuben, but Reuben got off the first shot.

"WHAT WAS THAT?" Rusty jumped, realizing that she'd been drowsing in her chair.

Quinn was sitting where she'd last seen him, at the table. "Hmm?"

"I thought I heard something."

"I didn't hear anything."

"I could swear—"

"The logs in the fireplace shifted. That's all."

"Oh." Chagrined by her nervousness, she relaxed again in her chair. "I must have dozed off. How long ago since they left?"

"Not long."

He got up and moved toward her, kneeling down on the hearth to add logs to the fire. The warmth seeped into Rusty's skin and her eyes drifted closed again. Sad and dirty as this cabin was, at least it provided a roof over her head and protection from the cold west wind. She was grateful for that. After spending days—

Her eyes popped open at his touch. Quinn, still kneeling in front of her, had his hand folded around her calf. "I thought you might want to prop up your leg again," he said.

His voice was as gentle as a saint's, but his eyes were Lucifer's own as they stared up at her from within their cavelike sockets. Terror gripped her, but common sense warned her not to show it.

"No, thank you. In fact," she said in a thin voice, "I think I'll walk around a bit to exercise it."

She reached for her crutches, but he grabbed them up first. "Let me help you."

Before she could protest, he caught her arm and pulled her out of the chair. He had caught her off guard and the momentum caused the front of her body to bump against his. She backed away instantly, but found that she couldn't go far because his other hand was at the small of her back, urging her forward.

"No!"

"I'm only trying to help you," he said smoothly, obviously enjoying her mounting distress.

"Then please let me go, Mr. Gawrylow. I can manage."

"Not without help. I'll take your husband's place. He told me to take care of you, didn't he?" He ran his hand over her hip and Rusty went cold with fear.

"Don't touch me like that." She tried to squirm away from him but his hands were everywhere. "Get your hands off me."

"What's wrong with my hands?" His expression suddenly turned mean. "Aren't they clean enough for you?"

"No…yes… I… I just meant that Cooper will—"

"Cooper won't do anything," he said with a sinister smile. "And from now on I'll touch you however I want."

He yanked her against him. This time there was no doubt about his intention. Rusty funneled all her strength into getting away from him. She placed the heels of her hands on his shoulders and arched her back, trying to push herself away and at the same time to dodge his kiss.

The crutches slid out from under her arms and fell to the floor. She had to support herself on her sore leg and a pain shot up the jagged scar. She cried out.

"Go ahead, scream. I won't mind." His breath was foul and hot against her face. She turned her head away, but he caught her jaw between iron fingers and pulled it back around. Just before his mouth made contact with hers, they heard thudding footsteps outside.

"Help me," Rusty screamed.

"Reuben?" the old man shouted. "Get in here."

Quinn turned his head toward the door, but it wasn't Reuben who came crashing through. Cooper's sweating face was a fierce mask of hatred and rage. His hair was littered with twigs and leaves. There were bleeding scratches on his cheeks and hands. His shirt was specked with blood. To Rusty, no one had ever looked better.

Feet wide apart, Cooper barked, "Let her go, you filthy animal."

Rusty collapsed to the floor when Gawrylow released her. He spun around. As he did so, he reached behind his back. Before Rusty fully realized what had happened, she heard a solid thunk. Then she saw the handle of Cooper's knife in the center of Quinn's chest. The blade was fully buried between his ribs.

The old man was wearing a startled expression. He groped for the handle of the knife. His searching fingers closed around it as he dropped to his knees. Then he fell face down onto the floor and was still.

Rusty gathered her arms and legs against her body, forming herself into a ball. She clapped her hands over her mouth and stared at the still form with wide, unfocusing eyes. Her breath was trapped in her lungs.

Cooper, knocking furniture aside, rushed across the room and crouched in front of her. "Are you all right?" He laid a hand on her shoulder. She recoiled in fright.

He froze. His eyes went as hard as slate as he said, "No need to thank me."

Gradually Rusty lowered her hands and released

her breath. She gazed up at Cooper, her lips white with fear. "You killed him." The words had no sound; she mouthed them.

"Before he killed me, you little fool. Look!" He pointed down at the dead man's back. There was a small handgun tucked into the waistband of his pants. "Don't you get it yet?" he roared. "They were going to waste me and keep you. They planned to share you between them."

She shuddered with revulsion. "No!"

"Oh, yeah," Cooper said, nodding his head. Apparently exasperated with her, he stood up and rolled the body over. Squeezing her eyes shut, Rusty averted her head. She heard the body being dragged across the floor and out the door. She heard Quinn's boots thump on the steps as Cooper dragged him down them.

She wasn't sure how long she stayed curled up in that fetal position on the floor. But she still hadn't moved when Cooper returned. He loomed over her. "Did he hurt you?"

Miserably she shook her head.

"Answer me, dammit! Did he hurt you?"

She raised her head and glared up at him. *"No!"*

"He was about to rape you. You *do* realize that, don't you? Or are the stars in your eyes still keeping you from seeing the light?"

Not stars, but tears filled her eyes. She was experiencing a delayed reaction to her horror. "What are you doing here? Why did you come back? Where's Reuben? What are you going to say to him when he gets back?"

"Nothing. Reuben won't be coming back."

She clamped her teeth over her quivering lower lip and closed her eyes. Tears rolled down her cheeks.

"You killed him, too, didn't you? That's his blood on you."

"Yes, dammit," he hissed, bending over her. "I shot him in self-defense. He walked me into the woods just far enough to separate us, then he turned a gun on me with every intention of killing me and making you his 'woman.'" Staring up at him, she shook her head in disbelief, which seemed to infuriate him. "And don't you dare pretend to be surprised. You had whipped them into a sexual froth and you know it."

"Me? How? What did I do?"

"Brushing your hair for God's sake!"

"'Brushing'—"

"Just being you. Just looking the way you do."

"Stop yelling at me!" she sobbed. "I didn't do anything."

"Except cause me to kill two men!" he shouted. "Think about that while I'm out burying them."

He stalked out. The fire in the fireplace burned out and the cabin grew cold. But Rusty didn't care.

SHE WAS STILL sitting in a heap on the floor and crying hard when he came back. She was tired. There wasn't a place on her body that didn't ache either from sleeping on the ground or walking on crutches or suffering Quinn Gawrylow's squeezing caresses.

She wanted good, honest food. She'd gladly trade her Maserati for a glass of milk. Her clothes had been ripped by tree branches or ravaged by this barbaric hoodlum she was marooned with. The fur coat she had prized so highly had been used as a litter.

And she had seen men die.

Five in the plane crash. Two at the hands of the man

who now threw himself down beside her. He roughly raised her head by placing his callused fingers beneath her chin.

"Get up," he ordered. "Dry your face. You're not going to spend the rest of the day sitting around crying like a baby."

"Go to hell," she spat, lifting her chin out of his grasp.

He was so furious, his lips hardly moved when he spoke. "Look, if you had a good thing going with Reuben and his pa, you should have told me. I'm sorry I ruined it for you."

"You bastard."

"I would have been all too glad to leave you in this paradise and strike out for the river by myself. But I think I should tell you that Reuben had a lot of children in mind. Of course you might not have ever known if the kids you hatched were his or his daddy's."

"Shut up!" She raised her hand to slap him.

He caught it in midair and they stared at each other for several tense seconds. Finally Cooper relaxed his fingers from around her wrist. Snarling angrily, he stood up and kicked a chair as far across the cabin as he could.

"It was either them or me," he said in a voice that vibrated with rage. "Reuben fired first. I got lucky and deflected his rifle just in time. I had no choice."

"You didn't have to kill them."

"No?"

An alternative didn't leap into her mind, but she was sure that if she thought about it long enough she would come up with one. Temporarily conceding, she lowered her eyes. "Why didn't you just keep going?"

His eyes narrowed to slits as he looked down at her. "Don't think I didn't consider it."

"Oh," she ground out. "I can't wait until I'm rid of you."

"Believe me, the feeling is mutual. But in the meantime we've got to tolerate each other. First thing on the agenda is to get this place cleaned up. I'm not spending another night in this stink hole."

Her jaw went slack with disbelief. Slowly her eyes roamed the grimy interior of the cabin. "Clean this place up? Is that what you said?"

"Yeah. We'd better get started, too. The day's getting away."

He righted the chair he'd just kicked over and made his way toward the pile of dingy bedding where Reuben had slept the night before. Rusty started laughing and her laughter was tinged with impending hysteria.

"You're not serious?"

"Like hell I'm not."

"We're spending the night here?"

"And every night from now on until we're rescued."

She came to her feet, propping herself up on one crutch while she watched him strip both beds and pile the bedding in the middle of the floor. "What about the river?"

"That might have all been a lie."

"The Mackenzie River is real, Cooper."

"But where is it from here?"

"You could keep walking in the direction they said until you found it."

"I could. I could also get terribly lost. Or injured and stranded. If you went with me, we might not make it out before the first real snow, in which case we'd probably die of exposure. If you stayed here and something happened to me, you'd die of starvation before the winter was over. And I'm not even sure the direction Reuben led me in was the right one. I've got 359 other choices from this cabin, and getting around to them all would take over a year."

Hands braced on his hips, he faced her. "None of those alternatives sounds very appealing to me. On the other hand if we clean this place up, we can survive. It's not the Beverly Hills Hotel, but it's shelter and there's a constant supply of fresh water."

She didn't appreciate his sarcasm and her mutinous expression let him know it. His whole demeanor suggested that she was foolish not to see all that without his having to explain it, and issued a challenge she wasn't about to back down from. She had been weak this morning, but she never would be again. Pushing up the sleeves of her sweater, she said, "What do you want me to do?"

He hitched his head backward. "Start with the stove."

Without another word, he gathered up the foul bedding and carried it outside.

Rusty attacked the black iron stove with a vengeance, scouring it from top to bottom, using more elbow grease than soap, since she had more of that. It was hard work, especially since she had to keep herself propped up on one crutch. She moved from the stove to the sink, then to the windows, then every stick of furniture got washed down.

After he had boiled the bedding in a caldron outside and hung it up to dry—or freeze, if the temperature turned much colder—Cooper came inside and washed the stones of the hearth. He found a colony of dead insects beneath the woodpile. They had no doubt died of old age since it was almost a certainty that the hearth had never been swept. Keeping the door and windows open to air the place out, he shored up the front porch and stacked firewood on the cabin's south side to protect it from the weather's brunt.

Rusty couldn't sweep the floor, so he did. But when he was finished, she got down on hands and knees and scrubbed it. Her sculptured nails broke off one by one. Where a mere chip would have sent her into a tizzy not long ago, she merely shrugged and went on with her scrubbing, taking satisfaction in the results of her labor.

Cooper brought in two beheaded and plucked birds—she didn't recognize the species—for their dinner. She had made an inventory of the Gawrylows' hoard and was pleased to find a fair amount of canned goods. They had apparently made their October trip to Yellowknife and were well stocked for the winter. A gourmet cook she wasn't, but it didn't take much talent to boil the fowl together with two cans of vegetables and a sprinkling of salt. By the time the stew was done, the aroma was making her mouth water. Darkness was settling in before Cooper carried in the bedding.

"Is it deloused?" she asked, turning from the stove.

"I think so. I boiled the hell out of it. I'm not sure it's quite dry, but if I leave it out any longer, it's going to freeze. We'll check it after dinner and if it's not dry, we'll hang it up in front of the fire."

He washed his hands at the sink, which was sparkling compared to what it had been.

They sat down to eat at the table Rusty had sanded clean. Cooper smiled when he unfolded what had once been a sock and was now acting as a napkin and placed it in his lap, but he didn't comment on her ingenuity. If he noticed the jar with the arrangement of autumn leaves serving as a centerpiece, he said nothing to indicate it. He ate two portions of the stew but didn't say a word about it.

Rusty was crushed. He could have said something nice—one single word of encouragement. Even a puppy needs to be patted on the head now and then.

She dejectedly carried their tin dishes to the sink. While she was pumping water over them, he moved up behind her. "You worked hard today."

His voice was soft and low and came from directly above her head. He was standing very close. His sheer physicality overwhelmed her. She felt tremulous. "So did you."

"I think we deserve a treat, don't you?"

Her stomach rose and fell as weightlessly as a balloon. Memory of the kiss he had given her that morning filled her mind, while a potent desire to repeat it flooded her veins. Slowly she turned around and gazed up at him. Breathlessly she asked, "What did you have in mind, Cooper?"

"A bath."

CHAPTER SIX

"A...BATH?" DOROTHY couldn't have said "Oz?" with any more awe and wistfulness.

"A real one. The works. Hot water, soap." He went to the door, opened it, and came back in rolling a large washtub. "I found this behind the cabin and cleaned it out."

She didn't remember feeling this grateful when she opened the present from her father and found her full-length, red fox coat folded amid tissue paper. She clasped her hands beneath her chin. "Oh, Cooper, thank you."

"Don't get gushy," he said querulously. "We'll get as disgusting as the Gawrylows if we don't bathe. Not every day, though."

Rusty didn't let him spoil her good mood. He didn't allow people to get even close enough to thank him. Well, that was his problem. He'd done something very thoughtful for her. She had thanked him. Beyond that, what else could she do? He must know how much this meant to her, even if he chose to act like a heel about it now.

She filled several pots and kettles with water from the pump. He carried them to the stove to heat them up, refueling the fire to hurry them along. He then dragged the tub across the wooden floor and placed it directly in front of the fireplace. The metal was icy cold, but in a few minutes the fire would warm it up.

Rusty watched him making all these preparations with expectation, then a growing concern. "What do I do about, uh…"

Saying nothing, expressionless, Cooper unfurled one of the rough muslin bed-sheets he'd boiled and aired that day. The ceiling of the cabin had bare beams. Apparently the Gawrylows had hung meat from it because there were several metal hooks screwed into the dark wood.

Cooper stood on a chair and pushed one of the sharp hooks through a corner of the sheet. Repositioning the chair several times, he soon had the sheet hanging like a curtain behind the tub.

"Thank you," Rusty said. She was glad to have the sheet there but couldn't help but notice that with the fireplace behind it, it was translucent. The tub was silhouetted against it. Anybody in the tub would be, too.

Cooper must have noticed that at the same time, because he shifted his eyes away from it and ran his hands nervously up and down his pants legs. "I think the water's just about ready."

Rusty assembled her precious cache of toiletries— a bar of scented soap, a small plastic bottle of shampoo, her razor—on the seat of the chair near the tub.

Earlier in the day, she had separated the meager clothing they had left and neatly folded and stacked it on separate shelves, one for her, one for Cooper. She took a fresh pair of long johns and a tank top from her stack now and draped them over the back of the chair.

When everything was ready, she stood awkwardly by while Cooper carefully carried the heavy pots of boiling water across the room and poured them into the tub. Steam rose out of it, but as far as Rusty was concerned it couldn't be too hot. She had four days' accumulation of grime and fatigue to soak away. Besides, she was accustomed to spending several minutes each day in her hot tub at home.

"What do I dry with?" she asked.

Cooper tossed her a coarse, dingy towel from the pile of bedding he'd carried in earlier. "I found a couple of these hanging from nails outside the cabin. I boiled them, too. They've never known fabric softener, but they're better than nothing."

The towel did feel more like sandpaper than terry cloth, but Rusty accepted it without comment.

"There, that should do it," Cooper said brusquely, emptying the contents of the last kettle into the tub. "Ease into it carefully. Don't scald yourself."

"Okay."

Standing at opposite sides of the tub, they faced each other. Their eyes met through the rising steam. The humidity was already curling Rusty's hair and making her complexion look dewy and rosy.

Cooper turned his back abruptly and impatiently swatted aside the curtain. It fell back into place. Rusty could hear his stamping, booted footsteps against the uneven flooring. He went outside and slammed the door closed behind him.

She sighed with resignation. He had a sour disposition and that's all there was to it. And while she was lolling in her first bath in four days, she certainly wasn't going to dwell on his personality flaws. She wouldn't let him spoil this for her, no matter how disagreeable he became.

Because she still avoided putting any weight on her leg, it was a challenge to get out of her clothes. When she had managed that, it was an even greater challenge to ease herself into the bathtub. She was finally able to do so by supporting herself on her arms and sitting down slowly, pulling her sore leg in behind her.

It felt more heavenly than she had allowed herself to anticipate. Cooper had been right to caution her; the water was hot, but deliciously so. The corrugated bottom of the tub felt odd against her buttocks and took some getting used to, but before long the luxury of being submerged in hot, soothing water took her mind off that one minor discomfort.

She immersed as much of herself as possible and rested her head against the rim. Her eyes slid closed. She was so relaxed that she didn't even flinch when she heard Cooper come back inside. She only frowned slightly when a breath of cold air reached her before he shut the door behind him.

Eventually she extended one dripping arm and took the bar of soap off the seat of the chair. She was tempted to lather herself liberally, wantonly, wastefully. But she thought better of it. This bar of soap might have to last a long time. Better not squander it, she decided, as she worked up an adequate lather and soaped herself all over.

Propping her feet one at a time on the rim of the tub, she shaved her legs, carefully maneuvering the razor around Cooper's stitching. With anguish she realized what an unsightly scar she was going to have but was ashamed of her vanity. She was lucky to be alive. As soon as she got back to Beverly Hills, she would have a plastic surgeon repair Cooper's well-intentioned, but unattractive, handiwork.

It struck her then that he was being awfully noisy. "Cooper, what are you doing?"

"Making up the beds," he said, grunting with the effort. "These frames are made of solid oak and weigh a ton."

"I can't wait to lie down on one."

"Don't expect it to be much better than the ground. There're no mattresses. Just canvas platforms like cots. But mattresses would have had lice, so it's just as well."

Laying aside her razor, she picked up the bottle of shampoo and after dunking her head beneath the water, squeezed out a dollop. The shampoo would have to be rationed even more sparingly than the soap. She worked it through her thick hair, scrubbing ruthlessly from her scalp to the ends. She dunked her head to rinse it, then wrung out as much water as she could.

Laying her head against the tub's rim again, she fanned her hair out behind her so it could begin to dry. It would drip on the floor, but water was probably the least offensive substance to ever be dripped on it.

Again, her eyes closed as she luxuriated in the warmth of the water, the floral fragrance of shampoo and soap, and the deliciousness of feeling clean again.

Eventually the water began to cool and she knew it was time to get out. Anyway, she doubted that Cooper would go to bed before she did. He must be exhausted after all he'd done since getting up before daybreak that morning. She had no idea what time it was. The crash had stopped both their watches. Time was measured by the sun coming up and going down. The days were short, but today had been long—emotionally as well as physically taxing.

She braced her arms on the rim of the tub and tried to push herself up. To her dismay, her arms collapsed like wet noodles. She had stayed in the hot water too long; her muscles were useless. Several times she tried, but to no avail. Her arms simply wouldn't support her. She devised other plans, but none of them worked because of her sore leg, which she couldn't put any weight on.

Finally, growing chilled and knowing that the inevitable couldn't be postponed indefinitely, she bashfully called his name.

"What?"

His irritable response wasn't too encouraging, but she had no choice. "I can't get out."

After a silence long enough for a telephone pole to stretch out in, he said, "Huh?"

Rusty squeezed her eyes shut and repeated, "I can't get out of the tub."

"Get out the same way you got in."

"I'm too weak from the hot water. My arms won't hold me up long enough to step out."

His curses were so scorching, she didn't know why the bed-sheet curtain didn't combust. When she heard his approaching footsteps, she crossed her arms over her breasts. Cool air fanned across her wet, bare back as he moved the curtain aside. She stared straight ahead into the fireplace, feeling his eyes on her as he moved toward the tub.

For a long time he just stood there, saying nothing. Rusty's lungs were almost ready to burst from internal tension by the time he said, "I'll slide my hands under your arms. Come up on your left leg. Then while I'm holding you up, lift it out of the tub and set it on the floor. Okay?"

His voice was low and of the same texture as the towel he'd given her to use—as rough as sandpaper. "Okay." She eased her arms slightly away from her body. Even though she'd been expecting it, the first touch of his fingertips against her slippery, wet skin, came as a shock. Not because it felt awful, but because it didn't.

And it only got better from there. Confident and strong, his hands slid into the notches of her armpits and cupped them supportively. He braced his legs wide apart, almost straddling the tub, and lifted her. She sucked in her breath sharply.

"What's the matter?"

"My...my underarms are sore," she told him breathlessly. "Because of the crutches." He muttered a curse. It was so vile she hoped she hadn't heard it correctly.

His hands slipped over her wet skin and encased her ribs. "Let's try it this way. Ready?"

Rusty, according to his instructions, supported herself on her left leg, letting the injured one dangle uselessly as he raised her out of the water.

"Okay so far?" She nodded. "Ready?" She replied in the same soundless way. He took all her weight on his hands as she lifted her left foot over the edge of the tub and set it on the floor.

"Oh!"

"What now?"

He was just about to release her when she made the exclamation and tipped forward slightly. With lightning reflexes, his arm slid around her, clasping her just below her breasts.

"The floor is cold."

"Christ, don't scare me like that."

"Sorry. It was a shock."

Each was thinking, "You can say that again."

Rusty groped for the back of the chair to lend her support and hastily clutched the towel to the front of her body. Of course that still left her back naked to his eyes, but she trusted that he was being a gentleman and wasn't taking advantage.

"All right?"

"Yes."

His hands moved from her front to her sides, but he didn't release her entirely. "Sure?"

"Yes," she answered thickly, "I'm fine."

He withdrew his hands. Rusty sighed with relief—as it turned out, prematurely.

"What the hell is this?" She gasped when his hand cupped the side of her hip. His thumb made a long, slow sweep across her buttock, sluicing off water. Then the other buttock was similarly examined. "What the devil happened to you? I thought you said he didn't hurt you?"

"I don't know what you mean." Breathless and dizzy, she turned her head and looked up at him over her shoulder. His brows were pulled together into a deep V and his mustache was curved downward with displeasure.

"You're black-and-blue."

Rusty looked over her shoulder and down the length of her back. The first thing that registered with her was that Cooper's dark hands against her pale flesh made a very sensuous picture. Only when he made another solicitous movement with his thumb did she see the bruises.

"Oh, those. They're from the ride in the travois."

His eyes swung up to hers and penetrated her with their heat. He kept his hands against her flesh. His voice was as soft as his touch. "You should have said something."

She became entranced with the movements of his mustache as his mouth formed words. Perhaps that's why she whispered, "Would saying something have changed anything?"

A strand of her hair got caught in the stubble on his chin. It connected them like a filament of light. Not that they needed it. Their stare was almost palpable. It lasted forever and wasn't broken until a log in the fireplace popped loudly. They both jumped guiltily.

Cooper resumed his broody expression and growled. "No. It wouldn't have changed anything."

Seconds later the drape fluttered back into place behind him. Rusty was trembling. *From the cold*, she averred. He had kept her standing here long enough to get chilled. She wrapped the towel around her and dried quickly. The cloth was so coarse it left her skin tingling. It chafed the delicate areas of her body, especially her nipples. When she finished drying, they were abnormally rosy and pointed. Achy. And throbbing. And hot.

"It's the *towel*," she muttered as she pulled on her silk long johns.

"What is it this time?" The cantankerous question came from the other side of the drape.

"What?"

"I heard you say something."

"I said this towel would make a great scouring pad."

"It was the best I could come up with."

"I wasn't being critical."

"That'd be a first."

She muttered something else beneath her breath, making sure he didn't overhear it this time, since it was an epithet grossly unflattering to his lineage and personality.

Aggravated, she ungracefully pulled the tank top over her head. Her nipples poked darkly against the clinging fabric. The silkiness, which should have felt soothing after the towel, only seemed to irritate them more.

She repacked her toiletries in their carrying case and dropped down into the chair. Bending at the waist, she flipped all her hair forward and rubbed it vigorously with the towel, alternately brushing it. Five minutes later, she flung her head back and her semidried hair settled against her shoulders in russet waves. It wasn't styled, but it was clean, and that was a definite improvement.

It was when she was replacing her hairbrush in the cosmetic kit that she noticed the condition of her nails. They had been jaggedly broken or torn away. She groaned audibly.

Within a heartbeat, the curtain was thrown back and Cooper was standing there. "What's the matter? Is it your leg? Is it—"

He broke off when he realized that Rusty wasn't in any pain. But even if that realization hadn't shut him up, the sight of her sitting silhouetted against the golden firelight, a halo of wavy cinnamon-colored hair wreathing her head like an aura would have. She was

wearing a top that was more alluring than concealing.
The shadows of her nipples drew his eyes like magnets.
Even now, he could feel the heaviness of her breasts
where they had rested on his forearms minutes ago.

His blood turned to molten lava, hot and thick and
rampant. It surged toward his sex where it collected
and produced the normal, but currently unwanted, reaction. It was painful in its intensity.

And since he couldn't alleviate it, he released his
sexual tension by another means: fury. His face grew
dark with menace. His heavy brows, more gold than
brown in the firelight, were intimidatingly drawn into
a frown over his eyes. Since he couldn't taste her with
his tongue—as he was dying to do—he'd use it to verbally lash her.

"You were groaning over your damn fingernails?"
he shouted.

"They're all chipped and broken," Rusty yelled back
at him.

"Better them than your neck, you little fool."

"Stop calling me that, Cooper. I'm not a fool."

"You couldn't even figure out that those two hillbil-
lies wanted to rape you."

Her mouth drew up into a sullen pout that only inflamed him further because he wanted to kiss it so
badly. His unquenchable desire prompted him to say
ugly, hurtful things. "You did all you could to entice
them, didn't you? Sitting near the fire when you know
what it does to your eyes and complexion. Brushing
your hair until it crackled. You know what that kind
of thing does to a man, don't you? You know it drives
him crazy with lust." Then, realizing that his tirade
was as good as a confession, he sneered, "I'm surprised

you didn't come out in that getup last night and flaunt yourself in front of Reuben, the poor jerk."

Rusty's eyes smarted with tears. His estimation of her was far lower than she had thought. Not only did he think she was useless, he thought she was no better than a whore.

"I didn't do anything on purpose. You know that, no matter what you say." Instinctively, in self-defense, she crossed her arms over her chest.

Suddenly he dropped to his knees in front of her and jerked her arms away. In the same motion, he whipped the lethal knife from its scabbard at his waist. Rusty squealed in fright when he clasped her left hand tightly and raised the glittering blade to it. He made a short, efficient job of paring her nails down even with the tops of her fingers. When he dropped that hand, she looked at it remorsefully.

"That looks awful."

"Well, I'm the only one here to see them and I don't give a damn. Give me your other hand."

She complied. She had no choice. In an arm-wrestling match, she could hardly win against him. And now her breasts were fair game for his condemning gaze again. But when his eyes glanced up from the bizarre manicure he was giving her, they weren't condemning. Nor were they cold with contempt. They were warm with masculine interest. A lot of interest. So much interest that Rusty's stomach took another of those elevator rides that never quite took it to the top or the bottom but kept it bobbing up and down somewhere in between.

Cooper took his time trimming the nails on her right hand, as if they needed more care and attention than those on her left. His face was on a level with her chest.

In spite of the awful things he'd said to her just moments ago, she wanted to run her fingers through his long, unruly hair.

As she watched his lips, set firmly in a scowl, she couldn't help but remember how soft they could become in a kiss—how warm and damp—and how marvelous his mustache had felt. If it had felt that good against her upper lip, how good would it feel against other parts of her body? Her neck? Her ear? Her areola—while his lips tugged at her nipple with the gentle fervency of a baby hungry for milk?

He finished cutting her nails and sheathed his knife. But he didn't release her hand. He held it, staring down at it, then laid it on her thigh, pressing it there with his own hand. Rusty thought her heart would explode from the pressure inside her chest.

He kept his head down, staring at the spot where his hand covered hers high on her thigh. His eyes looked closed from Rusty's angle. The lashes were thick and crescent shaped. She noticed that they, like his mustache and eyebrows, were tipped with gold. In the summertime his hair would be naturally streaked, bleached from the sun.

"Rusty."

He said her name. There was a slight creak in his voice, a groaning protest of the raw emotion behind his saying it. Rusty didn't move, but her heart was beating so fast and wildly that it stirred the silk that wasn't doing a very adequate job of covering her.

He removed his hand from hers and placed each of his on either side of the chair seat, bracketing her hips. His knuckles pressed into their flaring shape. He remained staring fixedly at her hand, which still lay on her thigh. He looked ready to lower his head and wearily rest his cheek against it, or to bend down and tenderly kiss it, or to nibble on the very fingers he'd just cut the nails from.

If he wanted to, Rusty wouldn't stop him. She knew that positively. Her body was warm and moist and receptive to the idea. She was ready for whatever happened.

No, she wasn't.

Because what happened was that Cooper came to his feet hastily. "You'd better get to bed."

Rusty was stunned by his about-face. The mood had been shattered, the intimacy dispelled. She felt like arguing, but didn't. What could she say? "Kiss me again, Cooper," "Touch me"? That would only confirm his low opinion of her.

Feeling rejected, she gathered her belongings, including the pile of dirty clothes she'd left beside the tub, and walked around the curtain. Each of the two beds had been spread with sheets and blankets. A fur pelt had been left at the foot of each. At home her bed was covered in designer sheets and piled with downy pillows, but it had never looked more inviting than this one.

She put her things away and sat down on the bed. In the meantime, Cooper had made several trips outside with buckets of bathwater. When the water level was low enough, he dragged the tub to the door and out onto the porch, then tipped it over the edge and emptied the rest of it. He brought the tub back into the room, replaced it behind the curtain, and from the pump in the sink began filling the pots and kettles again.

"Are you going to take a bath, too?"

"Any objections?"

"No."

"It's been a while since I chopped firewood and my back is sore. Besides that, I think I'm beginning to stink."

"I didn't notice."

He looked at her sharply, but when he could see that she was being honest, he came close to smiling. "You will now that you're clean."

The kettles had begun to boil. He lifted two of them off the stove and headed toward the tub.

"Do you want me to massage it?" Rusty asked guilelessly.

He stumbled, sloshed boiling water on his legs, and cursed. *"What?"*

"Massage it?" He gazed at her as though he'd been hit between the eyes with a two-by-four. "Your back."

"Oh, uh…" His eyes moved over her. The tank top left her throat and shoulders bare, cloaked only with a mass of reddish-brown curls. "No—" he refused curtly "—I told you to go to sleep. We've got more work to do tomorrow." He rudely returned to his task.

Not only was human courtesy impossible for him, he wouldn't let anybody be nice to him. Well he could rot, for all she cared!

Rusty angrily thrust her feet between the chilly sheets and lay down, but she didn't close her eyes. Instead she watched Cooper sit down on the edge of his bed and unlace his boots while he was waiting for more water to boil. He tossed his socks onto the pile of dirty clothing she had made and began unbuttoning his shirt. He was wearing only one today because he'd been working so hard outside. He pulled the tails of it from his jeans and took it off.

Rusty sprang to a sitting position. "What happened to you?"

He flung his shirt down onto the pile of clothes to be washed. He didn't have to ask what she was referring to. If it looked as bad as it felt, the bruise was noticeable even in the dim light.

"My shoulder came into contact with the barrel of Reuben's rifle. I had to deflect it that way, so my hands would be free to get my own rifle up."

Rusty winced. The fist-size bruise at the outer edge of his collarbone was black-and-blue and looked extremely painful. "Does it hurt?"

"Like hell."

"Did you take an aspirin?"

"No. We need to conserve them."

"But if you're hurting—"

"You aren't taking them for the bruises on your butt."

That remark shocked her speechless. But it didn't last long. After a moment she said stubbornly, "I still think two aspirin would help."

"I want to save them. You might have fever again."

"Oh, I see. You don't have any aspirin to take for your shoulder because I wasted them on my fever."

"I didn't say you wasted them. I said, oh—" Then he said a word that described something neither was in the mood to do, a word that should never be spoken aloud in polite company. "Go to sleep, will you?"

Wearing only his jeans, he went to the stove, apparently decided that the water was hot enough even though it wasn't quite boiling, and emptied it all into the tub. Rusty had lain back down, but she watched his shadow moving on the curtain as he shucked off his jeans and stepped naked into the tub. Her imagination got the night off because his shadow left nothing up to it, especially in profile.

She heard cursing as he lowered himself into the water. The tub didn't accommodate him as easily as it had her. How he expected her to go to sleep with all that splashing going on, she didn't know. He had splashed more water on the floor than was left in the bottom of the tub by the time he stood up to rinse off.

Rusty's throat went dry as she watched his shadow. He bent at the waist, repeatedly scooping handfuls of water over himself to rinse off the soap. When he stepped out, he dried with masculine carelessness. The only attention he gave his hair was to make one pass over it with the towel, then to comb his fingers through it. He finished by wrapping the towel around his waist.

He went through the laborious procedure of emptying the tub again. After the last trip to the porch, he left the tub outside. Rusty could tell he was shivering when he moved back to the fire and added several logs. Using the chair as his ladder, he took down the screen the same way he'd put it up. He folded the sheet, placed it on one of the several shelves against the wall, and blew out the lantern on the table. The last thing he did before sliding into his bed was yank the towel from around his waist.

During all that time, he never looked at Rusty. She was hurt that he hadn't even said good-night. But then, she might not have been able to answer him.

Her mouth was still dry.

COUNTING SHEEP DIDN'T HELP.

Reciting poetry didn't help, especially since the only poems he knew by heart were limericks of a licentious nature.

So Cooper lay there on his back, with his hands stacked beneath his head, staring at the ceiling, and wondering when his stiff manhood was going to stop tenting the covers and relax enough to let him fall asleep. He was exhausted. His overexerted muscles cried out for rest. But his sex wasn't listening.

Unlike the rest of him, it was feeling great. He felt like taps all over, but it felt like reveille: alert and alive and well. Too well.

In desperation, he put one hand beneath the covers. Maybe... He yanked his hand back. Nope. Uh-uh. Don't do that. Trying to press it down only made the problem worse.

Furious with Rusty for doing this to him, he rolled to his side. Even that movement created unwanted friction. He uttered an involuntary groaning sound, which he hastily turned into a cough.

What could he do? Nothing that wouldn't be humiliating. So he'd just have to think about something else.

But dammit, he'd tried. For hours, he'd tried. His thoughts eventually meandered back to her.

Her lips: soft.

Her mouth: vulnerable but curious, then hungry, opening to him.

He clenched his teeth, thinking of the way her mouth had closed around his seeking tongue. God, she tasted good. He'd wanted to go on and on, thrusting his tongue inside her, sending it a little farther into her mouth each time, until he decided exactly what it was she tasted like. It would be an impossible task and therefore endless—because she had her own unique taste.

He should have known better than to kiss her—not even for the sake of fooling the old man. Who had been fooling whom? he asked himself derisively. He had kissed her because he'd wanted to and he *had* known better. He had suspected that one kiss wouldn't satisfy him and now he knew that for sure.

What the hell? Why was he being so hard on himself? He was sleeplessly randy because she was the only woman around. Yeah, that was it.

Probably. Possibly. Maybe.

But the fact still remained that she had a knockout face. Sexy-as-hell hair. A body that begged to be mated. Breasts that were created for a man's enjoyment. A cute, squeezable derriere. Thighs that inspired instant arousal. And what lay nestled between them—

No! his mind warned him. Don't think about that or you'll have to do what you have miraculously, and with considerable self-discipline, refrained from doing tonight.

All right, that's enough. *Finis. No mas.* The end. Stop thinking like a sex-crazed kid at worst and a redneck sexist at best, and go to sleep.

He closed his eyes and concentrated so hard on keeping them closed that at first he thought the whimpering sound that issued from the other bed was his imagination. Then Rusty sprang up out of the covers like a jack-in-the-box. That wasn't his imagination. Nor was it something he could ignore by playing possum.

"Rusty?"

"What is that?"

Even with no more to light the room than the dying fire, he could see that her eyes were round and huge with fear. He thought she was having a nightmare. "Lie back down. Everything's okay."

She was breathing erratically and clutching the covers to her chest. "What is that noise?"

Had he made a noise? Had he failed to camouflage his groans? "Wha—"

But just as he was about to ask, the mourning, wailing sound came again. Rusty covered her ears and bent double. "I can't stand it," she cried.

Cooper tossed back the covers on his bed and reached hers in seconds. "Wolves, Rusty. Timber wolves. That's all. They're not as close as they sound and they can't hurt us."

Gently he unfolded her and eased her back until she was lying down again. But her face was far from restful. Her eyes apprehensively darted around the dark interior of the cabin as though it had been invaded by demons of the night.

"Wolves?"

"They smell the—"

"Bodies."

"Yes," he replied with regret.

"Oh, God." She covered her face with her hands.

"Shh, shh. They can't get to them because I covered the graves with rocks. They'll eventually go away. Hush, now, and go to sleep."

He'd been so miserable with his own problem that he'd paid scant attention to the barking of the pack that lurked in the woods surrounding the cabin. But he could see that Rusty's fear was genuine. She clasped his hand and drew it up under her chin as a child might hold his teddy bear to help ward off the terrors of a recent nightmare.

"I hate this place," she whispered.

"I know."

"I've tried to be brave."

"You have been."

She shook her head adamantly. "No, I'm a coward. My father saw it. He was the one who suggested that I return home ahead of schedule."

"Lots of people can't stand seeing animals killed."

"I broke down and cried today in front of you. You've known all along that I'm useless. I'm no good at this. And I don't want to be good at it." Her voice was defiant, incongruous with the tears that washed her cheeks. "You think I'm a terrible person."

"No, I don't."

"Yes, you do."

"No, honest."

"Then why did you accuse me of enticing those men?"

"I was angry."

"Why?"

Because you entice me, too, and I don't want to be enticed. He didn't tell her that. Instead he muttered, "Never mind."

"I want to go home. Where everything is safe and warm and *clean*."

He could argue that the streets of Los Angeles couldn't always been considered safe, but knew that now wasn't the time for teasing—even gentle teasing.

It went against his grain to compliment her, but he felt she'd earned it. "You've done exceptionally well."

She lifted watery eyes to his. "No, I haven't."

"Far better than I ever expected."

"Really?" she asked hopefully.

The breathlessness of her voice and the feminine appeal on her face was almost too much for him. "Really. Now, ignore the wolves and go back to sleep." He pulled his hand from her grasp and turned away. Before he could move, however, another wolf howled. She cried out and reached for him again, throwing herself against him when he turned back to her.

"I don't care if I am a coward. Hold me, Cooper. Please hold me."

Reflexively his arms went around her. Like that other time he had held her while she wept, he felt the same sense of helplessness steal over him. It was lunacy to hold her for any reason, but it would be abominably cruel to turn away. So even though it was as much agony as ecstasy, he drew her close and buried his lips in her wealth of hair.

As he spoke them, his words were sincere. He was sorry this had happened to her. He wished they would be rescued. He wanted her to be returned safely home. He was sorry she was frightened. If there was something he could do to get them out of their predicament, he would.

"You've done everything possible. But just hold me a minute longer," she begged.

"I will."

He continued to hold her. His arms remained around her. But he didn't move his hands. He didn't trust himself to rub them over her back and stop with that. He wanted to touch her all over. He wanted to knead her breasts and investigate the warm, soft place between her thighs. Desire made him shiver.

"You're freezing." Rusty ran her hands over the gooseflesh on his upper arms.

"I'm fine."

"Get under the covers."

"No."

"Don't be silly. You'll catch a cold. What's the big deal? We've slept together for the past three nights. Come on." She pulled back the covers.

"Uh-uh. I'm going back to my own bed."

"You said you'd hold me. Please. Just until I fall asleep."

"But, I'm—"

"Please, Cooper."

He swore, but slid beneath the covers with her. She cuddled against him, nuzzling her face against the fuzzy security of his chest. Her body became pliant against his. He gritted his teeth.

Seconds after she had relaxed against him, she pushed herself away. "Oh!" she exclaimed softly. "I forgot that you were—"

"Naked. That's right. But it's too late now, baby."

CHAPTER SEVEN

MASCULINE URGES GOVERNED him now. His mouth moved over hers in a deep, long, questing kiss while his body settled heavily against hers. Angling his head first to one side, then the other, he made heated love to her mouth with his greedy tongue.

Shock was Rusty's initial reaction. His wonderful nakedness was a stunning surprise. Then, before she could recover from that, she was swept up into his tempestuous kiss.

Her next reaction was spontaneous longing. It surged up through her middle, overwhelming her heart and mind, obliterating all else but the man who was ravishing her mouth so expertly. Her arms encircled his neck and drew him closer. Reflexively she arched against him, bringing her body in contact with his hard, rigid flesh.

Groaning in near pain, he buried his face in her neck. "God, it's so full it's about to burst."

"What do you want, Cooper?"

He laughed harshly. "That's obvious, isn't it?"

"I know; but, what do you want me to do?"

"Either touch me all over or don't touch me at all." His breath struck her face in hot, rapid gusts. "But whatever you decide, decide now."

Rusty hesitated only half a heartbeat before she ran

the fingers of one hand up through his hair and settled them against his scalp. She used the other to comb through the crisp hair on his chest, massaging the muscles that had beguiled her.

Their lips met in another rapacious kiss. He ran his tongue over her lower lip, then drew it between his lips and sucked it lightly. The sheer sexuality of it electrified her. He took her moaning whimper as encouragement and began kissing his way down her throat and chest. He wasn't a man to ask permission. Boldly he lowered his hand to her breast, cupped it, and pushed it up.

"I've been going out of my mind wanting you," he rasped. "I thought I'd go insane before I touched you, tasted you."

He opened his mouth over the smooth flesh that swelled above her tank top. He kissed it fervently, applying enough suction to draw it up against his teeth. He tickled it with his tongue at the same time he unhurriedly whisked his thumb back and forth across her nipple. When it began to respond and grow hard, he accelerated that fanning caress until Rusty was almost delirious.

"Stop, Cooper," she gasped. "I can't breathe."

"I don't want you to be able to breathe."

He lowered his head and, through the cloth of her tank top, flicked his tongue against her raised nipple, playfully nudging it. Rusty's heels ground into the bed beneath her and her back came off it. But even that revealing response didn't satisfy him.

"Say you want me," he said in a low, vibrating voice.

"Yes, I want you. Yes, yes."

Driven by a wild, uncontrollable hunger, heedless

of the consequences, she pushed him back and became the aggressor. Her lips moved down his throat and over his chest and stomach, striking as randomly as raindrops on parched earth. Each time her mouth touched his hair-smattered skin, she whispered his name. It became like a prayer, growing in fervency with each kiss.

"You're beautiful, beautiful," she whispered over his navel. Then, moving her head lower and rubbing her cheek in the hair that grew dense and dark, she said with a sigh, "Cooper."

The passion she'd unleashed stunned him. He tilted his head up and gazed down at her. Her hair was sweeping across his belly. Her breath was disturbing his body hair. The love words she was chanting had more erotic rhythm than any he'd ever heard. Her lips... God, her lips...were leaving dewy patches on his skin.

Her head moving over him was the most erotic, most beautiful sight he'd ever seen. And it scared the hell out of him. He pushed her away from him and rolled off the bed. Standing at the side of it, he trembled visibly, swearing beneath his breath.

Hard, passionate, mindless coupling he could handle, but not this. Not this. He didn't want any real yearning and feeling and emotion to be involved, thank you. He'd done every sensual thing that was physically possible to do with a woman. But no woman had ever expressed such honest longing. What Rusty had done suggested an intimacy between them that went beyond the physical.

He didn't need that. No romance. No love. No thanks.

He was temporarily responsible for Rusty Carlson's survival, but he damned sure wasn't going to assume responsibility for her emotional stability. If she wanted to mate, fine, but he didn't want her fooling herself into thinking that it meant something more than physical gratification. She could do whatever she wanted to with his body. He would permit, even welcome her, to indulge her most carnal desires. But that's where it stopped. No one was allowed to trespass on his emotions.

Rusty stared up at him, bewildered and hurt. "What's wrong?" Self-conscious now, she raised the sheet up to her chin.

"Nothing."

He crossed the room and tossed another log on the fire. It sent up a shower of sparks that threw a brief, but bright, glow into the room. In that light, she saw that he was still fully aroused.

He saw that her eyes were inquiring and disillusioned. "Go to sleep," he said crossly. "The wolves are gone. Besides, I told you they can't hurt you. Now stop being a crybaby and don't bother me again."

Returning to his own bed, he pulled the covers up around his ears. In seconds he was drenched with sweat. Damn her. His body was still on fire.

Damn her, why had she responded that way? So honestly. With no coyness. No affectation. Her mouth had been so receptive. Her kisses so generous. Her breasts so soft and her nipples so hard.

He clenched his teeth against the memories. Was he a fool? A damn fool for not taking what she had offered so unconditionally?

But that was the hitch. It wasn't unconditional. Otherwise he'd be lying between her silky thighs now instead of in a pool of his own sweat. That dazed expression on her face had told him that it meant more to her than simple rutting. She was reading things into it that he would never be able to deliver.

Oh, he could imbed himself deeply into that sweet feminine body and succeed in pleasing both of them physically. But he couldn't *feel*, and that's what she wanted. Maybe even what she deserved. He didn't have it to give. His heart was the Sahara of emotional wastelands.

No, better to hurt her now and get it over with. Better to be a bastard now than to take advantage of the situation. He didn't engage in long-term affairs. Certainly not in anything more. A relationship between them could go nowhere once they were rescued.

Until then, he'd live. Contrary to popular myth, a man couldn't die from being perpetually hard. It wouldn't be comfortable, but he'd live.

THE FOLLOWING MORNING, Rusty's eyes were so swollen from crying that she could barely open them. With an effort, she pried them apart and noticed that the cabin's other bed was empty. The covers had already been neatly smoothed into place.

Good. He wouldn't notice her puffy eyes until she had had a chance to bathe them in cold water. The weakness she'd exhibited last night made her furious with herself. Unreasonably, the crying wolves had frightened her. They personified all the threats surrounding her and made the precariousness of her situation very real.

For some inexplicable reason, her terror had manifested itself in desire. Cooper had responded. Then she had. Thank heaven he'd come to his senses before something drastic had happened.

Rusty only wished that she had been the one to come to her senses first. He might erroneously think that she'd wanted *him*—when in fact, what she had wanted was *someone*. He was just the only one around. And if he thought anything else, he was sorely mistaken.

Imitating him by making her bed—never let it be said that he was a superior survivor—she went to the sink and pumped enough water to bathe her face and brush her teeth. She dressed in the same pair of slacks she'd worn yesterday—air conditioning provided by Jack the Ripper, she thought peevishly—but put on a fresh flannel shirt. She brushed her hair and tied it back with a shoelace. It was when she was pulling on her socks that she realized she had been moving about without the aid of her crutches. There was very little soreness left in her leg. They might not be pretty, but Cooper's stitches had worked to heal her injury.

Not wanting to feel any kindness toward him, she moved to the stove and fed short sticks of firewood into it. She filled a kettle with water and spooned coffee into it, sadly thinking about the automatic coffee maker with the built-in digital timer that she had in her kitchen at home.

Forcibly tamping down a wave of homesickness, she began making a breakfast of oatmeal. Reading the directions on the side of the cylindrical box that she'd found among the food supplies, she was glad to discover that oatmeal didn't require any cooking skills beyond boiling water and pouring in the correct portion of oats.

Unfortunately her guess was off a trifle.

Cooper came stamping in and without preamble demanded, "Have you got breakfast ready yet?"

None too charitably, she answered, "Yes. Sit down."

She wanted to serve him a steaming bowl of creamy oatmeal like the ones in the commercials on TV. Instead, when she lifted the lid on the pot, she gazed down into a gooey mess about the color and consistency of setting concrete, except lumpier.

Dismayed, but determined not to show it, she squared her shoulders and dug out two spoonfuls. When she dumped them into the tin bowls, they landed in the bottom of them like lead. She carried the bowls to the table, set them on the rough wood plank with forceful disdain, and took her chair across from him.

"Coffee?" he said.

She bit her lip in consternation, but got up, poured their coffee and returned to the table without saying a single word. She let her body language convey her dislike for his lord-of-the-manor attitude.

He scooped up a bite of the oatmeal and weighed it in his spoon, eyeing her skeptically. Silently, she challenged him to say anything derogatory about her oatmeal. He put the bite in his mouth.

As though instructing him on what to do with it once it was there, Rusty took a bite of hers. She almost spat it out immediately. Instead, knowing he was watching her with his eagle eyes, she chewed it. It seemed to expand instead of get smaller. Finally she had no recourse but to swallow it to get rid of it. Her stomach must have thought she was eating golf balls. She swilled down a scalding gulp of coffee.

Cooper's spoon clattered against his bowl. "Is this the best you can do?"

Rusty wanted to come back with, "Was last night the best *you* could do?" But she reasoned that aiming such an insult at a man's lovemaking abilities might be justifiable grounds for homicide, so she judiciously said, "I don't cook that much at home."

"Too busy flitting from one expensive, fancy restaurant to another, I guess."

"Yes."

Making a terrible face, he forced down another swallow of the foul stuff. "This isn't that presalted, presweetened oatmeal that comes in the cute little packages with teddy bears and bunnies on them; this is the real stuff. Add salt to the water next time. Use only about half as much oatmeal, and then sprinkle sugar over it. But not too much. We've got to ration our supplies."

"If you know so much about cooking, Scoutmaster, why don't you do it?" she asked sweetly.

He shoved his bowl aside and propped his forearms on the table. "Because I've got to do the hunting and fishing and firewood cutting. But, now that I think about it, cooking is a whole lot easier. Want to swap? Or do you plan to make me do *all* the work while you lounge around and watch your fingernails grow back?"

In a flash and a scraping sound of wood on wood, Rusty was out of her chair and leaning across the table. "I don't mind doing my share of the work and you know it. What I *do* mind is having my best efforts criticized by you."

"If this is any indication of your best efforts, we'll be dead of starvation inside a week."

"I'll learn to do better," she shouted.

"It can't be soon enough for me."

"Oh!"

She spun away and when she did, the flannel shirt, which she'd left unbuttoned, flared open. Cooper's arm shot out and grabbed her arm.

"What's that?" Reaching inside the open shirt, he pulled down the strap of her tank top.

Rusty followed the direction of his gaze down to the slight discoloration on the upper curve of her breast. She looked at the round bruise, then lifted her eyes up to his. "That's where you…kissed…" Unable to go on, she made a helpless gesture with her hands. "Last night," she added huskily.

Cooper snatched his hand back, as guilty as Adam when caught sampling the forbidden fruit. Rusty could feel the blush rising in her neck. It spread as evenly and thoroughly as his eyes were moving over her. He noticed the rosy abrasions that his whiskered jaw had made around her mouth and against her face and throat. He grimaced with regret and raised his hand to his chin. When he rubbed it, the scratching noise filled the silence.

"Sorry."

"It's okay."

"Does it…do they hurt?"

"Not really."

"Did it, you know, when…?"

She shook her head. "I didn't notice then."

They quickly glanced away from each other. He moved to the window. It was drizzling outside. Occasionally a pellet of sleet would ping against the glass.

"I guess I should explain about last night," he said in a low, deep voice.

"No. No explanation is necessary, really."

"I don't want you to think I'm impotent or anything like that."

"I know you're not impotent."

His head snapped around and their gazes locked. "I don't guess I could keep it a secret that I was ready and able."

Rusty swallowed with difficulty and lowered her head. "No."

"That leaves willing." She kept her head bowed. "Well, aren't you even curious as to why I didn't go through with it?" he asked after a lengthy moment.

"I didn't say I wasn't curious. I only said that you didn't have to explain. We're strangers, after all. We owe each other no explanations."

"But you wondered." He pointed an accusing finger at her. "Don't deny that you wondered why I didn't finish it."

"I assumed that there is someone back home. A woman."

"No woman," he barked. At her shocked expression, he smiled crookedly. "No man, either."

She laughed uneasily. "That never occurred to me."

The injection of humor didn't last. His smile inverted itself into a frown. "I don't make sexual commitments."

Her chin went up a notch. "I don't remember asking for one."

"You didn't have to. If we… If I… With just the two of us here, for God knows how long, that's what it would amount to. We're already dependent on each other for everything else. We don't need to make the situation any more complicated than it already is."

"I couldn't agree with you more," she said breezily.

She had never taken rejection very well, but neither had she ever let her hurt feelings show. "I lost my head last night. I was frightened. More exhausted than I realized. You were there, you did the humane thing and rendered comfort. As a result, things got out of hand. That's all there was to it."

The lines running down either side of his mouth pulled in tighter. "Exactly. If we'd met anywhere else, we wouldn't have looked at each other twice."

"Hardly," she said, forcing a laugh. "You wouldn't exactly fit in with my cosmopolitan crowd. You'd stick out like a sore thumb."

"And you in your fancy clothes would be laughed off my mountain."

"So, fine," she said testily.

"Fine."

"It's settled."

"Right."

"We've got no problem."

One might wonder, then, why they were facing each other like pugilists squaring off. The air was redolent with animosity. They'd reached an agreement. They'd figuratively signed a peace treaty. But by all appearances they were still at war.

Cooper was the first to turn away and he did so with an angry jerk of his shoulders. He pulled on his coat and picked up his rifle. "I'm going to see what the stream has to offer in the way of fish."

"Are you planning to shoot them?" She nodded at his rifle.

He frowned at her sarcasm. "I rigged up a trotline while you were languishing in bed this morning." He didn't give her time to offer a rebuttal before he added,

"I also started a fire under that caldron outside. Do the laundry."

Rusty followed his gaze down to the tall pile of dirty clothes and looked at it with unconcealed astonishment. When she turned back to him, the spot he'd been standing in was empty. She hurried to the door as quickly as her limp would allow.

"I was going to do the laundry without you telling me to," she shouted at his retreating back. If he heard her, he gave no indication of it.

Cursing, Rusty slammed the door shut. She cleared the table. It took her almost half an hour to scrub clean the pot she'd cooked the oatmeal in. Next time she would remember to pour hot water in it as soon as she'd spooned the oatmeal out.

She then attacked their pile of dirty clothes with a vengeance. By the time he came back, she wanted to be finished with the chore she'd been summarily assigned. It was mandatory that she prove to him that last night's breakdown was a fluke.

After putting on her coat, she carried the first load of clothes outside and dropped it into the caldron. Previously, she had thought that such black iron pots suspended over smoldering coals existed only in movies. She used a smooth stick to swish the clothes around. When they were as clean as she thought they'd get, she lifted them out of the water with the stick and tossed them into a basket that Cooper had washed out the day before.

By the time she'd finished washing all the clothes using this archaic method, her arms were rubbery with fatigue. And by the time she had wrung them out and hung them up to dry on the wire that stretched from the corner of the house to the nearest tree, her arms felt as if they were about to fall off. Not only that, her wet hands were nearly frozen, as was her nose, which dripped constantly. Her leg, too, had begun to ache again.

A rewarding sense of accomplishment helped relieve some of her miseries. She took comfort in the thought of having done her job well. Once again inside the cabin, she warmed her hands by the fire. When circulation returned to them, she tugged off her boots and wearily climbed onto her bed. If anyone deserved a nap before dinner, it was she.

APPARENTLY SHE'D BEEN in a much deeper sleep than she had planned on. When Cooper came barging through the door shouting her name, she sprang up so suddenly that her head reeled dizzily and yellow dots exploded in front of her eyes.

"Rusty!" he shouted. "Rusty, did you— Dammit, what are you doing in bed?" His coat was open, his hair wild. His cheeks were ruddy. He was breathing hard, as though he'd been running.

"What am I doing in bed?" she asked around a huge yawn. "I was sleeping."

"Sleeping! *Sleeping!* Didn't you hear the plane?"

"Plane?"

"Stop repeating every damn word I say! Where's the flare gun?"

"The flare gun?"

He was all but foaming at the mouth. "Where's the flare gun? There's a plane buzzing overhead."

Her feet hit the floor. "Is it looking for us?"

"How the hell should I know?" He tore through the

cabin, uprighting everything he laid his hands on in his frantic search for the flare gun. "Where is that... here!" Brandishing the gun, he raced outside, leaped over the porch, and scanned the sky. In stocking feet, Rusty hobbled after him.

"Do you see it?"

"Shut up!" He cocked his head to one side while he listened carefully. The unmistakable hum of the engine reached them at the same time. They turned simultaneously and were met with a dismal sight.

It was an airplane, all right. Obviously a search plane, because it was flying low. But it was flying in the opposite direction. Firing the flares now would serve no purpose except to waste them. Two pairs of eyes remained on the diminishing speck until it grew too small to see and the whine of the engine could no longer be heard. It left a deafening silence in its wake. As the noise had died, so had their chances for a probable rescue.

Cooper came around slowly. His eyes looked cold and colorless and so laden with murderous intent that Rusty took a step backward.

"Just what the *hell* were you doing asleep?"

Rusty preferred him shouting. Ranting and raving she knew how to deal with and respond to. This soft, hissing, sinister-as-a-serpent voice terrified her. "I... I finished the wash," she said hastily. The words tripped over themselves. "I was exhausted. I had to lift—"

It suddenly occurred to her that she owed him no stuttering apologies. From the beginning, he'd assumed charge of the flare gun. It hadn't been out of his possession since they'd left the wrecked aircraft.

Belligerently, she placed her hands on her hips.

"How dare you blame this on *me!* Why did you go off without the flare gun?"

"Because I was mad as hell this morning when I left. I forgot it."

"So it's your fault the flare wasn't fired, not mine!"

"It was your fault that I was so damn mad when I left."

"If you can't control your short temper, how can you expect me to?"

His eyes turned dark. "Even if I'd had the gun and fired it, they could have missed it. But they damn sure could have seen smoke from our chimney. But, no. You needed a beauty rest. So you went to sleep and let the fire burn out."

"Why haven't you built a signal fire, a big one, one a potential rescuer couldn't miss?"

"I didn't think I'd need one. Not with a chimney. Of course I didn't count on you taking afternoon naps."

She faltered, then said defensively, "Chimney smoke wouldn't have attracted their attention anyway. That's nothing out of the ordinary."

"This far off the beaten track it is. They would have at least circled around to investigate."

Rusty groped for another valid alibi. "The wind is too strong for a column of smoke to form. Even if the fire had been going, they wouldn't have spotted our smoke."

"There was a *chance*."

"Not as good a chance as seeing a flare, if you had had the gun with you."

It would have been prudent not to point out his dereliction of duty at that particular moment. His lower lip disappeared beneath his mustache and he took a menacing step forward. "I could easily murder you for letting that plane go by."

She tossed her head back. "Why don't you? I'd rather you do that than keep harping about my shortcomings."

"But you provide me with such a wealth of material. You've got so many shortcomings that if we were stranded here for years I would never get around to harping on all of them."

Her cheeks grew pink with indignation. "I admit it! I'm not qualified to live in a rustic cabin in the middle of nowhere. It wasn't a life-style I chose for myself."

His chin jutted out. "You can't even cook."

"I've never wanted to or needed to. I'm a career woman," she said with fierce pride.

"Well, a helluva lot of good your career is doing me now."

"Me, me, me," Rusty shouted. "You've thought only of yourself through this whole ordeal."

"Ha! I should be so lucky. Instead I've had you to think about. You've been nothing but an albatross."

"It was not my fault that my leg got hurt."

"And I suppose you're going to say it wasn't your fault that those two men went dotty over you."

"It *wasn't*."

"No?" he sneered nastily. "Well, you haven't stopped putting out signals that you'd like to have me in your pants."

Later, Rusty couldn't believe she'd actually done it. She'd never guessed that she had a latent violent streak. Even as a child, she'd always given in to other children to avoid a confrontation. By nature she was a pacifist. She'd never been physically aggressive.

But at Cooper's intentionally hurtful words, she

launched herself at him, fingers curled into claws aimed for his smirking face. She never reached him. She came down hard on her injured leg. It buckled beneath her. Screaming with pain, she fell to the frozen ground.

Cooper was beside her instantly. He picked her up. She fought him so strenuously that he restrained her in an armlock. "Stop that or I'll knock you unconscious."

"You would, wouldn't you?" she asked, breathless from her efforts.

"Damn right. And I'd enjoy it."

Her struggles subsided, more out of weakness and pain than capitulation. He carried her indoors and set her down in the chair near the fire. Casting her a reproachful look, he knelt on the cold hearth and painstakingly coaxed the fire back to life.

"Does your leg still hurt?"

She shook her head no. It hurt like hell, but she'd have her tongue cut out before admitting it. She wasn't going to speak to him, not after what he'd said, which was patently untrue. Her refusal to speak was childish, but she clung to her resolution not to, even as he separated her torn pants leg, rolled down her sock, and examined the zigzagging incision on her shin.

"Stay off it for the rest of the day. Use your crutches if you move around." He patted her clothes into place, then stood up. "I'm going back to get the fish. I dropped them in my pell-mell rush to the cabin. I hope a bear hasn't already made them his dinner." At the door he turned back. "And I'll cook them if it's all the same to you. They look like good fish and you'd probably ruin them."

He slammed the door behind him.

THEY WERE GOOD FISH. Delicious, in fact. He'd cooked them in a skillet until they were falling-off-the-bones tender, crusty on the outside and flaky on the inside. Rusty regretted passing up the second one, but she wasn't about to devour it ravenously, as she had done the first. Cooper added insult to injury by eating it when she refused it. She wished he would choke on a bone and die. Instead, he complacently licked his fingers, smacking noisily, and patted his stomach.

"I'm stuffed."

Oh, boy, did she have some excellent comebacks for that leading line. But she maintained her stony silence.

"Clean up this mess," he said curtly, leaving the dirty table and stove to her.

She did as she was told. But not without making a terrible racket that echoed off the rafters. When she had finished, she threw herself down on her bed and gazed at the ceiling overhead. She didn't know if she were more hurt or angry. But whichever, Cooper Landry had coaxed more emotion from her than any other man ever had. Those emotions had run the gamut from gratitude to disgust.

He was the meanest, most spiteful human being she'd ever had the misfortune to meet, and she hated him with a passion that appalled her.

True, she had begged him to get into bed with her last night. But for comfort, not sex! She hadn't asked for it; she hadn't wanted it. It had just happened. He was bound to realize that. His puffed-up, colossal ego just kept him from admitting it.

Well, one thing was for certain: from now on she was going to be as modest as a nun. He'd see the skin of her face, possibly her neck, surely her hands, but

that was it. It wasn't going to be easy. Not living together in this—

Her thoughts came to an abrupt halt as she spied
something overhead that provided the solution to her
problem. There were hooks over her bed, exactly like
the ones Cooper had used to drape the curtain in front
of the bathtub.

Filled with sudden inspiration, she left the bed
quickly and retrieved an extra blanket from the shelf
against the wall. Completely ignoring Cooper, who she
knew was watching her covertly, she dragged a chair
across the floor and placed it beneath one of the hooks.

Standing on the chair, she had to stretch her calf
muscles—more than they'd ever been stretched in aer-
obics class—in order to reach the hook, but eventually
she managed it. Moving the chair directly beneath another hook, she repeated the procedure. When she was
done, she was left with a curtain of sorts around her
bed, which would give her privacy.

She shot her cabin mate a smug glance before she
ducked behind the blanket and let it fall into place behind her. There! Let him accuse her of asking for "it."

She shuddered at the memory of the crude thing
he'd said to her. Add *uncouth* to all his other disagreeable traits. She undressed and slid into bed. Because of
her nap, she couldn't fall asleep right away. Even after
she heard Cooper go to bed and his steady breathing
indicated that he was fast asleep, she lay there awake,
watching the myriad flickering patterns the fire cast
on the ceiling.

When the wolves began to howl, she rolled to her
side, covered her head with the blanket, and tried not
to listen. She clamped her finger between her teeth and

bit down hard to keep from crying, to keep from feeling lost and alone, and to keep herself from begging Cooper to hold her while she slept.

CHAPTER EIGHT

COOPER SAT AS perfectly still as a hunter in a deer stand. Motionless, feet planted far apart, elbows propped on widespread knees, fingers cupped around his chin. Above them, his eyes stared at her unblinkingly.

That was the first sight Rusty saw when she woke up the following morning. She registered surprise, but managed to keep from jumping out of her skin. Immediately she noticed that the screen she had so ingeniously devised and hung around her bed the night before had been torn down. The blanket was lying at the foot of her bed.

She levered herself up on one elbow and irritably pushed her hair out of her eyes. "What are you doing?"

"I need to talk to you."

"About what?"

"It snowed several inches last night."

She studied his expressionless face for a moment, then said with a great deal of pique. "If you're wanting to build a snowman, I'm not in the mood."

His eyes didn't waver, although she could tell that he was willfully restraining himself when he was sorely tempted to strangle her.

"The snowfall is important," he said calmly. "Once winter gets here our chances of being rescued are greatly reduced."

"I understand that," she replied in a serious tone befitting his observation. "What I don't understand is why it has such grave implications at this very minute."

"Because before we spend another day together, we've got to get some things straight, lay down some ground rules. If we're going to be marooned up here together all winter—which looks like a very real possibility—then we must reach an understanding on several points."

She sat up but kept the blanket raised to her chin. "Such as?"

"Such as no more pouting spells." His brows were drawn together in a straight, stern line of admonition. "I won't put up with that kind of brattiness from you."

"Oh, you won't?" she asked sweetly.

"No, I won't. You're not a child. Don't act like one."

"It's all right for you to insult me, but I'm supposed to turn the other cheek, is that it?"

For the first time, he looked away, apparently chagrined. "I probably shouldn't have said what I did yesterday."

"No, you shouldn't have. I don't know what evil thoughts you've cultivated in your dirty little mind, but don't blame me for them."

He gnawed on the corner of his mustache. "I was mad as hell at you."

"Why?"

"Mainly because I… I don't like you very much. But I still want to sleep with you. And by 'sleep' I don't mean just sleep." If he had slapped her, she couldn't have been more astounded. Her lips parted with a sudden intake of breath, but he didn't give her a chance to say anything. "Now isn't the time to beat around the bush or to mince words, right?"

"Right," she repeated hoarsely.

"I hope you can appreciate my honesty."

"I can."

"Okay, concede this point. We're physically attracted to each other. Bluntly stated, we want to get off together. It doesn't make any sense, but it's a fact." Rusty's gaze dropped to her lap. He waited until his patience gave out. "Well?"

"Well, what?"

"Say something for God's sake."

"I'll concede both points."

He let out a long breath. "All right then, knowing that, and knowing that it's unreasonable to do anything about it, and knowing, too, that it's going to be a helluva long winter, we've got some things to iron out. Agreed?"

"Agreed."

"First, we'll stop the mudslinging." Her russet eyes treated him to a frosty stare. Grudgingly he added, "I'll admit to being guilty of that more than you. Let's just promise not to be verbally abusive to each other from here on."

"I promise."

He nodded. "The weather will be our enemy. A fearsome one. It will require all our attention and energy. We can't afford the luxury of fighting each other. Our survival depends on living together. Our sanity depends on doing it peaceably."

"I'm listening."

He paused to collect his thoughts. "As I see it, our roles should be traditional."

"You Tarzan, me Jane."

"Sort of. I'll provide the food. You'll cook it."

"As you've so untactfully pointed out, I'm not a very good cook."

"You'll get better."

"I'll try."

"Don't get defensive if I offer you advice."

"Then don't make snide remarks about my lack of talent. I'm good at other things."

His eyes lowered to her lips. "I can't argue that." After a long, silent moment, he roused himself. "I don't expect you to wait on me hand and foot."

"I don't expect that from you, either. I want to pull my weight."

"I'll help you keep the cabin and our clothes clean."

"Thank you."

"I'll teach you to shoot more accurately so you can protect yourself when I'm gone."

"Gone?" she asked faintly, feeling that the rug had just been pulled out from under her.

He shrugged. "If the game gives out, if the stream freezes over, I might have to go in search of food."

She would face with fear and dread the times she might have to stay in the cabin alone, perhaps for days. Even a vulgar and insulting Cooper was better than no Cooper at all.

"And this is the most important point." He waited until he had her full attention, until her dazed eyes had refocused on him. "I'm the boss," he said, tapping his chest. "Don't let's kid ourselves. This is a life-or-death situation. You might know all there is to know about residential real estate and California chic and the life-styles of the rich and famous. But up here, all that knowledge isn't worth a damn. On your turf you can do whatever the hell you please and I say, more power to you, 'You've come a long way, baby,' and all that. But up here, you obey me."

She was stung by his implication that her field of expertise wasn't much use outside Beverly Hills. "As I recall, I haven't tried to usurp your position as the macho provider."

"Just see that you don't. In the wilderness there's no such thing as equality between the sexes."

He stood up and happened to catch sight of the blanket lying on the foot of the bed. "One more thing: No more silly screens. The cabin is too small and we're living too close together to play coy games like that. We've seen each other naked. We've touched each other naked. There're no more secrets. Besides," he said, raking his eyes over her, "if I wanted you bad enough, no damn blanket would keep me from you. And if rape was what I had in mind, I would have done it a long time ago."

Their eyes locked and held. Finally he turned his back. "It's time you got up. I've already started the coffee."

That morning the oatmeal was considerably better than it had been the day before. At least it didn't stick to the palate like a day-old peanut-butter sandwich. It had been frugally seasoned with salt and sugar. Cooper ate every bite of his, but didn't offer her a compliment.

She didn't take umbrage as she once would have done. His failure to criticize was tantamount to a compliment. They had only promised not to be verbally abusive; they hadn't promised to shower each other with flattery.

He went outside after breakfast and by the time he came in for a lunch of biscuits and canned soup, he had made himself a pair of snowshoes out of bent green-wood and woven dead vines. He strapped them to his boots and clumped around the cabin, modeling them for her. "These will make it a lot easier to navigate the ravine between here and the river."

He spent the afternoon away from the cabin. She straightened it, but the housekeeping didn't take more than half an hour. That left her with nothing to do but fret until she saw him through the window at dusk, making awkward progress toward the cabin in the homemade snowshoes.

She rushed out on the porch to greet him with a cup of hot coffee and a tentative smile, feeling slightly foolish for being so pleased to see him return safe and sound.

Unstrapping the snowshoes and propping them against the cabin's outside wall, he looked at her strangely and took the proffered coffee. "Thanks." He stared at her through the cloud of rising steam as he took a sip.

She noticed, as he held the cup to his lips, that they were chapped and that his hands were raw and red despite the shearling gloves he always wore when he was outdoors. She wanted to commiserate, but decided against it. His lecture that morning discouraged anything except mutual tolerance.

"Any luck at the stream?" she asked.

He nodded down toward the creel, which had belonged to the Gawrylows. "It's full. We'll leave some out to freeze and save them for days when I can't get down the ravine. And we should start filling containers with water in case the pump freezes up."

Nodding, she carried the basket of fish inside, proud

of the appetizing aroma of her stew. She had made it with dried beef found among the hermits' stock of canned food. Its aroma filled the cabin. Cooper ate two full bowls of it and made her day by saying, "Pretty good," at the conclusion of the meal.

THE DAYS FOLLOWED that basic pattern. He did his chores. She did hers. He helped her with hers. She helped him with his. They were scrupulously polite, if politely distant.

But while they could fill the short days with activity, the evenings seemed endless. They came early. First the sun sank below the tree line and cast the area surrounding the cabin in deep shadow, making outdoor chores hazardous and forcing them indoors.

The instant the sun was swallowed by the horizon, it was dark, even though it was still officially afternoon. Once dinner was eaten and the dishes were washed, there was little to do. There weren't enough inside chores to keep them occupied and separated. They had nothing to do except stare into the fire and avoid staring at each other—something that required supreme concentration on both their parts.

That first snowfall melted the next day, but the night following that, it snowed again and continued into the day. Because of the steadily dropping temperature and blowing snow, Cooper returned to the cabin earlier than usual, which made the evening stretch out unbearably long.

Rusty, her eyes swinging back and forth like twin pendulums, watched him as he paced the length of the cabin like a caged panther. The four walls were making her claustrophobic, and his restlessness only irritated her further. When she caught him scratching his chin, something she'd noticed him doing repeatedly, she asked with asperity, "What's the matter?"

He spun around as though spoiling for a fight and delighted that someone had finally picked one with him. "With what?"

"With you?"

"What do you mean?"

"Why do you keep scratching your chin?"

"Because it itches."

"Itches?"

"The beard. It's at the itchy stage."

"Well, that scratching is driving me crazy."

"Tough."

"Why don't you shave it off if it itches?"

"Because I don't have a razor, that's why."

"I—" She broke off when she realized that she was about to make a confession. Then, noticing that his eyes had narrowed suspiciously, she said haughtily, "I do. I have one. I brought it along and now I'll bet you're glad I did."

Leaving her chair near the fireplace, she went to the shelf where she had stored her toiletries. She treasured them as a miser did his bag of gold coins. She brought the plastic, disposable razor back to Cooper. And something else besides. "Put this on your lips." She passed him the tube of lip gloss. "I noticed that your lips are chapped."

He took the tube from her and rolled the stick of lip balm out. He seemed pressed to make several comments, but said none of them. She laughed at the awkward way he applied the gloss. When he was done, he handed the capped tube back to her. She gave him the razor. "Be my guest."

"Thanks." He turned the razor over in his hand, studying it from every angle. "You didn't by chance sneak some hand lotion, too, did you?"

She held up her hands. Like his, they had been ravaged by water, wind and cold. "Do these look like they've seen any lotion lately?"

His smiles were so rare that her heart melted beneath the one he flashed her now. Then, in what seemed like a reflexive gesture, he captured one of her hands and lightly kissed the backs of her fingers with lips made soft by shiny gloss.

His mustache tickled her fingers. And in a bizarre correlation that made absolutely no sense, it tickled the back of her throat as well. Her stomach executed a series of somersaults.

Suddenly realizing what he'd done, he dropped her hand. "I'll use the razor in the morning."

Rusty hadn't wanted him to let go of her hand. In fact, she'd been tempted to turn it and cover his mustache and lips with her palm. She wanted to feel their caress in that vulnerable spot. Her heart was pounding so hard she had difficulty speaking. "Why not shave now?"

"There's no mirror. With this much stubble, I'd lacerate myself."

"I could shave you."

For a moment neither of them said anything, only filled the narrow space between them with leaping arcs of sexual electricity. Rusty didn't know where the impulse had sprung from. It had just popped up from nowhere and she'd acted on it before thinking—maybe

because it had been days since they'd touched each
other for any reason. She was feeling deprived. As the
body gets hungry for a certain food when it needs the
vitamins and minerals it contains, she'd unconsciously
expressed her desire to touch him.

"All right." Cooper's permission was granted in a
ragged voice.

Nervous, now that he had agreed to her suggestion,
she clasped her hands at her waist. "Why...why don't
you sit over there by the fire. I'll bring the stuff."

"Okay."

"Roll the collar of your shirt in and tuck a towel inside," she said over her shoulder as she poured water
from the kettle on the stove into a shallow bowl. She
pulled a chair up close to his and set the bowl and razor
on the seat. She also got her bar of soap from the shelf,
and a spare towel.

"I'd better soak it first." He dipped the extra towel
into the bowl of hot water. "Ouch, damn," he cursed
when he tried to wring it out.

"It's hot."

"No foolin'?"

He juggled the scalding towel from one hand to
the other before finally slapping it against the lower
portion of his face, letting out a yelp when he did so.
He held it there, although Rusty didn't know how he
could stand it.

"Doesn't that burn?" Without removing the towel,
he nodded solemnly. "You do it to soften the whis-
kers, right?" Again, he nodded. "I'll try to work up a
good lather."

Tentatively she wet her hands in the bowl of hot
water and picked up the cake of soap. Cooper watched

her every move as she rubbed the soap between her hands until they were covered with honeysuckle-scented suds. The foam looked rich and creamy as she slid it between her palms. It oozed between her fingers, looking intensely sexy, although exactly why, he didn't know.

"Whenever you're ready," she said, moving behind him.

Gradually Cooper lowered the towel. Just as gradually, Rusty raised her hands to his face. Gazing down at him from her position above and behind him, the planes and ridges of his face looked even more harsh, more pronounced. But there was a vulnerability to his eyelashes that gave her enough courage to lay her palms against his prickly cheeks.

She felt him tense up in reaction to her touch. She didn't move her hands at first, but kept them still, resting lightly against his cheeks, while she waited to see if he was going to tell her that this wasn't a good idea.

It was a given that it wasn't a good idea.

She just wondered which one of them was going to admit it first and call a halt to the proceedings. But Cooper said nothing, and she didn't want to stop, so she began to rotate her hands over his cheeks.

The sensation of that scratchy surface against her palms was enticing. She moved her hands to encompass more area and found that the bones of his jaw were just as chiseled and rigid to the touch as they looked. His square chin had a shallow indentation in its center. She slipped the edge of her fingernail into it, but didn't investigate it nearly as long as she wanted to.

She ran her hands simultaneously down his throat, smoothing on the lather as she went. Her fingers glided over his Adam's apple and toward the base of his neck, where she felt his pulse pounding. Dragging her fingers back up his neck and over his chin again, she encountered his lower lip and, beyond it, the brush of his mustache.

She froze and drew in a quick, hopefully inaudible breath. "Sorry," she murmured. Removing her hands, she dipped them in the water to rinse them off. She leaned forward and inspected her handiwork from another angle. There was a speck of soap on his lower lip and some bubbles clinging to several of the blond hairs in his mustache.

With her wet finger, she whisked away that speck from his lip, then rubbed her finger over his mustache until the bubbles disappeared.

A low sound emanated from him. Rusty froze, but her eyes flew to his. "Get on with it," he growled.

With his face partially obscured by white foam, he shouldn't have posed any threat. But his eyes were alight. They glittered in the firelight. She could see the flames dancing in their depths and sensed a coiled violence over which he exercised tenuous control. It prompted her to step behind him again and out of harm's way.

"Don't cut me," he warned as she lifted the razor to his jaw.

"I won't if you'll be still and shut up."

"Have you ever done this before?"

"No."

"That's what I was afraid of."

He stopped talking as she drew the first swipe up his cheek. "So far so good," she said softly as she dipped the razor in the bowl. He mumbled something, trying to keep his mouth still, but Rusty didn't catch what he said. She was concentrating too hard on giving him a clean shave without nicking his skin. When the lower part of his face was clean, she let out a deep sigh of relief and satisfaction. "Smooth as a baby's bottom."

A laugh rolled up from the depths of his chest. Rusty had never heard him actually laugh with pure humor before. His infrequent laughs were usually tinged with cynicism. "Don't start bragging yet. You're not finished. Don't forget my neck. And for God sake, be careful with that blade."

"It's not that sharp."

"That's the worst kind."

She swished the razor in the water to dampen it, then placed one hand beneath his chin. "Tilt your head back."

He did. It rested heavily against her breasts. Rusty, unable to move for a moment, kept the razor poised above his throat. His Adam's apple bobbed with a hard, involuntary swallow. To take her mind off their position, she turned her attention to the task at hand, which only made matters worse. She had to come up on her toes and lean forward to see well. By the time she'd shaved his neck clean, his head was cushioned between her breasts and they were both keenly aware of it.

"There." She stepped back and dropped the razor as though it were the single piece of incriminating evidence in a murder trial.

He yanked the towel out of his collar and buried his face in it. For what seemed like hours he didn't move or lower the towel.

"How does it feel?" she asked.

"Great. It feels great."

Then, he stood up abruptly and tossed the towel onto the chair. Tearing his coat from the peg near the door, he pulled it on, ruthlessly shoving his arms into the sleeves.

"Where are you going?" Rusty asked anxiously.

"Outside."

"What for?"

He shot her a sizzling glance that wasn't in keeping with the blizzard blowing beyond the open door. "Believe me, you don't want to know."

HE CONTINUED TO behave in that volatile manner until noon the next day. All morning the weather had been prohibitive to beast and man, so they'd been snowbound in the cabin. For the most part, Cooper ignored her. She responded in kind. After several unsuccessful attempts to make conversation with him, she gave up and lapsed into a moody silence that matched his.

It was a relief when the snowy wind stopped its incessant howling and he announced that he was going to take a look around. She was concerned for his safety, but refrained from persuading him to stay indoors. They needed the breathing space away from each other.

Besides, she needed some privacy. Cooper wasn't the only one who'd been itching lately. The incision on her leg was giving her fits. As the skin began to knit, it had become tight and dry. Her clothing only aggravated it further. She decided that the stitches had to come out. She also decided that she was going to pull them out herself rather than involve Cooper, especially since their relationship was so rocky and his mood shifts so unpredictable.

He'd been gone only a few minutes when she stripped off all her clothes, having decided to use this opportunity to give herself a thorough sponge bath. When she finished washing, she sat down in front of the fire, wrapped in a blanket for warmth. She propped her injured leg over the knee of the other and examined it. How hard could it be to clip those stitches and pull them out?

Where before, the thought would have given her qualms the size of goose eggs, she approached the chore pragmatically. The first obstacle was to find something to clip the silk stitches with. The knife Cooper had given her was too cumbersome. The only thing in the cabin sharp enough and delicate enough was her razor.

It had seemed like a good idea, but when she held the razor lengthwise over the first stitch, poised and ready to saw into it, she realized that her hand was perspiring with apprehension. Drawing a deep breath, she touched the silk thread with the razor.

The door burst open and Cooper tramped through it, snowshoes and all. He'd covered his head with a fur pelt and was bundled up from his neck to his boots. His own breath had frozen on his mustache, making it appear ghostly white. Rusty emitted a squeak of alarm and momentary fright.

But her surprise couldn't compare to his. She was just as supernatural a vision as he, in an entirely different way. Silhouetted as she was against the fireplace, the flames shone through her hair. One leg was propped up, exposing a tantalizing length of naked thigh. The blanket she'd wrapped herself in after her sponge bath had slipped off her shoulder, revealing most of one breast. As his eyes fastened on it, the nipple grew taut with the chilly air he was letting in.

He closed the door. "What the hell are you doing sitting there like that?"

"I thought you'd be gone longer."

"I could have been anybody," he roared.

"Like who?"

"Like…like…"

Hell, he couldn't think of a single other person who might have barged in the way he just had, never guessing that he'd find a breathtaking sight like this one in a rude cabin in the Canadian wilds. He felt the front of his pants strain with his instant erection. Either she genuinely had no idea what effect she had on him, or she did know and was maliciously using it to slowly drive him crazy. Whichever, the result was the same.

Frustrated, he tore the pelt from his head and shook snow out of it. Gloves went flying. He tore at the tongs tying on his snowshoes. "Back to my original question, what the hell are you doing?"

"Taking my stitches out."

The peg in the wall caught the coat he tossed in that general direction. *"What?"*

His stance—that know-it-all, arrogant, condescending, masculine stance—grated on her like a pumice stone. Not to mention his superior tone of voice. She looked him directly in the eye. "They're itching. The wound has closed. It's time they came out."

"And you're using a razor?"

"What do you suggest?"

He crossed the floor in three angry strides, pulling his hunting knife from its scabbard as he came. When he dropped to his knees in front of her, she recoiled and drew the blanket tightly around herself. "You can't use *that!*"

His expression was forbearing as he unscrewed the handle of his knife and shook out several implements that Rusty hadn't known until now were in there. Among them was a tiny pair of scissors. Instead of being pleased, she was furious: "If you had those all along, why did you cut my fingernails with that bowie knife?"

"I felt like it. Now, give me your leg." He extended his hand.

"I'll do it."

"Give me your leg." He enunciated each word as he glared up at her from beneath his brows. "If you don't, I'll reach into that blanket and bring it out myself." His voice dropped to a seductive pitch. "No telling what I might encounter before I find it."

Mutinously she thrust her bare leg out from under the blanket. "Thank you," he said sarcastically.

"Your mustache is dripping on me."

The frost was beginning to melt. He wiped it dry on his shirt sleeve, but he didn't release her bare foot. It looked small and pale in his large hand. Rusty loved the feeling, but she fought against enjoying it. She waged a war within when he tucked her heel into the notch of his thighs. She gasped over the firm, solid bulge that filled her arch.

He raised sardonic eyes up to hers. "What's the matter?"

He was daring her to tell him. She would die before she even let him know she had noticed. "Nothing," she said nonchalantly. "Your hands are cold, that's all."

The glint in his eyes told her that he knew she was

lying. Grinning, he bent his head to his task. Clipping the silk threads presented no problems to either of them. Rusty was thinking that she could just as easily have done it herself. But when he picked up a small pair of tweezers and pinched the first clipped thread between them, she realized that the worst was yet to come.

"This won't hurt, but it might sting a little," he cautioned. He gave one swift tug to pull the stitch out. Reflexively Rusty's foot made a braking motion against him.

"Ah, God," he groaned. "Don't do that."

No, she wouldn't. She definitely would not. She would keep her foot as still as stone from now on, even if he had to tear the stitches out with his teeth.

By the time the tweezers had picked the last thread out, tears of tension and anxiety had filled her eyes. He'd been as gentle as he could be, and Rusty was grateful, but it hadn't been pleasant. She laid her hand on his shoulder. "Thanks, Cooper."

He shrugged her hand off. "Get dressed. And hurry up with dinner," he ordered with the graciousness of a caveman. "I'm starving."

Soon after that, he started drinking.

CHAPTER NINE

THE JUGS OF whiskey had been among the Gawrylows' supplies. Cooper had discovered them the day they cleaned out the cabin. He had smacked his lips with anticipation. That was before he tasted the whiskey. He had tossed back a healthy gulp and swallowed it without chewing—the stuff had looked viscous enough to chew. It was white lightning, moonshine, rotgut, and it had crashed and burned inside his stomach like a meteor.

Rusty had laughed at his coughing/wheezing spasm. He wasn't amused. After he'd recovered the use of his vocal cords, he had darkly informed her that it wasn't funny, that his esophagus had been seared.

Until now, he hadn't touched the jugs of whiskey. This time, there was nothing funny about his drinking it.

After he had built up the fire, he uncorked a jug of the smelly stuff. Rusty was surprised, but said nothing as he took a tentative swig. Then another. At first she thought he was drinking it in order to get warm. His expedition outside had been brief, but long enough to freeze his mustache. He was no doubt chilled to the marrow.

That excuse didn't serve for long, however. Cooper didn't stop with those first two drinks. He carried the jug with him to the chair in front of the fireplace and drank what must have equaled several cocktails before Rusty called him to the table. To her irritation, he brought the jug with him and poured an intemperate amount of the whiskey into his coffee mug. He sipped from it between bites of the rabbit stew she had cooked.

She weighed the advisability of cautioning him not to drink too much, but after a time, she felt constrained to say something; the regularity with which he drank from the tin mug was making her uneasy.

What if he passed out? He'd have to lie where he fell because she'd never be able to lift him. She remembered how much effort it had taken to drag him out of the crashed fuselage of the airplane. A great deal of her strength then had come from adrenaline. What if he ventured outside and got lost? A thousand dreadful possibilities elbowed their way through her mind.

Finally she said, "I thought you couldn't drink that."

He didn't take her concern at face value. He took it as a reprimand. "You don't think I'm man enough?"

"What?" she asked with bewilderment. "No. I mean yes, I think you're man enough. I thought you didn't like the taste of it."

"I'm not drinking it because I like the taste. I'm drinking it because we're out of the good stuff and this is all I've got."

He was itching for a fight. She could see the invitation to one in his eyes, hear it in his snarling inflection. Rusty was too smart to pull a lion's tail even if it was dangling outside the bars of the cage. And she was too smart to wave a red flag at Cooper when his face was as blatant a warning of trouble as a danger sign.

In his present mood he was better left alone and

unprovoked, although it was an effort for her to keep silent. She longed to point out how stupid it was to drink something that you didn't like just for the sake of getting drunk.

Which was apparently what he intended to do. He nearly overturned his chair as he pushed himself away from the table. Only trained reflexes that were as quick and sure as a striking rattler's kept the chair from landing on the floor. He moved back to the hearth. There he sipped and sulked while Rusty cleaned up their dinner dishes.

When she was finished, she swept the floor—more to give herself something to do than because it needed it. Unbelievable as it seemed, she'd come to take pride in how neatly she had arranged and maintained the cabin.

Eventually she ran out of chores and stood awkwardly in the center of the room while deciding what to do with herself. Cooper was hunched in his chair, broodily staring into the fireplace as he steadily drank. The most sensible thing to do would be to make herself scarce, but their cabin had only one room. A walk was out of the question. She wasn't a bit sleepy, but bed was her only alternative.

"I, uh, think I'll go to bed now, Cooper. Good night."

"Sit down."

Already on her way to her bed, she was brought up short. It wasn't so much what he'd said that halted her, but the manner in which he'd said it. She would prefer a strident command to that quiet, deadly request.

Turning, she looked at him inquisitively.

"Sit down," he repeated.

"I'm going—"

"Sit down."

His high-handedness sparked a rebellious response, but Rusty quelled it. She wasn't a doormat, but neither was she a dope. Only a dope would tangle with Cooper while he was in this frame of mind. Huffily, she crossed the room and dropped into the chair facing his. "You're drunk."

"You're right."

"Fine. Be ridiculous. Make a fool of yourself. I couldn't care less. But it's embarrassing to watch. So if you don't mind, I'd rather go to bed."

"I do mind. Stay where you are."

"Why? What difference does it make? What do you want?"

He took a sip from his cup, staring at her over the dented rim of it. "While I'm getting plashtered, I want to sit here and shtare at you and imagine you…" He drank from the cup again, then said around a juicy belch, "Naked."

Rusty came out of her chair as though an automatic spring had ejected her. Apparently no level of drunkenness could dull Cooper's reflexes. His arm shot out. He grabbed a handful of her sleeve, hauled her back, and pushed her into the chair.

"I told you to shtay where you are."

"Let go of me." Rusty wrested her arm free. She was as apprehensive now as she was angry. This wasn't a silly drunk's prank, or an argumentative drunk's unreasonableness. She tried convincing herself that Cooper wouldn't hurt her, but then she really didn't know, did she? Maybe alcohol was the catalyst that released his controlled violence. "Leave me alone," she said with affected courage.

"I don't plan on touching you."

"Then what?"

"Call this a masochistic kind of...self-fulfillment." His eyelids drooped suggestively. "I'm sure you can substitute the correct name for it."

Rusty went hot all over with embarrassment. "I know the correct name for *you*. Several, in fact."

He laughed. "Save them. I've heard them all. Instead of thinking up dirty names to call me," he said, after sipping from his mug, "let's talk about you. Your hair, for instance."

She crossed her arms over her middle and looked toward the ceiling, a living illustration of supreme boredom.

"You know what I thought about the first time I saw your hair?" He was undaunted by her uncooperative spirit and refusal to answer. Leaning forward from the waist, he whispered, "I thought about how good it would feel sweeping over my belly."

Rusty jerked her eyes back to his. His were glazed, and not entirely from liquor. They didn't have the vacuous look of the seasoned drunk. The dark centers of them were brilliant, fiery. His voice, too, was now clear. He wasn't slurring his words. He made it impossible for her to misunderstand him—even to pretend to.

"You were standing in the sunshine out on the tarmac. You were talking to a man...your father. But then I didn't know he was your father. I watched you hug him, kiss his cheek. I was thinking, 'That lucky bastard knows what it's like to play with her hair in bed.'"

"Don't, Cooper." Her fists were clenched at her sides. She was sitting as tall and straight as a rocket about to be launched.

"When you got on the plane, I wanted to reach out and touch your hair. I wanted to grab handfuls of it, use it to move your head down even with my thighs."

"Stop this!"

Abruptly he ceased speaking and took another draught of whiskey. If anything, his eyes grew darker, more sinister. "You like hearing that, don't you?"

"No."

"You like knowing you've got that kind of power over men."

"You're wrong. Very wrong. I felt extremely self-conscious about being the only woman on that airplane."

He muttered an obscenity and took another drink. "Like today?"

"Today? When?"

He set his cup aside without spilling a single drop. His coordination, like his reflexes, was still intact. He was a mean, nasty drunk, but he wasn't a sloppy one. He leaned forward, beyond the edge of his chair, putting his face within inches of hers.

"When I came in and found you bundled up naked in that blanket."

"That wasn't calculated. It was an error in judgment. I had no way of knowing you would come back so soon. You never do. You're usually away for hours at a time. That's why I decided to take a sponge bath while you were gone."

"I knew the minute I came through the door that you had bathed," he said in a low, thrumming voice. "I could smell the soap on your skin." His eyes moved down over her, as though seeing bare skin rather than her heavy, cable-knit sweater. "You favored me with a peek at your breast, didn't you?"

"No!"

"Like hell."

"I didn't! When I realized the blanket had slipped, I—"

"Too late. I saw it. Your nipple. Pink. Hard."

Rusty drew in several uneven breaths. This bizarre discussion was having a strange effect on her. "Don't say any more. We promised each other not to be abusive."

"I'm not being abusive. Maybe to myself, but not to you."

"Yes, yes, you are. Please, Cooper, stop this. You don't know—"

"What I'm saying? Yes, I do. I know exactly what I'm saying." He looked directly into her eyes. "I could kiss your nipples for a week and never get tired of doing it."

The whiskey huskiness of his voice barely made the words audible, but Rusty heard them. They intoxicated her. She swayed unsteadily under their impact. She whimpered and shut her eyes in the hopes of blocking out the outrageous words and the mental pictures they inspired.

His tongue moving over her flesh, soft and wet, tender and ardent, rough and exciting.

Her eyes popped open and she glared at him defensively. "Don't you dare speak to me like that."

"Why not?"

"I don't like it."

He gave her a smug and skeptical smile. "You don't like me telling you how I've wanted to put my hands all over you? How I've fantasized about your thighs being opened for me? How I've lain in that damn bed night after night listening to your breathing and wanting to be so deep inside you that—"

"Stop it!" Rusty leaped from her chair and pushed past him, trying to make good an escape out the door of the cabin. She would survive the bitter cold far better than she would his heat.

Cooper was too quick for her. She never reached the door. Before she'd taken two steps, he had her locked in an inescapable embrace. He arched her back as he bent over her. His breath struck her fearful features hotly.

"If it was my destiny to be stranded in this godforsaken place, why did it have to be with a woman who looked like you? Huh?" He shook her slightly as though expecting a logical explanation. "Why'd you have to be so damn beautiful? Sexy? Have a mouth designed for loving a man?"

Rusty tried to wiggle free. "I don't want this. Let me go."

"Why couldn't I be trapped here with someone ugly and sweet? Somebody I could have in bed and not live to regret it. Somebody who would be grateful for my attention. Not a shallow little tart who gets off by driving men crazy. Not a socialite. Not *you*."

"I'm warning you, Cooper." Gritting her teeth, she struggled against him.

"Somebody far less attractive, but *useful*. A woman who could cook." He smiled nastily. "I'll bet you cook all right. In bed. That's where you cook. I'll bet that's where you serve up your best dishes."

He slid his hands over her buttocks and brought her

up hard against himself, thrusting his hips forward and making contact with her lower body.

"Does it give you a thrill, knowing you do that to me?"

It gave her a thrill, but not the kind of which he spoke. This intimacy with his hardness stole her breath. She grabbed his shoulders for support. Her eyes clashed with his. For seconds, they held there.

Then Rusty broke their stare and shoved him away. She despised him for putting her through this. But she was also ashamed of her own, involuntary reaction to everything he'd said. It had been fleeting, but for a moment there, her choice could have gone either way.

"Keep away from me," she said in a voice that trembled with purpose. "I mean it. If you don't, I'll turn that knife you gave me on you. Do you hear me? Don't lay a hand on me again." She strode past him and threw herself face down on her bed, using the coarse sheet to cool her fevered cheeks.

Cooper was left standing in the center of the room. He raised both hands and plowed them through his long hair, painfully raking it back off his face. Then he slunk back to his chair in front of the fireplace and picked up the jug and his tin cup.

When Rusty dared to glance at him, he was still sitting there morosely sipping the whiskey.

SHE PANICKED THE following morning when she saw that his bed hadn't been slept in. Had he wandered out during the night? Had something terrible happened to him? Throwing off the covers—she didn't remember pulling them up over herself last night—she raced across the floor and flung open the door.

She slumped against the jamb in relief when she saw Cooper. He was splitting logs. The sky was clear. The sun was shining. What had been icicles hanging from the eaves the day before were now incessant drips. The temperature was comparatively mild. Cooper wasn't even wearing his coat. His shirttail was hanging out loose, and when he turned around Rusty saw that his shirt was unbuttoned.

He spotted her, but said nothing as he tossed several of the split logs onto the mounting pile near the edge of the porch. His face had a greenish cast and there were dark crescents beneath his bloodshot eyes.

Rusty stepped back inside, but left the door open to let in fresh air. It was still cold, but the sunshine had a cleansing effect. It seemed to dispel the hostility lurking in the shadows of the cabin.

Hastily Rusty rinsed her face and brushed her hair. The fire in the stove had gone out completely. By now she was skilled at adding kindling and starting a new one. In minutes she had one burning hot enough to boil the coffee.

For a change, she opened a canned ham and fried slices of it in a skillet. The aroma of cooking pork made her mouth water; she hoped it would tantalize Cooper's appetite, too. Instead of oatmeal, she cooked rice. She would have traded her virtue for a stick of margarine. Fortunately she didn't have an opportunity to barter it, so she settled for drizzling the ham drippings over the rice, which miraculously came out just right.

Splurging, she opened a can of peaches, put them in a bowl, and set them on the table with the rest of the food. She could no longer hear the crunching sound of splitting logs, so she assumed Cooper would be in shortly.

She was right. He came in moments later. His gait was considerably more awkward than usual. While he was washing his hands at the sink, Rusty took two aspirin tablets from the first-aid kit and laid them on his plate.

He stared down at them when he reached the table, then took them with the glass of water beside his plate. "Thanks." Gingerly he settled himself into his chair.

"You're welcome." Rusty knew better than to laugh, but the careful way he was moving was indicative of how severe his hangover was. She poured a cup of strong, black coffee and passed it to him. His hand was shaking as he reached for it. The log-splitting exercise had been self-imposed punishment for his whiskey-drinking binge. She was glad he hadn't chopped off a toe. Or worse.

"How do you feel?"

Without moving his head, he looked over at her. "My eyelashes hurt."

She held back her smile. She also resisted the compulsion to reach across the table and lift the sweaty strands of hair off his forehead. "Can you eat?"

"I think so. I should be able to. I spent what seemed like hours, uh, out back. If the lining of my stomach is still there, it's all that's left."

While he sat with his shoulders hunched and his hands resting carefully on either side of his plate where he'd planted them, she dished up the food. She even cut his ham into bite-size pieces before scooting the plate in front of him. Taking a deep breath, he picked up his fork and took a tentative bite. When he was certain that it was going to stay down, he took another, then another, and was soon eating normally.

"This is good," he said after several minutes of silence.

"Thank you. Better than oatmeal, for a change."

"Yeah."

"I noticed the weather is much warmer."

Actually, what she had noticed was that the exercise had caused the hair on his chest to curl damply. He'd rebuttoned most of the buttons on his shirt before coming to the table, but it was open far enough for her to get a glimpse of that impressive chest.

"We might get lucky and have a few more days of this before the next storm blows through."

"That would be nice."

"Hmm. I could get a lot done around here."

They'd never had a pointless, polite conversation before. This exchange of meaningless chitchat was more awkward than any of their arguments had been, so both dropped it. In a silence so profound they could hear the water dripping off the eaves outside, they finished their meal and drank their second cups of coffee.

When Rusty stood up to clear the table, Cooper said, "I think the aspirin helped. My headache's almost gone."

"I'm glad."

He cleared his throat loudly and fiddled with the knife and fork he'd laid on his empty plate. "Look, about last night, I, uh, I don't have an excuse for it."

She smiled at him with understanding. "If I could have stood the taste of that whiskey, I might have gotten drunk myself. There have been numerous times since the crash when I've wanted that kind of escape. You don't have to apologize."

Moving back to the table, she reached for his plate. He caught her hand. The gesture, unlike anything else he'd done since she met him, was unsure, hesitant. "I'm trying to apologize to you for the things I said."

Staring down at the crown of his head, where his hair grew around a boyish swirl, Rusty asked softly, "Did you mean them, Cooper?"

She knew what she was doing. She was inviting him to make love to her. She wanted him to. There was no sense in fooling herself any longer. He appealed to her like no man ever had. And apparently the attraction was mutual.

They would never maintain their sanity if they didn't satisfy this physical craving. They might live through the winter without becoming lovers, but by spring they would both be raving maniacs. This passionate wanting, unreasonable as it was, could no longer be suppressed.

A relationship between them would be unworkable under ordinary circumstances. Their circumstances were far from ordinary. It simply wasn't practical to examine whether their life-styles or politics or philosophies were compatible. It didn't matter. What mattered—very much so—was a basic human need for intimacy with the opposite sex.

Cooper raised his head slowly. "What did you say?"

"I asked if you meant them—the things you said."

His eyes didn't even flicker. "Yes. I meant them."

He was a man of action, not of words. He reached up and curled his fingers around the back of her neck, pulling her head down for his kiss. He made a sound like that of a feasting wild animal as he used his lips to rub hers apart. His tongue went searching inside her mouth. Rusty welcomed it.

He stood up, stumbling and off balance. This time his chair did topple backward. It landed on the floor with a crash. Neither of them noticed. His arms slid around her waist, hers around his neck. He drew her body tightly against his. Where hers was bowed, his arched to complement it.

"Oh, God." He tore his mouth from hers and pressed it against her neck. The fingers of one hand ravaged her hair, threading through it and weaving it between his fingers. It became hopelessly ensnared in his grip, which was exactly what he wanted. He pulled her head back and stared down into her face. His was taut with desire.

She met his gaze without shyness. "Kiss me again, Cooper."

His mouth claimed hers again, hotly and hungrily. It drew breath from her. As he kissed her, his hand moved to the front of her slacks. He fumbled with the button and zipper until they were undone. When his hand slid into the elastic waistband of her panties, Rusty gasped. She had thought there would be a sensual buildup, a flirtatious progression, extended foreplay.

She didn't regret that there wouldn't be. His boldness, his impatience, was a powerful aphrodisiac. It set off explosions of desire deep within her. She tilted her hips forward and filled his palm with her softness.

He muttered swearwords that were in themselves arousing because they so explicitly expressed the height of his arousal. Like a Rod Stewart song, they were viscerally sexy; one couldn't hear them without thinking of a male and a female mating.

He struggled with the fly of his jeans until his manhood was freed—a hot, hard fullness probing between her thighs. "I feel your hair against me," he rasped in her ear. "It's so soft."

The erotic message made Rusty weak. She leaned back against the edge of the table and lowered her hands to his hips, inside his jeans. "Please, Cooper, now."

One swift and sure stroke planted him solidly inside her. She gasped at the splendid pleasure/pain. He caught his breath and held it. They clung together like the survivors of a catastrophe—which, in fact, they were—as though their very existence depended on never letting go of each other. Oneness was essential to survival.

It was impossible to say who moved first. Perhaps it was simultaneous. After that initial instant of sheer delight in his total possession, Cooper began to delve deeper yet. He ground his hips against hers, extending himself, stretching her, his goal seemingly to be to reach the very nucleus of her soul.

Rusty, crying out in ecstasy, flung her head back. He randomly kissed her exposed throat and moved his mouth over her breasts, though she was still wearing her sweater.

But love play was unnecessary. Nothing could heighten this fire. Cooper's plunging body became hotter and harder with each savage thrust.

Then he had no choice in the matter.

"You're a very beautiful woman."

Rusty gazed up at her lover. One of her arms was

folded beneath her head. The other hand was draped over his shoulder. Her pose was provocative. She wanted it to be. She didn't mind that her breasts were fully revealed and wantonly inviting. She wanted to display them for his entertainment. She enjoyed seeing his eyes turn lambent every time he looked at them and their pouting tips.

Maybe he'd been right all along. She'd shown a marked lack of modesty since she'd met him. Maybe she had been deliberately seductive because she had wanted him from the beginning. She had wanted this—this languishing aftermath of a coupling that had left her replete.

"You think I'm beautiful?" she asked coyly, running her fingers through his hair and smiling like the cat who had just lapped up the cream.

"You know I do."

"You don't have to sound so angry about it."

His fingers trailed down the groove between her ribs all the way to her navel. "I am, though. I didn't want to give in to your charms. I lost the battle with my own lust."

"I'm glad you did." She raised her head and kissed his mouth softly.

He dusted his fingertips over her navel. "For the time being, so am I."

Rusty didn't want them to be restricted to a time limit. "Why 'for the time being'?"

It hadn't taken them long to undress and make up the pallet in front of the fire. Stretched out naked on the pile of furs, hair a rumpled heap of reddish curls, lips rosy and wet from frequent kissing, eyes drowsy with lovemaking, Rusty looked like a conquering vandal's battle prize. Cooper had never waxed poetic, surely not right after having sex. The thought brought an involuntary smile to his lips.

He surveyed her alluring body. "Never mind."

"Tell me."

"It has something to do with you and me and who we are. But I really don't want to talk about that now." He bent his head low and kissed the ginger curls between her thighs. They were damp. They smelled and tasted of himself and he felt his body respond. Her low moan worked as surely as a velvet-fisted caress on his rising sex. He sighed his pleasure. "Did you know that you're very small?" he whispered into the fleecy delta. Her thighs relaxed and parted. His fingers slipped inside her.

"I am?"

"Yes."

"I'm not all that experienced."

He gazed down at her doubtfully, but her face was guileless. Abruptly he asked, "How many?"

"How indelicate!"

"How many?"

Rusty wrestled with her decision to tell him. Finally, eyes evasive, she said quietly, "Less than I could count on one hand."

"In a year?"

"Total."

Cooper stared down at her, searching for any trace of duplicity in her eyes. God, he wanted to believe her, but couldn't. His probing caress was telling him what his mind wasn't ready to accept, what he should have known the moment he entered her, but couldn't reconcile with his image of her.

"Less than five?"

"Yes."

"Less than three?" She looked away. "Just one?" She nodded. His heart did an odd little dance, and the emotion that surged through him felt like happiness. But he'd known so little of it, he couldn't be sure. "And you didn't live with him, did you, Rusty?"

"No." She tossed her head to one side and bit her lower lip at his thumb's indolent stroking. The callused pad of it had been gifted with a magical and intuitive touch that paid honor to a woman's body.

"Why not?"

"My father and brother wouldn't have approved."

"Does everything you do have to meet with your father's approval?"

"Yes... No... I... I... Cooper, please stop," she gasped breathlessly. "I can't think while you're doing that."

"So don't think."

"But I don't want to...to, you know...oh, please... no..."

AFTER THE LAST shimmering beam of light had finally burned out, she opened her eyes and met his teasing smile. "That wasn't so bad, was it?"

She discovered that she had just enough energy to answer his smile and reach up and touch his mustache with her fingertips. "I didn't want to do that so soon. I wanted to look at you some more."

"I guess that ends the discussion of you and your father."

Her brows drew into a frown. "It's very complex, Cooper. He was devastated when Jeff was killed. So was

I. Jeff was…" She searched for the all-encompassing word. "He was wonderful. He could do everything."

Cooper brushed her lips with his mustache. "Not everything," he said mysteriously. "He couldn't—" He bent down and whispered what Jeff couldn't do with him, using a street word that brought color rising all the way to Rusty's hairline. But she blushed with pleasure, not with affront. "So, see? There's no reason for you to feel inferior to your brother."

Before she could expound on the subject, he sealed her lips closed with an arousing, eating kiss. "Now, what was that about looking at me?"

Her breath was insufficient. She drew in a deep, long one before saying, "I haven't looked my fill." Her eyes, shining as brightly as copper pennies, roved down his chest. She lifted her hand to touch him, glanced up at him as though asking permission, then laid her fingers against the springy hair.

"Go on, coward. I don't bite." The glance she gave him was eloquently sensual. He laughed. "Touché. I do. But not all the time." He leaned down and whispered, "Only when I'm buried inside the sweetest silk I've ever found between two thighs."

While she explored, he nibbled her ear and took love bites out of her neck. When her fingers flitted across his nipple, he sucked in a sharp breath. She jerked her hand back quickly. He recaptured it and pressed it back against his chest.

"That wasn't alarming or painful," he explained in a hoarse, thick voice. "It's like connecting two live wires. I wasn't prepared for the shock. Do it again. All you want."

She did. And more. She dallied with him until his

breath became choppy. "Something else needs your attention, but we'd better not," he said, catching her hand on its downward slide. "Not if we want to take this one slow and easy."

"Let me touch you."

Against such a breathy request, he exercised no willpower. He squeezed his eyes shut and withstood her curious caresses until he couldn't bear anymore. Then he lifted her hand off him and satisfied them both with a fervent kiss.

"My turn." One of her arms was still bent behind her head. Her breasts rose off her chest, perfect domes crowned with delicate, pink crests. He covered each with a hand and squeezed. "Too hard?" he asked in response to Rusty's change in facial expression.

"Too wonderful." She sighed.

"That night I kissed you...here..." He touched the curving softness of her breast.

"Yes?"

"I meant to make the mark."

Her sleepy eyelids opened wide. "You did? Why?"

"Because I'm mean, that's why."

"No, you're not. You just want everyone to think you are."

"It works, doesn't it?"

She smiled. "Sometimes. Sometimes I've thought you were very mean. Other times I knew you were feeling a lot of pain and that being deliberately mean was your only way of coping with it. I think it goes back to your days as a POW."

"Maybe."

"Cooper?"

"Hmm?"

"Make another mark if you want to."

His eyes darted up to hers. Then he moved above her and kissed her mouth thoroughly while his hands continued to massage her breasts. He brushed her wet and swollen lips with his mustache before dragging it down her neck, nipping her lightly with his teeth as he went. He kissed his way across her collarbone and down her chest until he reached the upper curve of her breast.

"I'm responsible for the bruises on your bottom. Then the passion mark. I guess in a primitive way I wanted to brand you mine. I don't have to put a mark on you now," he said, moving his lips lightly over her skin. "You belong to me. For a little while, anyway."

Rusty wanted to take issue with his choice of words and tell him that she would belong to him for as long as he liked, but his roving lips emptied her mind of the correct phrases. He kissed every inch of her breasts, avoiding the nipples. Then he licked them all over and at once, like a greedy child with a quickly melting ice-cream cone. When Rusty didn't think she could stand any more, she clutched handfuls of his hair and pulled his mouth directly above one of the achy, stiff peaks.

His tongue flicked over it, lightly, deftly, until her head was thrashing from side to side. He used his mustache to tickle and tease. When he closed his lips around her nipple and surrounded it with the scalding, tugging pressure of his mouth, she cried his name out loud.

"Oh, baby, you're nice." He moved his head from one side of her body to the other. His mouth was ravenous, but tender.

"Cooper?"

"Hmm?"

"Cooper?"

"Hmm?"

"Cooper?" She curled her fingers around his ears and pulled his head up even with hers. "Why'd you do it?"

"Do what?"

He avoided looking at her by staring at a spot beyond the top of her head. "You know what." She wet her lips anxiously. "Why did you…withdraw…before…?"

She felt apprehensive and disappointed, just as she had earlier when, at the last possible heartbeat, he'd cheated her out of the ultimate high, that of feeling him come inside her.

He became perfectly still. For a moment she was afraid she'd made him angry and that he was going to leave the pallet. After a long, tense moment, he cut his eyes back to hers. "I guess you're due an explanation." She said nothing. He released her name on a sigh. "We might be here for a long time. I don't think either of us wants or needs another mouth to feed."

"A baby?" Her voice was hushed with awe. She played with the idea of having a baby and didn't find it repugnant at all. In fact her lips formed a winsome smile. "I hadn't thought of that."

"Well, I had. We're both young, healthy adults. I know you're not using a contraceptive because I know everything that we brought into this cabin with us. Am I right?"

"Yes," she said timidly, like a child confessing a small transgression.

"I didn't pack anything to take with me to the hunting lodge."

"But it probably won't even happen."

"We can't be sure. I'm taking no chances. So—"

"But if it should," she interrupted excitedly, "we'd be found before the child was born."

"Probably, but—"

"Even if we weren't, I'd be the one responsible for feeding it."

This talk about a child had his stomach churning. His mouth was set in its familiar, firm, hard line. It softened now when he saw how earnest Rusty was. Almost naive. "That's just it," he said roughly, his mouth moving toward her breasts. "I can't stand the thought of sharing you with anyone."

"But—"

"I'm sorry. That's the way it's got to be."

She wanted to protest and pursue the argument. But he used his hands and lips and tongue with such prurient talent that they dissolved in a mutual, simultaneous orgasm before she realized that once again he had withdrawn from her just in time.

They kept each other so sated with sex that they didn't get hungry or cold or tired. They made love all that day and into the evening. Finally, exhausted, they wrapped themselves in fur and each other, and slept.

Only the unexpected rat-a-tat drumbeat of helicopter blades could have disturbed their dreams.

CHAPTER TEN

HE WAS GOING to miss the chopper. He knew that. He always did. But he kept running anyway. He always did that, too. Jungle foliage blocked his path. He clawed his way through it toward the clearing. He was running so hard his lungs were on fire. His breathing sounded loud to his own ears.

But he could still hear the rotating blades of the chopper. Close. So close. Noisy.

I've got to make it this time, he cried to himself. I've got to make it or I'll be captured again.

But he knew he wouldn't make it, although he kept running. Running. Running...

As always, after having the nightmare, Cooper sat up, chest heaving with exertion and drenched with sweat. God, it had been real this time. The racket of those chopper blades seemed—

Suddenly he realized that he could still hear the helicopter. Was he awake? Yes, he was. There lay Rusty, sleeping peacefully beside him. This wasn't Nam; this was Canada. And, by God, he heard a helicopter!

He scrambled to his feet and crossed the cabin's chilly floor with running footsteps. Since the day they'd missed the search plane, the flare gun had remained on a shelf next to the door. He grabbed it on his way out. When he dashed across the porch and leaped to the ground, he was still naked, but the flare gun was clutched tightly in his right hand.

Shading his eyes with his left, he scanned the sky. The sun was brilliant and just even with the tops of the trees. His eyes teared because it was so bright. He couldn't see a damn thing. He only had six flares. He mustn't waste them. Each one had to count. But he could still hear the chopper. So he acted on impulse and fired two of the flares directly overhead.

"Cooper, is it—"

"A chopper."

Rusty ran out onto the porch and tossed him a pair of jeans. When she had awakened, first with the intuitive knowledge that her lover was no longer lying beside her, then with the sound of the helicopter, she had hastily pulled on her tattered slacks and bulky sweater. Now she, too, shaded her eyes and searched the sky in every direction.

"He must have seen the flares," Cooper cried excitedly. "He's coming back."

"I don't see him. How do you know?"

"I recognize the sound."

Apparently he did. Within seconds, the helicopter swept over the tops of the trees and hovered above the cabin. Cooper and Rusty began waving their arms and shouting, even though it was obvious that they'd been spotted by the two men sitting in the chopper. They could even see their wide smiles through the bubble.

"They see us! Oh, Cooper, Cooper!"

Rusty launched herself against him. He caught her in a fierce bear hug and, lifting her off her feet, swung her around. "We made it, baby, we made it!"

The clearing surrounding the cabin was large

enough to accommodate the helicopter. It set down. Hand in hand, Rusty and Cooper ran toward it. She was heedless of the twinge of pain in her leg. The pilot in the right-hand chair unbuckled his seat belt and stepped out. Ducking under the rotating blades, he ran to meet them.

"Miz Carlson, ma'am?" His Southern accent was as thick as corn syrup. Rusty bobbed her head up and down, suddenly shy and speechless. Timidly she clung to Cooper's arm.

"Cooper Landry," Cooper said, sticking out his hand and pumping the pilot's in a hearty handshake. "We're damn sure glad to see you guys."

"We're kinda glad to see you, too. Miz Carlson's daddy hired us to look for her. The authorities weren't doing the job to his satisfaction."

"That sounds like Father," Rusty shouted over the clapping sound of the turning blades.

"Y'all the only ones who made it?" They nodded somberly. "Well, unless y'all want to stick around, let's git you home. Your daddy sure is gonna be glad to see ya."

At the mention of the young woman's father, the congenial pilot gave Cooper a worried glance, taking in his unfastened jeans. It was obvious that they'd been pulled on in haste and that the man wearing them was naked underneath. Rusty had the debauched, disheveled look of a woman who'd been making love all night. The pilot summed up the situation readily enough; it didn't have to be spelled out to him.

They returned to the cabin only long enough to dress properly. Cooper retrieved his expensive hunting rifle. Beyond that, they came away empty-handed.

As she went through the door for the last time, Rusty gave the cabin a wistful backward glance. Originally she had despised the place. Now that she was leaving it, she felt a trace of sadness.

Cooper didn't seem to share her sentiment. He and the pilot were laughing and joking, having discovered that they were veterans of the same war and that their tours of duty had overlapped. Rusty had to run to catch up with them. When she did, Cooper slipped an arm around her shoulders and smiled down at her. That made everything all right. Or at least better.

"I'm Mike," the pilot told them as he assisted them into their seats. "And that's my twin brother Pat." The other pilot saluted them.

"Pat and Mike?" Cooper shouted. "You gotta be kidding?"

That seemed hilariously funny and they were all laughing uncontrollably as the chopper lifted off the ground and skimmed the tops of the trees before gaining altitude.

"The crash site was spotted by a search plane several days ago," Mike shouted back at them and pointed down.

Rusty viewed the sight. She was surprised that they had covered so much distance on foot, especially with Cooper dragging her in the handmade travois. She would never have survived if it hadn't been for him. What if he had died in the crash? Shuddering at the thought, she laid her head on his shoulder. He placed his arm around her and pulled her close. Her hand curled around the inside of his thigh in a subconscious gesture of trust.

"The other five died on impact," Cooper told the pilots. "Rusty and I were sitting in the last row. I guess that's why we lived through it."

"When the report came back that the plane wasn't burned or anything, Mr. Carlson insisted on searching for survivors," Mike said. "He hired my brother and me out of Atlanta. We specialize in rescue missions." He propped his elbow on the back of his seat and turned his head to address them. "How'd you happen onto the cabin?"

Cooper and Rusty exchanged a troubled glance. "We'll save that story and tell it only once, if you don't mind," Cooper said.

Mike nodded. "I'm gonna radio that you've been rescued. Lots of people have been lookin' for ya. The weather's been a real bitch. Sorry, Miz Carlson."

"That's okay."

"We were grounded until yesterday when the weather cleared. Didn't see anything. Then got an early start again this morning."

"Where are you taking us?" Cooper asked.

"Yellowknife."

"Is my father there?"

Mike shook his head. "He's in L.A. My guess is that he'll have y'all hustled down there before the day is out."

That was good news to Rusty. She couldn't say why, but she had dreaded having to relate the details of her ordeal to her father. Knowing that she wouldn't have to face him right away came as a relief—perhaps because of what had happened last night. She hadn't had time to analyze it. She wanted to savor the experience she had had with Cooper.

Their rescue had been an intrusion. She'd been glad

about it, of course. Still, she wanted to be alone with her thoughts. The only person she wanted to distract her was Cooper. With that thought, the uncharacteristic shyness stole over her again and she snuggled against him.

He seemed to read her mind. He tipped her face up and peered at her closely. Bending his head, he kissed her soundly on the lips, then pressed her head against his chest. He gathered her hair in a gentle fist. His actions were both protective and possessive.

They stayed in that position for the remainder of the flight. Neither pilot tried to engage them in conversation, but respected their need for privacy. Pertinent questions could wait.

"You've drawn quite a crowd." Mike glanced at them over his shoulder and nodded toward the ground as they approached the airport, which was small when compared to metropolitan airports, but large enough to accommodate jet aircraft.

Rusty and Cooper saw that the airport below was teeming with people. The milling crowd was showing no respect for restricted areas of the tarmac. Vans labeled as portable television-broadcast units were parked end to end. In this remote area of the Northwest Territories, such media hype was virtually unheard of.

Cooper muttered a curse. "Who the hell is responsible for this?"

"The plane crash made big news," Mike told him with an apologetic smile. "Y'all were the only survivors. I reckon everybody wants to hear what y'all've got to say about it."

The instant Pat set the chopper down, the crowd of reporters surged forward against the temporary barriers. Policemen had a difficult time forcing them back. Several official-looking men ran forward. The helicopter's twirling blades plastered their business suits against their bodies and slapped their neckties against their faces. The rotors finally wound down.

Mike jumped to the concrete and helped Rusty climb down. She cowered bashfully against the side of the helicopter until Cooper jumped down beside her. Then, after profusely thanking the twin pilots from Georgia, they moved forward. Their hands were clasped together tightly.

The men who greeted them were representatives of the Canadian Aviation Safety Board and the National Transportation Safety Board. The U.S. agency had been invited to investigate the crash since the passengers involved were all American.

The bureaucrats deferentially welcomed Cooper and Rusty back to civilization and escorted them past the squirming, shouting wall of reporters whose behavior was anything but civilized. They bombarded them with questions fired as rapidly as machine-gun bullets.

The dazed survivors were escorted through one of the building's employee entrances, down a corridor, and into a private suite of offices that had been provided for their use.

"Your father has been notified, Miss Carlson."

"Thank you very much."

"He was delighted to hear that you are well," the smiling official told her. "Mr. Landry, is there anyone we should notify for you?"

"No."

Rusty had turned to him, curious to hear his reply. He had never mentioned a family, so she had assumed that there was none. It seemed terribly sad to her that no one had been waiting for Cooper's return. She longed to reach out and lay a compassionate hand along his cheek. But the officials were crowded around them.

One stepped forward. "I understand you were the only two to survive the crash."

"Yes. The others died immediately."

"We've notified their families. Some are outside. They want to speak with you." Rusty's face turned as white as the knuckles of her fingers, which were still linked with Cooper's. "But that can wait," the man said hastily, sensing her distress. "Can you give us a clue as to the cause of the crash?"

"I'm not a pilot," Cooper said shortly. "The storm was a factor, I'm sure. The pilots did everything they could."

"Then you wouldn't blame the crash on them?" the man probed.

"May I have a glass of water, please?" Rusty asked softly.

"And something to eat," Cooper said in that same clipped tone. "We haven't had any food this morning. Not even coffee."

"Surely, right away." Someone was dispatched to order them a breakfast.

"And you'd better bring in the proper authorities. I've got the deaths of two men to report."

"What two men?"

"The ones I killed." Everyone froze. He had succeeded in winning their undivided attention. "I'm sure someone should be notified. But first, how about that coffee?" Cooper's voice rang with authority and impatience. It was almost amusing how it galvanized everyone into action. For the next hour, the officials flapped around them like headless chickens.

They were brought huge breakfasts of steak and eggs. More than anything on the tray Rusty enjoyed the fresh orange juice. She couldn't drink enough of it. As they ate, they answered the endless rounds of questions. Pat and Mike were brought in to verify the location of the cabin relative to the crash site. While the weather was still cooperating, crews were dispatched to view the wreckage and exhume the bodies that Cooper had buried.

In the midst of the chaos a telephone receiver was thrust into Rusty's hand and her father's voice boomed into her ear. "Rusty, thank God. Are you all right?"

Tears filled her eyes. For a moment she couldn't speak. "I'm fine. Fine. My leg feels much better."

"Your leg! What happened to your leg? Nobody told me anything about your leg."

She explained as best she could in brief, disjointed phrases. "But it's fine, really."

"I'm not taking your word for it. Don't worry about anything," he told her. "I'll handle everything from here. You'll be brought to L.A. tonight and I'll be at the airport to meet you. It's a miracle that you survived."

She glanced at Cooper, and said softly, "Yes, a miracle."

Around noon they were taken across the street to a motel and assigned rooms in which to shower and change into clothes provided by the Canadian government.

At the door to her room, Rusty reluctantly let go of Cooper's arm. She couldn't bear to let him out of her sight. She felt alien, apart. None of this seemed real. Everything and everybody swam toward her like distorted faces out of a dream. She had difficulty matching words to concepts. Everything was strange—except Cooper. Cooper alone was her reality.

He seemed no more pleased with the arrangements than she, but it would hardly be suitable for them to share a motel room. He squeezed her hand and said, "I'll be right next door."

He watched her enter her room and safely close and lock the door before he went to his own. Once inside, he dropped into the only chair and covered his face with his hands.

"Now what?" he asked the four walls.

If only he had held off for one more night. If only she hadn't asked that question of him yesterday morning after breakfast. If only she hadn't been so desirable in the first place. If only they hadn't been on the same airplane. If only it hadn't crashed. If only some of the others had survived and they hadn't been alone.

He could come up with thousands of "if onlys," and the bottom line would still be that they'd made love all day yesterday and last night until the wee hours.

He didn't regret it—not a single breathless second of it.

But he didn't know how in the hell he was going to handle it from here. Rightfully, he should pretend that it hadn't happened and ignore the shining recognition of mutual passion in her eyes. But that was just it: he couldn't ignore her melting looks.

Nor could he callously disregard her dependency on him. The rules they'd laid down in the cabin were still in effect. She hadn't acclimated yet. She was apprehensive. She had just survived a trauma. He couldn't subject her to another one so soon. She wasn't tough like him; she had to be treated with delicacy and tact. After the rough time he'd given her, he thought she deserved that much consideration.

Of course he was reconciled to having to turn his back on her. He wished she would turn hers on him first. That would relieve him of the responsibility of hurting her.

But dammit, she wouldn't. And he couldn't. Not yet. Not until it was absolutely necessary for them to part. Until then, even though he knew it was foolhardy, he'd go on being her Lancelot, her protector and lover.

God, he loved the role.

It was just too damn bad it was temporary.

THE HOT SHOWER felt wonderful and worked to revive her physically and mentally. She scrubbed her hair with shampoo twice and rinsed it until it squeaked. When she stepped out of the tub, she felt almost normal.

But she wasn't. Normally she wouldn't have noticed how soft the motel towels were. She would have taken soft towels for granted. She was changed in other ways, too. When she propped her foot on the edge of the tub to dry, she noticed the unsightly, jagged scar running down her shin. She bore other scars. Deeper ones. They were indelibly engraved on her soul. Rusty Carlson would never be the same.

The clothes she'd been given were inexpensive and way oversize, but they made her feel human and feminine again. The shoes fit, but they felt odd and unusually light on her feet. It was the first time in weeks that she'd worn anything but hiking boots. Almost a week at the lodge and almost two since the crash.

Two weeks? Is that all it had been?

When she emerged from the motel room, Cooper was waiting outside her door. He had showered and shaved. His hair was still damp and well combed. The new clothes looked out of place on his rangy body.

They approached each other warily, shyly, almost apologetically. Then their eyes met, the familiarity sparked. And something else, too.

"You're different," Rusty whispered.

He shook his head. "No, I'm not. I might look different, but I haven't changed."

He took her hand and drew her aside, giving the people who would have rushed to cluster around them a "back off" glance. They moved out of hearing distance. Cooper said, "In all this confusion, I haven't had a chance to tell you something."

Clean and smelling like soap and shaving cream, mouth giving off the fresh scent of peppermint, he was very handsome. Her eyes moved hungrily over him, unable to take in this new Cooper. "What?"

He leaned closer. "I love the way your tongue feels flicking over my navel."

Rusty sucked in a startled breath. Her eyes darted toward the group that was huddled a discreet distance away. They were all watching them curiously. "You're outrageous."

"And I don't give a damn." He inched even closer. "Let's give them something to speculate about." He curled his hand around her throat and placed his thumb beneath her chin to tilt it up.

Then he kissed her unsparingly. He took what he wanted and gave more than she would have had the audacity to ask for. Nor was he in any hurry. His tongue plumbed her mouth slowly and deliciously in a purely sexual rhythm.

When he finally pulled away, he growled, "I want to kiss you like that all over, but," he shot a look in the direction of their astounded observers, "that'll have to wait."

They were driven back to the airport, but Rusty never remembered leaving the motel. Cooper's kiss had entranced her.

THE HOURS OF the afternoon dragged on forever. They were catered another meal. Rusty ordered an enormous chef's salad. She was starved for cold, crisp, fresh vegetables, but found that she could only eat half of it.

Her lack of appetite was partially due to the breakfast she'd eaten only hours before, but mostly to her anxiety over the interrogation she and Cooper were put through regarding the deaths of Quinn and Reuben Gawrylow.

A court reporter was brought in to take down Cooper's testimony. He told how they had met the two recluses, were given shelter by them, promised rescue, and then were attacked. "Our lives were in danger," he said. "I had no choice. It was self-defense."

Rusty gauged the reactions of the policemen and saw that they weren't convinced. They murmured among themselves and kept casting suspicious glances toward Cooper. They began asking him about his stint in Vietnam and brought up the fact that he was a former POW. They asked him to recount the events leading to his escape from the prison camp. He refused, saying that it had no bearing on this issue.

"But you were forced to...to..."

"Kill?" Cooper asked with ruthless candor. "Yes. I killed a lot of them on my way out of there. And I'd do it again."

Telling looks were exchanged. Someone coughed uncomfortably.

"He's leaving out a vital point," Rusty said abruptly. Every eye in the room turned to her.

"Rusty, no," he said. His eyes speared into hers in a silent plea for caution and discretion. "You don't have to."

She looked back at him lovingly. "Yes, I do. You're trying to spare me. I appreciate it. But I can't let them think you killed those two men without strong motivation." She faced her listeners. "They, the Gawrylows, were going to kill Cooper and... and keep me."

Shock registered on the faces encircling the table where she was seated with Cooper. "How do you know that, Ms. Carlson?"

"She just knows it, okay? You might suspect me of lying, but you have no reason to think she is."

Rusty laid a restraining hand on Cooper's arm. "The older one, Quinn, attacked me." In plain language, she told them what Gawrylow had done to her that morning in the cabin. "My leg was still seriously injured. I was virtually helpless. Cooper returned just in time to prevent a rape. Gawrylow reached for a gun. If Cooper hadn't acted when and how he did, he would have been killed instead of Gawrylow. And I would still be at the old man's mercy."

She exchanged a long stare of understanding with Cooper. She had never deliberately inflamed the hermits. He had known that all along. He silently asked her to forgive him his insults and she silently asked him to forgive her for ever being afraid of him.

Cooper's hand splayed wide over the top of her head and moved it to his chest. His arms wrapped around her. Ignoring everybody else in the room, they held each other tight, rocking slightly back and forth.

Half an hour later, Cooper was relieved of all legal responsibility for the deaths of the Gawrylows. Facing them now was their meeting with the victims' families. The weeping, somber group was led into the office. For nearly an hour Rusty and Cooper spoke with them and provided what information they could. The bereaved derived some comfort from the fact that their loved ones had died immediately and without having suffered. They tearfully thanked the survivors for sharing their knowledge about the crash. It was a moving experience for everyone involved.

The meeting with the media was something altogether different. When Rusty and Cooper were escorted into the large room that had been set up for the press conference, they were greeted by a restless crowd. A pall of tobacco smoke obscured the ceiling.

Seated behind a table with microphones, they answered the barrage of questions as thoroughly, but as concisely, as possible. Some of the questions were silly, some were intelligent, and some were painfully personal. When one gauche reporter asked what it was like to share a cabin with a total stranger, Cooper turned to one of the officials and said, "That's it. Get Rusty out of here."

The bureaucrat didn't move fast enough to suit him. Taking it upon himself to remove Rusty from the carnival atmosphere, he slipped his arm beneath hers and assisted her out of her chair. As they made their way toward the exit, a man came rushing up and shoved a business card into Cooper's face. It identified him as a reporter for a newsmagazine. He offered them an enormous sum of money for exclusive rights to their story.

"But if that's not enough," he stammered hastily when Cooper glared at him with icy malevolence, "we'll up the ante. I don't suppose you took any pictures, did you?"

Emitting a feral growl, Cooper pushed the reporter aside and told him what he could do with his magazine, using descriptive words that couldn't be misunderstood.

By the time they were boarded onto the L.A.-bound jet, Rusty was so exhausted she could barely walk. Her right leg was aching. Cooper had to practically carry her aboard. He buckled her into her first-class seat next to the window and took the aisle seat beside her. He asked the flight attendant to bring a snifter of brandy immediately.

"Aren't you having any?" Rusty asked after taking a few fiery and restorative sips.

He shook his head. "I've sworn off the booze for a while." The corner of his mouth lifted into a slight smile.

"You're very handsome, Mr. Landry," she remarked softly, gazing up at him as though seeing him for the first time.

He removed the snifter from her listless fingers. "That's the brandy talking."

"No, you are." She raised her hand and touched his hair. It slid through her fingers silkily.

"I'm glad you think so."

"Dinner, Ms. Carlson, Mr. Landry?"

They were surprised to realize that the airplane was already airborne. They'd been so preoccupied with each other that they hadn't even noticed the takeoff. Which was just as well. The helicopter ride hadn't been so bad for her because she hadn't had time to anticipate it. But as the day stretched out, the thought of flying to Los Angeles had filled Rusty with apprehension. It would be a while, if ever, before she was a completely comfortable flyer.

"Dinner, Rusty?" Cooper asked. She shook her head. To the flight attendant he said, "No, thanks. They fed us several times today."

"Buzz me if you need anything," she said graciously before moving down the aisle. They were the only passengers in the first-class cabin. When the flight attendant returned to the galley, they were left alone for the first time since being rescued.

"You know, it's funny," Rusty said musingly, "we were together so much that I thought I'd welcome the time when we could be apart. I thought I missed being with other people—" she fingered the pocket of his shirt "—but I hated the crowds today. All that pushing and shoving. And every time I lost sight of you, I panicked."

"Natural," he whispered as he tucked a strand of hair behind her ear. "You've been dependent on me for so long, you're in the habit. That'll go away."

She angled her head back. "Will it, Cooper?"

"Won't it?"

"I'm not sure I want it to."

He said her name softly before his lips settled against hers. He kissed her ardently, as though this might be his last chance. There was a desperation behind his kiss. It persisted when Rusty looped her arms around his neck and buried her face in the hollow of his shoulder.

"You saved my life. Have I thanked you? Have I told you that I would have died without you?"

Cooper was frantically kissing her neck, her ears, her hair. "You don't need to thank me. I wanted to protect you, to take care of you."

"You did. Well. Very well." They kissed again until they were forced to break apart breathlessly. "Touch me."

He watched her lips whisper the words. They were still glistening from their kiss. "Touch you? Here? Now?"

She nodded rapidly. "Please, Cooper. I'm frightened. I need to know you're here—really and truly here."

He opened the coat that the Canadian government had supplied and slipped his hand inside. He covered her breast. It felt womanly and warm and full beneath her sweater.

He laid his cheek against hers and whispered, "Your nipple is already hard."

"Hmm."

His fingers played with the tight little bead through the knit. "You don't seem surprised."

"I'm not."

"Are they always like this? Where were you when I was fourteen?"

She laughed softly. "No, they're not always like this. I was thinking about last night."

"Last night lasted a lifetime. Be specific."

"Remember when…" She whispered a sultry reminder.

"Lord, yes," he groaned, "but don't talk about that now."

"Why?"

"If you do, you'll have to sit on my lap."

She touched him. "To cover this?"

"No, Rusty," he said through gritted teeth. And when he told her what they would be doing if she sat on his lap, she chastely removed her hand.

"I don't think that would be proper at all. For that matter, neither is what you're doing. Maybe you'd better stop." He withdrew his hand from her sweater. By now both her breasts were showing up hard and pointed beneath it. They gazed at each other, their eyes reflecting a sense of loss. "I wish we hadn't been so stubborn. I wish we'd made love before last night."

He sighed deeply. "I've thought about that, too."

A sob rose in her throat. "Hold me, Cooper." He clasped her tightly and burrowed his face in her hair. "Don't let me go."

"I won't. Not now."

"Not ever. Promise."

Sleep claimed her before she got his promise. It also spared her from seeing the bleak expression on his face.

IT SEEMED THAT the entire population of the city was waiting for their arrival at LAX. They had landed only briefly in Seattle and hadn't had to deplane. None of the boarding passengers had joined them in first class. That takeoff had been uneventful.

Now, anticipating a mob scene, the senior flight attendant advised them to let all the other passengers disembark first. Rusty welcomed the delay. She was terribly nervous. Her palms were wet with perspiration. Jitters like this were foreign to her. At ease on every social occasion, she couldn't imagine why she was sick with anxiety now. She didn't want to release her grip on Cooper's arm, although she kept flashing insincere, confident smiles up at him. If only she could slip back into her regular life without a lot of fuss.

But it wasn't going to be that easy. The moment she stepped through the opening of the jet way and entered the terminal, her worst expectations were realized. She was momentarily blinded by television lights. Microphones were poked into her face. Someone inadvertently bumped her sore shin with a camera bag. The noise was deafening. But out of that cacophony, a familiar voice beckoned her. She turned toward it.

"Father?"

Within seconds she was smothered in his embrace. Her arm was jostled away from Cooper's. Even as she returned her father's hug, she groped for Cooper's hand, but she couldn't find it. The separation left her panicked.

"Let me review the damage," Bill Carlson said, pushing his daughter away and holding her at arm's length. The reporters widened the circle around them, but cameras snapped pictures of this moving reunion. "Not too bad, under the circumstances." He whipped the coat from around her shoulders. "As grateful as I am to the charitable Canadian government for taking such good care of you today, I think you'll feel much better in this."

One of his lackeys materialized and produced a huge box, from which Carlson shook out a full-length red fox coat exactly like the one she'd been wearing when the plane crashed. "I heard about your coat, darling," he said as he proudly draped the fur around her shoulders, "so I wanted to replace it."

Oohs and aahs rose out of the crowd. Reporters pressed closer to take pictures. The coat was gorgeous but far too heavy for the balmy southern California evening. It felt like chain mail weighting her down. But Rusty was oblivious to it, to everything, as her eyes frantically probed the circle of light surrounding her in search of Cooper. "Father, I want you to meet—"

"Don't worry about your leg. It will be seen to by expert doctors. I've arranged a room for you at the hospital. We're going there immediately."

"But Cooper—"

"Oh, yes, Cooper Landry, isn't it? The man who also survived the crash. I'm grateful to him, of course. He saved your life. I'll never forget that." Carlson spoke in a booming voice that was guaranteed to be overhead by the newspaper reporters and picked up by microphones.

Diplomatically his assistant wielded the long coatbox to clear a path for them through the throng of media people. "Ladies and gentlemen, you'll be notified if anything else comes out about the story," Carlson told them as he ushered Rusty toward a golf cart that was waiting to transport them through the terminal.

Rusty looked everywhere, but she didn't see Cooper. Finally she spotted his broad-shouldered form walking away from the scene. A couple of reporters were in hot pursuit. "Cooper!" The cart lurched forward and she grabbed the seat beneath her for balance. "Cooper!" she called again. He couldn't hear her above the din.

She wanted to leap off the cart and chase after him, but it was already in motion and her father was speaking to her. She tried to assimilate his words and make sense of them, but it seemed that he was speaking gibberish.

She fought down her rising panic as the cart rolled down the concourse, beeping pedestrians out of the way. Finally Cooper was swallowed up by the crowd and she lost sight of him altogether.

Once they were inside the limousine and cruising toward the private hospital where Carlson had arranged for a room, he clasped Rusty's clammy hand. "I was very afraid for you, Rusty. I thought I'd lost you, too."

She rested her head on her father's shoulder and squeezed his arm. "I know. I was as worried about how you'd take the news of the crash as I was about my own safety."

"About our tiff that day you left—"

"Please, Father, don't let's even think about that now." She lifted her head and smiled up at him. "I might not have survived the gutting of that ram, but I survived a plane crash."

He chuckled. "I don't know if you remember this— you were very young—but Jeff sneaked out of his cabin at Boy Scout camp one summer. He spent the entire night in the woods. He got lost and wasn't found until well into the next day. But that little scrapper wasn't the least bit scared. When we found him, he had made camp and was calmly fishing for his dinner."

Rusty returned her head to his shoulder, her smile gradually fading. "Cooper did all that for me."

She felt the sudden tension in her father's body. He usually bristled like that when something didn't meet

with his approval. "What kind of man is this Cooper
Landry, Rusty?"

"What kind?"

"A Vietnam veteran, I understand."

"Yes. He was a POW, too, but managed to escape."

"Did he...handle you well?"

Ah, yes, she was thinking. But she capped the foun-
tain of passionate memories that bubbled inside her
like uncorked champagne. "Yes, Father. Very well. I
wouldn't have survived without him."

She didn't want to tell him about her personal involvement with Cooper so soon after her return. Her
father would have to be apprised of her feelings gradually. They might be met with resistance, because Bill
Carlson was an opinionated man.

He was also intuitive. One didn't easily pull the
wool over his eyes. Keeping her tone as casual as possible, Rusty said, "Will you try to locate him for me
tonight?" It wasn't an unusual request. Her father had
contacts all over the city. "Let him know where I am.
We got separated at the airport."

"Why is it even necessary for you to see this man
again?"

He might just as well have asked her why it was necessary for her to go on breathing. "I want to thank him
properly for saving my life," she said as a diversion.

"I'll see what I can do," Carlson told her just as the
chauffeur wheeled under the porte cochere of the private clinic.

Even though her father had paved the way, it was
two hours later before Rusty was left alone in her plush
room. Decorated with original works of art and con-
temporary furniture, it resembled a chic apartment

more than it did a hospital room. She lay in a firm, comfortable, mechanized bed with soft pillows beneath her head. She was wearing a new designer nightgown, one of several her father had packed in the suitcase that had been waiting for her when she checked in. All her favorite cosmetics and toiletries had been placed in the bathroom. She had the staff at her beck and call. All she had to do was pick up the phone on her nightstand.

She was miserable.

For one thing, her leg was sore as a result of the surgeon's examination. As a safety precaution X rays had been taken, but they revealed no broken bones. "Cooper said nothing was broken," she quietly informed the doctor. He had frowned over the jagged scar. When he lamented the crude stitching that had been done, Rusty jumped to Cooper's defense. "He was trying to save my leg," she snapped.

Suddenly she was fiercely proud of that scar and not all that excited about seeing it erased, which, she was told, would require at least three reconstructive operations—maybe more. To her, the scar was like a badge of courage.

Besides, Cooper had spent a great deal of time with it the night before, kissing the raised, puckered skin and telling her that it didn't turn him off in the slightest and, in fact, made him "horny as hell" every time he looked at it. She had contemplated telling *that* to the pompous plastic surgeon.

She hadn't. Indeed, she hadn't said much of anything. She simply didn't have the energy. All she could think about was how blessed it was going to be when she was left alone to go to sleep.

But now that she had the opportunity, she couldn't.

Doubts and fears and unhappiness were keeping her awake. Where was Cooper? Why hadn't he followed her? It had been a circus at the airport, but surely he could have stayed with her if he'd really wanted to.

When the nurse came in offering her a sedative, she gladly swallowed the pill. Otherwise she knew she'd never fall asleep without Cooper's hard, warm presence embracing her.

CHAPTER ELEVEN

"I MEAN, MY GOD! We couldn't believe it! Our Rusty in a plane crash!"

"It must have been dreadful."

Rusty looked up from the pillows of her hospital bed at the two well-dressed women and wished they would vanish in a puff of smoke. As soon as her breakfast tray had been carried out by an efficient and ebullient nurse, her two friends had breezed into her room.

Reeking of exotic perfume and avid curiosity, they said they wanted to be the first to commiserate. Rusty suspected that what they really wanted was to be the first to hear the delicious details of her "Canadian caper," as one had called it.

"No, I couldn't say it was much fun," Rusty said tiredly.

She had awakened long before breakfast was served. She was accustomed to waking up with the sun now. Thanks to the tranquilizing pill she'd been given the night before, she had slept soundly. Her lack of animation stemmed from dejection more than fatigue. Her spirits were at an extremely low ebb, and her friends' efforts to raise them were having the opposite effect.

"As soon as you get out of here, we're treating you to a day of self-indulgence at the salon. Hair, skin, massage. Just look at your poor nails." One lifted her listless hand, clicking her tongue against the roof of her mouth. "They're ravaged."

Rusty smiled wanly, remembering how upset she'd been when Cooper had pared off her fingernails with his hunting knife. "I didn't get around to having a manicure." It was meant to be facetious, but her friends were nodding sympathetically. "I was too busy trying to stay alive."

One shook her intentionally tousled blond head and shuddered delicately, causing the Hermès scarf around her neck to slip. The dozen or so silver bangle bracelets on her wrist jingled like the harness on a Christmas reindeer. "You were so brave, Rusty. I think I would rather have died than go through all that you did."

Rusty was about to refute that remark, when she remembered that not too long ago she could have said something that shallow. "I always thought I would, too. You'd be amazed how strong the human animal's survival instincts are. In a situation like the one I was in, they take over."

But her friends weren't interested in philosophy. They wanted to hear the nitty-gritty. The get-down-and-get-dirty good stuff. One was sitting on the foot of Rusty's bed; the other was leaning forward from the chair beside it. They looked like scavenger birds perched and ready to pick her bones clean the second she succumbed.

The story of the crash and the events following it had appeared on the front page of that morning's newspaper. The writer had, with only a few minor errors, meticulously chronicled Rusty's and Cooper's ordeal. The piece had been serious in tone and journalistically sound. But the public had a penchant for reading between the lines; it wanted to hear what had been omitted. Her friends included, the public wanted the facts fleshed out.

"Was it just *awful*? When the sun went down wasn't it terrifyingly dark?"

"We had several lanterns in the cabin."

"No, I mean outside."

"Before you got to the cabin. When you had to sleep outdoors in the woods."

Rusty sighed wearily. "Yes, it was dark. But we had a fire."

"What did you eat?"

"Rabbits, mostly."

"Rabbits! I'd *die*."

"I didn't," Rusty snapped. "And neither would you."

Now, why had she gone and done that? Why hadn't she just left it alone? They were looking wounded and confused, having no idea why she had jumped down their throats. Why hadn't she said something cute, something glib, such as telling them that rabbit meat is served in some of the finest restaurants?

Following on the heels of that thought, of course, came one of Cooper. A pang of longing for him seized her. "I'm awfully tired," she said, feeling the need to cry and not wanting to have to explain why.

But subtlety didn't work with this duo. They didn't pick up on the hint to leave. "And your poor leg." The one with the bracelets clapped her hand to her cheek in horror. "Is the doctor sure he can fix it?"

Rusty closed her eyes as she answered, "Reasonably sure."

"How many operations will it take to get rid of that hideous scar?" Rusty felt the air stir against her face as the other friend waved frantically to the untactful speaker. "Oh, I didn't mean it that way. It's not that hideous. I mean—"

"I know what you mean," Rusty said, opening her eyes. "It is hideous, but it's better than a stump, and for a while I was afraid that's what I'd end up with. If Cooper—"

She broke off, having inadvertently spoken his name. Now that it was out, the carrion birds flocked to it, grasping it in their avidly curious talons.

"Cooper?" one asked innocently. "The man who survived the crash with you?"

"Yes."

The two women exchanged a glance, as though mentally tossing a coin to see who was going to pose the first of numerous questions about him.

"I saw him on the TV news last night. My God, Rusty, he's gorgeous!"

"'Gorgeous'?"

"Well not gorgeous in the *perfect* sense. Not *model* gorgeous. I mean rugged, manly, sweaty, hairy, sexy kind of gorgeous."

"He saved my life," Rusty said softly.

"I know, my dear. But if one's life must be saved, better it be by someone who looks like your Cooper Landry. That mustache!" She grinned wickedly and licked her chops. "Is what they say of mustaches true? Remember the joke?"

Rusty did remember the joke. Her cheeks went pink while her lips went pale. What they said about mustaches *was* true.

"Are his shoulders really this broad?" The friend held her hands a yard apart.

"He's rather brawny, yes," Rusty admitted helplessly. "But he—"

"Are his hips really this narrow?" The hands closed to less than a foot apart. The ladies giggled.

Rusty wanted to scream. "He knew things to do that I would never have thought about. He built a travois, using my fur coat, and dragged me away from the crash site—for miles. I didn't even realize how far until I saw the distance from the helicopter."

"There's something deliciously dangerous about him." One friend gave a delicate shiver. She hadn't heard a single word Rusty had said. "Something threatening in his eyes. I've always found that primitive streak wildly sexy."

The one sitting in the chair closed her eyes in a near swoon. "Stop. You're making me hot."

"This morning's paper said he killed two men in a fight over you."

Rusty nearly got out of her bed. "That's not what the paper said at all!"

"I put two and two together."

"It was self-defense!"

"Honey, calm down." She patted Rusty's hand. "If you say it was self-defense, then it was self-defense." She winked down at Rusty. "Listen, my hubby knows Bill Friedkin. He thinks your story would make a terrific movie. He and Friedkin are having lunch next week and—"

"A movie!" Rusty was aghast over the thought. "Oh, no. Please tell him not to say anything. I don't want anything to come of this. I just want to forget about it and get on with my life."

"We didn't mean to upset you, Rusty." The one who

had been sitting in the chair rose to stand beside the bed. She laid a comforting hand on Rusty's shoulder. "It's just that we're your two best friends. If there *was* something dreadful that you wanted to discuss, some— you know—*personal* aspect of the disaster that you couldn't tell your father, we wanted to make ourselves available."

"Like what?" Rusty shrugged off her friend's hand and glared up at them. They exchanged another telling glance.

"Well, you *were* alone with that man for almost two weeks."

"And?" Rusty asked tetchily.

"And," she said, drawing a deep breath, "the paper said it was a one-room cabin."

"So?"

"Come on, Rusty." The friend's patience gave out. "The situation lends itself to all kinds of speculation. You're a very attractive young woman, and he's positively yummy and certainly virile. You're both single. You were hurt. He nursed you. You were almost totally dependent on him. You thought you might be stranded up there for the duration of the winter."

The other took up the slack and said excitedly, "Living together like that, in such close proximity, in the wilderness—well, it's positively the most romantic thing I ever heard of. You know what we're getting at."

"Yes, I know what you're getting at." Rusty's voice was cold, but her brown eyes were smoldering. "You want to know if I slept with Cooper."

Just then the door swung open and the topic of their discussion came striding in. Rusty's heart nearly jumped out of her chest. Her friends spun around, reacting to the radiant smile that broke across her face. He barely took notice of them. His gray eyes found and locked upon Rusty. The sizzling look they exchanged should have answered any questions regarding their level of intimacy.

Rusty finally composed herself enough to speak. "Uh, Cooper, these are two of my closest friends." She introduced them by name. He gave each of the women a disinterested, terse nod to acknowledge the introductions.

"Oh, Mr. Landry, I'm *so* honored to meet you," one of them gushed, round-eyed and breathless. "The *Times* said that you are an escaped POW. That just blows my mind. I mean, all that you've been through already. Then to survive a plane crash."

"Rusty claims that you saved her life."

"My husband and I would like to give the two of you an intimate little dinner party when Rusty gets up and around. Please say you'll let us."

"When did you decide that?" the other asked with pique. "*I* wanted to give them a dinner party."

"I spoke first."

The silly chatter was irritating and embarrassing. Their squabbling made them sound like the two stepsisters in *Cinderella*. "I'm sure Cooper can't stay long," Rusty interrupted, noticing that he was growing increasingly impatient. As was she. Now that he was here, she wanted to get rid of her so-called friends so she could be alone with him.

"We've stayed long enough," one of them said as she gathered up her handbag and coat. She bent over Rusty and kissed the air just above her cheek, whispering, "You sly thing, you. You won't get away with this. I want to know *everything*."

The other one leaned down and said, "I'm sure he was well worth the plane crash. He's divine. So raw. So... Well, I'm sure I don't have to tell *you*."

They stopped on their way to the door to say good-bye to Cooper. One even tapped his chest with a flirtatious hand as she reminded him about the dinner party she was planning in his honor. They glided out, smiling smugly at Rusty over their shoulders before the door closed on them.

Cooper watched them go, then approached the bed. "I'm not going to any damned dinner party."

"I didn't expect you to. Once the novelty has worn off, I'll advise her to drop that idea."

Looking at him proved to be hazardous. She was dismayed to feel tears stinging her eyes. Self-consciously she brushed them off her cheeks.

"Something wrong?"

"No, I'm..." She hesitated to tell him, but decided to take the plunge. The time for secrets between them was long past. Bravely she lifted her eyes back to his. "I'm just very glad to see you."

He didn't touch her, although he might just as well have. His gaze was as possessive as a caress. It passed down her form lying beneath the thin blanket, then moved back up again. It lingered on her breasts, which were seductively outlined by the clinging silk nightgown.

She nervously raised her hand and fiddled with the lace neckline. "The, uh, the gown was waiting here for me when I checked in."

"It's nice."

"Anything is better than long johns."

"You look all right in long johns."

Her smile wavered. He was here. She could see him, smell his soapy clean smell, hear his voice. He was wearing new clothes—slacks and a casual shirt and jacket. But they weren't responsible for his distant attitude. She didn't want to acknowledge it, but it was undeniably there—as obvious to her as an unbreachable wall.

"Thank you for coming to see me," she said for lack of anything better. "I asked my father to locate you and tell you where I was."

"Your father didn't tell me anything. I found you on my own."

She took heart. He'd been looking for her. Maybe all night. Maybe while she'd lain sleeping a drug-induced sleep, he'd been combing the city streets in a frantic search.

But then he shot down her soaring hopes by adding, "It was in the morning paper that you were here. I understand that a plastic surgeon is going to correct the stitches I made."

"I defended your stitching."

He shrugged indifferently. "It worked, that's all I care about."

"That's all I care about, too."

"Sure."

"It is!" She sat up straighter, angry over his righteous condescension. "It wasn't my idea to come straight here from the airport. It was my father's. I would rather have gone home, checked my mail, watered my plants, slept in my own bed."

"You're a big girl. Why didn't you?"

"I just told you. Father had made these arrangements. I couldn't demand that he change them."

"How come?"

"Don't be obtuse. And why shouldn't I want this scar removed?" she cried angrily.

He glanced away, gnawing on the corner of his mustache. "You should. Of course you should."

Slumping with misery, Rusty settled back on her pillows and blotted her eyes with the corner of the sheet. "What's wrong with us? Why are we behaving like this?"

His head came back around. He wore a sad expression, as though her naiveté was to be pitied. "You shouldn't have to go through the rest of your life with that scar on your leg. I didn't mean to suggest that you should."

"I'm not talking about the scar, Cooper. I'm talking about everything. Why did you disappear at the airport last night?"

"I was there, in plain sight."

"But you weren't with me. I called out. Didn't you hear me?"

He didn't answer directly. "You didn't seem to be lacking attention."

"I wanted *your* attention. I had it until we stepped off the airplane."

"We could hardly do in that crowd what we were doing on the airplane." His eyes raked down her insultingly. "Besides, you were otherwise occupied." His mouth was set in a cynical smirk again. It looked unfamiliar now because Rusty hadn't seen that expression since they'd made love.

She was bewildered. Where and when had things

between them gone wrong? "What did you expect to happen when we arrived in L.A.? We were and are news, Cooper. It wasn't my fault that the reporters were there. And my father. He was worried sick about me. He helped fund our rescue. Did you think he'd treat my return casually?"

"No." He raked his fingers through his hair. "But did it have to be such a goddamn sideshow? Why the big production? That coat, for instance."

"That was a very thoughtful thing for him to do."

It embarrassed her even now to recall her father's flamboyant gesture, but she sprang to defend him. The coat had been an expression of his love and joy at having her safely returned to him. That it had been a tasteless display of affluence wasn't the point. It was aggravating that Cooper couldn't see that and simply overlook her father's idiosyncrasies.

Cooper was moving around the room restlessly, as though he found it confining. His motions were abrupt and self-conscious, like those of a man ill at ease because his clothes didn't fit him well. "Look, I've got to go."

"Go? Now? Why? Where are you going?"

"Home."

"To Rogers Gap?"

"Yeah. Back to where I belong. I've got a ranch to look after. No telling what shape I'll find it in when I get there." Almost as an afterthought he glanced down at her right leg. "What about your leg? Is it going to be all right?"

"Eventually," she replied dully. *He's leaving. He's going. Away from me. Possibly forever.* "It's going to take a series of operations. The first of them is being done tomorrow."

"I hope I didn't do you more harm than good."

Her throat was tight with emotion. "You didn't."

"Well, I guess this is goodbye." He edged toward the door, trying not to make it look like an escape.

"Maybe sometime I can drive up to Rogers Gap and say hello. You never can tell when I might get up that way."

"Yeah, sure. That'd be great." His forced smile told her otherwise.

"How…how often do you come to L.A.?"

"Not very often," he was honest enough to say. "Well, so long, Rusty." Turning on the heels of his new shoes, he reached for the door handle.

"Cooper, wait!" He turned back. She was sitting up in bed, poised to chase after him if necessary. "Is this how it's going to end?"

He nodded curtly.

"It can't. Not after what we've been through together."

"It has to."

She shook her head so adamantly that her hair flew in every direction. "You don't fool me anymore. You're being insensitive to protect yourself. You're fighting it. I know you are. You want to hold me just as much as I want to hold you."

His jaw knotted as he ground his teeth together. At his sides, his hands formed fists. He warred with himself for several seconds before losing the battle.

He lunged across the room and pulled her roughly into his arms. Lowering himself onto the side of the bed, he hugged her against him tightly. With their arms wrapped around each other, they rocked together. His face was buried in the cinnamon-colored hair. Hers was nestled against his throat.

"Rusty, Rusty."

Thrilling to the anguish in his voice, she told him, "I couldn't go to sleep last night without a sedative. I kept listening for your breathing. I missed being held in your arms."

"I missed feeling your bottom against my lap."

He bent his head at the same moment she lifted hers and their mouths sought each other. Their kiss was desperate with desire. He plowed all ten fingers through her hair and held her head still while he made love to her open mouth with his tongue.

"I wanted you so bad last night, I thought I'd die," he groaned when they moved apart.

"You didn't want to be separated from me?"

"Not that way."

"Then why didn't you answer me when I called out to you at the airport? You heard me, didn't you?"

He looked chagrined, but nodded his head yes. "I couldn't be a performer in that circus, Rusty. I couldn't get away from there fast enough. When I came home from Nam, I was treated like a hero." He rubbed a strand of her hair between his fingers while he reflected on the painful past. "I didn't feel like a hero. I'd been living in hell. In the bowels of hell. Some of the things I'd had to do... Well, they weren't very heroic. They didn't deserve a spotlight and accolades. *I* didn't deserve them. I just wanted to be left alone so I could forget it."

He tilted her head back and pierced her with a silvery-gray stare. "I don't deserve or want a spotlight now, either. I did what was necessary to save our lives. Any man would have."

She touched his mustache lovingly. "Not any man, Cooper."

He shrugged away the compliment. "I've had more experience at surviving than most, that's all."

"You just won't take the credit you deserve, will you?"

"Is that what you want, Rusty? Credit for surviving?"

She thought of her father. She would have enjoyed hearing a few words of praise for her bravery. Instead he had talked about Jeff's Boy Scout escapade and told her how well her brother had reacted to a potentially fatal situation. Comparing her to Jeff hadn't been malicious on her father's part. He hadn't meant to point out how she fell short of Jeff's example. But that's what it had amounted to. What would it take, she wondered, to win her father's approval?

But for some reason, winning his approval didn't seem as important as it once had been. In fact, it didn't seem important at all. She was far more interested in what Cooper thought of her.

"I don't want credit, Cooper. I want..." She stopped short of saying "you." Instead, she laid her cheek against his chest. "Why didn't you come after me? Don't you want me anymore?"

He laid his hand over her breast and stroked it with his fingertips. "Yes, I want you." The need that made his voice sound like tearing cloth wasn't strictly physical.

Rusty perceived the depth of his need because she felt it too. It came out of an emptiness that gnawed at her when he wasn't there. It caused her own imploring inflection. "Then why?"

"I didn't follow you last night because I wanted to speed up the inevitable."

"The inevitable?"

"Rusty," he whispered, "this sexual dependency we feel for each other is textbook normal. It's common among people who have survived a crisis together. Even hostages and kidnap victims sometimes begin to feel an unnatural affection for their captors."

"I know all that. The Stockholm syndrome. But this is different."

"Is it?" His brows lowered skeptically. "A child loves whoever feeds him. Even a wild animal becomes friendly with someone who leaves food out for it. I took care of you. It was only human nature that you attach more significance—"

Suddenly and angrily, she pushed him away. Her hair was a vibrant halo of indignation, her eyes bright with challenge. "Don't you dare reduce what happened between us with psychological patter. It's crap. What I feel for you is real."

"I never said it wasn't real." Her feistiness excited him. He liked her best when she was defiant. He yanked her against him. "We've always had this going for us." He cupped her breast again and impertinently swept his thumb across the tip.

She wilted, murmuring a weak "Don't," which he disregarded. He continued to fondle her. Her eyes slid shut.

"We get close. I get hard. You get creamy. Every damned time. It happened the first time we laid eyes on each other in the airplane. Am I right?"

"Yes," she admitted.

"I wanted you then, before we ever left the ground."

"But you didn't even smile, or speak to me, or encourage me to speak to you."

"That's right."

"Why?" She couldn't take any more of his caresses and stay sensible. She moved his hand aside. "Tell me why."

"Because I guessed then what I know for fact now: we live worlds apart. And I'm not referring to geography."

"I know what you're talking about. You think I'm silly and superficial, like those friends of mine you just met. I'm not!"

She laid her hands on his forearms and appealed to him earnestly. "They irritated me, too. Do you know why? Because I saw myself—the way I used to be. I was judging them just as you did me when we first met.

"But please be tolerant toward them. Toward me. This is Beverly Hills. Nothing is real. There are areas of this city I couldn't relate to. The Gawrylows' cabin was beyond my realm of comprehension. But I'm changed. I really am. I'm not like them anymore."

"You never were, Rusty. I thought so. I know better now." He framed her face between his hands. "But that's the life you know. It's the crowd you run with. I couldn't. Wouldn't. Wouldn't even want to try. And you wouldn't belong in my life."

Hurt by the painful truth of what he was saying, she reacted with anger and threw off his hands. "Your life! What life? Shut away from the rest of the world? Alone and lonely? Using bitterness like an armor? You call that a life? You're right, Cooper. I couldn't live like that. The chip on my shoulder would be too heavy to bear."

His lower lip narrowed to a thin, harsh line beneath his mustache. She knew she'd hit home, but there was no victory in it.

"So there you have it," he said. "That's what I've been trying to tell you. In bed we're great, but we'd never make a life together."

"Because you're too damned stubborn to try! Have you even considered a compromise?"

"No. I don't want any part of this scene." He spread his hands wide to encompass the luxurious room and all that lay beyond the wide window.

Rusty aimed an accusing finger at him. "You're a snob."

"A snob?"

"Yes, a snob. You snub society because you feel superior to the masses. Superior and righteous because of the war and your imprisonment. Scornful because you see all that's wrong with the world. Locked up there on your solitary mountain, you play God by looking down on all of us who have the guts to tolerate each other despite our human failings."

"It's not like that," he ground out.

"Isn't it? Aren't you just a trifle self-righteous and judgmental? If there's so much wrong with our world, if you ridicule it that much, why don't you do something to change it? What are you accomplishing by withdrawing from it? Society didn't shun you. You shunned it."

"I didn't leave her until she—"

"Her?"

Cooper's face cleared of all emotion and became as

wooden and smooth as a mask. The light in his eyes flickered out. They became hard and implacable.

Shocked, Rusty laid a hand against her pounding heart. *A woman was at the source of Cooper's cynicism.* Who? When? A hundred questions raced through her mind. She wanted to ask all of them, but for the time being she was occupied only with enduring his icy, hostile stare. He was furious with himself and with her. She had goaded him into resurrecting something he had wanted to keep dead and buried.

Her overactive heart pumped jealousy through her system as rich and red as her blood. Some woman had wielded enough influence over Cooper to alter the course of his life. He might have been a happy-go-lucky chap before this unnamed she-wolf got her claws into him. For his bitterness to be this lasting, she must have been some woman. He was still feeling her influence. Had he loved her that much? Rusty asked herself dismally.

A man like Cooper Landry wouldn't go long without having a woman. But Rusty had imagined his affairs to be fleeting, physical gratification and little else. It had never occurred to her that he'd been seriously involved with someone. But he had been, and her departure from his life had been wrenching and painful.

"Who was she?"

"Forget it."

"Did you meet her before you went to Vietnam?"

"Drop it, Rusty."

"Did she marry someone else while you were a prisoner?"

"I said to forget it."

"Did you love her?"

"Look, she was good in the sack, but not as hot as you, okay? Is that what you're itching to know—how the two of you compare? Well, let's see. She wasn't a redhead, so she lacked your fiery spirit. She had a great body, but it didn't come close to yours."

"Stop it!"

"Her breasts were fuller, but no more responsive. Nipples? Larger and darker. Thighs? Hers were just as smooth, but not nearly as strong as yours." He stared at the spot where hers came together. "Yours can squeeze the life out of a man."

She covered her mouth to trap a sob of anguish and outrage. Her breath was coming as hard and fast as his. They glared at each other with an animosity as fierce as the passion they'd shared while making love.

It was into that seething atmosphere that Bill Carlson made his inopportune entrance. "Rusty?"

She jumped at her father's voice. "Father!" His name came out as a gusty exhalation. "Come…good morning. This…" She discovered that her mouth was dry and the hand she raised to gesture toward Cooper was trembling. "This is Cooper Landry."

"Ah, Mr. Landry." Carlson extended his hand. Cooper shook it. He did so firmly, but with a noticeable lack of enthusiasm and a great deal of dislike. "I've had several people trying to track you down." Cooper offered no explanations as to his whereabouts overnight, so Carlson blustered on. "I wanted to thank you for saving my daughter's life."

"No thanks is necessary."

"Of course it is. She means the world to me. The way she tells it, you meant the difference between her

life and death. In fact she's the one who urged me to
locate you last night."

Cooper glanced down at Rusty, then back at Carlson, who was reaching into the breast pocket of his suit
coat. He withdrew a white envelope. "Rusty wanted to
say thank-you in a special way."

He handed the envelope to Cooper. Cooper opened
it and glanced inside. He stared at the contents for a
long moment before lifting his eyes to Rusty. They
were frigid with contempt. One corner of his mustache curled into a nasty smile. Then, in one vicious
motion, he ripped the envelope and the cashier's check
inside in half. He tossed the two halves into the valley of her thighs.

"Thanks all the same, Miss Carlson, but on our last
night together I was paid in full for my services."

CHAPTER TWELVE

TURNING BACK TO his daughter after watching Cooper storm from the room, Carlson said, "What an unpleasant individual."

"Father, how could you have offered him money?" Rusty cried in dismay.

"I thought you wanted and expected me to."

"Whatever gave you that impression? Cooper... Mr. Landry... He is a proud man. Do you think he saved my life for profit?"

"I wouldn't be surprised. He's an unlikeable character from what I've heard of him."

"You asked around?"

"Certainly. As soon as he was identified as the man with you when you were rescued. Being marooned with him couldn't have been easy for you."

"We had our differences," Rusty replied with a rueful smile. "But he could have deserted me and saved himself at any time."

"He wasn't about to. Not when there might be a reward for saving you."

"He didn't know that."

"He's clever. He deduced that I'd spare no expense to rescue you if you were still alive. Maybe he was offended by the amount." He picked up the ripped check and studied it. "I thought it was a generous reward, but maybe he's greedier than I suspected."

Rusty closed her eyes and let her head fall back onto the pillows in defeat. "Father, he doesn't want your money. He's all too glad to be rid of me."

"The feeling is mutual." Carlson sat down on the edge of her bed. "However, it's unfortunate that we can't capitalize on your mishap."

Her eyes came open again. "'Capitalize'? What in the world are you talking about?"

"Don't jump to conclusions until you've heard me out."

She'd already jumped to several conclusions, none of which were to her liking. "You're not referring to a movie are you?" When her friend had mentioned the idea, she'd been appalled.

Carlson patted her hand. "Nothing so crass, my dear. We've got more style than that."

"Then, what?"

"One of your problems has always been your lack of vision, Rusty." Affectionately, he cuffed her on the chin. "Your brother would have immediately seen the enterprising possibilities this situation has opened up to us."

As usual, the comparison to her brother left her feeling inferior. "Like what?"

Patiently Carlson explained. "You've made a name for yourself in real estate. And not by riding my coattails, either. I might have placed a few opportunities in your path, but you took advantage of them."

"Thank you, but what is this leading to, Father?"

"In your own right, you're something of a celebrity in this town." She shook her head scoffingly. "I mean it. Your name is well-known in important circles. And in recent days your name and picture have appeared in newspapers and on television. You've been made into a sort of folk heroine. That kind of free publicity is as good as money in the bank. I propose that we use this disaster to our advantage."

On the verge of panic, Rusty wet her lips. "You mean promote the fact that I survived an airplane crash to generate business?"

"What could it hurt?"

"You must be joking!" He wasn't. There was nothing in either his expression or demeanor to indicate that he was only fooling. She bowed her head, shaking it. "No, Father. Absolutely not. The idea doesn't appeal to me at all."

"Don't say no right away," he said patronizingly. "I'll get our advertising agency to work up a few ideas. I promise not to move on any of them until you've been consulted and I have your approval."

He was suddenly a stranger to her. The voice, the face, the polished manner—all were familiar. But she didn't really know the heart and soul of the man behind the veneer. She didn't know him at all.

"I'll never approve. That plane crash killed five people. *Five men*, Father. I met their families—their grieving widows and children and parents. I talked to them. I offered them my heartfelt condolences. To turn their misfortune to my own advantage—" she shuddered with repugnance "—no, Father. That's something I can't do."

Bill Carlson pulled on his lower lip, as he always did when he was deep in thought. "Very well. For the time being, we'll table that idea. But another has occurred to me."

He pressed both her hands between his. Rusty got the distinct impression that she was being restrained as a precautionary measure, as if what he was about to suggest would precipitate a fit.

"As I've told you, I had Mr. Landry thoroughly checked out yesterday. He owns a large ranch in a beautiful area of the Sierras."

"So he's said."

"No one has developed the land around it."

"That's the beauty of it. The region has remained virtually untouched. I fail to see what that has to do with us."

"Rusty, what's the matter with you?" he asked teasingly. "Have you become a conservationist after two weeks in the woods? You're not going to circulate petitions accusing builders of raping the land every time a new tract of homes goes up, are you?"

"Of course not, Father." His teasing bordered on criticism. There was a trace of reproach behind his smile. Rusty didn't want to disappoint him, but she hastened to eliminate any ideas he was nursing regarding Cooper and enterprise. "I hope you aren't considering any commercial development in Mr. Landry's part of the state. I can promise you, he wouldn't welcome it. In fact he'd fight you."

"Are you sure? How does the idea of a partnership strike you?"

She stared at him incredulously. "A partnership between Cooper and me?"

Carlson nodded. "He's a war veteran. That's very promotable. You survived a plane crash together and endured unbelievable hardships in the Canadian wilds before you were rescued. That, too, has high drama and marketability. The buying public will eat it up."

Everyone, even her own father, seemed to regard the plane crash and the life-threatening experiences following it as a grand adventure, a melodrama starring Cooper and herself in the principal roles—*The African Queen* set in a different time and locale.

Carlson was too caught up in his plans to notice Rusty's negative reaction to them. "I could make a few calls and by dark today put together a group of investors who would love to build condos in that area. There's a ski lift at this Rogers Gap, but it's ill-managed. We'd modernize and improve that and build around it.

"We'd bring Landry into it, of course. That would smooth the way with the other locals. He's not a mixer, but my investigators reported back that he wields a lot of influence. His name means something up there. Once the condos are under construction, you could start selling them. We'd all stand to make millions."

Her objections to his proposal were too many to enumerate, so she didn't even try. She had to shoot down the idea before it even took off. "Father, in case you didn't get the message a minute ago, Mr. Landry isn't interested in making money." She picked up the two halves of the check and shook them in front of his face as a reminder. "Making money off a real-estate venture will be anathema to him. He loves that country up there. He wants it left alone, kept the way it is, unspoiled by land developers. He loves the way nature developed it."

"He might play lip service to that Walden Pond philosophy," her father remarked skeptically. "But every man has his price, Rusty."

"Not Cooper Landry."

Carlson stroked his daughter's cheek. "Your naiveté is endearing."

The twinkle in his eyes was familiar and alarming. It indicated that he was on the scent of a Big Deal. In a community of capitalist sharks, her father was among those with the most deadly jaws. She grasped his hand and squeezed it hard. "Promise me, *promise*, that you won't do this. You don't know him."

"And you do?" The glint in his eyes dimmed and the lids narrowed. Gradually she released his hands. He backed away from her suspiciously, as though he'd just learned that what was confining her to the hospital bed might be contagious.

"I haven't posed any questions that might have been embarrassing for you to answer, Rusty. I wanted to spare us both that. However, I'm not blind. Landry is almost a caricature of the macho male. He's the kind of belligerent loner that women swoon over and fancy themselves able to tame."

He cupped her chin and tilted it up so he could read her eyes. "Surely you're too intelligent to fall for a pair of broad shoulders and a broody disposition. I hope that you didn't form any sort of emotional attachment to this man. That would be most unfortunate."

Unwittingly her father had echoed Cooper's theory—that their feelings were due largely to their dependency on each other. "Under the circumstances, wouldn't forming an attachment to him be natural?"

"Yes. But the circumstances have changed. You're no longer isolated with Landry in the wilderness;

you're home. You have a life here that mustn't be jeopardized by a juvenile infatuation. Whatever happened up there," he said, hitching his perfectly groomed head in the direction of the window, "is over and should be forgotten."

Cooper had said as much, too. But it wasn't over. Not by a long shot. And it couldn't be forgotten. What she felt for him wasn't going to weaken and eventually die from lack of nurturing. She hadn't formed a psychological dependency on him that would disappear as she gradually resumed her previous life.

She'd fallen in love. Cooper was no longer her provider and protector, but something so much more. He was the man she loved. Whether they were together or apart, that would never change.

"Don't worry, Father. I know exactly what I feel for Mr. Landry." That was the truth. Let her father draw his own conclusions.

"Good girl," Carlson said, patting her shoulder. "I knew I could count on you to come out of this stronger and smarter than ever. Just like your brother, you've got your head on straight."

SHE HAD BEEN home for a week after spending almost a week in the hospital recovering from the first operation on her shin. The scar didn't look much better than it had before the surgery, but the doctor had assured her that after the series of operations, it would be virtually undetectable.

Aside from a little tenderness in her leg, she felt perfectly fine. The bandages had been removed, but the surgeon had advised her to keep clothing off the leg and to continue to use crutches for support.

She had regained the few pounds she'd lost after the
plane crash. She spent a half hour or so each day lying
in the sun on the redwood deck of her pool to restore
her light tan. Her friends had been true to their promise, and since she couldn't easily get to a salon, they'd
brought the salon to her. A hairdresser had trimmed
and conditioned and restored her hair to its usual glossy
sheen. A manicurist had resculptured her nails. She'd
also massaged a pound of cream into Rusty's dry,
rough hands.

As she watched the manicurist smoothing away the
scaly redness, Rusty thought about the laundry she had
washed by hand, then hung up to dry on a crude outdoor clothesline. It had always been a contest to see if
the clothes would dry before they froze. It hadn't been
all that bad. Not really. Or did memory always make
things seem better than they actually had been?

That could be applied to everything. Had Cooper's
kisses really been that earth-moving? Had his arms and
whispered words been that comforting in the darkest
hours of the night? If not, why did she wake up frequently, yearning for his nearness, his warmth?

She had never been so lonely.

Not that she was ever alone—at least not for prolonged periods of time. Friends dropped in to bring tri-
fling presents that would hopefully amuse her because
she seemed so morose. Physically she was coming
along nicely, but her spirits hadn't bounced back yet.

Friends and associates were worried about her. Since
the airplane crash, she was not her usual, jovial self at
all. They kept her stuffed with everything from Godiva
chocolates to carry-out tacos to covered dishes from
Beverly Hills's finest restaurants, prepared especially

for her by the head chefs who knew personally what her favorite foods were.

She had lots of time on her hands, but she was never idle. Her father's prediction had come true: she was suddenly a celebrity real-estate agent. Everybody in town who wanted to sell or buy sought her advice on the fluctuating market trends. Each day she took calls from prospective clients, including an impressive number of movie and television people. Her ear grew sore from the hours spent on the telephone. Ordinarily she would have leaped over the moon for a client list of this caliber. Instead she was plagued with an uncharacteristic ennui that she couldn't explain or overcome.

Her father hadn't said any more about developing the area around Rogers Gap. She hoped that idea was officially a dead issue. He came by her house each day, ostensibly to check on her progress. But Rusty suspected, perhaps unfairly, that her father was more interested in quickly harvesting this crop of new business than in her recovery.

The lines around his mouth became tense with impatience, and his jocular encouragement for her to get back to work was beginning to sound forced. Even though she was following doctor's orders, she knew that she was stretching her recovery time for as long as she could. She was determined, however, not to return to her office until she felt good and ready.

On this particular afternoon, she groaned in dread when the doorbell pealed through her house. Her father had called earlier to say that because of a business commitment he wouldn't be able to come by that day. Rusty had been relieved. She loved her father but had welcomed the break from his daily visit, which never failed to exhaust her.

Obviously his meeting had been canceled and she wasn't going to get a reprieve after all.

Hooking her arms over her crutches, she hobbled down the hallway toward her front door. She'd lived in this house for three years. It was a small, white stucco building with a red tile roof, very southern California in design, tucked into an undercliff and shrouded with vividly blooming bougainvillea. Rusty had fallen in love with it the minute she saw it.

Propping herself up on one crutch, she unlatched and opened the door.

Cooper said nothing. Neither did she. They just stared at each other for a long time before she silently moved aside. He stepped through the arched doorway. Rusty closed the door and turned to face him.

"Hi."

"Hi."

"What are you doing here?"

"I came to see about your leg." He looked down at her shin. She stuck it out for his inspection. "It doesn't look much better."

"It will." His skeptical gaze moved up to meet hers. "The doctor has promised it will," she said defensively.

He still seemed doubtful, but let the subject drop. He took in his surroundings, pivoting slowly. "I like your house."

"Thank you."

"It's a lot like mine."

"Really?"

"Mine looks sturdier, maybe. Not decorated as

fancy. But they're similar. Large rooms. Lots of windows."

She felt she had recovered enough to move. Upon seeing him, her one good knee, which she relied on for support, had threatened to buckle beneath her. Now, she felt confident enough to move forward and indicated for him to follow her. "Come on in. Would you like something to drink?"

"Something soft."

"Lemonade?"

"Fine."

"It'll only take a minute to make."

"Don't bother."

"No bother. I was thirsty for some anyway."

She maneuvered herself through the dining room and into the kitchen at the back of the house. He followed. "Sit down." She nodded toward the butcher-block table that formed an island in the center of the kitchen and moved toward the refrigerator.

"Can I help?" he asked.

"No thanks. I've had practice."

She turned her head, ready with a smile, and caught him staring at the backs of her legs. Thinking that she was going to be alone all day, she'd dressed in a ragged pair of cutoffs and hadn't bothered with shoes. The tails of a chambray shirt were knotted at her waist. She'd pulled her hair up into a high, scraggly ponytail. The effect was a Beverly Hills version of Daisy Mae.

Caught staring at her smooth, bare legs, Cooper shifted guiltily in his chair. "Does it hurt?"

"What?"

"Your leg."

"Oh. No. Well, some. Off and on. I'm not supposed to walk or drive or anything like that yet."

"Have you gone back to work?"

Her ponytail swished against her neck as she shook her head. "I'm conducting some business here by telephone. The messenger services love me. I've kept them busy. But I haven't quite felt up to dressing and going to the office."

She took a can of lemonade concentrate out of the refrigerator where she'd had it thawing. "Have you been busy since you got home?"

She poured the thick pink concentrate into a pitcher and added a bottle of chilled club soda. When some of it splashed on the back of her hand, she raised it to her mouth and sucked it off. That's when she turned with the question still in her eyes.

Like a hawk, Cooper was watching every move. He was staring at her mouth. Slowly, she lowered her hand and turned back to her task. Her hands were trembling as she took glasses down out of the cabinet and filled them with ice cubes.

"Yeah, I've been busy."

"How was everything when you got back?"

"Okay. A neighbor had been feeding my livestock. Guess he would have gone on doing that indefinitely if I'd never turned up."

"That's a good neighbor." She had wanted to inject some levity into the conversation, but her voice sounded bright and brittle. It didn't fit the atmosphere, which was as heavy and oppressive as a New Orleans summer. The air was sultry; she couldn't draw enough of it into her lungs.

"Don't you have any help running your ranch?" she asked.

"Off and on. Temporary hands. Most of them are ski bums who only work to support their habit. When they run out of money they work a few days so they can buy lift tickets and food. The system works for both them and me."

"Because you don't like a lot of people around."

"Right."

An abysmal depression came over her. She staved it off by asking, "Do you ski?"

"Some. Do you?"

"Yes. Or I did." She glanced down at her leg. "I may have to sit this season out."

"Maybe not. Since the bone wasn't broken."

"Maybe."

And that, it seemed, was all they had to say. By tacit agreement, they ended the inane small talk and did what they really wanted to do—look at each other.

His hair had been cut, but was still unfashionably long. She liked the way it brushed the collar of his casual shirt. His jaw and chin were smoothly shaven, but if one single hair in his mustache had been altered, she couldn't tell it. The lower lip beneath it was as stern and unyielding as ever. If anything, the grooves bracketing his mouth looked deeper, making his face appear more unrelievedly masculine. She couldn't help but wonder what particular worry had carved those lines deeper.

His clothes weren't haute couture, but he would turn heads on Rodeo Drive and be a refreshing change from the dapper dressers. Blue jeans still did more for a male physique than any other garment ever sewn together. They did more for Cooper's body than for most.

Of course, there was more to work with—so much more that the bulging denim between his thighs made Rusty's stomach flutter.

His cotton shirt was stretched over a chest she still dreamed about. The sleeves had been rolled back to reveal his strong forearms. He had carried a brown leather bomber jacket in with him. It was now draped over the back of his chair, forgotten. Indeed, he seemed to have forgotten everything except the woman standing only a few feet, yet seemingly light-years, away from him.

His eyes tracked down her body, stripping her as they went. As though he were actually peeling away layer after layer of clothing, her skin began to burn with fever. By the time his eyes paused on the uneven, stringy hems of her cutoffs, where the soft threads tickled her bare thighs, Rusty was warm and moist.

His gaze moved back up to her face and the desire he saw registered there reflected his own. His eyes were like magnets drawing her into their field. On her crutches, she closed the distance between them, never breaking their stare. He didn't either. As she drew nearer, he had to tilt his head back to maintain eye contact. It seemed to take a lifetime but was actually only a few seconds before she stood directly in front of him, leaning on her crutches for support.

She said, "I can't believe you're really here."

Groaning, he lowered his head and pressed it hard against her breasts. "Rusty. Damn you. I couldn't stay away."

Overwhelming emotions caused her eyes to close. Her head tipped forward in total surrender to her love for this complex man. She whispered his name.

He folded his arms around her waist and nuzzled his face in the soft, fragrant valley between her breasts. His hands opened wide over her back, drawing her body closer even though she couldn't move her feet.

"I've missed you," she admitted hoarsely. She didn't expect him to make a similar confession, and he didn't. But the ardency of his embrace was unspoken evidence of how much he'd missed her. "I'd hear your voice and turn, expecting you to be there. Or I'd start to say something to you before I realized you weren't there."

"God, you smell good." Openmouthed, he gnawed on the soft inner curves of her breasts, catching cloth and all between his strong, white teeth.

"You smell like the mountains," she told him, kissing his hair.

"I've got to have—" he was frantically untying the knot at her waist "—just one—" it came undone and he ripped the buttons apart "—bite." His mouth fastened on the fleshy part of her breast, which was overflowing the cup of her brassiere.

At the first hot contact of his mouth with her skin, she arched her back and moaned. Her knuckles turned white where they gripped the handles of her crutches. She longed to drop them and plunge her fingers into his hair. She felt it dusting her skin when he turned his head and kissed her other breast. He took gentle love bites through the sheer cups of her brassiere and delicately sipped at the tips.

She released a keening sound much like a sob. It was both frustrating and thrilling not to have the use of her hands. The sense of helplessness was titillating. "Cooper," she gasped imploringly.

He reached around her and unhooked her bra strap,

working it down as far as it would go before the straps
got caught in her sleeves. But that was sufficient. He
had completely uncovered her. His eyes drank their fill
before his lips surrounded one taut, pink crest and drew
it into his mouth. He sucked it lovingly, then sponged
the very tip of it with his tongue before drying it with
his mustache. His whole face moved over her breasts,
rubbing them with cheek and chin and mouth and nose
and brow. Rusty, leaning precariously on her crutches,
chanted his name with religious fervor.

"Tell me what you want. Anything," he said huskily. "Tell me."

"I want you."

"Woman, you've got me. What do you want?"

"To touch. To be touched."

"Where?"

"Cooper..."

"Where?"

"You know where," she cried.

He brusquely unsnapped her cutoffs and slid down
the zipper. Her brief panties did little more than cover
the triangle of curls. He wanted to smile, but his face
was too set with passion, so he couldn't. He merely
growled his approval as he pulled down the panties
along with her cutoffs. He kissed the gingery down.

Rusty's strength deserted her. She let go of the
crutches. They clattered to the floor. She fell forward slightly, breaking her fall by placing her hands
on Cooper's shoulders. As she did so, he slid off the
seat of the chair and sank to his knees in front of her.

She caught her lower lip between her teeth to keep
from screaming with pleasure as he parted her dewy

flesh with his thumbs and buried his tongue in the softness.

He didn't stop there. He didn't stop at all. Not after the first wave of ecstasy swept over her. Not even after the second had claimed her. He didn't stop until her body was glistening with a fine sheen of perspiration, until tendrils of russet hair were clinging damply to her temples and cheeks and neck, until she was quivering with aftershocks.

Only then did he rise to his feet and take her in his arms. "Which way?" His face was softer than she'd ever seen it as it bent over hers. The guarded chill was no longer in his eyes. In its place were sparks of some strong emotion she dared to hope was love.

She raised her hand and pointed in the general direction of the bedroom. He found it without difficulty. Since she'd spent a great deal of time in that room recently, it had a homey, lived-in aspect that apparently appealed to him. He smiled as he carried her through the doorway. Gently he stood her on her left leg and threw back the covers on the bed. "Lie down."

She did, watching as he went into the bathroom. She heard water running. Moments later, he came back carrying a damp cloth. He didn't say a word, but his eyes spoke volumes as he drew her into a sitting position and eased off her blouse. Removing her brassiere only required sliding the straps off her arms. She sat before him totally naked, and marvelously unashamed.

He ran the cool, damp cloth over her arms and shoulders and around her neck. After he had eased her back onto the pillows, he raised her arms over her head and washed the shallow cups of her armpits. She

purred in surprised satisfaction; he ducked his head
and kissed her moaning mouth.

He moved the cloth over her chest, then her breasts.
Her nipples drew up again and he smiled. He touched
a rosy whisker-burn on her tender flesh.

"I always seem to leave a mark on you," he said with
a trace of regret. "I'm sorry."

"I'm not."

His eyes glowed hotly as they moved down her
stomach to her navel. He licked the sweat out of it before bathing the rest of her abdomen with the cloth.
Then he washed her legs, being careful of her new
scar. "Turn over."

Rusty gazed up at him inquisitively, but she turned
over on her stomach and rested her cheek on her
stacked hands. Leisurely, he washed her entire back
with the cloth. At the small of her back, he paused, then
ran the cloth over the cheeks of her bottom.

"Hmm," she sighed.

"That's for me to say."

"Go right ahead."

"Hmm." He spent far more time than was necessary
to wash away any perspiration. He sponged the backs
of her legs all the way down to the soles of her feet,
which he discovered were ticklish. On his way back
up, he lingered to taste the backs of her knees.

"Just relax a minute," he told her as he left the bed
to undress.

"Easy for you to say. You haven't been subjected to
heavy petting."

"Brace yourself, baby. You've got more coming."

Rusty wasn't quite braced for him to lie naked and
warm along the length of her back. She drew in a jag-

ged breath and shivered with the startling impact of his hair-roughened skin against the smoothness of her back. His opened thighs sandwiched hers. Her bottom fit snugly against his sex. It was solid with desire and as smooth as velvet-sheathed steel as it rubbed against her.

He covered the backs of her hands with his palms, interlacing their fingers, and used his nose to move aside her ponytail so his lips could get to her ear.

"I can't do anything for wanting you," he whispered gruffly. "Can't work. Sleep. Eat. There's no comfort in my getaway house anymore. You ruined it for me. The mountains aren't beautiful anymore. Your face has blinded me to them."

He rocked against her and made an upward thrust, settling himself more firmly against her. "I thought I'd work you out of my system, but so far I've failed. I even went to Vegas and bought a woman for the evening. When we got to the hotel room, I just sat there staring at her and drinking, trying to work up desire. She practiced some of her fanciest tricks, but I felt nothing. I couldn't do it. Didn't want to. Finally I sent her home before she became as disgusted with me as I was with myself."

He buried his face in the back of her neck. "You redheaded witch, what'd you do to me up there? I was fine, understand? Fine, until you came along with your wet-satin mouth and silky skin. Now my life isn't worth a damn. All I can think about, see, hear, touch, smell, taste, is you. *You.*"

He rolled her over and pinned her beneath him. His mouth slanted against hers. He parted her lips with his hard, invasive, possessive tongue. "I've got to have you. Got to. Now."

He ground his body against hers as though to meld them into one. Nudging her knees apart and giving one long, smooth, plunging motion of his hips, he delved into the giving folds of her womanhood.

Groaning with pleasure, he lowered his head to her chest. He called upon every prince of Heaven and hell to release him from his torment. His breath fell hot and labored on her breasts and when the nipples responded, he loved them with his mouth.

His skin was flushed. It burned her hands as she moved them over the rippling, supple muscles of his back and hips. She cupped his hard buttocks and drew him deeper yet. He moaned her name and brought their mouths together again. His kiss was carnally symbolic.

Rusty didn't feel vanquished by his virile power, though she could well have. On the contrary, she felt free and unfettered, strong enough to fly, to soar to the limits of the universe. Just as her body was opened to him, so was her heart and soul. Love poured out of them abundantly. He must feel it. He must know.

She was sure he did, because he was saying her name in cadence to his thrusts. His voice was raw with emotion. But a heartbeat before he lost his ability to reason, she felt him about to withdraw.

"No! Don't you dare."

"Yes, Rusty, yes."

"I love you, Cooper." She crossed her ankles at the small of his back. "I want you. All of you."

"No, no," he groaned in misery as well as ecstasy.

"I love you."

Clenching his teeth and baring them, he threw his head back and surrendered to orgasm with a long, low, primal groan that worked its way up from the bottom of his soul. He filled this woman who loved him with his hot, rich seed.

CHAPTER THIRTEEN

SWEAT DRIPPED FROM his face. He was drenched in it. His body hair was curled with it. He collapsed atop her. She held him tightly. Her maternal instinct asserted itself; she wanted to cuddle him like a child.

It was an endless forever before he regained enough strength to move, but neither was in a hurry for him to leave her. Finally he rolled away from her and lay on his back, replete. Rusty gazed at his beloved face. His eyes were closed. The lines on either side of his stern mouth had relaxed considerably since he'd come through her front door.

She laid her head on his chest and smoothed her hand over his stomach, combing through the crinkled, damp hair. "It wasn't just me you withdrew from, was it?" Somehow she knew that this was the first time in a long time that Cooper had completed the love act.

"No."

"It wasn't because I might get pregnant, was it?"

"No, it wasn't."

"Why did you make love that way, Cooper?" He opened his eyes. She stared down into them. They were guarded. He, who she had assumed was fearless, was afraid of her, a naked woman, lying helplessly beside him, utterly fascinated by him and under his spell. What threat could she possibly represent?

"Why did you impose that kind of discipline on yourself?" she asked gently. "Tell me."

He stared at the ceiling. "There was a woman."

Ah, *the* woman, Rusty thought.

"Her name was Melody. I met her soon after I got back from Nam. I was messed up. Bitter. Angry. She—" he made a helpless gesture "—she put things back into perspective, gave focus to my life. I was attending college on the GI bill. We were going to get married as soon as I finished. I thought that everything was going well for us. It was."

He closed his eyes again and Rusty knew he was approaching the difficult part of the story. "Then she got pregnant. Without my knowledge, she had an abortion." His hands curled into fists and his jaw grew rigid with fury. Rusty actually jumped when he turned to her abruptly.

"She killed my baby. After all the death I'd seen, she…" His breathing became so harsh that Rusty was afraid he'd go into cardiac arrest. She laid a comforting hand on his chest and softly spoke his name.

"I'm so sorry, Cooper, darling. I'm so sorry."

He breathed deeply, until he had filled his lungs with sufficient air. "Yeah."

"You've been angry at her ever since."

"At first. But then I came to hate her too much to be angry at her. I'd shared so many confidences with her. She knew what was going on inside my head, how I felt about things. She'd urged me to talk about the prison camp and everything that happened there."

"Did you feel that she abused that confidence?"

"Abused and betrayed it." With the pad of his thumb, he caught a tear rolling down Rusty's cheek and swept it away. "She'd held me in her arms while I cried like a baby, telling her about buddies I'd seen...killed," he finished in a hoarse whisper.

"I'd told her about the hell I went through to escape and then what I did to survive until I was rescued. Even after that, after I'd described how I'd lain in a heap of rotting, stinking corpses to keep from being recaptured—"

"Cooper, don't." Rusty reached for him and drew him close.

"She went out and had our baby destroyed. After I'd seen babies torn apart, probably had killed some myself, she—"

"Shh, shh. Don't."

Rusty cradled his head against her breasts and crooned to him as she smoothed his hair. Tears blurred her vision. She felt his suffering, and wished she could take it all on herself. She kissed the crown of his head. "I'm sorry, my darling. So very sorry."

"I left Melody. I moved to the mountains, bought my livestock, built my house."

And a wall around your heart, Rusty thought sadly. No wonder he'd spurned society. He'd been betrayed twice—once by his country, which didn't want to be reminded of its mistake, and then by the woman he had loved and trusted.

"You didn't take a chance on any woman getting pregnant by you again."

He worked his head free and looked into her eyes. "That's right. Not until now." He placed his hands on either side of her face. "Until you. And I couldn't stop myself from filling you." He kissed her hard. "I wanted it to last forever."

Smiling, she turned her head and bit the meaty part of his hand just below his thumb. "I thought it was going to."

He smiled, too, looking boyishly pleased with himself. "Really?"

Rusty laughed. "Really."

He slid his hand between her thighs and worked his fingers through the nest of russet curls before intimately palming her sex. "I left a special mark on you this time. You're carrying part of me inside you." He raised his head off the pillow and brushed his mouth across her kiss-swollen lips.

"That's what I wanted. I wouldn't have let you leave me this time."

"Oh, no?" There was an arrogant, teasing glint in his eyes. "What would you have done?"

"I would have given you one hell of a fight. That's how much I wanted you. All of you."

He pulled her lower lip between his teeth and worried it deliciously with his tongue. "One of the things I like most about you…" His mouth went for her neck.

"Yes?"

"Is that you always look like you've just been royally…" He finished his sentence with a gutter word that only he could make sound sexy.

"Cooper!" Pretending to be offended, Rusty sat back on her heels and placed her hands on her hips.

He laughed. The wonderful, rare sound of his laughter was so encouraging that she assumed an even prissier expression. He only laughed harder. His laughter was real, not tainted by cynicism. She wanted to draw it around her like a blanket. She wanted to bask in it as one would the first hot day of summer. She'd made

Cooper Landry laugh. That was no small feat, particularly in the past few years. Probably few could lay claim to having made this man laugh.

His mouth was still split into a wide grin beneath his mustache. He mimicked her in an old maid's whine. "Coo-per!" Piqued by his imitation of her, she smacked his bare thigh. "Hey, it's not my fault that you've got bedroom hair and smoky brown eyes." He reached out and ran his thumb along her lower lip. "I can't help it if your mouth always looks recently kissed and begging for more; if your breasts are always aquiver."

"'Aquiver'?" she asked breathlessly as he cupped one.

"Hmm. Is it my fault that your nipples are always primed and ready?"

"In fact it is."

That, he liked. Smiling, he plucked at the dusky pearl, rolling it gently between his fingers.

"But primed and ready for what, Cooper?"

He leaned forward and, using his lips and tongue, demonstrated.

Rusty felt the familiar sensations unwinding in her midsection like a spool of silk ribbon. Sighing, she clasped his head and pushed it away from her. He looked at her in bewilderment, but didn't resist as she pressed him back against the pillows. "What are we doing?" he asked.

"I'm going to make love to you for a change."

"I thought you just did."

She shook her tousled head. At some point her ponytail had come down. "You made love to me."

"What's the difference?"

Smiling a feline smile, her eyes full of promise, she stretched out alongside him and began nibbling his neck. "Wait and see."

IN THE PEACEFUL aftermath, they lay together, their arms and legs entangled. "I thought only hookers knew how to do that right." His voice was still scratchy from crying out her name, and he barely had the energy to strum her spine with his fingertips.

"Did I do it right?"

He tilted his head back and gazed down at the woman who lay sprawled across his chest. "Don't you know?"

Her eyes were glazed with love as she looked up at him and shook her head with shy uncertainty.

"That's the first time you ever…?" She nodded yes. He hissed a soft curse and drew her up for a gentle, loving kiss. "Yeah. You did it just fine," he said with a trace of humor when he finally released her lips. "Just fine."

After a long silence, Rusty asked him, "What kind of family life did you have?"

"Family life?" As he collected his thoughts, he absently rubbed his leg against her left one, ever careful not to bump the sore one. "It's been so long ago I barely remember. Practically all I remember of my dad was that he went to work every day. He was a salesman. His job finally caused a massive heart attack that killed him instantly. I was still in elementary school."

"Mother never got over being mad at him for dying prematurely and leaving her a widow. She never got over being mad at me for…existing, I guess. Anyway, all I meant to her was a liability. She had to work to support us."

"She never remarried?"

"No."

His mother had probably blamed her blameless son for that, too. Rusty could paint in the numbered spaces and get the complete picture. Cooper had grown up unloved. It was little wonder that now, when a hand was extended to him in kindness, he bit it instead of accepting it. He didn't believe in human kindness and love. He'd never experienced them. His personal relationships had been fouled with pain, disillusionment, and betrayal.

"I joined the Marines as soon as I graduated from high school. Mother died during my first year in Nam. Breast cancer. She was the kind of woman who was too stubborn to have that lump checked before it was too late."

Rusty stroked his chin with her thumbnail, occasionally dipping it into the vertical cleft. She was filled with remorse for the lonely, unloved child he'd been. Such unhappiness. By comparison she'd had it so easy.

"My mother died, too."

"And then you lost your brother."

"Yes. Jeff."

"Tell me about him."

"He was terrific," she said with an affectionate smile. "Everybody liked him. He was friendly—the kind of person who never met a stranger. People were automatically drawn to him. He had outstanding leadership qualities. He could make people laugh. He could do everything."

"You've been reminded of that often enough."

Quickly her head popped up. "What's that supposed to mean?"

Cooper seemed to weigh the advisability of pursuing this conversation, but apparently decided in favor of it. "Doesn't your father continually hold your brother up as an example for you to follow?"

"Jeff had a promising future in real estate. My father wants that for me, too."

"But is it *your* future he wants for you, or your brother's future?"

She disengaged herself and swung her legs over the side of the bed. "I don't know what you mean."

Cooper caught a handful of her hair to keep her from leaving the bed. He came up on his knees behind her where she sat on the edge of it. "Like hell you don't, Rusty. Everything you've said about your father and brother leads me to believe that you're expected to fill Jeff's shoes."

"My father only wants me to do well."

"What *he* considers well. You're a beautiful, intelligent woman. A loving daughter. You have a career, and you're successful. Isn't that enough for him?"

"No! I mean, yes, of course it's enough. It's just that he wants me to live up to my potential."

"Or Jeff's." She tried to move away, but he held her back by her shoulders. "Like that hunting trip to Great Bear Lake."

"I told you that that was my idea, not Father's."

"But why did you feel that it was necessary to go? Why was it your responsibility to uphold the tradition he had shared with Jeff? You only went because you thought it might please your father."

"What's wrong with that?"

"Nothing. If it was strictly a gesture of self-sacrifice, of love. But by going, I think you set out to prove something to him; I think that you wanted your father to see that you're as marvelous as Jeff was."

"Well, I failed."

"That's my point!" he shouted. "You don't like hunting and fishing. So what? Why should that make you a failure?"

She managed to wrest herself free. Once she was on her feet, she spun around to face him. "You don't understand, Cooper."

"Obviously I don't. I don't see why being exactly what you are isn't enough for your father. Why do you continually have to prove yourself to him? He lost his son: unfortunate; tragic. But he's still got a daughter. And he's trying to shape her into something she isn't. You're both obsessed with Jeff. Whatever else he did, I'm fairly sure he didn't walk on water."

Rusty aimed an accusing finger at him. "You're a fine one to preach about other people's obsessions. You nurse your hurt obsessively. You actually take pleasure in your despair."

"That's nuts."

"Precisely. It's easier for you to sit up there on your mountain than it is to mix with other human beings. Then you might have to open yourself up a little, let people get a peek at the man you are inside. And that terrifies you, doesn't it? Because you might be found out. Somebody might discover that you're not the hard, cold, unfeeling bastard you pretend to be. Someone might decide that you're capable of giving and receiving love."

"Baby, I gave up on the idea of love a long time ago."

"Then what was that all about?" She gestured toward the bed.

"Sex." He made the word sound as dirty as possible.

Rusty recoiled from the ugliness of his tone, but tossed her head back proudly. "Not to me. I love you, Cooper."

"So you said."

"I meant it!"

"You were in the throes of passion when you said it. That doesn't count."

"You don't believe that I love you?"

"No. There's no such thing."

"Oh, there is." She played her trump card. "You still love your unborn child."

"Shut up."

"You grieve for it still because you loved it. You still love all those men you saw die in that prisoner-of-war camp."

"Rusty…" He came off the bed and loomed over her threateningly.

"You watched your mother spend her life nursing her anger and bitterness. She thrived on her misfortune. Do you want to waste your life like that?"

"Better that than to live like you, constantly striving to be someone you're not."

Hostility crackled between them. It was so strong that at first they didn't even notice the doorbell. It wasn't until Bill Carlson called out his daughter's name that they realized they weren't alone.

"Rusty!"

"Yes, Father." She dropped back onto the edge of the bed and started yanking on her clothes.

"Is everything okay? Whose beat-up old car is that out front?"

"I'll be right out, Father."

Cooper was pulling on his clothes with considerably more composure than she. She couldn't help but wonder if this was the first time he had found himself in an awkward situation like this, maybe with the untimely appearance of a husband.

Once they were dressed, he helped her to her feet and handed her her crutches. Together they went through the bedroom door and down the hall. Red-faced, knowing that her hair was in wild tumble and that she smelled muskily of sex, Rusty entered the living room.

Her father was impatiently pacing the hardwood floor. When he turned around and saw Cooper, his face went taut with disapproval. He treated Cooper to a frigid stare before casting his judgmental eyes on his daughter.

"I hated to let a day go by without coming to see you."

"Thank you, Father, but it really isn't necessary for you to stop by every day."

"So I see."

"You...you remember Mr. Landry."

The two men nodded to each other coolly, taking each other's measure like opposing champion warriors who would decide the outcome of a battle. Cooper kept his mouth stubbornly shut. Rusty couldn't speak; she was too embarrassed. Carlson was the first to break the stressful silence.

"Actually, this is an opportune meeting," he said.

"I have something to discuss with both of you. Shall we sit down?"

"Surely," Rusty said, flustered. "I'm sorry. Uh, Cooper?" She gestured toward a chair. He hesitated, then dropped into the overstuffed armchair. His insolence grated on her raw nerves. She gave him a baleful look, but he was staring at her father. He'd watched the Gawrylow men with that same kind of suspicious caution. The memory disturbed Rusty. What correlation between them and her father was he making in his mind? She moved toward a chair near Carlson.

"What do you want to discuss with us, Father?"

"That land deal I mentioned to you a few weeks ago."

Rusty's lungs caved in. She could feel each membrane giving way, collapsing one on top of the other. Her cheeks paled, and her palms became immediately slick with nervous perspiration. A choir of funeral bells started tolling in her ears. "I thought we had that all settled."

Carlson chuckled amiably. "Not quite. But now we do. Now the investors have had a chance to put some concrete ideas on paper. They'd like to present these ideas for Mr. Landry's consideration."

"Somebody want to tell me what the hell is going on?" Cooper rudely interrupted.

"No."

"Of course." Carlson overrode his daughter's negative reply and seized the floor. In his typically genial manner, he outlined his ideas for developing the area around Rogers Gap into an exclusive ski resort.

Summing up, he said, "Before we're done, working

with only the most innovative architects and builders, it will rival Aspen, Vail, Keystone, anything in the Rockies or around Lake Tahoe. In several years I'll bet we could swing the Winter Olympics our way." Leaning back in his chair and smiling expansively, he said, "Well, Mr. Landry, what do you think?"

Cooper, who hadn't so much as blinked an eye during Carlson's recital, slowly rolled off his slouching spine and came to his feet. He circled the island of furniture several times as though considering the proposal from every angle. Since he owned some of the land that would be used—Carlson had done his homework—and had been offered the salaried, figurehead position as local coordinator of the project, he stood to make a great deal of money.

Carlson glanced at his daughter and winked, assured of capitulation.

"What do I think?" Cooper repeated.

"That's what I asked," Carlson said jovially.

Cooper looked him straight in the eye. "I think *you* are full of garbage, and I think your *idea* sucks." He dumped those words in the middle of the floor like a ton of bricks, then added, "And for your information, so does your daughter."

He gave Rusty a look that should have turned her to stone. He didn't even deign to slam the door shut behind himself after he stamped out. They heard his car roar to life, then the crunch of gravel as he steered out of her driveway.

Carlson harrumphed and said, "Well, I see that I was right about him all along."

Knowing that she would never recover from the

wound Cooper had inflicted on her, Rusty said dully, "You couldn't be more wrong, Father."

"He's crude."

"Honest."

"A man without ambition or social graces."

"Without pretenses."

"And apparently without morals. He took advantage of your solitude and confinement."

She laughed softly. "I don't remember exactly who dragged whom into the bedroom, but he certainly didn't force me into bed with him."

"So you *are* lovers?"

"Not anymore," she said tearfully.

Cooper thought she had betrayed him, too, just like that other woman, Melody. He thought she had been her father's instrument, using bedroom tactics to turn a profit. He would never forgive her, because he didn't believe that she loved him.

"You've been his lover all this time? Behind my back?"

She started to point out that at the ripe old age of twenty-seven she shouldn't have to account to her father for her private life. But what was the use? What did it matter? The starch had gone out of her. She felt sapped of strength, of energy, of the will to live.

"When we were in Canada, yes. We became lovers. When he left my hospital room that day, he went home and hasn't been back since. Not until this afternoon."

"Then apparently he has more sense than I gave him credit for. He realizes that the two of you are completely incompatible. Like most women, you're looking at the situation through a pink fog of romance. You're letting your emotions rule you instead of your head. I thought you were above that female frailty."

"Well, I'm not, Father. A female is what I happen to be. And I have all the frailties, as well as all the strengths, that go with being a woman."

He came to his feet and crossed the room. He gave her a conciliatory hug. She was standing on her crutches so he didn't notice how stiffly she held herself in resistance to his embrace. "I can see that Mr. Landry has upset you again. He truly is a scoundrel to have said what he did about you. You're better off without him, Rusty, believe me.

"However," he continued briskly, "we won't let his lack of charm keep us from doing business with him. I intend to move forward with our plans in spite of his objections to them."

"Father, I beg you—"

He laid a finger against her lips. "Hush, now. Let's not talk anymore tonight. Tomorrow you'll feel better. You're still emotionally overwrought. Having surgery so soon after the plane crash probably wasn't such a good idea. It's perfectly understandable that you're not quite yourself. One of these days you'll come to your senses and return to being the old Rusty. I have every confidence that you won't disappoint me."

He kissed her forehead. "Good night, my dear. Look over this proposal," he said, withdrawing a file folder from his lizard briefcase and laying it on the coffee table. "I'll drop by tomorrow morning, eager to hear your opinion."

After he left, Rusty locked up her house and returned to the bedroom. She bathed, languishing in a hot bubble bath. She'd taken one every day since the doctor had said it was okay to get her leg wet. But once she was dried, lotioned, and powdered, she still hadn't rid her body of the traces of Cooper's lovemaking.

She was pleasantly sore between her thighs. The blemish he'd left on her breast still showed up rosily, as indelible as a tattoo. Her lips were tender and puffy. Every time she wet them with her tongue, she could taste him.

Looking at herself in the mirror, she admitted that he was right. She *did* look as if she'd just been engaged in rowdy lovemaking.

Her bed seemed as large and empty as a football field during the off-season. The linens still smelled like Cooper. In her mind she relived every moment they'd spent together that afternoon—the giving and taking of pleasure; the exchange of erotic dialogue. Even now, his whispered, naughty words echoed through her mind, causing her to flush hotly all over.

She yearned for him and could find no comfort in the thought that her life would be a series of empty days and joyless nights like this one.

She'd have her work, of course.

And her father.

Her wide circle of friends.

Her social activities.

It wouldn't be enough.

There was a great big hole where the man she loved should be.

She sat up in bed and clutched the sheet against her, as though the realization she'd just had would get away from her if she didn't hold on to it until she could act upon it.

Her choices were clear. She could either roll over

and play dead. Or she could fight for him. Her main adversary would be Cooper himself. He was mule-headed and mistrustful. But eventually she would wear him down and convince him that she loved him and that he loved her.

Yes, he did! He could deny it until he gasped his dying breath, but she would never believe that he didn't love her—because right after her father had made that hateful disclosure, just before Cooper's face had hardened with contempt, she'd seen incredible pain there. She wouldn't have the power to hurt him that badly unless he loved her.

She lay back down, glowing in her resolution and knowing exactly what she had to do the following morning.

HER FATHER WAS taken off-guard. A strategist as shrewd as General Patton, he had slipped up. He hadn't expected a surprise attack.

When she made her unannounced appearance in his office the next morning, he glanced up from his highly polished, white lacquered desk and exclaimed, "Why, Rusty! What...what a lovely surprise."

"Good morning, Father."

"What are you doing out? Not that the reason matters. I'm delighted to see you up and around."

"I had to see you and didn't want to wait to be worked into your busy schedule."

He chose to ignore the note of censure in her voice and walked around his desk with his hands outstretched to take hers. "You're feeling much better—I can tell. Did Mrs. Watkins offer you coffee?"

"She did, but I declined."

He regarded her casual clothes. "Apparently you're not going to your office."

"No, I'm not."

He cocked his head to one side, obviously waiting for an explanation. When none was forthcoming he asked, "Where are your crutches?"

"In my car."

"You drove here? I didn't think—"

"Yes, I drove myself. I wanted to walk in here under my own steam and stand on my own two feet."

He backed away from her and propped his hips against the edge of his desk. Casually he crossed his ankles and folded his arms over his middle. Rusty recognized the stance. It was the tactical one he assumed when he was backed into a corner but didn't want his rivals to know that he was. "I take it you read the proposal." With a smooth motion of his head, he indicated the folder she was carrying under her arm.

"I did."

"And?"

She ripped the folder in two. Tossing the remnants on the glassy surface of his desk, she said, "Lay off Cooper Landry. Drop the Rogers Gap project. Today."

He laughed at her sophomoric gesture and shrugged helplessly, spreading his arms wide in appeal. "It's a little late for that, Rusty dear. The ball has already started rolling."

"Stop it from rolling."

"I can't."

"Then you're in a real jam with these investors you collected, Father—" she leaned forward "—because I'm going to privately and publicly resist you on this. I'll have every conservationist group in the country beating down your door in protest. I don't think you want that."

"Rusty, for Heaven's sake, come to your senses," he hissed.

"I did. Sometime between midnight and 2:00 a.m., I realized that there's something much more important to me than any real-estate deal. Even more important to me than winning your approval."

"Landry?"

"Yes." Her voice rang with conviction. She was not to be swayed.

But Carlson tried. "You'd give up everything you've worked for to have him?"

"Loving Cooper doesn't take anything away from what I've done in the past or will do in the future. Love this strong can only embellish, not tear down."

"Do you realize how ridiculous you sound?"

She didn't take offense. Instead she laughed. "I guess I do. Lovers often babble nonsensically, don't they?"

"This is no laughing matter, Rusty. If you do this, it's an irreversible decision. Once you give up your position here, that's it."

"I don't think so, Father," she said, calling his bluff. "Think how bad it would be for business if you fired your most effective employee." She produced a key from the pocket of her nylon windbreaker. "To my office." She slid the key across his desk. "I'll be taking an indefinite leave of absence."

"You're making a fool of yourself."

"I made a fool of myself at Great Bear Lake. I did that for love, too." She turned on her heels and headed for the door.

"Where are you going?" Bill Carlson barked. He wasn't accustomed to someone walking out on him.

"To Rogers Gap."

"And do what?"

Rusty faced her father. She loved him. Very much. But she could no longer sacrifice her own happiness for his. With staunch conviction she said, "I'm going to do something that Jeff could never do: I'm going to have a baby."

CHAPTER FOURTEEN

RUSTY STOOD ON the cliff and breathed deeply of the cool, crisp air. She never tired of the scenery. It was constant, and yet ever changing. Today the sky was like a blue china bowl turned upside down over the earth. Snow still capped the mountain peaks against the horizon. The trees ranged in color from the blue-green of the evergreens to the delicate green of trees on the verge of spring budding.

"Aren't you cold?"

Her husband came up behind her and wrapped his arms around her. She snuggled against him. "Not now. How's the foal?"

"He's having breakfast—to his and his mother's mutual contentment."

She smiled and tilted her head to one side. He inched down the turtleneck of her sweater and kissed her beneath her ear. "How's the other new mother on the place?"

"I'm not a new mother yet." She glowed with pleasure as he ran his large hands over her swollen abdomen.

"Looks that way to me."

"You think this new figure of mine is amusing, don't you?" She frowned at him over her shoulder, but it was hard to maintain that expression when he was gazing at her with such evident love.

"I love it."

"I love you."

They kissed. "I love you, too," he whispered when he lifted his mouth off hers. Words he had found impossible to say before, now came easily to his lips. She had taught him how to love again.

"You had no choice."

"Yeah, I remember that night you showed up on my threshold looking as bedraggled as a homeless kitten in a rainstorm."

"Considering what I'd just come through I thought I looked pretty good."

"I didn't know whether to kiss you or paddle you."

"You did both."

"Yeah, but the paddling didn't come until much later."

They laughed together, but he was serious when he said, "No fooling, I couldn't believe you drove all that way alone through that kind of weather. Didn't you listen to your car radio? Didn't you hear the storm reports? You escorted in the first heavy snowstorm of the season. Every time I think about it, I shudder." He pulled her closer, crossing his hands over her breasts and nuzzling his face in her hair.

"I had to see you right then, before I lost my nerve. I would have gone through hell to get here."

"You very nearly did."

"At the time, it didn't seem so bad. Besides, I had survived a plane crash. What was a little snow?"

"Hardly a 'little snow.' And driving with your injured leg too."

She shrugged dismissively. To their delight the gesture caused her breasts to rise and fall against his hands. Murmuring his appreciation, he covered them completely and massaged them gently, aware of the discomfort they'd been giving her lately as a result of her pregnancy.

"Tender?" he asked.

"A little."

"Want me to stop?"

"Not on your life."

Satisfied with her answer, he propped his chin on the top of her head and continued to massage her.

"I'm glad the operations on my leg have to be postponed until after the baby gets here," she said. "That is, if you don't mind looking at my unsightly scar."

"I always close my eyes when we're making love."

"I know. So do I."

"Then how do you know mine are closed?" he teased. They laughed again, because neither of them closed their eyes while they were making love; they were too busy looking at each other, looking at themselves together, and gauging each other's level of passion.

As they watched a hawk lazily circling in downward spirals, Cooper asked, "Remember what you said to me the instant I opened the door that night?"

"I said, 'You're going to let me love you, Cooper Landry, if it kills you.'"

He chuckled at the memory and his heart grew warm, as it had that night, when he thought about the courage it had taken for her to come to him and make that bizarre announcement. "What would you have done if I had slammed the door in your face?"

"But you didn't."

"Assuming I had."

She pondered that for a moment. "I'd have barged in anyway, stripped off all my clothes, pledged everlasting love and devotion, and threatened you with violence if you didn't love me back."

"That's what you did."

"Oh, yeah," she said around a giggle. "Well, I'd have just kept on doing that until you stopped refusing."

He planted his lips against her ear. "You went down on bended knee and asked me to marry you and give you a baby."

"How well your memory serves you."

"And that's not all you did while you were on your knees."

She turned in his arms and said sweetly, "I didn't hear you complaining. Or were all those garbled phrases coming out of your mouth complaints?"

He laughed, throwing back his head and releasing a genuine burst of humor—something he did frequently now. There were times when he lapsed into the moody, withdrawn man he'd been. His mind carried him back to haunting phases of his life where she couldn't go. Her reward lay in the fact that she could bring him out again. Patiently, lovingly, she was eradicating his disturbing memories and replacing them with happy ones.

Now she kissed his strong, tanned throat and said, "We'd better go in and get ready for our trip to L.A."

They made one round-trip a month to the city, during which they spent two or three days at Rusty's house. While there, they ate in fine restaurants, went to concerts and movies, shopped, and even attended an occasional social gathering. Rusty stayed in touch with her old friends, but was delighted with the new friendships Cooper and she had cultivated as a couple. When he wanted to, he could ooze charm and engage in conversation on a wide range of subjects.

Also while they were there, she handled business matters that demanded her attention. Since her marriage, she'd been promoted to vice-president in her father's real-estate company.

Cooper worked as a volunteer counselor in a veterans' therapy group. He'd initiated several self-help programs that were being emulated in other parts of the country.

Now, with their arms around each other's waist, they walked back toward the house that was nestled in a grove of pines. It overlooked a spectacular valley. Horses and cattle grazed in the mountain pastures below the timberline.

"You know," he said as they entered their glass-walled bedroom, "talking about that night you arrived has gotten me all hot and bothered." He peeled off his shirt.

"You're always hot and bothered." Rusty peeled her sweater over her head. She never wore a bra when they were at home alone.

Eyeing her enlarged breasts, he unsnapped his jeans and swaggered toward her. "And it's always your fault."

"Do you still desire me, even though I'm mis-shapen?" She gestured at her rounded tummy.

For an answer, he took her hand and pulled it into his open fly. She squeezed his full manhood. He groaned softly. "I desire you." Bending his knees, he kissed one of her creamy breasts. "As long as you're you, I'll love you, Rusty."

"I'm glad," she sighed. "Because, just like after the plane crash, you're stuck with me."

* * * * *

A SECRET
SPLENDOR

CHAPTER ONE

SHE'S HERE AGAIN, Drew McCasslin thought as he slammed his racket against the tennis ball. For the third time that week she was sitting at the same table, the one nearest the ledge overlooking the tennis courts. The table's brightly striped umbrella partially shaded her face.

She hadn't been there when he and Gary started playing, but he'd known the moment she walked out onto the patio, which was an extension of the club's outdoor snack and cocktail bar. He had missed a ball when he let his attention wander to the graceful way she smoothed her skirt beneath her hips and thighs as she sat down.

"Better every day," Gary said to him as they met at the net to catch their breath, take a swig of Gatorade and towel mop rivers of sweat that saturated sweatbands couldn't absorb.

"Not good enough," Drew replied before taking a long pull at the bottle of lemon drink. Over the bottle's length, he eyed the woman sitting on the patio above them. Ever since the first day he had seen her there, she had inspired his curiosity.

She was bent over the table tapping a pencil against a tablet in a manner that he now associated with her. What the devil was she always writing down?

Slowly, he lowered the bottle from his mouth, and his blue eyes narrowed with suspicion. Could she be another bloodsucking reporter? God forbid. But it wouldn't be unlike an enterprising tabloid publication to send bait like that to trap him into an interview.

"Drew? Did you hear me?"

"Huh?" He swung his eyes back to his tennis opponent. A friendly opponent for once. "I'm sorry. What did you say?"

"I said your stamina has improved since last week. You're running my ass all over the court, and you're barely winded."

Drew's eyes crinkled at the corners as he smiled, obscuring the tiny white lines in his bronzed face. It was a smile reminiscent of the days before he had learned the definition of tragedy. "You're good, but you're not Gerulaitis *or* Borg *or* McEnroe *or* Tanner. Sorry, chum, but I have to be a helluva lot better than you before I'm ready again for the big fellows. And I'm not there by a long shot. No pun intended." The once-famous grin flashed again in the Hawaiian sunlight.

"Thanks," Gary said dryly. "I can't wait for the day I'm stumbling over my tongue and you've still got enough energy to jump the net when the match is over."

Drew slapped him on the shoulder. "That's the spirit," he gibed goadingly. He picked up his racket and twirled it with the absentminded finesse that had come from years of thinking of it as an extension of his hand.

A cheer and hearty applause erupted from a group of female spectators. They were clustered on the other side of the fence surrounding the courts. Their vocal approval increased as Drew walked back to the baseline.

"Your fans are out in full force today," Gary said with a taunting inflection.

"Damn groupies," Drew grumbled as he turned around and glared at the women who clung to the fence like hungry zoo animals at mealtime. And he was the feast. He scowled at them angrily, but that only seemed to stir them rather than to repel them. They called outrageous endearments to him and flirted shamelessly. One, wearing a brief halter top, peeled the side back to flaunt a heavy breast with his name, decorated with flowers and hearts and lovebirds, tattooed on it. Another had a bandanna, the kind he wore as a trademark sweatband around his forehead every time he played, tied high around the top of her thigh. He looked away in disgust.

He forced himself to concentrate on the ball as he bounced it idly, planning his serve, plotting to fire the ball across the net to bounce in the back corner of the serve box and spin out to the left, Gary's weak backhand side. One of Drew's "fans" called out a lewd invitation, and he gritted his teeth. Didn't they know that the last thing he was interested in was a woman? My God, Ellie had only been dead...

Dammit, McCasslin, don't think about Ellie, he warned himself. He couldn't think about Ellie when he tried to play or his game went straight to hell....

"Mr. McCasslin?"

"You've got him," he had said cheerfully into the telephone receiver that sunny day in paradise when the last thing a man would expect was for his wife to die in the tangle of metal and glass of a car crash.

"Are you alone?"

Drew had pulled the receiver from his ear and looked at it in puzzled amusement. He laughed out loud. "Yes, I'm alone except for my son. Is this going to be an obscene phone call?" He'd meant it as a joke. He'd had no idea how obscene the call would actually be.

"Mr. McCasslin, I'm Lieutenant Scott with Honolulu P.D. There's been an accident."

He didn't remember much after that....

Now HE TOOK up the ball and bounced it in his hand as though weighing it. Actually, he was trying to erase his mind, to wipe it clean of memories that made his insides churn. His eyes gravitated to the woman still sitting at the patio table. Her cheek was resting on her palm as she stared vacantly into space. She seemed impervious to everything going on around her. Didn't she hear all the commotion from the women at the fence? Wasn't she the least bit curious about him?

Apparently not. She hadn't so much as glanced at the tennis court. Unaccountably, he resented her indifference, which was irrational, since all he'd wanted for the year since Ellie's death was to be left alone.

"Hey, Drew," called out a singsong voice from the gathered fans, "when you're through playing with your balls, you can play with something of mine."

The *double entendre* was so blatant and so crudely bold that Drew's blood boiled, and when his serve sliced through the air, it was but a blur. For the rest of the set, he kept up that kind of anger-inspired play. When it was over, he'd granted Gary only two points.

Draping a towel around his neck, Gary wheezed, "If I'd known that all it took to get you to play championship tennis was a dirty suggestion from one of your groupies, I'd have rented them by the hour weeks ago."

Drew had already gathered up his tennis bag, zipped his racket into its holder and was heading toward the stairs that led to the patio overlooking the courts. "Most of them could be rented by the hour, I'm sure."

"Don't be too hard on them. They're your fans."

"I could do with more fans who are sports writers or commentators. Among them, I don't have one. All they do is tell the world that I'm washed up. Finished. Drunk all the time."

"You *were* drunk all the time."

Drew stopped on the step above Gary and whipped around to confront him angrily. His friend's face was guileless, open and damnably honest. What he'd said was true. Drew's anger dissolved in the face of such forthright friendship. "I was, wasn't I?" he asked on an embarrassed sigh.

"But not anymore. Today you were the old Drew. Blistering serves. Damn! Every time one came near me, I saw my life flash before my eyes." Drew laughed. "Well-thought-out maneuvers, strategy to take advantage of my weak left side."

A grin split Drew's mobile mouth. "I didn't think you'd notice."

"Like hell."

They were laughing companionably as they took the last few stairs up to the patio. Drew saw at once that she was still there, a sheaf of papers strewn over the table top, a glass of mineral water at her right hand. She was scribbling furiously on a yellow legal pad. He was going to walk past her table. It was on his way to the lockers, and he would only call attention to himself if he avoided passing where she was sitting.

They were almost beside her when she glanced up at them. The glance was a reflex action, as though they had disturbed her train of thought and she was looking up involuntarily to determine the source of that interruption. But she looked directly at Drew, directly into his eyes, and the impact of her gaze made his eyes narrow on her and his ears close to Gary's chatter.

Her eyes dropped immediately back to her paper, but not before Drew had seen that they were incredibly green and surrounded by dark, bristly lashes.

That was when he made up his mind. He'd make a wager with himself. If she was still there when he came out of the locker room, he'd speak to her. If not, well, nothing was lost. He wasn't really interested in meeting a woman, any woman. It was just that this one intrigued him. If he was honest with himself, he'd have to admit that the main reason she piqued his curiosity was because she was so *un*curious about him.

Yes, he'd leave it to chance. If she was still there when he came out of the locker room, he'd at least say hello. No harm in that.

One other thing, he reminded himself. *Don't linger in the shower.*

ARDEN'S HEART WAS booming like a kettledrum.

It had been a full five minutes since he'd walked within touching distance, since she'd seen his face up close and in the flesh for the first time, and still her heart hadn't quieted. She blotted her palms with the damp napkin knotted in her fists. Ice rattled in her glass when she took a sip of her lime-refreshed mineral water.

He had looked straight at her. Their eyes had met. Briefly, briefly. Yet it had been like lightning striking her to see Drew McCasslin for the first time, knowing the bond that linked them together. Total strangers to each other, yet with a common secret they would share throughout their lives.

She looked down at the court where he had just played with such brilliance. A few months before, she'd known little about tennis, especially professional tennis. Now she was almost expert in her wealth of knowledge on the subject. Certainly she had a vast amount of knowledge on the career of Drew McCasslin.

A group of four ladies came onto the court, looking ridiculous in their designer tennis clothes and extravagant gold and diamond jewelry. She smiled at them indulgently, remembering Ronald's urging that she join the tennis league at their club in Los Angeles.

"That's not me, Ron. I'm not athletic. I'm not a participator, a joiner."

"You'd rather sit in the house all day writing those little verses that you lock away and don't let anyone see. For God's sake, Arden, you don't have to play *well*. I don't care if you can play tennis or not. It's just good for my professional image, not to mention the valuable contacts you could make if you're an active member of the club. Socialize with the other doctors' wives."

He'd settled for bridge. She never was a master of the game, but she played well enough to be invited to all the tournaments sponsored by the country club, and that satisfied Ronald's demands that she mix and mingle with what he considered suitable friends for a prominent doctor's wife.

Then Joey had come along and provided her with a

viable excuse for curtailing her social activities. Joey had provided her with excuses for many things. Some, she wished she could forget. Would her son, her adorable, painfully sweet, innocent son, have understood that one life-altering decision? Would he have forgiven what she couldn't forgive herself?

She'd asked his forgiveness the day the pitifully small casket was lowered into the short grave. She'd asked God's forgiveness, too, for the bitterness she felt at watching an intelligent, beautiful child waste away in a hospital bed while other robust children played and ran and got into mischief.

Shaking herself out of her emotional reverie, she took another sip of water and mentally toasted herself for playing it just right with Drew McCasslin. It was public knowledge that since he'd retreated to his carefully guarded estate on this island, he'd avoided interviews and shunned publicity of any kind.

For days, Arden had occupied herself with thinking of a way to approach him. On the long flight over from the mainland and even after her arrival on Maui, she had discarded one plan after another. The only positive thing she'd done was to acquire a room at the resort and club where he worked out every day. His privacy had been guaranteed him by the management. This was the first day since she'd been watching him that he hadn't entered the locker room from the metal door that opened directly onto the courts.

Her only option had been to play it subtly, to make herself visible and see what happened. She would pretend to ignore him. It wasn't hard to see that his more forward fans irritated him.

And today he'd noticed her. Instinctively, she knew

it. She'd given an impression of casual disinterest, but she'd been aware of every move he made. He'd glanced in her direction several times, especially after executing an outstanding move. He'd never caught her eyes on him. A famous personality like Drew McCasslin wasn't used to being ignored.

In his case, such conceit was justifiable. His blond hair was too long, but it suited his dashing good looks. His trim physique didn't show the ravages of his recent bout with alcohol. The tropically tanned arms and legs, which moved with the precision and power of a well-oiled machine, were the epitome of masculine grace, and contrasting with the bronzed skin was an eye-catching dusting of tawny body hair. He was somewhat broader of chest than most tennis players, but that flaw was readily forgiven by anyone who watched the play of those muscles under his tailored white T-shirts.

It was obvious that since the tragic death of his wife, Drew McCasslin had just as soon women not notice his virile appeal. No, she had played it just right, Arden congratulated herself. Today he had looked at her. Maybe tomorrow—

"You must have a lot of friends and relatives."

Startled by the masculine voice, Arden swiveled around; to her dismay, she found herself staring into the fly of a pair of white shorts. The sculpted bulge behind that fly could only be produced by either very brief and very tight underwear or a jock strap. Either possibility sent a hot current rushing through her body.

She dragged her eyes away from Drew McCasslin's crotch and let them scale the long torso, which was clothed in a royal-blue nylon windbreaker zipped only halfway up to reveal a coppery chest furred with golden hair. His smile was an orthodontist's dream. Straight white teeth were set in a jaw too strong to be anything but stubborn. The blue eyes were as dazzling as they were reported to be.

"I beg your pardon?" she asked in a voice she hoped didn't betray her disabling nervousness.

"You're busy writing an awful lot of something. I thought it might be postcards home. 'Wish you were here.' That sort of thing."

His voice was clear, a true baritone in pitch, unaccented, his tone strangely intimate.

She smiled, remembering her act of nonchalant indifference. "No. Not postcards. There really is no one home to miss me."

"Then no one could mind if I joined you."

"*I* could mind."

"Do you?"

Elated but not daring to show it, she paused only a heartbeat before saying, "No. I guess not."

He tossed his canvas bag beneath the chair opposite hers and sat down. Reaching across the paper-strewn table, he said, "Drew McCasslin."

She took the extended hand into her own. "Arden Gentry." She was touching him! Looking at their clasped hands, at his flesh against hers, she marveled over the wonder of this being their first physical contact when—

"Are you on vacation?" he asked politely.

She released his hand and sat back in her chair, trying to dispel a feeling of lightheadedness. "Partially. A mixture of business and pleasure."

He signaled the waiter from behind the outdoor bar.

"Do you care for another?" he asked, indicating her glass.

"Pineapple juice this time," she said, smiling.

"You're a foreigner, all right. You haven't had time to grow sick of the stuff."

She wished he weren't quite so attractive when he smiled. His blatant sex appeal distracted her from the reason why she had wanted to make his acquaintance, gain his confidence, if possible, become his friend.

"The lady wants pineapple juice, and I want about four glasses of water, please," he told the waiter.

"Yessir, Mr. McCasslin. You were playing well today."

"Thank you. Hurry with the water. I'm all sweated out."

"Yessir."

"You did play well," Arden said when the waiter hurried off to get Drew's order.

He studied her face for a time before he said, "I didn't think you noticed the match at all."

"I would have to be blind and deaf not to. I don't know much about tennis, but I know you're playing better now than you were several months ago."

"Then you knew who I was?"

"Yes. I'd seen you on television once or twice." He seemed boyishly crestfallen, and Arden's smile widened. "You're a celebrity, Mr. McCasslin," she whispered reassuringly. "People all over the world know your name."

"And most of those people don't make any bones about staring at me when I'm in public." It was a gently spoken challenge.

"Like your cheerleading section down there?" She

nodded toward the fenced-off area where the groupies had collected. They had since dispersed.

He groaned. "Would you believe I began working out here because I was promised anonymity and privacy? It's also about the best court on Maui. But we didn't take into account the fact that guests of the resort have access to the courts. When word gets out that I'm practicing—" He sighed in exasperation. "Well, you see what happens."

"Most men would be flattered by such adoration."

He scoffed at that and quickly changed the subject. "What is all this, anyway?" he asked of the papers scattered across the table.

"Notes. I'm a free-lance writer."

His retreat was instantaneous and physical, though he didn't move. His eyes became cold and implacable. The sensuous curve of his lips thinned into a line of aggravation. Around the frosted glass of water the waiter had just delivered, his fingers flexed in anger. "I see," he said tersely.

She lowered her eyes and picked at the paper doily under her glass of juice. "I don't think you do. I'm a writer, not a reporter. I'm not after an interview. You initiated this conversation, not I, Mr. McCasslin."

When he didn't respond, she lifted her thick, dark lashes and looked at him. He was as he had been before, smiling slightly, friendly, yet guarded, just as she was. "Call me Drew, please."

He had laid down the terms of the truce, and she accepted it. "All right, Drew. And I'm Arden."

"What kind of writer? Novelist?"

She laughed. "Not yet. Maybe someday. Right now I'm trying to peddle anything and everything until I find my niche. I'd always wanted to come to the islands but never had. I lined up several articles to write to help subsidize my trip. This way I can stay longer, see more and not have to worry about the drain on my bank account."

He liked the sound of her voice, the way her head tilted first one way then another as she talked. It made her dark hair move against her neck and bare shoulders. The wind off the ocean lifted sun-reddened strands and tossed them playfully about her face before letting them rest against skin that had been in the islands long enough to be tinted a beautiful apricot but not long enough to take on that lined, leathery look that he found repulsive. Arden Gentry had exceedingly touchable skin. And hair. And lips.

He cleared his throat. "Articles on what?"

She went on to explain that she was doing one for the travel section of the *Los Angeles Times,* another for a fashion magazine. She was also going to interview a local botanist and do an article for a gardening publication. He barely listened.

For the first time since he'd met Ellie, he was interested in a woman. It surprised him because he had never thought he'd want to be deeply involved with a woman again. Not that this would go beyond sharing a drink or casual conversation. But having met Arden, he felt that he might one day get over Ellie's death and actually seek another female companion.

He couldn't help being conscious of Arden Gentry physically. He'd have to be a blind eunuch not to be. She was a beautiful woman. And she had a serenity about her that he found appealing. He tried to concentrate on that and on her soft voice and keep his mind off other aspects of her.

From the moment he'd sat down, he'd tried not to look at her breasts and speculate whether that firm shape came from a strapless bra beneath her green cotton sundress or whether she had such a figure naturally. *What the hell. Go ahead and look.*

He voted strongly in favor of the latter theory. For with the caress of the cool wind, he could detect the merest puckering of her nipples. He felt stirrings of desire that he thought had been buried with Ellie and didn't know if he was ashamed or glad to feel them again.

He hadn't admired a woman's body since the last time he'd made love with Ellie. Gross displays of flesh did nothing to turn him on. He had the same interest in a woman's body as any man, but this…this was something different. It wasn't merely the flesh he found himself liking about Arden, but a personality, an evident intelligence, a certain disregard for his fame.

A spark of his old mischievousness flared. It made him wonder what she'd do if he leaned toward her and said, "Arden, please don't take offense, but for the first time since my wife died, I'm not disgusted by the way my body is responding to a woman."

There had been women. Bodies. Nothing more. Procured for him by well-intentioned friends who thought that erotically talented hands and mouths would cure him of all ills. If he could remember the drunken encounters later, he'd become sick with disgust for himself.

One night in Paris, where he'd publicly disgraced himself with a humiliating defeat on the courts, he'd found his own woman. She was the most sordid of whores. She was the punishment he doled out to himself. His penance. Later, when he was sober enough, he'd wept and hoped to God he hadn't been infected with something he'd have to be terribly embarrassed about.

That had been the turning point. The last chapter in the suicidal dissipation of Drew McCasslin. No one could save him but himself.

And then, besides himself, there was Matt to consider.

"How long have you lived in the islands?"

Arden's question yanked him back into the much brighter present. "Most of my adult life. After I began winning and making money on endorsements, it seemed like the ideal place for a bachelor to live. I was living in Honolulu when I met Ellie. She—"

His words came to an abrupt halt. He looked down into his water glass, and his shoulders assumed a defensive hunch. "I know about your wife, Drew," Arden said softly. "You don't have to apologize for mentioning her."

He saw in her eyes a compassion that was unlike the morbid curiosity he was accustomed to reading in inquiring faces. That alone compelled him to continue. "Her father was a naval officer stationed at Pearl. Eleanor Elizabeth Davidson. I told her it was too much for a woman her size—she was petite—to carry the name of a first lady and a queen."

"So you dubbed her Ellie." Arden was smiling encouragingly.

He answered with a chuckle. "Yeah, much to the irritation of her parents." He took a sip of water and drew idle circles in the condensation on the side of the glass. "Anyway, after she was killed, I wanted a change of scenery, so I moved here to Maui where it's much more isolated. I wanted to protect my privacy and shelter Matt from all the curiosity seekers."

Arden's whole body went still. "Matt?"

"My son." Drew beamed.

Her throat throbbed with the thudding of her heart, but she managed to reply. "Oh, yes. I've read about him, too."

"He's terrific. Smartest, cutest kid in the world. This morning, he—" Drew bit off his sentence. "Forgive me. I get carried away when I talk about him."

"You won't bore me," she said quickly.

"Given half a chance, yes, I will. Suffice it to say that he's been the one thing in my life recently that I could take pride in. We live right on the beach. He loves it."

Arden, striving for control, stared out at the horizon. The sun was a brassy reflection on the surface of the ocean. It hurt one's eyes to look at it from this angle. The island of Molokai was a gray-blue shadow against the northwestern horizon. Palm trees swayed with rhythmic grace in the gentle wind. Frothy white waves rolled in to kiss the sandy beach before receding.

"I can see why you'd want to live here. It's lovely."

"It's been great for me. A healing place, both mentally and physically."

He wondered why he was talking so openly to this woman. But he knew why. She inspired confidence and radiated understanding. A thick, sun-bleached brow arched quizzically over one of his eyes as a thought struck him. "You said there was no one at home to miss you. You aren't married?"

"I was. I'm divorced."

"No children?"

"A son. Joey." She faced him squarely. "He died."

He muttered an expletive before he sighed and said, "I'm sorry. I know how painful inadvertent reminders can be."

"Don't be sorry. The only thing I hate is when friends *won't* talk about him, as though he didn't exist."

"I've run into that, too. People avoid speaking Ellie's name, almost as though they're afraid I'll collapse into tears and embarrass them or something."

"Yes," Arden said. "I want Joey to be remembered. He was a beautiful child. Fun. Sweet."

"What happened? Accident?"

"No. When he was four months old, he contracted meningitis. It damaged his kidneys. He was on dialysis from then on, and I thought he'd live a fairly normal life, but…" Her voice faded into nothingness, and they were quiet for long moments, not even aware of the peripheral noises around them—laughter from a table on the other side of the patio, the whirring of the blender the bartender was using, a gleeful shout from the tennis courts below. "He got worse. There were complications, and before a suitable organ became available for a transplant, he died."

"Your husband?" Drew asked softly.

When had he taken her hand? She didn't remember. But suddenly she became aware of his holding it, rubbing the back of her knuckles with his thumb. "We were divorced before Joey's death. He more or less left Joey in my care."

"Mr. Gentry sounds like a real son of a bitch."

Arden laughed. His name wasn't Gentry, but she couldn't agree with Drew more. "You're right, he is."

They laughed softly and privately until they became aware of it. With the awareness came a flustered embarrassment. He released her hand promptly and leaned down to pick up his gear. "I've distracted you from your work long enough. Besides, I promised to baby-sit this afternoon so my housekeeper can go shopping."

"You have a housekeeper who tends to Matt? Is she…good with him?" Anxiety made her voice breathless.

"I don't know what I'd do without her. We had Mrs. Laani before Matt came along. When Ellie died, she took over and moved here with me. I trust her completely."

Arden could feel the taut muscles of her body easing with relief. "It's fortunate you have someone like her."

He stood and extended his hand. "I've enjoyed it, Arden."

She shook his hand. "So have I."

He seemed reluctant to let go of her hand. When he did, his fingertips lightly dragged against her palm. He wanted to do that to her cheek, to the underside of her arm, to her shoulder. He wanted to do what her hair did, sweep the skin of her neck and chest with seductive caresses. "I hope you enjoy the rest of your trip."

Her heartbeat had accelerated; there was a tickling sensation in the back of her throat. "I'm sure I will."

"Well, goodbye."

"Goodbye, Drew."

He took three steps away from her before coming to a stop. He weighed his decision for a few seconds before turning back. He was going to do something he hadn't done since he'd met Ellie Davidson. He was going to ask for a date.

"Uh, listen, I was wondering if you'd be around to-morrow."

"I don't know," Arden said with cool tact. Actually, she was holding her breath, offering up a silent prayer. "Why?"

"Well, Gary and I play tomorrow morning." He shifted from one sneakered foot to the other. "And I was thinking that if you were going to be around, maybe you could watch a game or two and then we could have lunch somewhere here at the resort."

She lowered her eyes, almost closing them in ju-bilation.

"If you'd rather not—" he began.

"No," she said quickly, lifting her head again. "I mean, yes, that would be… I'd like that."

"Great!" he said, his confidence flooding back. Why the hell did it matter so much that she'd consented? He could have a woman anytime he wanted one. And not for lunch. But it had been damned important for Arden to say yes. "Then I'll see you here sometime around noon?" he asked, trying to steal a glance at the legs primly crossed beneath the table. Maybe she had thick ankles.

"I'll be here."

Her ankles were gorgeous. "'Bye." His lips opened wide over a devastating smile.

"'Bye." She hoped her own lips weren't visibly trem-bling when she returned it.

His easy, athletic stride carried him quickly across the patio. She watched him go, admiring the effort-less way he moved and the athletic shape of his body.

She liked him! And she was so glad she did. He was a nice man. An extraordinary man, to be sure, but a man. Not a faceless, nameless question mark in her mind any longer. A man with an identity and a personality. A man who had experienced love and pain and bore them both well.

She had won his trust, and that gave her a twinge of guilt. Would he have invited her to lunch if she'd told him who she was? Would he have been as eager to see her again if he knew she had been the woman artificially impregnated with his semen? Would he have confided in her so openly if she had come right out and said, "I'm the surrogate mother you and Ellie hired. I bore your son"?

CHAPTER TWO

IN HER ABSENCE, the maid had cleaned her room and left the air conditioner going full blast. Dropping her purse and notebook on a table, Arden first adjusted the thermostat on the wall, then slid open the wide glass door that led out to her private ocean-front terrace. The room was exorbitantly expensive, but the view was well worth every penny.

She drew in a great breath, and as she quelled it, breathed a name: Drew McCasslin. Her quarry. At last she had met him, talked to him, heard him speak her son's name. Matt.

It didn't take her long to peel off the sundress and wrap herself in a terry robe. She stepped out into the embracing Hawaiian warmth and sat down in one of two chairs on the terrace. Propping her heels against the seat of the chair, she rested her chin on her knees as she stared out at the seascape.

Drew had assumed that Gentry was her married name. What he didn't know was that she'd thrown off that name like an animal shedding old skin as soon as she had filed for divorce. She wanted nothing to do with Ronald Lowery, even his hateful name.

Just when she'd think the anger was finally gone, it would sneak up and grab her, as it was doing now. It was as silent and intangible as a fog, but just as blanketing, just as blinding, just as suffocating.

Would she never forget the humiliation of that night he had first broached the subject? She had been in the kitchen of their Beverly Hills home preparing dinner. It was a rare evening when Ron came home directly after office hours. But that afternoon he'd called saying that no babies were due, he'd made hospital rounds early and he'd be leaving the office in time to have dinner with her. In a marriage that had quickly proved disappointing for Arden, even having dinner together was an event. If Ron was going to try to make things better, Arden would do her part.

"What's the occasion?" she had asked when he came in carrying a bottle of vintage wine.

He kissed her peremptorily on the cheek. "A celebration of sorts," he said offhandedly. She knew from experience that he liked to keep secrets, not for the pleasure they would eventually bring someone else, but because they gave him a sense of superiority. She'd learned long ago not to press him for information. More often than not, his surprises were unpleasant.

"The pot roast will be done in a minute. Why don't you go in and see Joey? He's in the den watching 'Sesame Street.'"

"For God's sake, Arden. I just got home. The last thing I want to do is listen to Joey's chatter. Fix me a drink."

Stupidly, she had obeyed. As was her habit. "Joey's your son, Ron," she said as she handed him his Scotch and water. "He worships you, but you do so few things together."

"He can't do normal things."

She hated the way he dashed down his drink and then shoved the glass toward her with an unspoken command to refill it. "That's why it's even more important that you find—"

"Christ! I should have known that if I came home with good news, you'd have to spoil it with your bitching. I'll be in the living room. Call me when dinner's ready. *Our* dinner. I want to talk to you about something important, so feed Joey ahead of time and put him to bed."

With that, he had stalked out of the room, and Arden had taken immense pleasure in noting that his pants bagged in the seat. When she had met Ron as a medical student, he'd been proud of his athletic physique. Too many cocktail parties later, his stomach was no longer flat and trim. His buttocks were getting flatter and his hips wider. He wasn't nearly as suave and debonair as he used to be. And he knew it. All he had to fall back on now was the gynecological practice that he had sacrificed everything else for. Even her love.

She made an effort that night to be congenial and attractive when she called him into the dining room for dinner. Joey had been shuttled away after a hasty and insincere kiss from his father. The meal she'd prepared was sumptuous. In those days, she had taken pleasure in cooking.

"Well, now," she said, smiling across the table at her husband as he finished his second slice of apple pie, "are you going to tell me what we're celebrating?"

"The end to all our problems," he said expansively.

The end to all her problems would be to see Joey completely well and living the normal life of a three-year-old. But she asked politely, "What problems? The clinic's going well, isn't it?"

"Yeah, but…" He sighed. "Arden, you know lately I've needed to…relax, have some fun. All I hear day in and day out is women griping about cramps or screaming in labor."

Arden swallowed a tart rebuke. Her father hadn't felt that way about the practice he'd spent a lifetime making one of the finest in Los Angeles. He hadn't felt intolerance of his patients' pain, imagined or not, the way Ron did.

"I've been gambling a little, and well…" He shrugged and grinned at her with what he considered to be boyish appeal. "I'm busted. In debt up to my armpits."

It took her a moment or two to absorb what he'd just said. Then a full minute to fight down her panic. Her first thought was Joey. His medical care was incredibly expensive. "How…how much in debt?"

"Enough that I might have to sell the practice or put it in hock so deep I'd never get it out no matter how many brats I deliver."

The dinner she'd just eaten almost came up. "Oh, my God. My father's practice."

"Goddammit!" Ron roared, slamming his fist down on the table so hard that china and crystal clattered. "It's not *his,* it's *mine.* Mine, do you hear me? He was a country doctor with outmoded methods until I converted that women's clinic into a modernized—"

"Factory. That's how you run it. Without compassion or feeling for the women you treat."

"I help them."

"Oh, granted, you're a fine doctor. One of the best.

But you have no emotion, Ron. You don't see that woman you're treating as a person. You only care about her checkbook."

"You don't mind living here and being a member of the grandest country club—"

"*You* wanted the house and the club, not me."

"When a woman leaves my office, she feels on top of the world."

"You have a terrific bedside manner. I know that, Ron. I'm not stupid. But it's all for show. You can charm a person into thinking you care for them."

He settled back in his chair, his legs stretched out in front of him, ankles crossed. His expression was sly. "Speaking from experience?" he drawled.

She lowered her eyes to her plate. It hadn't taken long after their marriage for her to realize that all his romancing and professions of love had been to gain himself, not a loving wife, but a well-established, well-paying practice. "Yes. I know why you married me. You wanted my father's clinic. I think you purposely badgered him until he had his stroke and died. Now you have everything you want." Her anger had been building up to this point. Now she ended on a shout. "And now you're telling me that you're about to lose it all because you've gambled it away!"

"As usual, you're jumping to conclusions and not listening to half of what I'm saying." He poured a generous glass of wine and downed it. "I've been given an opportunity to make a lot of money."

"How? Drugs?"

He glowered at her but continued. "Do you remember when I got that baby for a couple to adopt about a year ago? They wanted no hassle, no red tape, just a baby with legal documents."

"I remember," she said cautiously. What was he considering? Black-market babies? It wouldn't be beyond him. She shuddered.

"I had an appointment with friends of theirs today. A *secret* appointment. Very hush-hush. Because they're celebrities." He paused dramatically, and she knew he wanted her to beg him for their identity. Later, she would regret that she hadn't. "This couple wants a baby more than any I've seen. They've tried everything for her to get pregnant. Nothing's worked, but he's been checked out. A loaded pistol if I've ever seen one," he said lewdly. Arden listened stoically, with no change of expression. "I said I'd see what I could do about finding them a baby to adopt with no hassle. But the woman said no dice. She wants this to be her husband's baby."

"I'm not sure I follow you."

"The fruit of his loins, his seed," he intoned theatrically. "They want me to find them a suitable surrogate mother and impregnate her with his sperm. *Presto!* They have a baby."

"I've heard of surrogate mothers. How do you feel about it? Can it work? Would you do it for them?"

He laughed. "Hell, yes, I'll do it for them for the money they're talking about. One hundred thousand dollars. Fifty for the mother. Fifty for me."

Arden gasped. "One hundred... They must be *wealthy* celebrities."

"All they demand is a healthy baby and absolute secrecy. Secrecy, Arden. Nonreportable income. They've said they'll pay me in cash."

It was unethical, if not illegal. She couldn't imagine any woman consenting to such subterfuge. "Where will you find a woman willing to have a baby, only to give it up?"

His eyes bored into hers, and a chill slithered down her spine. For ponderous moments, they stared at each other over the corner of the table. "I don't think I'll have to look too far," he said.

Her face drained of all color. Surely he couldn't mean *her*. His own wife! "Ron," she said, hating the note of desperation and panic in her voice, "you're not suggesting that I—"

"Exactly."

She bolted out of her chair and spun away, but he was a step behind her, nearly wrenching her arm out of its socket when he spun her around to face him. His face was florid, and he showered her with spittle as he growled, "Think for once, Arden. If you do this for me, we get all the money. I…we don't have to divide it with anyone."

"I'll try to forget we ever had this conversation, Ron. Please let go of my arm. You're hurting me."

"You'll hurt even more if your sweet tush gets booted out of this house you love to seclude yourself in. And what about Joey? His treatments are eating us alive. And your precious father's legacy. Are you going to let it go down the tubes because of your sterling principles?"

She yanked her arm free and would have run from him, but what he'd said made her think despite the insanity of it all. She couldn't let Ron gamble away her father's life's work. And Joey! What would they do if they couldn't afford his medical bills?

"I'm sure this…this couple didn't have their doctor's wife in mind when they sought you out."

"They'd never know. They don't want to know the mother and don't want her to know them. They intend to pass the kid off as their own. All they want is a healthy woman to deliver them a healthy baby. A vessel."

"Is that all I am to you, Ron? A means of bailing you out? A money-making *vessel?*"

"Take it from one who knows. You're not using that equipment for anything else. You might just as well have a baby with it."

Her whole body sagged under the weight of his insult. It was true. The infrequency of sex between them was an ongoing argument. Arden didn't have an aversion to sex. She had grown up educated to it by her father's frankness, with a respect for its sanctity, with a healthy anticipation for it. What she did have an aversion to was Ron's kind of sex. It was without foreplay, without tenderness, without love. She had submitted for years until she couldn't stand any more and had begun to make frequent excuses.

Rather than begin that stale argument, which invariably led to his near raping her, she said, "I don't want to have a baby. Another man's baby. I have Joey to consider. I'm worn out half the time when I come in from the hospital. I don't think I'm physically up to it. Certainly not psychologically."

"You're up to it if you make up your mind that you are. And forget that crap about another man's baby. It's a biological process. Sperm and egg. Slam, bam, one baby coming up."

She turned away in revulsion. How could he be so

callous about a miracle he witnessed every day? She didn't know why she was even standing there discussing this with him, except that maybe she saw it as her way out, too.

"What would we tell people? I mean, when I came home from the hospital without a baby."

"We'd tell them that the baby had been stillborn, that we were devastated and wanted no funeral service, no memorial. Nothing."

"But what about the hospital staff? There are strict rules forbidding doctors to treat family members. How do you make the switch, give my...the baby to a woman who wasn't pregnant and pass mine off as dead?"

"Don't worry about any of that, Arden," he said impatiently. "I'll take care of all those details. Money shuts people up. The delivery-room nurses are loyal. They'll do what I tell them to do."

Apparently, he was accustomed to such intrigue, pulling off deals. Such things were foreign to Arden, and the scope of possible repercussions made her uncomfortable.

"How do we...do it?"

Now that he thought she was going to comply, his excitement heightened. "First we have to make sure you're not pregnant." He smirked a nasty grin. "But then that would be almost impossible, wouldn't it? I'll show them your medical history, which is without blemish. You had no trouble with your first pregnancy. We sign a contract. I do the procedure at the office."

"What if I don't conceive?"

"You'll conceive. I'll see to it."

She shivered. "I have to think about this, Ron."

"What's to think—" he began on a shout. But when

he saw her chin lift stubbornly, he softened his approach and relied on his charm. "Sure. I know. Give yourself a few days, but they want an answer by the end of the week."

She told him her answer the next morning. He was thrilled. Then she stated her conditions.

"You *what?*" he snarled.

"I said that I want half the money upon delivery, along with divorce papers, signed, sealed and delivered. There will be no intimacies between us until I deliver. As soon as I leave the hospital with my money, I never want to see you again."

"You won't leave me, baby. If anyone gets dumped around here, it will be you! You care too much about the clinic's reputation to leave me."

"I did. While Father was alive, it was everything it was supposed to be. I strongly suspect that under your auspices it will gradually begin to crumble. I won't be there to see it. It's no longer something I can take pride in." She drew herself up straight. "You used me to get the clinic. Now do with it as you will. I'll have this baby because the money will allow me and Joey to be free of you. You've used me for the last time, Dr. Ronald Lowery."

He'd met all her terms. He never told her, but Arden was fairly certain that his creditors were pressuring him. A desperate man didn't have any choice but to accept conditions. When she left the hospital that day, feeling soiled and used and empty, but free, she hadn't regretted her decision. The money her nine months' job had earned her would enable her to take better care of Joey.

But now, almost two years later, she had ambivalent feelings about her decision to bear the child of a stranger. The McCasslins had had their heartfelt wish granted when she bore a baby boy. He had enriched their lives and given Drew an anchor to cling to, a reason for living when the rest of his world fell apart. Shouldn't that alone absolve Arden of any guilt she felt? Why did she continue to fault herself? In any event, it was too late now to alter history.

She hadn't moved as she reviewed the event that had finally brought her to that lovely island. Now she stood up and stretched muscles that were stiff from having been in one position so long. She spent a quiet evening in her room, writing some, mostly wondering when she would tell Drew McCasslin who she was and how she could ask him to let her see her son.

"HI." HE JOGGED over to the edge of the court and looked up at her where she sat at her customary table near the ledge. "You look as cool as a cucumber."

"And you look as hot as hell."

He laughed, surprised. "And that's exactly how I feel. Gary's giving me a run for my money."

"I'd say he's getting his money's worth, too." Arden had been watching the strenuous match for the last two games, and Drew was playing at what she knew must have been his full potential before grief and too much alcohol crippled his game.

He seemed pleased that she'd noticed. "Yeah, well, I've managed to get in a few good shots," he conceded humbly. "I'm working up a hearty appetite for lunch."

"Don't rush on my account. I'm enjoying the exhibition."

He bowed at the waist and trotted back onto the

court, calling to an exhausted-looking Gary that rest time was over. Drew took the next game without granting a point. On Gary's serve, however, the club pro came back with a vengeance. The game went to deuce several times before Drew took two points in a row to win the match.

Ignoring the cheering girls who had again collected like bright butterflies against the fence, he comically staggered over to the wall and looked up at Arden. "Isn't the matador supposed to throw the lady the bull's ear or tail or something to dedicate the bullfight to her?"

She laughed. "I think so, yes. But please don't cut off Gary's ear."

"I don't have anything to throw you except a tennis ball. Or a sweaty towel."

"I prefer the ball."

He tossed it up to her, and she caught it deftly, bowing her head over it in regal acceptance. "Order me four glasses of water and I'll be with you in a minute."

Arden watched as he slung his bag over his shoulder and loped off in the direction of the locker room. He waved at her once before disappearing through the thick metal doors.

Had he ever thought about the woman who had borne his child? she wondered as she signaled the waiter and ordered his water and another glass of iced tea for herself. Had he ever considered how she must have felt carrying a part of him in her body? Intimacy without intimacy.

THE DAY RON determined she was fertile—he had taken her temperature with a specialized thermometer for several days in a row—he told her to come to his office after hours. Naked and vulnerable, she had lain on the examination table, her feet propped in stirrups while he inserted what he called a cervical cup. Then he injected the frozen seminal fluid into the receptacle. It would hold the fluid against the door of her womb until she painlessly extracted it at home. With any luck, the results would be positive.

"You're getting no more excited over this than you do over the real thing, Arden," he said, leering down at her.

"Just hurry and finish," she said wearily. His lurid jokes no longer had the power to provoke her.

"Aren't you the least bit curious? Hmm? Don't you wonder what he looks like? Who he is? I have to admit he's a handsome fellow. Are you wishing you could get a little turned on beforehand so it would seem more official?" His hand grasped her breast and squeezed painfully. "I could accommodate you. Everyone's gone home."

She slapped his hand away, and he laughed cruelly. Did he truly think that slack-lipped, insinuating smile was going to send her into the throes of passion? She looked away as a lone tear rolled down her temple. "Just finish, please."

"We do it again tomorrow," he said when she sat up.

"Tomorrow?"

"And the next day. Three days while you could be ovulating." He leaned against the table and stroked her thigh. "Then we sit back and wait and see."

She prayed that she'd conceive on that first attempt. After subjecting herself to Ron's lewdness, she didn't think she could stand to go through with it again next month. Her prayers had been answered. Within six weeks, Ron was certain that she was pregnant. He informed the couple that their surrogate mother had conceived. He told Arden they were ecstatic.

"You be damn sure to take care of yourself," he warned. "I don't want anything to mess this up now."

"Nor do I," she had said, closing the door to the bedroom in his face.

She didn't think about the life she was carrying as a baby, a personality, a human being. She thought of it only as a means to let her and Joey have a better chance at happiness, free of Ron's greed and selfishness.

During the weeks of morning sickness and on the long, exhausting days she drove Joey to and from the hospital, she tried not to resent the fetus she could never let herself love. When friends congratulated her and Ron on the pregnancy, she forced herself to smile and accept their good wishes and Ron's proprietary arm around her shoulders.

The day she first felt the infant move, she knew a moment of incredible joy. It was quickly suppressed, pushed aside, hidden in some secret corner of her mind. Only at night, alone in her room, as she spread soothing lotion on her distended abdomen did she allow herself to wonder about the child. Would it be male or female? Blue eyed or brown? Or would it inherit her green eyes?

And that was when she'd begun to wonder about the father, about whose seed she carried. What was he like? Was he kind? Would he be a good parent? Did he love his wife? Surely he did. She loved him enough to let another woman bear his child. Had they been lying together when he collected—

"PENNY FOR THEM."

"Oh!" Arden gasped, flattened her hand over her chest and whirled around to see the subject of her thoughts leaning down over her, smiling. His hand was on the top of her chair, close to her bare back.

"I'm sorry," he said, genuinely contrite. "I didn't mean to scare you."

"No, no. It's okay." She knew her cheeks were burning and that she looked as disconcerted as she felt. "I was a million miles away."

"I hope the daydream was worth the trip."

His eyes were unbelievably blue against his dark tan, and they were ringed with thick, brown lashes, gilded on the tips. His teeth flashed whitely. He smelled wonderfully of soap and an elusive and expensive cologne. Apparently, he intended to let the sun dry his hair. Damp strands lay rakishly on his forehead.

Because of what she'd been thinking, Arden didn't want to see him as a man with a face and a body. A handsome face. A sexy body. Her cheeks burned as she thought of that life-generating injection Ron had made into her body. She looked away, wetting her lips nervously. "It wasn't really a daydream," she said lightly, dismissively, she hoped. "Just musings. The surroundings are hypnotic. The lull of the surf. The sighing of the wind. You know."

He relaxed in the chair across from hers. He was wearing ivory-colored slacks and a navy polo shirt. He took a long drink from one of the glasses of ice water and said, "Sometimes I can go down to the beach in front of my house, particularly in the evenings, and sit for an hour or more without ever knowing that time has passed. It's like sleeping, except I'm not asleep."

"I think our minds have a way of shutting down when they know we need escape."

"Ah-ha, so that's what you were doing? Trying to escape me."

Arden laughed, thinking that no woman in her right mind would want to escape a man who looked like him when he smiled. "No. Not before you buy my lunch, anyway," she teased.

"That sounds like Matt. He demands a treat before he grants a hug and a kiss." When he saw her startled expression, he cursed under his breath. "Arden, ah... hell. Arden, I didn't mean that the way it sounded. There are no strings attached to this lunch. I mean..."

"I know what you meant," she said, smiling again. "And I didn't take offense. Truly."

He partially lowered one eyelid as he assessed her mouth, making no secret of the fact that it appealed to him. "It bears thinking about, though, doesn't it? Kissing, that is."

"I don't know," she said gruffly.

She had debated all morning over what to wear. Now she wished she hadn't been quite so adventurous. For months after Joey's death, she had wallowed in misery, letting herself become slovenly. Before she embarked on this mission, she had exercised diligently, begun eating right, worked on her nails, her complexion, had her hair cut and bought a new wardrobe of coordinates that stretched her limited budget. She was amazed at the results. Had Ron repressed her that much? She looked better than she ever had. That day was no exception.

The black, elasticized, strapless tube top clung provocatively to her breasts, detailing every nuance of their shape. The trim white skirt was fashionably cut and buttoned down the left side from waist to hem. She'd left the buttons undone halfway up her thigh. Her legs looked tanned and silky against the white cloth. Her sandals were flat-heeled black patent leather and had thongs that wrapped around her ankles. Her only jewelry was a white bangle bracelet and large white hoops in her ears.

Standing in front of the mirror in her room, she had thought she looked smart. Smart and chic. Why was she now feeling she had dressed seductively?

Because Drew's eyes, taking a long, appraising tour with evident appreciation for everything he saw, made her feel seductive. She knew he could detect the hardening of her nipples. She'd never thought of herself as a sensual person, but now, with those azure eyes lazily tracking her, every sensory receptor in her body seemed to be going wild.

"Maybe we should start with lunch and go on from there," he said when his eyes eventually returned to hers.

"All right."

CHAPTER THREE

HE ESCORTED HER to one of the restaurants in the resort. With a deference reserved for VIPs, the maître d' seated them at an ocean-view table. Though the luncheon diners were dressed in casual clothes for the most part, there was an underlying elegance to the room with its mint-green and peach décor, black lacquered chairs and vases of fresh flowers scattered throughout.

"Cocktails, sir?" the waiter asked.

"Arden?"

"A virgin Mary, please."

"Perrier and lime," Drew said to the waiter, who backed away with a silent nod.

Drew reached for a bread stick, snapped it in two and handed her one half. "Did you order that on my account?" he asked in clipped tones.

"What?" She bristled at his curtness. "The drink?"

"The drink that isn't really a 'drink.' If you want something else, order it." He had the appearance of a tightly wound coil about to spring. "I promise not to grab it from you and guzzle it down. I'm past the sweating-and-shaking stage." As though to prove that, he was taking inordinate care in buttering his half of the bread stick.

Arden set her bread stick on the plate and folded her

clenched hands in her lap. "I'll order what I please, Mr. McCasslin." Her frigid declaration brought his head up. "If anyone knows your name, he knows you had a drinking problem. But please don't talk to me like I'm some missionary who has appointed herself to rescue you from demon rum. If I didn't think you were past your sweating-and-shaking stage, I wouldn't be here with you in the first place."

"I've made you mad."

"Yes, you have. And I'll thank you never to do my thinking for me again."

The waiter brought their drinks and placed menus in front of them. Arden stared levelly at Drew across the table. She was nettled and was making no secret of it.

"I'm sorry," he said when the waiter withdrew. "I'm sensitive to criticism, even though lately I've deserved every word of it. I've become the classic paranoid, looking for slights when none are there."

She was studying the pattern of the silver and cursing herself for being so prickly. Did she want to win his friendship or scare him off? When she lifted her green eyes, they had softened considerably. "I'm sorry, too. For years I let my husband do my thinking and speaking for me. It's a dangerous rut for a woman, or anyone, to get into. I think we touched sore spots at the same time." Diplomatically, she smiled and lifted her glass. "Besides, I *like* tomato juice."

Laughing, he raised his own glass and clinked it against hers. "To the loveliest lady on the island. From now on, I'll take everything you say or do at face value."

She wished he had composed another toast, one that had less to do with honesty, but she smiled back at him.

"What do you like to eat?" He opened the embossed menu.

"Name it."

"Liver."

She burst out with a spontaneous laugh. "That's the one thing I *won't* eat in any form or fashion."

His grin was wide and white and wonderful. "Good. I can't stand the stuff, either. I think this friendship was predestined."

As Arden scanned the menu, she couldn't help thinking that Matt would probably grow up hating liver, too.

She ordered a shrimp salad that was served in a fresh pineapple boat garnished with avocado and orchids. It was almost too pretty to eat. Drew had a small fillet and garden salad. During lunch, they got acquainted. When asked, Arden told him that her parents were dead, that her mother had died while Arden was studying creative writing at UCLA and that her doctor father had died of a stroke a few years after that. She went into no details, especially on her father's gynecological practice.

Drew had grown up in Oregon, where his mother still lived. His father had died some years before. Drew had begun playing tennis in junior high school.

"That was before very many public schools had tennis teams. When the coach saw that I had a knack for the game, he asked me to be on the new team he was setting up. I really preferred baseball, but he kept pressuring me, so I gave in. I soon became obsessed with getting better. By the time I got to high school, I was winning local tournaments."

"But you went on to college."

"Yes, much to the consternation of my manager, Ham Davis, who took me on in my sophomore year. Exams were always getting in the way of practice and play, but I knew my body wouldn't let me play tennis, at least not competitively, the rest of my life, so I thought I'd better prepare for the day when I couldn't."

"You caught up, though, didn't you? Once you started playing the circuits, you were an instant winner." She plopped the last chunk of papaya into her mouth. They had ordered fresh fruit compotes for dessert and were finishing them and sipping coffee.

"I had some good years." He shrugged modestly. "I had the advantage of a few years' maturity, too, and didn't stay out all night and carouse like some players do the first time they tour." He took a sip of coffee. "The system is unbalanced. When you first start out, it's expensive as hell. Transportation, lodging, food. Then, when you make it, when you're winning prize money and getting endorsement contracts, everything's paid for."

He shook his head, laughing. "I risked losing some valuable contracts when even the best of tennis shoes couldn't keep me from stumbling onto the court after a drinking binge."

"You'll get them back."

His head came up to search her eyes. "That's what Ham says. Do you really think so?"

Was her opinion so important to him, or did he need any form of encouragement? "Yes. Once they see you play the way you've been playing, once you've won a tournament or two, you'll be back on top."

"There are younger guys every day to take my place."

"Can't hold a candle," she said with a dismissive wave of her hand.

He smiled crookedly. "I wish I had your confidence in me."

"Uh, Mr. McCasslin, excuse us, but…"

A dark scowl wrinkled Drew's thick blond brows as he turned in his chair to see the couple standing timorously behind him. They wore matching Hawaiian shirts in a gaudy floral print and labeled themselves tourists in myriad, unmistakable ways. "Yes?" At best, Drew's greeting was chilly.

"We…uh…" The lady hesitated. "We were wondering if you'd give us your autograph for our son. We're from Albuquerque, and he's just now getting into tennis, and he thinks you're wonderful."

"He has a poster of you in his room," the man said. "He—"

"I don't have anything to write on," Drew said, and rudely turned his back on them.

"I do," Arden chimed in, noticing the embarrassed, discomfited expressions on their sunburned faces. She reached into her bag and took out the tennis ball Drew had tossed her from the court. "Why don't you sign this for them, Drew?" she suggested softly, extending the ball to him.

At first, his eyes were hooded and rebellious, and she thought he might very well tell her to mind her own damn business. But when he saw the gentle chastisement in her eyes, he smiled and reached for the ball. Taking the pen the woman had found in her purse, he scrawled his signature on the fuzzy surface of the tennis ball.

"Thank you so much, Mr. McCasslin. I can't tell you what this souvenir will mean to our son. He—"

"Come on, Lois, and let the man enjoy his lunch. We hated to bother you, Mr. McCasslin, but we just wanted to tell you we can't wait to see you play again. Good luck."

Drew stood and shook hands with the man and kissed the lady's hand, an action that almost caused her to faint, if her fluttering eyelashes were any indication. "Good luck to your son, too. Have a nice vacation."

They ambled away, studying their precious souvenir and murmuring how nice he'd been and that all those reporters who said he was nasty and belligerent were wrong.

Drew looked over at Arden, and she prepared herself for a blistering put-down. Instead, his voice was husky when he asked, "Are you finished?" When she nodded, he put his hand under her elbow and helped her from her chair. They left the restaurant and didn't speak until they were wending their way through the landscaped pathways that connected the various buildings of the resort.

"Thank you," he said simply.

She stopped on the path and looked up at him. "For what?"

"For subtly warning me that I was behaving like a bastard."

She found his eyes too compelling to look into, so she studied the third button on his shirt, but was instantly distracted by the wedge of chest hair above it. "I shouldn't have interfered."

"I'm damn glad you did. You see, that's another thing I'm overly sensitive about. For months after Ellie died, I was hounded by reporters for a 'comment' every time I stuck my nose out the door. Soon I became furious whenever someone even recognized me in public."

"I can imagine that having such a high public profile can be trying." What did that hair feel like to touch? It was a gorgeous golden color against his tanned skin.

"Under the best of circumstances it's trying. Under the worst, it's hell. When I was at my lowest, I had crowds jeering at me from the spectator stands, throwing things at me because I was playing so badly. Irrationally, I blamed them. My fans were deserting me because I drank, and I drank because my fans were deserting me. It was a vicious cycle. I'm still wary when people approach me, thinking they may very well have an insult to throw in my face."

"What I just witnessed was nothing short of unabashed hero worship." Forcing her eyes away from his chest and her mind from the erotic thoughts it incurred, she looked up at him. "You've still got thousands of fans just waiting for you to get back on the circuit."

He stared down into her sincere face for a long while and almost got lost in the swirling green depths of her eyes. She smelled of flowers. She looked both cool and assured, yet warm and giving. He raised his hand, intending to touch the sable hair that blew gently against her cheek, but changed his mind and dropped it back to his side. At last, he said, "Meeting you is one of the nicest things that's happened to me in a long time, Arden."

"I'm glad," she said, meaning it.

"I'll walk you to your room."

They went through the lobby of the main building. At the elevator, he said, "Wait here for me. I'll be right back."

Before she could wonder what he was doing, he had dashed off. She punched the up button but had to let two empty elevators go before he came running back carrying something wrapped in white paper. "Sorry," he said breathlessly. "Which floor?"

They took the elevator up, and Arden's female curiosity over his package was killing her. His eyes were dancing. If this was to be a surprise, she wasn't going to spoil it for him.

At her door, she stuck out her hand. "Thank you for a lovely lunch."

He didn't take her hand. He unwrapped the paper and shook out a plumeria and orchid lei. Dropping the wrapping negligently on the hallway floor, he held the lei over her head.

"You've probably been presented with dozens of these since you've been here, but I wanted to give you one."

The heady fragrance of the flowers and his nearness made oxygen scarce. Her senses reeled. Emotion congested her throat, but she managed to strangle out, "No. I've never had one. Thank you. The flowers are beautiful."

"You enhance the flowers."

He slipped the ring of perfect blossoms over her head and settled it gently on her bare shoulders. The fragile petals were dewy and cool against her skin. He didn't withdraw his hands but laid them lightly on her shoulders. Confusion and conflicting emotions swamped her, and she bowed her head.

The man and everything about him overwhelmed her, filled her head, her heart. He subjected her body to a lethargy that was foreign, but so delicious. She longed to succumb to it and sag against his hardness. The flowers lying on her breast trembled with her erratic heartbeat. Tentatively, she touched them with palsied fingers.

In her peripheral vision, she saw his fingers reaching toward hers, and then they brushed, touched, entwined. His were dark with springy golden hairs on the knuckles. They were warm, sure, strong. She raised her head and looked at him with eyes as dew-sparkled as the flowers.

"Aloha," he whispered. He leaned down and kissed her first on one cheek, then the other. He rested his lips against the corner of hers. There, with his beard-roughened cheek lightly touching her, he sighed her name. "Arden."

His thumbs traveled over her collarbone, while his breath fanned her temple and teased her ear. "Now that lunch has been dispensed with…"

Oh, no! she groaned silently as her heart sank. *Here comes the sleazy proposition.*

He pulled back and released her shoulders. "How about dinner?"

EVEN AS SHE dressed for the evening, she knew she should have begged off when Drew asked her for the date. It would have been logical for her to have said, "I'm sorry, and it sounds wonderful, but I should stay here tonight and work on an article."

Instead, she had heard herself say, "I'd love to, Drew." He had smiled and turned toward the elevator. She had entered her room in a cloud of romantic feeling. It hadn't taken long, however, for her to remember why she had contrived to meet Drew.

For a few minutes, while his hands had been touching her and his breath stirring her hair, she had forgotten her son. She had been thinking of Drew not as her son's father but solely as a man, a man she realized she was dangerously attracted to.

After her dismal marriage and hideous sex life with Ron, she had thought she'd never be interested in having a relationship with a man again. It came as a shock to her how much she was anticipating another few hours in Drew's company. And for all the wrong reasons.

It would have served her purpose better had Drew not been so sexually appealing…and widowed…and lonely himself. Wouldn't it have made her task less complicated to find her child's parents both alive and well, the father a jolly sort? Short, soft, round and balding? At the outset, the looks and personalities of the couple hadn't been a factor. She'd been interested only in locating the child she'd given birth to but had never seen. It hadn't been easy.

It was like opening a wound every time she remembered the gray, rainy day she had buried Joey. Never in her life, not even after the deaths of her father and mother, had she felt so alone. After obtaining her divorce, she had devoted herself to taking care of Joey. For the last few months of his life, he had been hospitalized. She watched him deteriorate with each day and struggled against praying for the death of another child so Joey might have the needed kidney. God couldn't be expected to grant such a prayer, so she never actually verbalized it.

When at last the time came, he had died as sweetly as he had lived, asking her please not to cry, saying that he would save her a bed next to his in heaven. For hours after he'd breathed his last, she held his thin hand in hers and stared into his peaceful face, memorizing it.

Ron had put on a performance of abject grief at the funeral service for those few of his friends who had attended. Arden was sickened by his hypocrisy. Valiantly, Joey had hid his disappointment each time Ron failed to come to the hospital to see him, as promised.

After the funeral, Ron cornered her. "Do you still have any of that money you screwed me out of?"

"That's none of your business. I earned that money."

"Goddam you, I need it."

She couldn't help noticing that the ravages of dissipation were becoming more and more pronounced. He wore desperation like a banner. It generated not the least amount of compassion in her.

"That's your problem."

"For God's sake, Arden. Help me. Just this once, and I promise—"

She had slammed the limousine door in his face and demanded that the driver leave immediately. Even at his son's funeral, Ron's thoughts were only for himself.

For the next several months, she was so immersed in grief that she didn't know one day from the next. She lived in a vacuum of despair. Only on paper could she communicate her feelings, reconcile herself to them. An essay she wrote on losing a child was sold to a ladies' magazine, and it won public acclaim. She was asked to write others but had no ambition to do so. She felt that she was only filling time until her own death, for she had nothing else to live for.

Except that other child.

It came to her quietly one day. She *did* have a reason

for living. Somewhere in the world, she had another child. It was at that point she made up her mind to find it. Never was it her intention to disrupt the child's life. She wouldn't be that cruel to parents who had gone to such great lengths to get that child. She only wanted to see it. To know its name, its sex. She had asked Ron to give her anesthesia just before the moment of delivery so she'd never remember the birth itself or inadvertently learn anything about the child she had borne for someone else.

"What do you mean there are no records?" she had demanded in frustration on her first attempt to gain information.

The administrator's face remained unperturbed. "I mean, Mrs. Lowery, that your records seem to have been misplaced and I've yet to locate them. In a hospital this size, these things happen."

"Especially when an influential doctor asks you or pays you to 'misplace' a file. And my name is Ms. Gentry!"

It was the same story everywhere. Birth records both at city hall and at the hospital had mysteriously disappeared. But to Arden it was no mystery at all who was responsible for such a puzzling loss of efficiency.

She didn't know the attorney who had drawn up the official papers. But he had to have been hired by Ron and therefore wouldn't tell her a thing if she found him. Ron, guessing correctly that after Joey's death she'd feel compelled to locate her second child, had gone before her, putting everyone involved on guard against feeding her one scrap of information.

The obstetric nurse who had helped her through her

labor was her last resort. She found the nurse working in a charity clinic that specialized in abortions.

Arden could detect her fear immediately when the nurse spotted her as she left the clinic one afternoon. "Do you remember me?" Arden began without preface.

The nurse's furtive eyes darted around the parking lot as though looking for some means of escape. "Yes," she whispered fearfully.

"You know what happened to my baby," Arden guessed, intuitively knowing the statement to be a fact.

"No!" Earnest as the answer was, Arden knew she was lying.

"Miss Hancock," she pleaded, "please tell me anything you know. A name. Please. That's all I ask. Just a name."

"I can't," the woman cried, and covered her face with her hands. "I can't. He…he watches me, told me that if I ever said anything to you, he'd tell them about me."

"Who watches you? My ex-husband?" The woman jerked her head up and down in confirmation. "What is he using to blackmail you? Don't be afraid of him. I can help you. We can turn him over to the police—"

"No! My God, no. You don't…" She choked back racking sobs. "You don't understand. I was on… I had a little trouble with Percodan. He found out about it. He had me fired from the hospital, but got me a job here. And…" Her narrow shoulders shook. "And he said if I ever told you anything, he'd turn me over to the police."

"But if you're clean now. If you…" Arden's voice trailed off when she read the guilty admission in the woman's shattered face.

"Not just me. My old man would die without…his medicine. I have to get it for him."

It was useless to pursue that channel. Arden sank back into a black pit of self-pity and despair. One day bled into another with no real differences between them. That was why she was sitting on her living-room sofa staring vacantly into the television screen one Saturday afternoon. How long she'd been there, she didn't know. What she was watching, she couldn't have said.

But suddenly something caught her attention. A face. A familiar face the camera loomed toward. And just as closely, Arden's brain focused on it. Shaking off the leaden depression, she turned up the volume on the set. The program was a sports show. The day's featured event was a tennis tournament. Atlanta? Somewhere. Men's singles match.

She knew that face! Handsome. Blond. Broad white grin. Where? When? The hospital? Yes, yes! The day she left with nothing but a purse with fifty thousand dollars cash in it. There had been a commotion on the outside steps. Reporters with microphones and cameras. Television crews crawling over the marble steps for better vantage points.

They were all there to see the beautiful couple leaving the hospital with their new baby. The tall blond man with the dazzling smile had a protective arm around his petite, equally blond wife, who was holding a squirming bundle of flannel. Arden remembered the joy they radiated and had known a stab of envy at the loving way the man smiled down at the woman and child. Tears had blurred her eyes as she shoved her way through the crowd toward the taxi that had been called for her. She had refused Ron's offer to take her home.

She hadn't thought of that scene until then. And *this* was the man. She listened to what the commentator was saying as the man's body arched into his serve.

"Drew McCasslin seems to be making a heroic effort here today after his crushing defeat in Memphis last week. We've seen a steady decline in his performance over the past several months."

"Much of that has to do with the personal tragedy he suffered this year," another off-camera voice said charitably.

"No doubt."

Drew McCasslin lost the point, and Arden read on his lips a vile expletive that should never have been televised. Apparently, the director thought so, too. He picked up another camera angle that showed McCasslin at the baseline, concentrating on the ball he was bouncing methodically. The serve was brilliantly executed, but the line referee called it out.

McCasslin axed his aluminum racket against the court and lunged toward the referee's high chair shouting vicious curses and insults. The television network judiciously went into a commercial break. After the virtues of an American-made car had been touted, they rejoined the match.

Arden hung on to every word as the commentators smugly excused McCasslin's behavior as a result of his grief over losing his wife in a grisly automobile accident in Honolulu, where the couple lived with their infant son. McCasslin played, surly and belligerent, and lost the match.

Arden went to bed that night thinking about the professional tennis player and wondering why she was so intrigued by him, having only seen him once. It came to her in the middle of the night that she *had* seen him more than once. She sat bolt upright in bed, her heart racing, her mind spinning out of control. She couldn't grasp the thoughts before they eluded her.

Slinging off the covers, she paced the room, pounding her temples with agitated fists. "Think, Arden," she commanded herself. "Think." For some reason, it was terribly important that she remember.

With agonizing slowness, the pieces fell into place. She'd been in pain. Lights, moving lights. That was it! She was being rolled down a hospital corridor on a gurney, and lights flashed by overhead. She'd been on her way to the delivery room. It was almost over. All she had to do was deliver the baby and she'd be free of Ron forever.

She'd seen the couple out of the corner of her eye as she was pushed past a shadowed hallway. The light had caught on their two blond heads. She'd turned her head slightly. Neither of them noticed her. They were smiling, clinging to each other happily, whispering excitedly and secretively. What was wrong with that picture? Something, but what? *What?*

"Remember, Arden," she whispered as she slumped down on the side of the bed and clasped her head with both hands. "They were happy just like any other couple having a baby. They—"

Everything stopped at once. Her breathing. Her heartbeat. Her whirling thoughts. Then they started up again, sluggishly, gaining momentum as the dot of light at the end of a dark tunnel grew larger until the conclusion blasted into her mind. *The woman hadn't been pregnant!*

She hadn't been in labor. She'd been standing out in

the hall talking in excited whispers with her husband. They had had about them an air of secrecy, like children plotting a marvelous prank.

The McCasslins were wealthy. They were recognized worldwide. He was handsome, as Ron had said the father of her baby was. They had left the hospital with a newborn child the same day Arden had left.

She had had their baby.

Arden wrapped her arms around herself and rolled back and forth on the bed in solitary celebration. She knew she was right. She had to be. All the pieces fit.

She sobered considerably as she remembered the other fact she'd learned that day. Mrs. McCasslin was dead. Arden's son—the sports announcers had said Drew McCasslin had an infant son—was being reared without the loving care of a mother and by a father who wasn't mentally or physically stable.

Drew McCasslin became Arden's obsession. For months, she read everything she could about him, past and present, spending hours in the public library poring over microfilms of sports pages that featured stories about his heyday. Daily, she read of his decline.

Then, one day, she read that he had gone into semi-retirement. His manager was quoted as having said, "Drew knows his game has slipped. He's going to concentrate on restoring it and spending time with his son at their new home on Maui."

That was when Arden had begun planning to go to Hawaii to somehow meet Drew McCasslin.

"And now that you've met him, what are you going to do about him?" she asked her mirror image.

She hadn't counted on being susceptible to his

charm and good looks. "Remember why you're here, Arden. Stay objective," she told her reflection.

But it mocked her from the mirror. She didn't look like a woman striving for objectivity. The strapless jade silk dress did nothing to disguise her figure. The fuchsia belt encircled a trim waist and drew attention to the round curves above and below it. The cream-colored blazer she wore over the sheath only made more suggestive the expanse of bare shoulders it covered. She was wearing the lei instead of jewelry. The flowers almost matched the color of her belt. She had pulled her hair back into a neat chignon, but its severity was compromised by wavy tendrils that had escaped to lie on her neck and to form a soft brush of bangs over her forehead.

The woman who looked back at her with smoky green eyes looked like a prime candidate for a tempestuous love affair.

"My God," she whispered as she pressed cold, trembling fingers to her forehead. "I've got to stop thinking of him this way. I'll ruin everything. And I've got to stop him from thinking of me as a…a…woman."

He would need discouraging. She knew that with every feminine instinct she possessed.

He had loved his wife. Probably still did. But everything about him spoke of intense virility. He wasn't the kind of man who could live without a complementing feminine presence for long.

The electricity between them—and she could no longer convince herself that it wasn't there—threatened her plan. The plan had been to meet him and win his confidence as a friend. When she had proved she didn't mean to threaten his relationship with his son, she would tell him who she was and make her request. "I would be forever grateful if you'd let me see my son now and then."

Hold that thought, she told herself when she heard his knock on her door. *Objectivity,* she reminded herself, and resolved to put away any other thoughts about Drew McCasslin.

It was impossible, however, to keep that promise to herself when he looked so handsome in tailored navy slacks, a beige sport coat that was almost the same color as his collar-length hair and a baby-blue shirt that matched his eyes.

Those eyes were doing their fair share of looking. They went all the way from the top of her head to the heels of her lizard sandals and back up again. They stopped short of her face and paused in the vicinity of the lei. Arden got the distinct impression they weren't looking at the blossoms but at the shape of her breasts beneath them.

"You do a lot for those flowers," he said in a gravelly voice that confirmed what she had suspected.

"Thank you."

"You're welcome." Only then did he lift his eyes to hers and smile. "Ready?"

CHAPTER FOUR

THEY HAD DINNER dates each night after that for the next three. Arden knew she was making the difficult impossible, but couldn't bring herself to refuse his invitations. She and Drew were growing closer, true, but in the wrong way. There was no room in her scheme for romance. So, on the fourth night, she begged off, using the lame excuse of working on her article about the chances of tropical-plant survival in less tropical climes, an article she'd already mailed.

Instead of directing her thoughts away from Drew, she spent that evening wondering where and with whom he was having dinner. Was he home with Matt? With a friend? With another woman? She doubted it was the last. When they were together, she held his undivided attention.

"Am I moving too fast, monopolizing your vacation time, horning in on someone else's territory?" he had asked when she declined his dinner invitation. The question was spoken lightly, almost jokingly, but she knew by the frown wrinkling his eyebrows that he was serious.

"No, Drew, it's nothing like that. I told you the day I met you, there is no one I'm accountable to. It's just that I think we might need a night away from each other. I don't want to monopolize your time, either. And I really do have work to do." Skeptically, grudgingly, he had accepted her refusal.

She was terrified of what was happening to her each time they were together. She was flirting with disaster and knew it well, but the hours she wasn't with him had become colorless and monotonous. He had never kissed her except for that one time when he gave her the lei. Beyond common courtesies, he never touched her. Yet he made her feel giddy and young and beautiful. All those emotions were symptoms of falling in love. And that simply couldn't be. She had come to Maui to see her son. That was her main goal, and Drew McCasslin was only the means to that end.

Still…

The morning after their evening apart, she meandered in the direction of the tennis courts, swearing to herself that she wasn't going there to see him. He might not even be playing.

He was guzzling Gatorade when he spotted her. He tossed the bottle to Gary and trotted over to her.

"Hi. I was going to call you later. Dinner tonight? Please."

"Yes."

His rapid-fire invitation and her spontaneous acceptance surprised and delighted them both. They laughed together softly, shyly, all the while drinking in the sight of each other.

"I'll pick you up at seven-thirty."

"Fine."

"Are you going to watch me play?"

"For a while, then I must go back to my room to work."

"And I promised Matt I'd play with him on the beach."

Whenever he mentioned the boy's name, her heart lurched with eagerness. "I'm not keeping you away from him too much, am I?"

"I don't leave in the evenings until he's bedded down for the night. He doesn't miss me. He makes sure I'm the second one in the house awake every morning."

She laughed. "Joey used to do that, too. He'd come into my bedroom and peel open my eyelids, asking if I was awake."

"I thought only Matt knew that trick!" They laughed together again; then he said, "I'm losing momentum. I need to get back, but I'll see you tonight."

"Play well."

"I'm trying."

"You *are*."

He winked at her before rejoining the patient Gary, who hadn't wasted his time, but had been flirting with their covey of spectators. Arden wondered if she looked like just another groupie to anyone observing her and Drew. The thought made her uneasy. *Was* she just another groupie?

SHE WASN'T QUITE ready when Drew knocked on her door. Despite her subconscious thoughts about him all afternoon, she had become inspired and had worked fast and furiously on one of her articles. She'd barely allowed time for a bath and shampoo before he arrived.

She was still zipping the back of her dress as she raced for the door. "I'm sorry," she said breathlessly as she pulled it open. He was leaning indolently against the jamb as though she hadn't kept him waiting a full minute already.

He took in her flushed cheeks, stockinged feet and general appearance of disarray and smiled. "It was worth the wait."

"Come in. I'll be ready as soon as I get on my shoes and jewelry. Did you make reservations? I hope we don't lose—"

"Arden," he said, closing the door behind him and catching her by both shoulders. "It's okay. We've got plenty of time."

She took a deep breath. "Right. I'll slow down."

"Good." He laughed and released her. He took a cursory look around the room, finally focusing his gaze on her as she stepped into high-heeled sandals. Flattening one hand against the wall to brace herself, she lifted one slender foot to adjust the strap. Her movement was graceful, innately feminine and unconsciously provocative.

He took in the smooth length of silk-encased legs. The muscles of her calves were clearly, but softly, defined as she stood on the balls of her feet. They would fit in the palm of his hand perfectly, he thought.

Catching a glimpse of the weblike lace that bordered the hem of her slip, he smiled at the sheer womanliness of it. And as she leaned down, he couldn't help noticing the precious weight of her breasts filling and pulling taut the bodice of her dress. The deep V neckline revealed the shadowy velvet cleft between her breasts. Mentally, he placed his lips there and pressed them against the fullness on each side of it. Immediately aroused, he ordered his unwilling eyes to safer ground.

Her hair always seemed soft and touchable even

when it was pulled back. That night she'd worn it loose, and his fingers tingled with the desire to caress the dark strands, to test their silkiness and then to see if her complexion was as soft as it looked. All over.

"There," she said, pushing herself away from the wall and going to the long, low bureau opposite the king-size bed.

Drew hadn't allowed himself to think about the bed, to think about the alluring body he was examining so closely lying naked on that bed.

"Jewelry." She was rummaging through a satin travel jewelry carrier.

Her sleeveless dress was of some clingy, soft aqua material that conformed to nicely rounded but not over-developed hips. Anything she wore looked terrific, no matter how dressy or casual. He thought she could be wearing jeans and a sweatshirt and give them as much class as an *haute couture* ensemble. She'd also look great in nothing at all.

Damn! He was thinking about what he'd promised himself he wasn't going to think about.

Her fingers worked deftly to clip gold earrings onto lobes he now fantasized about touching with his tongue. His heart began to hammer when her breasts lifted and swelled above her dress as she raised her arms to clasp a slender gold chain around her neck.

"Here. Let me," he said unsteadily. He moved up behind her. For a moment, before his fingers took the ends of the chain from hers, they stared at each other in the mirror. Her arms were still raised, her breasts still high and voluptuous, the tender undersides of her arms displayed, making her pose both wanton and vulnerable.

She lowered her arms slowly as he took the chain

from her hands and ducked his head to work the intricate clasp. When it was fastened, she hurried to move away.

"Wait." His hands gently held her. "Your zipper's stuck."

"Oh." She barely had enough air to utter the word. In her effort to make the sound, it came out as a soft exclamation.

With tantalizing slowness, he eased the zipper down. Air cooled the flushed skin of her back. Motionless, not daring to draw a breath and break the sensuous spell, she stood, letting him draw the tab of the zipper all the way to her waist. His eyes, matching the leisureliness of his hand, charted its descent. The bare expanse of smooth skin let him know that there was no bra between her and the bodice of the dress.

Again, his eyes met hers in the mirror. They were dark and smoldering, like the purest of blue flame. And in her own eyes was the glassy sheen of desire.

His tense body radiated silent sexual messages. She knew that if she moved back but a fraction of an inch and let her hips brush the front of his trousers, she'd feel him hard and primed with passion. She doubted they would go to dinner. It was her decision.

But going to bed with Drew was out of the question. Bringing sexual involvement into this already untenable situation would be lunacy. And in some secret corner of her mind, she feared she might be disappointed. Or worse, he might be. Ron's scathing criticism of her sexual prowess haunted her.

It would be best to keep things on an even footing. Friendly. Wasn't it possible for a male and female to be nothing more than platonic friends? Wasn't that what she'd originally wanted from Drew McCasslin?

Wisely, judiciously, with cowardice, she lowered her head and shook it slightly. He got the message and pulled the zipper up. "A loose thread got caught. All done."

"Thank you," she said, stepping away.

She wasn't going to get off that easily.

"Arden?"

She picked up her purse before turning to face him. "Yes?"

"It's been a long time since I've been around feminine clutter, watched a woman I care for dress. I didn't realize until now how much I've missed living with a woman."

She looked away, out the wide windows where palm trees were blackly etched silhouettes against an indigo sky. "Living alone has disadvantages for a woman, too."

He took a step closer. "Like what?" It was a low, urgent whisper.

This had to stop. And it was up to her to see that it did. She raised her eyes to his, forced them to twinkle mischievously and determinedly grinned a gamine smile. "Like not having someone around to unstick a zipper."

His disappointment in her answer showed in the slight relaxing of his shoulders, but he smiled a gracious surrender, alleviating the crackling tension in the room. "See? What would all you liberated women do without us?"

That cheerful, bantering mood stayed with them as he drove his Seville along Maui's narrow highways.

The Kaanapali Beach area was one of the few developed regions on the island. It was studded with elegant hotels, restaurants and clubs.

Drew brought his car to a stop under the porte cochere of the Hyatt.

"Ever been in here?" he asked as he joined her on the curb after a valet had assisted her out of the car.

"No, but I wanted to see it before I went home."

"Prepare yourself. It's like no other hotel in the world."

That was readily apparent. Most other hotel lobbies had ceilings. This one did not. The ceiling of the lobby, which was many stories high, was a starry sky. The lobby was landscaped to represent a rain forest, profuse with tropical trees and blooming plants. When it did rain, the effect was true to life. The areas that were covered were elegantly decorated with huge Chinese vases that dwarfed even Drew. Priceless rugs and oriental antiques gave the hotel a palatial aspect without detracting from the casual, homey atmosphere.

They crossed the immense lobby, Drew giving her far too little time to gaze into the elaborate shops and galleries before whisking her down a curved staircase into the Swan Court.

"I feel like a country bumpkin in the city for the first time. Is my mouth hanging open?"

"I like bumpkins," he said, and squeezed her waist. "And your mouth, like the rest of you tonight, looks delectable."

She was glad the maître d' chose that moment to escort them to a candlelit table beside the pond, where swans glided across the surface with the haughty disdain of royalty. As were most of the restaurants on the island, this one was open-air. It looked out on a small lake complete with waterfall and lava rocks.

The patrons were dressed in evening clothes, and Arden was glad she'd selected her dressiest dress to wear. Drew seemed to guess her thoughts. "Don't be too impressed," he whispered from behind his menu. "In the mornings, this room is swarming with people in swimsuits and thongs at the breakfast buffet."

She let the ambience of the room soak into her and was only vaguely aware of Drew signaling the waiter.

"Would you like wine with dinner, Arden?"

She met his challenging stare levelly. "Yes, thank you."

He ordered an expensive bottle of white wine. She refused to show her surprise. In all the time they'd been together, he'd never drunk anything alcoholic.

"I drink an occasional glass of wine at dinner," he said.

"I didn't ask."

"No, but you were probably wondering if I can handle it."

"I asked you once before not to do my thinking for me. You're a big boy. You know if you can 'handle' it or not."

"You're not afraid that I'll go on a binge and become drunk and disorderly?" He was teasing.

She tossed down her own gauntlet. Leaning toward him, she whispered, "Maybe I'd like you to become a little disorderly." Moths had an instinct for flying directly into flames.

Drew's eyes narrowed seductively. "It wouldn't take even a sip of wine to make me completely unruly."

She backed off before her wings could be singed. "But I trust you not to."

He allowed her retreat. The tone of his voice told her he was willing to change the subject. "You have every reason to be concerned. I've been drunk and disorderly more this last year than I've been sober. I don't think I'll ever live it down." He clenched his teeth as strongly as he clenched the fist that lightly thumped the tabletop. "God, I'd give anything to undo some of the things I did."

Arden was well acquainted with the frustration and self-loathing he was feeling. Decisions were made; decisions were regretted. Most were irrevocable. "We all make mistakes, Drew, and later wish we could redo it all. We can't. We have to live with our decisions." Her voice became painfully introspective when she added, "Sometimes for life."

He chuckled softly. "That sounds so defeatist, hopeless. Don't you think we're given second chances to make things right again?"

"Yes. Thank God, yes. I think we *make* our second chances. We either try to turn our mistakes around or learn to live with them."

"That's the loser's way. To give in."

"Yes. And you're a winner."

"I couldn't live with the garbage I'd made of my life. I had to do something about it."

"So did I," she muttered to herself.

"Pardon?"

Should she tell him now? Now? He'd brought up the subject of personal failures and attempts to rectify them. He was doing that in his own life. Surely he'd understand her own desire to correct her mistakes.

Wouldn't he? What if he didn't? What if he stormed out
and left her alone and she never saw him again? She
would never see Matt, either. No. Better to wait until
after she'd at least seen her son once. Then she'd tell
Drew she was Matt's mother. Then, not now.

She sat up straighter and flashed him a brilliant
smile. "Why are we having this gloomy conversation?
Here comes the wine. Let's not dwell on past mistakes
tonight."

Their veal was scrumptious, as were all the dishes
that went with it. They had only the one bottle of wine,
and half of it was left when they finally brought the
two-hour dinner to an end. Full and satisfied, yet feeling as light as a feather, Arden seemed to float up the
staircase. She wasn't drunk on wine but on the romantic atmosphere and the magnetism of the man beside her.

At the lobby cocktail bar, a pianist was playing love
ballads on a white baby grand. An ocean breeze swept
through the lobby, stirring the leaves of the trees and
carrying with it the perfume of pikaki and plumeria.

They paused beneath a softly glowing lamp. "Enjoy
the dinner?" he asked, taking both her hands in his and
swinging them back and forth.

"Um-huh." She was looking at his hair and wondering what it would feel like to run her hands through it,
to twist it around her fingers when passion rendered
her mindless. She contemplated his mouth. The most
erotic scene she'd ever seen in a motion picture was
a camera-close view of a man's mouth on a woman's
breast. She remembered vividly the tender flicking of
his tongue as it circled a dusky areola, the flexing of
his cheeks as he gently sucked the nipple, the moist ca-

ress of his lips on the soft flesh. That was what looking at Drew's mouth brought to mind, and her whole body flushed hotly with the fantasy.

Ron had never taken time for such foreplay, and never asked what she'd like. She probably wouldn't have liked it with Ron. She thought she'd like it very much with Drew.

"What?"

"What?"

"Did you say something?" Drew asked. His eyes were scanning the features of her face, lingering on one a long while before moving to another.

"No," she whispered. "I didn't say anything."

"Oh. I thought you said something." He was studying her mouth now, and if she had blushed at her own fantasy, she would have disintegrated with embarrassment had she known where *his* fantasy placed *her* mouth. To safeguard his sanity, he pulled a curtain over the erotically detailed mental picture. "What would you like to do?"

"Do? I don't know. What do you want to do?"

Oh, God, don't ask! "Go dancing?"

"That sounds fun," she said, coughing lightly and making an unnecessary straightening gesture down the front of her dress. Activity. That was what they needed. When they stood still, they became absorbed in each other to the exclusion of everything else.

"There's a club downstairs. I've never been there, but we can give it a try."

"Fine."

He led her down yet another staircase, this one brass banistered and reminiscent of the turn of the century. Pushing open the tufted leather door, they were greeted by a smiling hostess, a blast of disco music, a rumble of conversation and laughter and a cloud of tobacco smoke.

Drew looked down at her in silent query. She looked up with the same question in her eyes. Simultaneously, they turned on their heels and went back up the stairs. They were laughing by the time they reached the lobby.

"We must be getting old," Drew said. "The music of that single piano sounds better to me."

"To me, too."

"And I don't want to shout to be heard." He leaned down and placed his lips on her ear to whisper, "I may say something I wouldn't want anyone else to hear." When he pulled back, the burning glow in his eyes reinforced the intimacy of his words. A shiver of excitement feathered up Arden's spine. "Would you like something to drink?"

She shook her head. "Why don't you show me the pool?"

Clasping her hand and linking their fingers, he led her out onto the terraced rock pathways that wound through a veritable Garden of Eden. The paths were lit by widely spaced torches. Their flames flickered drastically in the wind. The swimming pools were an architectural masterpiece built on several levels around a lava-rock grotto.

Arden responded appreciatively to everything he pointed out, but she didn't really care what he said or what she saw. It was marvelous to hear his voice near her ear, to catch the fragrance of his warm breath, to feel the protective strength of his hard body as he directed her footsteps with subtle movements. Her pulse seemed to beat with the pagan rhythm of the surf as it pounded the shore only yards away.

Lovers lurked in the shadows, embracing, whispering. It was tacitly understood that privacy was the goal of anyone walking through the garden at that time of night. And when Drew stopped and pulled her behind a sheltering rock draped with a clinging vine, she made no protest.

"May I have this dance?" he asked with mock formality.

She laughed, trying to keep a straight face as she answered, "Yes, you may." She walked into his arms, and for the first time since they met, she knew the thrill of holding him, of being held.

He held her in the traditional waltz position, his arm around her waist and their joined palms at shoulder level. Her hand rested on his other shoulder. They couldn't move much without sacrificing this precious, private space, and both knew the invitation to dance had been issued only to provide them with an excuse to hold each other. So they swayed to the rhythm of the mood music wafting from the piano in the lobby bar.

Minutes ticked by, and one song drifted into another, and still they clung together, their eyes never wavering from each other's face. Their bodies, looking deceptively serene, were raging on the inside, clamoring for closer contact, yearning and straining until finally her breasts brushed against his chest.

He uttered a small groan and closed his eyes in exquisite pleasure. When they opened again, hers had been shuttered by the most fragile, lavishly fringed eyelids he'd ever seen. He wanted to kiss them. Instead, he brought his hand up from her waist and increased the pressure on her back until first the delicate crests, then the full mounds of her breasts were flattened against his chest.

Her eyes opened slumberously, and she moved her hand from his shoulder to the back of his neck. Her fingers threaded through the adorably shaggy blond hair that lay on his collar. Never taking his eyes from hers, he brought the hand he held to his mouth and brushed the knuckles with his lips. Back and forth, he caressed that dainty ridge, leaving it moist with the vapor of his breath.

Gradually, he lifted her arm and placed it over his shoulder and behind his neck. Then his hand glided down the underside of her arm, down her ribs and around to her back. He drew her close.

"You know how hard it's been for me to keep my hands off you, don't you?"

"Yes," she said throatily, responsively arching her body to meet his.

"I've wanted so badly to hold you, Arden."

"And I've wanted so badly to be held."

"All you had to do was ask," he whispered before he buried his face in her hair, nuzzling her with his nose and chin and mouth. "You smell so good, feel wonderful. Your complexion is beautiful. Honest to God, I've imagined every inch of it. I've wanted to see you, touch you, taste you."

A tremulous sigh shook her whole body as she nestled her face in the curve of his throat. Her hands tightened around his neck, and she took a step closer. His rasping groan of ecstasy was emitted through tightly clamped jaws. One of his hands stole down her back, paused briefly at her waist, then lowered to conform to the curve of her buttocks. Without separating himself from her, he managed to alternate their feet until one of his legs rested between hers, one of hers between his.

He was hard. And warm. So warm. Arden felt his heat searing through their clothes, burning into her body and melting it against his. Holding her still with one hand on her hip, he rubbed himself against her. Her sharp, startled cry was muffled against his shirtfront.

"I'm sorry, Arden. I don't mean to be crude, but God, it feels so good."

"Drew—"

"Do you want me to stop?"

"Drew." She threw her head back to look boldly into his face. "No." She shuddered. "No." Then, a bit hysterically, a bit deliriously, and quite desperately, she begged, "Kiss me."

His mouth came down on hers with the same kind of desperation she had voiced. It was a violent kiss, an explosive release of pent-up longing and withheld emotion. His lips ground into hers almost brutally, but she welcomed the rough caress, for she'd never felt more alive. She was a butterfly bursting free of a dreary chrysalis, a prisoner of despair and dark unhappiness seeing the light of life for the first time.

He lifted his head and looked down at her with shining blue eyes. His breath was ragged, labored. It matched hers. She could feel his rigid virility against that part of her that seemed to be throbbing with joy.

By an act of will, he controlled his raging impulses and let his hand come up to cradle her jaw with heartfelt tenderness. He ran the pad of his thumb along her bruised lower lip and frowned his regret. She smiled her forgiveness.

When next his lips met hers, it was with the merest touch. He skimmed over them with soft, moist lips whose comforting caresses became a gently building torment.

"Drew." His name was a plea from the bottom of her soul.

"I was rough. I didn't mean to be."

"I know."

"You make me wild with need of you."

"Take what you want."

A moan of animal pleasure rumbled in his chest as his mouth descended once again. His tongue was a sweet aggressor. It traced her bottom lip, bathing it with the nectar of his own mouth. She picked it up with her own tongue and murmured her approval. He placed his mouth against hers and opened his lips slowly. She did the same. For long moments, they waited there, savoring their expectation, their accelerated pulses, their aroused sexes.

Then his tongue pressed home, embedding itself snugly in her mouth. He withdrew, pressed again. Again and again, until Arden thought for certain she would die. She could feel her body flowering open, preparing for love. Her nipples grew hard and sensitive against the cool, sensuous cloth of her dress.

His kiss became playful. His tongue darted around her mouth. He teased, explored, stroked, probed, at varying tempos and angles and with such skill that she clung to him weakly and called his name softly when she had to tear her mouth free to breathe.

The heels of his hands inched up her ribs to find the sides of her breasts. With soft pressure, he squeezed them together. They nearly overflowed the V of her neckline, and he whispered accolades to them. He pressed hot kisses into the fragrant flesh. His tongue delved into the deep cleavage in a caress so evocative that Arden's body was washed with a delightful sense of shame.

She had needed this all her adult life. She had needed a man to show her what it was to be adored, loved for what she was, admired for her femininity. Not until she met Drew had she thought of herself as an attractive woman. From the beginning, his every look, every gesture, had told her he thought she was extremely sexy and desirable. He'd been honest and forthright about it from the beginning.

But she hadn't been.

What she was feeling now was pure and honest, but would he believe that later? When he learned she was Matt's mother, she would have so many things to answer for. Did she want to add luring him sexually to that list? The thought sickened her. She had to reverse this headlong plunge into sexual involvement immediately or forever be the object of his scorn.

"Drew," she murmured against his lips, which had returned to hers.

"Hmm?" He was lost in his caress.

"Drew," she repeated more stridently, and placed her hands against his shoulders. "Don't—" His hand was sliding beneath the strap of her dress, easing it down. She panicked. If she didn't stop this now, she wouldn't be able to. Her only resource was to make him angry. He was beyond reasoning with.

"Stop it!" She slapped his hand away and yanked herself free of his embrace.

His face registered total bewilderment. He blinked

his eyes rapidly until he could focus on her clearly. She watched as his initial befuddlement changed to irritation. "All right," he said tightly, "you don't have to treat me like a disobedient child. I had every right to think you were enjoying my kisses."

She avoided looking at him. "Kisses, yes, but I'm not one of the groupies you—"

"Is that all you think this is?" He raked a hand through his hair and worked with frustrated, ineffectual fingers at his necktie. "Is it?" he demanded.

Angering him had been her intent, but she hadn't counted on contending with such a volatile temper. She stammered to explain. "I... I—"

"Well, okay, then, but what sets you apart from the others? Huh? You've been more than available, and there were no strings attached. What else was I supposed to think? Or are you different because you never intended to go 'all the way'? No sex, just spiritual support for my much-publicized lost soul." He was furious. "Was that it? Was I a charitable case you took on?"

Arden was finding it difficult to keep a leash on her own temper. "As I pointed out to you the first day, you approached me, not the other way around. As for taking you on as a 'case,' I don't care if you go straight to hell or drink yourself to death or stumble and fall on every tennis court in the world. I frankly doubt if you're worth saving."

He ignored her, cocking his head to one side as if seeing her in a new light. "Maybe you're not so different, after all. Groupies want to sleep with a celebrity to elevate their own egos. Was sleeping with me going to shore up your shattered confidence after a failed marriage?" He thrust his face to within an inch of hers. "What's the matter? Chicken out?"

Fury bathed her world red. "You conceited ass. I'm not some frustrated divorcée. I was all too glad to get rid of the man I had. And I'll think long and hard before wanting another one. And if my confidence *were* shattered, which it's not, it would take a lot more than sleeping with a washed-up tennis bum to restore it. You can keep what's in your pants, Mr. McCasslin. I've lived without it for thirty-one years. I think I can go at least another thirty-one."

She whirled away from him and stumbled down the darkened path. He caught up with her and growled, "You're going the wrong way."

She tried to wrench her arm free, but he wouldn't let her. She wasn't going to engage in an undignified tug-of-war, so she let herself be escorted through the lobby. They waited in hostile silence for his car to be brought around. Not one word was said on the drive back to the resort where she was staying.

"I can find my way, thank you," she said as she pushed open the door the instant he braked the car to a stop. Not looking back, she rushed to the elevator and to her room. He didn't follow her.

Only when her anger had been spent in a fit of door slamming, drawer rattling and cursing did she realize what she'd done.

Matt!

She had ruined all chances of meeting him now. Tears rolled down her cheeks in torrents, and she pledged to herself repeatedly that it wasn't for losing Drew but only for losing her son again.

HER EYES WERE puffy and burning when she tried to pry them open the next morning. She rolled over and burrowed her face in the pillow. When the second loud knock sounded on her door, she groaned, "Go away, maid."

A third knock, more imperious, shook the whole room. Arden cursed the maid's ambition. She saw that her only option was to go to the door and tell the maid to come back later.

She rolled out of bed, groping for the walls, since her eyes seemed to have been glued shut with tears. They came open wide when she peered through the peephole and saw Drew standing on the other side of the door. She watched as he knocked again. This time, he said, "Arden, open this door."

"Not on your life."

"So you *are* awake."

She appreciated his cheerful tone of voice as much as she would appreciate a splinter under her thumbnail. "I don't want to see you, Drew."

"Well, I want to see you. To apologize. Now open the door or everyone on this floor is going to hear an apology that will wake them up faster than a good strong cup of coffee."

She gnawed at her bottom lip while she weighed her options. She wasn't up to seeing him. The night before, he had been insulting, and she wasn't ready to forgive him. And even if she were, she knew she looked like the devil. Her eyes were probably red and swollen and her hair tangled. When she met him face-to-face again, she wanted to be at her haughtiest best.

On the other hand, she'd deliberately made him angry. No man, no matter how easygoing normally, could be expected to be in the best of humor after being sexually thwarted. She had spent half the night tearfully berating herself for letting her relationship with Drew jeopardize her chances of seeing Matt. Swallowing her pride was a small price to pay for that, wasn't it?

She flipped open the dead-bolt lock and opened the door a crack. "I'm not dressed."

"You're dressed," he said, taking in the collar and sleeves of her blue-and-white striped oxford-cloth nightshirt.

"If you insist on seeing me, I'll meet you in the lobby. Give me—"

"Haven't got the time." His grin was both devilish and winning. "Come on, Arden. Let me in."

Reluctantly, she opened the door and preceded him into the room. The door was closed softly behind him. He took in her dishabille in one lazy glance. Her bare feet and legs made her feel nervous and uncomfortable. The nightshirt wasn't revealing, but she suddenly wished the hem fell below the middle of her thighs. Self-consciously, she crossed her arms over her chest and tried to look bored.

"You're right. I'm a conceited ass." He brushed past her and went to the window, opening the drapes without her permission and flooding the room with a blinding sunlight that made her squint.

"I was acting like a horny teenager, grappling and groping in the dark. Hell—" He sighed, rubbing the back of his neck "—no wonder you thought I saw you as no more than a groupie. That's how I was treating you. And when you said no, I don't know why I said the things I did. I didn't mean them. They weren't accurate, and I knew it." He glanced over his shoulder to see that her militant stance hadn't relaxed one iota.

"The only excuse I can offer," he went on, "is that soon after Ellie died, I was surrounded by women who thought they could cure me of my grief. I got the impression they saw themselves as some kind of sexual social workers out to save me from my self-destruction. And to them I'd be no more than a notch on the bedpost."

Arden lowered her arms and relaxed her posture. She'd had that same kind of response from men after her divorce. Friends of Ron's, divorced themselves, began calling, offering her their "help." "No, thank you," she had said until they finally gave up.

"Anyway," Drew was saying, "that's why I had to see you first thing this morning. The minute I pulled away from here last night, I knew I'd acted like a jerk. You should have kicked me in the groin or something."

"I thought about it."

He laughed. "Well, it might not have changed my mind immediately, but you would have gotten my attention."

She laughed, too.

"Now that we're friends again," he said hurriedly, clapping his hands together, "why don't you go over to Oahu with me for a few days?"

"What—"

"Just a minute," he said, holding up both hands to ward off her objections. "There are still no strings attached. I'll only be there a few days. I've got a suite of rooms reserved. Maybe you'll get an idea for an article." It was a weak argument, but he was in a rush to convince her.

"But I can't just move out of here. I—"

"I'm not suggesting you do. Pack only what you'll need. We'll tell the manager that you'll be gone for a few days but want to keep the room."

He stepped closer and clasped her hands. "I like the way you look in that nightshirt," he said in a sexy drawl, "with your hair all mussed up and your cheeks blushing pink. You have the sweetest mouth I've ever tasted. And I really can't believe I was stupid enough to let a good thing like last night end so badly."

"You're a bully, did you know that? You have your nerve coming in here this morning after the things you said to me last night, telling me how good I look when I know I must look like hell." Her outburst made him smile, and that fueled her anger. "Do you always get your way?"

"I'm a competitor, Arden, and I like to win." The fierceness in his eyes told her she was his next goal. While she was held dumbstruck by his handsome appeal and the earnestness of his expression, he urged softly, "Come to Honolulu with me. We'll get to know each other better."

She wanted nothing more, but knew she was only letting herself in for more trouble. Taking a deep breath, she shook her head. "Drew, I don't think—"

"Please. Besides, it'll give you a chance to know Matt."

CHAPTER FIVE

SECONDS TICKED BY while she stared at him speechlessly. The arsenal of arguments she had been stockpiling in her mind tumbled. Finally, she stammered, "M-Matt's going?"

"Yeah, he's the main reason we're going. It's time for a checkup at the pediatrician. He needs a booster shot. And Mrs. Laani was complaining the other day that he's growing so fast he doesn't have any clothes. She's planning an extensive shopping trip."

Arden's mind was thrown into chaos. It was going to happen! She was going to see her son, spend time, *days,* with him. For months, she had waited for this moment, dreamed about it, imagined how she'd feel. But the panic that seized her now was unpredicted. That was all she felt—cold, blind panic. Now that what she'd prayed for was here, she was terrified of it.

She began trying to talk her way out of it. "This is a family trip, and I wouldn't want to interfere. He... Matt might not like me. Mrs., uh, Laani, is it? She might resent your bringing a...me along."

"It *is* a family trip, but I happen to be the head of the family. Mrs. Laani lectures me on just about everything, including the deficiency of a nice—and I stress nice—lady in my life. She's eager to meet you. And Matt's only twenty months old. He loves anyone who feeds him." His hands cupped her head. "Please come, Arden. If I didn't think it was a good idea, I wouldn't have asked." His voice deepened perceptibly. "I don't want to be away from you even for a few days."

Oh, God, why wasn't she jumping up and down with glee? Why was she hesitating? Did she feel guilty? Was that the emotion that had a stranglehold on her heart and wouldn't let go to make room for others? Drew was gazing down at her with naked longing. He was looking at her as a woman he was growing romantically attached to, not as the surrogate mother he and his beloved wife had hired. How long could she go on tricking him?

"Drew, I'm not sure going with you is a good idea."

"Are you still angry about last night?"

"No, but—"

"I don't blame you for being mad. I said terrible, insulting things." His thumb stroked her cheekbone. "I was wrong, but everything you said was true. I behaved like an ass. I am conceited. I am accustomed to getting my way and am likely to throw temper tantrums if I don't. I am a washed-up tennis bum."

"No! That's not true. I said that to deliberately hurt. No other reason."

He sighed. "Whether it's true or not remains to be seen. What I am is a man who finds himself attracted to a woman when he never thought he'd feel that way again. I'm scared as hell of you, Arden, and of what I'm feeling. Don't make it so damn hard on me. I'm trying to adjust to being a human being again, to act like one and not like a wounded animal. Sometimes I have lapses. Last night was one of those times."

"I'm not playing coy, Drew."

"I know that."

"I wasn't last night, either."

He kissed her gently. "I know that, too."

"There's a reason why I shouldn't go."

"You've given me no reason. I don't think there is one. Not a valid one, anyway. Come with us. The plane leaves in an hour."

"What?" she gasped, shoving him aside and checking the digital clock on the bedside table. "An hour! Oh, Drew... I can't... Why didn't you say... I'll never get ready—" She stopped abruptly when she realized she'd just consented.

He laughed at her startled expression, and dropping down on the bed, picked up the telephone. "You'd better hurry. I'll call down for coffee."

By the time she stepped out of the shower, he was tapping on the bathroom door. "Room service." She eased the door open a crack and took a cup of coffee from him. "Thirty minutes," he said. "Want me to toss a few things in a suitcase for you?"

The thought of his handling her intimate garments set off a chain reaction that ended in a flush of warmth between her thighs. "No. I'll be out in a jiffy."

She sipped the coffee and tried to keep her hands from shaking while she applied her makeup. She told herself her jittery nerves were the result of a short, virtually sleepless night. But not a little of her tenseness had to do with standing naked only a few feet and one door away from Drew. And most of it had to do with the fact that in less than an hour she'd meet the son she'd carried for nine months but had never seen.

Drew was dressed in a pair of casual khaki slacks and a loosely woven white cotton sweater with wide sleeves that he'd pushed up to his elbows. Arden had taken a pair of raw silk slacks and a matching top with dolman sleeves into the bathroom with her. She wound her hair into a loose French braid down the back of her head and tucked the ends under at the nape. Not great, but the best she could do in a hurry.

When she came out of the steamy bathroom, she looked nervously toward Drew, who was slouched in a chair near the glass terrace door perusing the morning newspaper. He tipped down a corner of the paper to look at her and whistled long and low. "How'd you do that so fast? Take casual clothes, shorts, swimsuit, something to wear to dinner, but nothing fancy."

She began folding things into a shoulder bag, her mind clicking off the accessories that went with each outfit. She became all thumbs and butterfingers when she began packing her underwear into the bag. Though he still held the paper up in front of him, Drew's eyes weren't on the print. Arden could feel him watching her every move as she packed lacy panties and flimsy brassieres. When she shot him an accusing glare, he flashed her a broad, guileless grin.

"All set," she said as she zipped the bag, in which she'd managed to cram not only clothes but also makeup, jewelry caches and shoes.

"Amazing," he said, standing up and glancing at his wafer-thin watch. "And just on time. We're meeting Mrs. Laani and Matt at the airport. Mo, who takes care of the grounds of the house, is going to drive them. We'll take the resort's limo, if that's okay. I hated to leave my car at the airport for that long."

"That's fine." She set a natural-straw hat with a wide, floppy brim over her head and slid on large square sunglasses. "Remember, I'm accustomed to traveling on a shoestring budget."

"You certainly don't look like it," he said as he carried her bag down the hall toward the elevator. He took in every fashionable detail as they waited for the elevator. "I approve," he said softly.

"Thank you," she whispered back.

Once inside the cubicle, he said, "I forgot something."

"You left something in the room?"

"No. I forgot this." He bent his knees to put his height on a level with hers, tilted his head under the brim of her hat and slanted his mouth over hers.

His lips moved but a little, but she felt their sweet pressure all along her body. His tongue barely breached her lips to touch the tip of hers, but he could have been teasing her fingertips, her nipples, secret places deep inside her, for she felt the titillating caress in all those places.

When he pulled back, she was exceedingly warm and tingling. "You fogged up my sunglasses," she said in a husky voice.

"Sorry?"

She shook her head. He was well into a second kiss when the elevator door whooshed open. Flustered, Arden said, "I've got to make arrangements about my room."

"I'll save us a place in the limo."

She waded through the crowd at the concierge's desk. Naturally, it was jammed that time of day, with guests either checking out or checking in or making reservations for various excursions via land, sea or air to other parts of the island. She cast several anxious glances over her shoulder toward the front doors before it was finally her turn.

Hastily, she explained that she wanted to pay for the days she had occupied her room but wanted to keep it until she returned in three days. After repeating her request several times, she finally made herself understood over the hubbub. The harried clerk found her registration card, ran her credit card through his machine, smiled at her toothily, wished her a good trip and expressed his gratitude for her business. She felt uneasily that she'd been dismissed, but before she could get the clerk's attention again, Drew was calling to her.

"Arden, the limo's waiting."

"I'm coming," she called back, and made her way through the crowd until he clasped her hand and pulled her toward the door.

"No problems?"

"No."

"Good. We're barely going to make it."

Once they were seated in the limo and speeding toward the airport, she realized that in just a few minutes she would see her son. Her heart was pounding in her chest, and her breathing was shallow.

"You're not scared of flying, are you?" Drew asked, mistaking the source of her obvious nervousness.

"No. I don't mind flying, although I prefer the larger jets."

"I like the smaller airplanes because I can see more. Besides, this airport, such as it is, is only five minutes from home. And it's a good commuter airline. I know just about everyone on staff by now."

Kaanapali Airport, as Drew had said, wasn't much compared to major-city airports. The building was about the size of a self-service gas station. But it was a beehive of activity. As each plane landed and disgorged its nine passengers, another would be taking off.

The resort's van pulled up with a jarring halt. Drew hauled her bag onto his shoulder, stepped out ahead of her and offered her a hand to help her down.

"They should be somewhere… Ah, there they are." His chin lifted, indicating that Arden should look behind her. She drew in a great amount of air, squeezed her eyes shut momentarily and turned around. She had to lock her trembling knees to keep them from buckling under her. Drew hadn't noticed. He was walking away from her toward a grove of trees. "Matt," he shouted.

Arden saw him, and her heart turned over.

He was wearing a white shirt and a pair of bright red shorts with a bib and shoulder straps that crisscrossed over his back. White knee socks encased stocky calves. He had on white high-topped shoes. The pumping chubby legs came to a weaving halt when Matt heard his father's voice, and he turned around, squealed and came racing back in the opposite direction toward Drew. A woman in a white uniform, who was as wide as she was tall, came huffing along behind him on amazingly small feet for someone her size.

Arden had eyes only for the blond boy who almost toppled over in his excitement before he barreled into his father's legs and was swooped over the tall man's head.

"Hey, you little dynamo, slow down or you're going to skin your knees again," Drew said, shaking the boy, whose peals of laughter filled the morning air.

"Up, up," he shouted.

"Later," Drew said, swinging him down to hold him

in the crook of his arm. "I want you to meet a lady, Arden," he said, turning to the pale, transfixed woman beside him, "this is Matt."

Her eyes were rapacious, trying to devour as much of him as she could. She searched for something familiar but found little. His coloring was his father's: blond hair, blue eyes. There was a squareness to his chin that reminded her a little of her father.

She saw none of herself, but she could not have been more certain that this was her son. She knew by the way her breasts expanded, as though filling with the milk that had never been allowed to come. She knew by the contracting of her womb as she remembered each time she felt the movement of a fist or a foot or laughed at a case of prenatal hiccups that echoed through her own body. She knew because of her yearning to touch him, to clutch his sweet, young, healthy body to her.

"Hi, Matt," she rasped out.

The child stared back at her with candid curiosity. "Say *aloha,* Matt," his father directed him, nudging his stomach.

"O-ha," he mumbled before turning in Drew's arms and shyly burying his face against his father's neck.

Drew closed his arms tight around his son and rubbed his back. He looked at Arden over Matt's blond curls. "We're still working on etiquette," he said, smiling apologetically.

"Mr. McCasslin, I thought I'd let him run off some energy before the airplane ride," the nurse panted as she came up to them.

"Good idea. Mrs. Laani, I want you to meet Ms. Gentry. She's our guest for the next several days."

"*Aloha,* Mrs. Laani," Arden said, dragging her eyes

away from the soft skin on her son's nape. She used to tickle Joey there with her mouth. "Getting sugar," she called it.

The middle-aged Polynesian woman was eyeing her with open curiosity. She seemed to like what she saw, for her round, unlined face split into a broad grin.

"*Aloha,* Ms. Gentry. I'm glad you're coming with us. Sometimes two men are too much for me to handle."

"Fine," Drew said. "Your job is to handle Matt. Let Arden handle me."

Arden blushed beneath her hat, but Mrs. Laani laughed gustily. Arden liked her instantly. Despite her size, she was neat to a fault, her uniform crisply starched. Her hair was cut short and permanently curled to form a dark, silver-threaded wreath around her head.

One of the employees of the commuter airline stepped out onto the porch. "Mr. McCasslin, we're ready for your party to board now."

"Did you get all the luggage on board?" Drew asked the attendant, who checked them off the passenger list.

"Yes, sir, we sure did."

"Add this," he said, handing the man Arden's bag.

"I don't mind carrying it on board," she offered.

"No, ma'am," the attendant said. "The seats are too small. All luggage has to go in the back."

A man in shirtsleeves, whom Arden determined was their pilot, slapped Drew on the back. "When are you going to treat me to another match? I finally recovered from the last one." As they chatted, they made their way onto the tarmac to the waiting plane. Drew was still carrying Matt on his shoulders. Arden had yet to take her eyes off him. She was grateful that the confusion of boarding the airplane provided her with an opportunity to stare at him without anyone noticing.

Mrs. Laani's bulk could barely squeeze through the narrow door of the aircraft. She sank into one of the seats in the back so she wouldn't have to wedge herself through the aisle.

"Care to ride in the copilot's chair this morning?" the pilot asked Drew.

He grinned boyishly. "You know that's my favorite seat." He turned to Arden. "Do you mind sitting beside Matt?"

She shook her head, not trusting herself to speak. She took the window seat so Matt wouldn't feel so confined. Drew buckled him into the seat beside hers and just behind his. "There we go, hotshot. You can be the navigator, okay?"

Matt smiled, revealing eight pearly teeth. His excitement wavered when the pilot started the noisy engines. His back went ramrod straight, his eyes widened, and his lower lip began to tremble. Arden placed her hand on his knee, and when he looked up at her fearfully, she smiled. Drew turned around, winked at the boy and reached back to pat him on the head.

Matt sat still and stiff until the plane gained altitude and he was convinced he was in no immediate danger. Only one stranger had boarded the plane with them, and he had fallen asleep immediately. As had Mrs. Laani. Matt grew restless and strained against his seat belt. After first checking with Drew and the pilot, Arden released it.

"Just don't let him crawl around too much," Drew told her. "If he gets too rambunctious, pass him up here."

"No. He'll be fine." Drew went back to his conversation with the pilot, and she devoted her attention to Matt, as she had longed to do. In typical little-boy fashion he couldn't sit still. He twisted and turned in his seat, tried to stand up, wobbled unsteadily and sat back down. He investigated everything.

Arden watched each movement, adored it and savored it for the time when she'd have to leave him again. She hadn't made plans beyond this point, beyond getting to see her son. But she knew she couldn't uproot him from the life he had. She couldn't do that to his father, and she knew it wouldn't be best for Matt, either. For right now, she only wanted to love Matt, silently and secretly, but love him as only a mother could.

When she patted her lap, he paused for only a moment before climbing up into it. He studied her closely and reached out and poked the lens of her glasses with a damp fist.

"Thanks," she joked as she took the glasses off to clean the smudged lens. "Between you and your dad, I'm having a hard time seeing out of these."

He grinned and pointed toward the back of Drew's head. "Dad."

"Yes," she exclaimed, laughing. She touched his cheek and marveled at how soft it was. His hair, too, curled softly around her fingers. It was only several shades away from platinum, and as he grew older, it would darken to the wheat color of Drew's. Lovingly, she ran her hands over his dimpled arms and let him wrap tight, damp fists around her fingers. Quoting a nonsense rhyme, she made a game of squeezing his knees until he giggled. "A good child, a good child /

As I suppose you be, / Will neither laugh nor cry / At
the tickling of your knee."

When he didn't resist, she pulled him into her arms
and held him close. She hugged him as tight as he'd
allow. He smelled of baby soap and clean clothes and
sunshine. Mrs. Laani took good care of him. He was
spotless; his fingernails were well trimmed. Arden
loved the sturdiness of his body. Joey had been so pitifully frail. When she left Matt, she'd leave knowing
that he was healthy and normal.

And like any normal, healthy little boy, he rebelled
against so much affection. He squirmed away from
her, taking her hat off in the process. Playfully, she
placed the hat on his head, and it all but swallowed him.
They played peekaboo from under the floppy brim for
a while. Inspired, she put the glasses on his nose. He
had to hold his head still to keep them from slipping
off, and she could see his eyes rolling back and forth
behind the lenses to watch her as she took a compact
from her purse. When she held the mirror up to him,
he crowed with glee.

"Dad, Dad," he called, getting to his feet in Arden's
lap and hitting Drew on the head. The hat and glasses
were knocked askew, but Matt didn't notice.

Drew turned around and burst out laughing at the
comical sight. "You look worse than E.T. in the wedding dress," he hooted. Matt bobbed up and down until
he became a little too wild and had to be calmed down.
When he eventually tired of the hat and glasses, Arden
placed them in his chair and took him back on her lap.

The droning motors of the plane and her gentle maternal stroking of his hair lulled him, and soon his
head was resting heavily on her breasts. She couldn't

believe that she'd been blessed with this moment. It was more than she had allowed herself to hope for. He liked her, trusted her instinctively, enough to fall asleep against her.

She could feel the rapid beating of his heart against hers and thought of the irrevocable and eternal bond that bound them. There was none other like it in the universe, that between mother and child. Her body had nourished him, breathed for him, sheltered him. Emotion such as she'd never known welled up inside.

Drew glanced at them and did a double take when he saw the rapt attention Arden was giving his son. She was absorbed in the small hand she held in hers, massaging the tiny knuckles. As though she sensed him watching her, she raised her head, and he was further startled to see tears pooling in her eyes. She smiled at him tremulously, then once again lowered her eyes to the boy sleeping on her bosom.

The pilot landed the plane expertly and taxied toward the terminal. As soon as he cut the engines, he excused himself and hurried to the back of the aircraft to assist Mrs. Laani out. The other passenger left as soon as he located his briefcase.

Drew eased himself down on the edge of the seat next to Arden's. He studied her for a moment with probing blue eyes before he spoke. "I see you two have taken to each other."

"I hope so. He's dear, Drew. So dear. A wonderful little boy."

"I think so."

Lightly, she ruffled the blond curls. "Was he a good baby?"

"Ellie and I didn't have anything to compare him

to, but we thought so. He was hard to come by. We wouldn't have cared if he'd squalled all the time."

Her next question would be like stepping off a high diving board into a vat of fire. The quantity of adrenaline that pumped through her veins was the same as if she were. "Ellie had a difficult time having him?"

There followed a significant pause. She continued to stare down at the sleeping child, noting each eyelash that rested on his flushed cheeks.

"Not exactly," Drew said slowly. "She had a hard time conceiving him."

"Oh." It relieved her conscience somewhat to know that Drew had chosen to lie, also. How far could she fish before he became suspicious? "Does he look like his mother?"

"Ellie was blond," he answered noncommittally. "I think he takes more after me, though."

Arden looked up at him then and smiled, though there were still tears in her eyes. "As a proud father, you're biased."

"I'm sure that has a lot to do with it," he answered with a hint of self-mockery. "I can't really tell how much he looks like his...mother."

Arden looked away again, quickly, before he could see her wounded expression. But he saw the tear that rolled down her cheek. Raising her head with a gentle fist under her chin, he lifted away the tear with his fingertip.

"Because of the son you lost?" The question was asked with such tenderness and compassion that a new, unnamed emotion blossomed in her chest. She was stunned by it. Stunned and frightened.

Now, now, she said to herself. He had presented her

with the perfect opportunity to tell him that she had just now *found* her son, that she had borne this boy whose life Drew treasured. But the words wouldn't come. He might yank her son away and never let her see him again. He might think that she'd been using him all this time to get to her son.

Wasn't that what she had done?

No, no! She cared as much for the father now as she did for her child. She couldn't hurt Drew, not when he had just gotten his life back in order and regained his self-confidence. No. She couldn't tell him yet. Later. When the time was right, she'd know it.

"Yes," she said. "Because of the son I lost."

Drew nodded in understanding. Matt's breath whistled through his cherubic mouth. He had left a trickle of saliva on Arden's top.

"He's getting your blouse wet," Drew whispered in the still silence. He couldn't have honestly said which he found the most captivating, his son's sweet mouth or the sweet place it rested against. Her breast was plumped out from the weight of Matt's head and looked maternal and comforting, and he longed to touch it, to stroke its full softness.

"I don't mind." And she didn't. She didn't care if the child irreparably stained every garment she owned as long as she could continue to hold him.

Entranced, she watched as Drew's index finger reached toward his son's cheek. He brushed it lovingly, then moved toward the open baby lips and picked up the beads of moisture that lingered there. Fascinated both by what she was seeing and the love that was bubbling inside her, she watched the finger trail slowly from the child's mouth to the wet spot on her breast.

He touched it, but had she not been watching, she might not have known it, so light was that touch. Then, moving with excruciating slowness, he turned his hands and cradled his son's head, placing the back of his hand against Arden's breast.

A shudder of emotion rippled through her, and a soft half sob escaped her trembling lips. Her eyes were made blind by collecting tears. Drew's head snapped up, and his blue eyes pierced into her wide green ones.

"Arden, don't cry anymore." Without moving anything but his head, he joined their mouths together. This kiss wasn't restrained like the one in the elevator earlier that morning. This one was rife with emotions, any one of which would have been sufficient to tear down all their defenses.

His tongue delved deeply and was received into the snug warmth of her mouth. Without thinking about it, her hand came up and pressed Matt's head to her breast, trapping Drew's hand between them. Now she was holding them both. The son. The father. So long dreamed about, speculated on. Ever elusive. Now her flesh could feel them both; her senses could luxuriate in the sounds, smells and sights of them. Their bodies were the most beautiful in the world to her. With one, she had created the other.

Drew groaned softly, and his lips twisted over hers. With his fingers, he caressed his son's head. It wasn't accidental that his fingers were also moving against Arden's nipple with the same pressure his tongue applied inside her mouth. His passion coursed through her, down her throat and straight into her body until it touched her femininity and bathed it with liquid heat. And she knew then what it would have been like had they made Matt in the conventional way, and she felt cheated, bereft at not having had the full knowledge of that miracle.

"God," Drew moaned as he pulled away at last, lifting the still-sleeping Matt into his arms. "If you go on kissing me like that, I'll start crying myself. And for an entirely different reason."

He helped her out of the airplane into the balmy sunlight. The sleeping Matt was draped over his shoulder. With his free hand, Drew clasped hers, and they made their way to the terminal.

THEIR SUITE OF rooms at the Sheraton was spacious and faced the ocean with an unrestricted view of Diamond Head. There was a sitting room that separated the room Mrs. Laani and Matt would share from Drew's bedroom. Arden had the room across the hall from his.

"Here's a key to the suite if you should need one," he said on their way up in the elevator. "Make yourself at home anytime." He pressed the key into her palm, making his meaning implicitly clear. When Arden had the nerve to glance at Mrs. Laani, she saw that the woman was beaming a smile. Arden knew they'd both be disappointed if they expected her to use the key.

They got the worst over first. As soon as they had eaten lunch and Matt had taken a short nap, Drew and Mrs. Laani left with him for his appointment with the pediatrician.

Under the hotel's wide breezeway, as they were getting into the car Drew had leased at the airport, he clasped Arden's hand. "We'll be back in about an hour. You're sure you'll be all right?"

"Yes, but I wouldn't mind going along." In fact, she

wanted desperately to go with them but knew it would seem unnatural to press the issue.

"That's generous of you, but I wouldn't force this on anyone." Drew laughed. "Matt's not the most cooperative of patients. Shop, sightsee and we'll meet you back in the suite by five o'clock."

"Okay," she said resignedly. He kissed her quickly on the cheek, and they sped away.

Matt was obviously miffed at both Mrs. Laani and his father when they brought him back to the hotel. He treated them as enemies who had put him through a terrible ordeal. He would have nothing to do with either of them during the early dinner they ate at one of the coffee shops in the hotel complex. Only Arden was allowed to cater to him.

"You're only making it worse," Drew said as she fed ice cream to Matt after his dinner. "He'll think you're his fairy godmother or something."

Arden almost dropped the spoon but managed to recover. She looked pleadingly at Mrs. Laani and Drew. "Let me spoil him. He's had a hard day."

The child was querulous with everyone by the time dinner was over, and Drew firmly suggested they make it an early night.

"As soon as Matt's in bed," Mrs. Laani said, "I'd like to go out for a while. My sister wanted me to come see her and meet my niece's fiancé."

"That's fine with me," Drew said.

"Why don't you go on now?" Arden rushed to say. "I don't mind putting Matt to bed. In fact, I'd love to. There's no sense in your postponing your visit."

"Are you sure you know what you're letting yourself in for?" Drew asked her, his brows creasing over skeptical eyes.

"Yes." Arden turned to Mrs. Laani. "Go on. Matt and I will get along fine."

It was settled, and Mrs. Laani left a few minutes later. Between the two of them, Drew and Arden managed to get the cross little boy bathed and snapped into pajamas. Arden almost regretted that he was so fractious and sleepy. She would have loved to have played with him longer.

It was she who laid him in the portable crib the hotel had provided and patted his back until he fell asleep. Drew had already withdrawn into the other room. She stayed by the crib until Drew called to her.

When she joined him in the sitting room, he was leaning back in the sofa with his feet stretched out in front of him. He had changed into a pair of shorts and a T-shirt. He was barefoot. Arden admired the bunched muscles in his arms and legs, the rippling ridges of muscle on his chest. She loved, too, the way his body hair shone golden against his bronzed skin in the soft lamplight.

"Come here and crash," he said, extending his hand. "I'd get up and come get you, but I'm pooped."

She laughed and sank down beside him on the sofa. "A big strapping boy like you being worn out by one twenty-month-old!" she teased.

He grunted. "He can wear me out faster than a tennis match. Incidentally, I've got to practice while I'm here. Want to watch me tomorrow morning?"

"Of course."

"We'll make good our escape before Matt realizes we're gone. Mrs. Laani can take him to the park or

something. Right now I'm feeling very jealous of my
son for absorbing so much of your attention." He turned
to face her, letting his eyes take in her pleasantly rumpled appearance. As he had been sure she would, she
made even domesticity look elegant.

"You shouldn't," she said, wishing she had the courage to brush the wayward strands of hair from his forehead. "The reason I like him so much is because he's
related to you."

His eyes gleamed with pleasure. "Is that right?"

"That's right." It was true. She loved Matt not only
because he was her son but also because he was Drew's.
It only stood to reason that she loved Drew, as well.
But what kind of love? Was it merely because he was
Matt's father? No. She was in love with this man, and
it had nothing to do with Matt.

He was looking at her in the same intense way she
was surveying him. "This is twice today my son has
gotten you wet." His finger traced the damp patterns
that Matt's body, wet from his bath, had left on the
casual blouse that had replaced her traveling clothes.

His hand paused at the top curve of her breast, and
his eyes met hers. "From the very beginning, you were
no casual pickup, no quick lay. Tell me you know that."

Shaking her head and closing her eyes briefly, she
said, "Yes, I know that." She dared to meet his gaze
again, knowing as she did that she was making an
error in judgment. Her conscience screamed at her, but
she ignored it because she wanted him so badly. "Last
night, I was afraid."

"Of me?"

"Of...this."

"And now?"

She shook her head, and his face tightened with emotion. His hand moved down, over the swelling mound of her breast. He looked at what he touched in a way that endeared him to her. She got as much pleasure from watching the delight in his eyes as she did from the stirring way his hand caressed her. When he raised his head, his eyes were smoldering with desire, and he held her captive in that swirling inferno. He was looking directly into her eyes when his fingertip grazed the tip of her breast. It ripened beneath his touch. They cried each other's names simultaneously.

His mouth came down hard on hers as his arms enfolded her. She locked her hands behind his neck and opened her lips to his tongue. It mated with hers, rubbing and pressing and thrusting, intimating the most primitive of lovemaking.

"God, but you're sweet," he whispered against her throat. He nuzzled her neck, left tiny love bites on the fragile skin, tasted her with the tip of his tongue.

He palmed the generous fullness of her breast, kneaded it tenderly, then sought the nipple with his thumb. He worried it to tight perfection before ducking his head and taking it between his lips. Even through her clothes, the moist fury of his mouth surrounded her, drove her mad with its sensuous tugging cadence.

She lay back against the cushions, urged down by his reclining weight. His desire strained against the cloth of his shorts. She felt it against her thigh and thrilled to it. Her hands slipped under his T-shirt and began working it up even as he began to unbutton her blouse. His mouth returned to hers for quick sipping kisses. "I want to love you. Now, Ellie, now."

Arden froze.

Drew jerked upright when he heard the words leave his mouth. *What had he said?* It took only one look at Arden's chalky face to know.

He vaulted off the couch to his feet. The heels of his hands dug viciously into his eye sockets as his face contorted into a feral scowl of rage and agony.

When he could no longer contain it, a vile expletive erupted from his mouth.

CHAPTER SIX

THEY WERE PETRIFIED by shock. Drew's blasting curse had left a vacuum of silence behind it, like the absence of oxygen immediately following an explosion, like the sulfurous charge in the air after lightning has struck. They were held paralyzed in that deadly quiet void.

When at last he spoke, his voice carried a great weariness with it. "I'm sorry, Arden." He raised his arms in helpless appeal. "Dammit, what else can I say but that I'm sorry?"

Arden stood like a somnambulist, swayed slightly, but at last was able to propel herself toward the door, rearranging her clothes as she went.

"Arden." He said her name softly, apologetically, but when she didn't turn around, he repeated it with more force. When she didn't stop then, he lunged after her. "Arden," he said, grabbing her arm and turning her around. "Listen—"

"Let me go, Drew." She kept her head averted, her voice iron hard and cold.

"Not until you've listened to an explanation."

She laughed without humor. It was a hollow, lifeless sound. "I think this poignant scene is self-explanatory." She struggled against his tenacious hold. Had she not been so civilized, she would have clawed, kicked. She was frantic to get away. "Let me go," she shouted.

"I don't belong here. I don't know why I'm here. It's wrong. Let me go." She was bordering on hysteria but couldn't contain it and fought the manacle of his hand around her upper arm.

"You *do* belong here because I invited you. I want you here with me and Matt."

"You want Ellie here!" she screamed up at him.

His face, which had been working with anger at himself and frustration over her misunderstanding, went completely blank. Her cruel words erased all expression. The steely fingers around her arm relaxed, and his arm fell to his side. "Ellie *is* here," he whispered. "That's the problem."

He returned to the sofa with trudging footsteps. Slumping down onto it, he laid his head against the back cushions and closed his eyes.

The moment Arden flung her hateful accusation in his face, she would have given heaven and earth to recall it. As he turned away from her, she reached out a comforting hand, but pulled it back. The last thing he would want now was her pity. But she couldn't leave without saying something.

"What I said was unforgivable, Drew."

He scoffed with the same bitterness she had shown only moments before. "What *I* said was unforgivable. I know you feel insulted. Don't. You should feel flattered." He opened his eyes and looked at her. "I'd like to explain."

"You don't have to."

"I want to." His tone was determined. She nodded.

He stood up and walked to the wide glass door. Sliding it open, he let the scent and sound of the Pacific Ocean fill the suddenly stifling room. "Honolulu is where Ellie and I met, where we lived when we were married. I can't come back here without having a million places and things remind me of her or something she said or something we did."

"I know what that's like. After Joey died, sometimes the memories were so strong, I would think I'd hear his voice."

He shook his head in aggravation. "She's been on my mind since we arrived. We used to take Matt to the pediatrician together, you see. Tomorrow I'm taking him to visit her parents." Arden didn't want to acknowledge the stab of envy that pierced through her. "And all day, I've felt like…like I was being unfaithful to Ellie."

"Because of me?"

"Yes."

Sorry as she was about what she'd said to him, she felt he'd slapped her in the face again. "Is that supposed to make me feel better?" she asked scathingly. He pivoted around, and she saw again that flicker of impatience in his eyes. Actually, she preferred it to the haunted vacancy that had been there moments before.

"It might if you wouldn't fly off the handle, if you'd let me tell you a few things before you jump to conclusions."

"You make me sound like an unscrupulous home wrecker."

"Dammit, will you *listen?*" He muttered a curse and shoved strands of hair off his forehead. "There have been other women, Arden. Since Ellie and before you."

"I'm feeling better all the time."

He frowned at her sarcasm before going on. "Too many women. One-night stands. Faceless, nameless women that I was later glad I couldn't remember." He closed the distance between them and peered closely into her eyes to emphasize his next point. "They meant nothing. Nothing," he said, slicing the air with his hands. "My desire for them was a biological function, nothing more. What I did with those women could be described in the coarsest of terms because that's all it was. I didn't feel I had betrayed Ellie, at least not our love, because there was no emotional involvement for me."

He took a breath that expanded his chest almost enough to touch her. His voice lowered in pitch and volume. "You're the first woman I've felt guilty about."

Her outrage receding, she wet her lips nervously. "Why?"

"Because with you there *is* an emotional involvement. With you it wouldn't be just…" He searched for a less abrasive word, shrugged and said bluntly, "Screwing." He placed his hands on her shoulders and drew her closer. "It would be loving. I'm falling in love with you, Arden. I'm surprised by it. Actually dismayed. And I don't quite know how to handle it."

She swallowed the knot in her throat. "You still love Ellie." There was no inquiry in her voice; it was a simple statement of fact.

"I'll always love her. She was a part of my life. But I swear to God I'm not trying to replace her with you. The two of you are too totally different. Nothing alike. So please don't think that because I spoke her name while I was loving you, I superimposed her image over your body. I wasn't thinking of her. I was immersed in you, only you."

He brought his hands up to her face and alternately

stroked her cheekbones with his thumbs. "It's just that this is the first time since her death that my heart has been an integral part of having sex. Speaking her name was a conditioned reflex, because I haven't felt that emotional and spiritual rush since I last held Ellie. Not until you. Don't assign any Freudian implications to it, please."

"I reacted out of conditioned reflex, too. My pride was stung," she cried. "Any woman's would have been."

"Or any man's. I'm not diminishing my error. Believe me, I know I was ghastly. I just want you to know where it was coming from. Tell me you understand."

When he was close like this, she couldn't think, so she stepped away from him and stared out the glass door herself. She wondered if he would be telling her all this if he knew who she was. If she identified herself as the surrogate mother he and Ellie had hired, would he still want to make love to her? How could she ever hurt him and risk losing him by telling him the truth?

"I do understand, Drew. You and Ellie had a rare and special marriage." She could have added, "She loved you enough to let another woman have your child."

"Yes, we did. I was faithful to our vows." He laughed softly. "On tour, that's not always easy. There are opportunities every day. Whatever you want, it's available."

He came to stand beside her, propping himself in the doorframe by leaning into it with his shoulder. "Ellie traveled with me when she could, but not all the time. Sometimes I wanted sex. Badly. And there were plenty of women who would have obliged. But I knew how rotten I'd feel afterward. And it would be more than just feeling guilty for being unfaithful. After having experienced sex as a part of love, I really didn't want it any other way. I didn't want it reduced to a merely physical exercise."

He glanced at her quickly. "I'm not a saint. There were times when I was strongly tempted. Particularly if I'd played well, won a match and wanted to celebrate. The adrenaline would be pumping, and I'd want…want to make love."

She looked away, out over the ceaseless surf. Quietly, she said, "I can see how one would go with the other. How physical stamina would give you more energy…make you…"

His laughter this time was genuine, and he cupped her chin with his hand and turned her face back to his. "I know what you're thinking, Ms. Gentry."

"I'm not thinking—"

"You're thinking that since I was playing well that first day we met and since you were sitting there on that patio all cool and serene and appealing as hell, I automatically wanted to hop in the sack with you and work off some excess energy."

She blushed and hated herself for being so transparent. Drew smiled wider, knowing he'd been right on target. "Well, I'll admit I was aroused from that first day. I've given making love to you a lot of thought since we met, particularly after our first lunch date. You looked so untouchably sophisticated, yet you nearly drove me to distraction in that little black top that fit like a second skin over your breasts."

She gasped softly in surprise, but he continued. "Arden, here," he touched the fly of his shorts, "I've been ready to make love since I first saw you. Here," he touched his temple, "I know it's time I loved again.

It's here," he said, indicating his heart, "that I'm in conflict."

"You don't hold a monopoly on that," she said, brushing past him and going back into the room. "Hasn't it occurred to you that this might be different for me, too?" She whirled on him. "I'm not accustomed to accompanying men on three-day vacations." Her eyes darted past him as she said in a quieter tone, "The only man I've slept with was my husband. Before or after we were married. It was a lousy marriage. In every way." She hazarded a look toward him. He was listening closely, his eyes trained on her.

"He and I didn't love each other the way you and Ellie were lucky enough to. And when the marriage was over, I gave all the love I had to give to Joey. When I lost him, too, I felt empty, depleted of emotion, a shell with no soul inside. Until…" She raked her bottom lip with her teeth and cautioned herself not to reveal too much.

"Anyway, I'm not ready to gamble with my heart, either. I've lost my parents, my husband, such as he was, and my son. I don't know that I'm ready to risk loving anyone else."

"The odds don't look particularly promising when you're risking it on a has-been tennis bum and his orphaned son."

"Don't say that about yourself," she said fiercely. "You're *not* a has-been and certainly not a bum. And Matt is—"

She broke off when she saw the grin tilting up one side of Drew's lips. "You've just put your foot in it, Arden. You care more than you want to admit."

She lowered her eyes in chagrin. When she raised

her eyes again, he could see that they were brimming with tears. "I'm afraid, Drew."

He went to her and wrapped his arms around her. His large, strong hand cradled her head and pressed it into his shoulder. "What are you afraid of?"

Afraid that if you find out who I am you won't believe how much I've come to love you. I wanted my son, but now I think I want you more, and that's wrong of me. Isn't it? I don't know. I don't know.

"I'm afraid to let myself love again."

He pulled away only far enough to look down into her face. He squeezed his hand between their bodies and placed it over her heart. "You have so much love to give. I can feel it, beating here, trying to get out. Don't be afraid to let it go." He lowered his head, and his lips made a pass across her brow as his hand cupped her breast and made a caressing circular motion. "God, Arden, but it would be easy and right for us to love each other."

Yes, it would be so easy. Her body gravitated toward his as naturally as the river flowed toward the falls. And just as perilously, she wanted to hurl herself over the cliff of conscience and principle.

But would it be *right*? Would he feel it was right if he knew that their meeting hadn't been dictated by fate but had been contrived by her for the purpose of finding her son? She tamped out the fires of desire that were already rekindling.

His lips hovered above hers, but she placed her fingers over them. "Don't, Drew. Not now. If we ever make love, I want everything to be perfect. It wasn't that way for me with my husband." Before she could say more, his mouth stopped her. It was a kiss that promised loving him would be beyond her previous experience and her wildest imagination.

Shakily, she went on when he lifted his lips from hers. "Until such a time, we have our private wars to wage. I don't want you to blame me for any guilt feelings you might have over Ellie."

"You're not to blame," he whispered into her hair. "I blame only myself."

She maneuvered her mouth away from the seductive persuasion of his. "Let's continue being just close friends for the present. Please?"

He sighed his disappointment, but she knew he was going to agree. His smile was wry. "You're making it hard on me." His nose nuzzled her ear. "In case you didn't catch it, there's a pun in there."

"I caught it," she said dryly, pushing him away. "It was in exceedingly bad taste."

"I told you I wasn't a saint."

"Then I'd better clear out while my virtue is still intact. What time do you practice in the morning?" They arranged to meet and have a quick cup of coffee before driving to the courts.

At the door, he caught her waist with both hands. They were indomitably possessive as they squeezed lightly. His eyes swept her breasts and lingered. She focused on the hollow of his throat.

"Arden, do you honestly believe we're going to remain just good friends?"

Her eyes took in the sensuous shape of his mouth. "No."

His voice was slurred with longing when he replied, "Neither do I."

THEY WERE FRIENDLY the next morning when they met, the tension of the evening before having been dispelled. Drew kissed her briefly on the mouth as he cheerfully greeted her. When they arrived at the courts at the appointed time, he introduced her to his opponent. Bart Samson was a retired professional, Drew's senior by fifteen years, but he could still play a mean game of tennis.

They played on municipal courts, which surprised Arden, but she didn't remark on it. She sat on the splintery bleachers and watched the match. She had brought along a tablet and pen, should she want to work on an article, but took very few notes. Drew's superb game held her attention.

"Thanks for the workout, Bart," Drew said to the man as they strolled toward the parking lot when they were through.

The older man ran a towel over his face and around the back of his neck. "Thank *you*. You whipped me, but it was great tennis." He looked at Arden before he said, "Why don't you meet me at Waialee tomorrow? This—" he indicated the less than perfect courts "—isn't where someone of your caliber should be playing. Everyone at the country club would love to see you again, Drew."

"Thanks, Bart, but no. Not yet." He took Arden's hand. "If you'd rather not play here with me, I'll understand," he said frostily.

"I don't deserve that," Bart replied quietly and without rancor. "Here, tomorrow morning at eight." He nodded to Arden before sliding into his Mercedes and starting the motor.

They were almost back at the hotel before Arden

said, "You and Ellie were members of Waialee Country Club, weren't you?"

"Yes, why?" he asked, momentarily taking his eyes off the rush-hour traffic.

"Nothing. I just wondered."

At the next stoplight, he leaned toward her. "My not wanting to play there has nothing to do with Ellie or you or our old friends seeing you and me together. They'd all be delighted with you, I'm sure. The reason I don't want to play there is because I made a spectacle of myself the last time. I'm not ready to face the club set yet. Okay?"

"Not okay. You should go back and play there with your head held high. Talk to old friends. You've got absolutely nothing to be ashamed of, Drew."

He studied her for a time, grudgingly admiring the wisdom of what she said and appreciating her vote of confidence in him. "Give me a kiss."

"No."

"Because I'm sweaty and stinky?"

"No. Because the light turned green about thirty seconds ago and all the cars behind us are honking."

He cursed softly as he released the brake and continued the drive back to the hotel, scowling at Arden's soft chuckles. The moment they opened the door of the suite, they knew something was wrong. Matt, tears streaming down his face, came running to his father, arms outstretched.

Drew scooped him up. "What the hell...?"

"Mrs. Laani!" Arden cried, crossing the room swiftly when she saw the woman lying on her back on the sofa, one forearm across her eyes, the other across her stomach. She was moaning pitiably. "Mrs. Laani,"

Arden repeated, going down on her knees beside the sofa and touching the woman's arm, "are you ill?"

"I'm so sick," she groaned. "The baby, he's hungry and wet…but, I'm sorry, Mr. McCasslin," she said when Drew walked into her range of vision. "I couldn't get up. My stomach." She closed her eyes again in misery.

Matt had stopped crying and was hiccuping against Drew's shoulder. "Do you need to go to the doctor? Could it be appendicitis?"

"No. I had my appendix out years ago. It's…at my sister's house. They all had this virus. I guess I caught it. I don't want Matt to get sick."

Arden was touched over Mrs. Laani's concern for the child. "Don't worry about him. He'll be fine. We need to get you feeling better. Can I get you something?"

"You're a nice *wahine*," she said, squeezing Arden's hand. "Thank you, but I don't want anything except to get out of here and keep all of you from catching this. Mr. McCasslin, I called my sister and asked if I could stay with her until I'm well. My brother-in-law is coming to pick me up. I hate to desert you, but—"

"That's all right," Arden said, intervening again. "I can take care of Matt. When is your brother-in-law coming to get you?"

"He should be downstairs now."

"Drew, give Matt to me and I'll get him some breakfast. You help Mrs. Laani down to the lobby. Is that her bag? Here, carry it for her."

"Yes, ma'am," he said as he followed her instructions. Despite his worry over his able housekeeper, whom he'd never seen in less than perfect health, his eyes were twinkling with amusement at the way Arden was taking charge.

They were still sparkling when he returned after escorting Mrs. Laani down to meet her brother-in-law. Arden was helping Matt eat his cereal. There was a small refrigerator in the suite, and Mrs. Laani had stocked it with juice, milk, fruit, cheese and snacks so Matt wouldn't have to be taken to a restaurant for every meal. The hotel management had provided them with a small assortment of dishes and silverware.

"How is she?" Arden asked.

"Miserable, but relieved that she's separating herself from Matt. He was her main worry. She expects that if she lives for the next twenty-four hours, she'll survive."

"I think so, too. It's probably just a bug."

"And in the meantime—"

"I'll take care of Matt."

"I can't let you do that."

"Why not? Don't you trust me with him?"

He placed his hands on his hips in exasperation. "Yes, I trust you with him, but I didn't bring you along to take over as nursemaid."

Feeling glowingly content, with her child on her lap and his father looking ruggedly handsome in his sweat-damp tennis clothes, she cocked her head to one side and asked impishly, "Why *did* you bring me along?"

"To woo you into bed with me."

She laughed. "Well, before you proceed, would you please go take a shower?"

He looked down at himself, grinned abashedly and said, "Oh, yeah. That might be a good idea."

By the time Drew had showered, she had Matt bathed and dressed. "If you'll give me just a few minutes, I'll be ready, too." She'd told him she needed some things for Matt, and they'd decided to make a short shopping expedition. "Let me pop into my room and I'll be right back."

"I was meaning to talk to you about that."

"About what?" she paused to ask as she was sailing out the door.

"About your room. Wouldn't it be more convenient if you moved in here?"

She fixed him with a doubtful stare. "Convenient for whom?"

His smile fell on her like warm sunshine. "For you. And Matt, of course."

"Oh, of course."

"Think about it," he said, shrugging with feigned nonchalance.

"I already have. The answer is no."

She met them in the designated place in the lobby ten minutes later, looking amazingly well put together after having dressed so quickly. "I like those stretchy little tops you wear," Drew said in her ear as he draped an arm around her shoulders. Matt was walking with independent importance a few steps ahead of them.

"This is a sundress," she said, smiling her pleasure.

"Yeah, but it's made like that top you had on that day at lunch. I loved it because—"

"I know. You've already told me."

"Because it—"

"It's high fashion."

"Because it shows your nipples when they contract. Like now."

"Stop it." She tried to sound indignant and failed.

"It makes me wonder what color they are and how they'll feel against my tongue."

She made a whimpering sound. "Please, Drew, stop talking that way."

"Okay. I will. But only because those two sailors are ogling you in a way that makes me want to knock their heads together. The last thing they need to see is that limpid look in your eyes. It's the biggest come-on I've ever seen, and a man would have to be dead not to notice it." He all but snarled at the two hapless sailors as they walked past them. Then he hissed in her ear, "You've got great legs, too." She laughed.

He was highly irritated that one of the items on the shopping list was disposable diapers. "Matt's supply is running low," Arden explained.

"I want to get him out of diapers, but Mrs. Laani says he's not ready to potty train yet."

"And she's right. It can be traumatic if you try to train a child too early."

"I know," he grumbled, shoving his hands into the pockets of his navy blue shorts. The lean muscles of his thighs looked sculpted. "It's just that he'll seem officially a son when we can go into the men's room together."

She rolled her eyes heavenward. "The male ego. I can't believe it. I've changed him numerous times and seen him in the bathtub twice. He's officially your *son*."

Drew's eyebrows arched wickedly. "You think he inherited something from me?"

Her cheeks flamed scarlet. She spoke over his hearty laughter. "He might train more quickly if you'd take him into the bathroom with you now and again. Maybe he'd begin to get the idea."

"You're changing the subject."

"You're right."

He kissed her soundly but quickly. "I'll take your suggestion to heart—it sounds like a good idea that I should have thought of myself."

When they returned to the hotel, Arden carrying their parcels and Drew carrying Matt, it was time to clean him up for lunch with Ellie's parents. Arden was dismayed to find that most of her belongings had been moved into the bedroom formerly occupied by Mrs. Laani.

"Remind me to compliment the manager of the hotel on his staff's efficiency."

"Drew," she said, rounding on him, "I won't stay here with you tonight."

"Not with *me*. With Matt. He's in a strange place. He'll feel better with someone in the room with him."

"Then you sleep with him."

He placed an index finger over her lips. "You're too smart for your own good." His eyes followed his finger as it moved over her lips. "Please. Nothing will happen that you don't want to happen. I promise."

In the end, she relented. Actually, being able to spend the night in the same room with her son was like being given a gift.

"You can go with us," Drew repeated for the third time when he and Matt were ready to leave for lunch.

She shook her head as she ran a fine brush through Matt's curls. "No, Drew. I couldn't."

"It wouldn't matter to me. I'd like for them to meet you."

She could tell by his inflection that it was important she believe him. "Thank you for that. But I wouldn't want to spring up from nowhere and probably spoil the visit for them. I know they're looking forward to it."

"They are. Matt's their one-and-only grandchild."

Then they don't really have one, do they? she thought to herself. "Was Ellie an only child?"

"Yes. She moved to the mainland to wait for…until Matt was born. They wanted her to…uh…to have him here, but she wanted to have him in Los Angeles. Anyway, when we brought him home, they were ecstatic. He'll be a demon tonight. They spoil him rotten."

So, even Ellie's parents didn't know that her pregnancy had been a hoax. Did anyone know besides Drew and herself? And Ron, of course.

"What will you do while we're gone?" he asked her.

"Work on an article. I checked with the hotel, and they have a spare typewriter they'll let me use." Drew had discouraged her from carting her portable along. "Or I may go to the pool and work on my tan."

"Wear something modest. I don't want a stray man with dishonorable intentions to get the idea you're available and take it upon himself to make your acquaintance."

She propped her fists on her hips. "That's how I met you."

"That's what scares me."

THE SUN WAS hot, baking into her body. It felt marvelous. The breeze off the ocean was cooling, so only her skin, lightly glossed with tanning lotion, was warm from the afternoon sun. She had tuned out the sounds of laughing tourists, playful children, boisterous teenagers, and listened only to the pounding surf.

Its rhythm was so hypnotic that she could almost feel her body undulating to the beat.

Was it the surf that caused that restlessness in the lower part of her body? Or was it the thought of Drew's kisses, his caressing hands, his tongue in her mouth and licking her skin? He had introduced her to a world of sensuality she'd never known before. Until she met him, she had thought that sphere existed only in the imaginations of poets and dreamers, romantics who wished life could be better than it was. But this world of sight and sound and smell and taste and breathless excitement did exist. If one was fortunate enough to find the right partner to share it. It wasn't a world that could be experienced alone.

For much of her life, she'd been alone. Now her life was so full it frightened her. She was with her living son. *Her son*. And she loved him as passionately as she had loved Joey. She took advantage of every excuse to touch him, to snuggle him to her, to breathe in his delicious smell, to marvel over his powers of reasoning and his physical dexterity.

And she was coming to love, even more passionately, the man who had fathered him.

She was both joyful and sad. Joyful over having found them and loved them. Sad because she knew she couldn't have them. Everyone she had ever loved, she had lost. They would be lost to her, too. The day would come when she'd have to give them up. But until that day, she'd bask in their presence.

"Oh!" she exclaimed, coming bolt upright on her beach towel and knocking Matt down into the sand on his bottom.

"Code," he shrieked, giggling and shaking another ice cube onto her bare stomach.

She gasped again, sucking in her stomach and reaching for his cup of ice at the same time. "Yes, it's 'code,' and as smart as you are, I don't think you could have thought up this prank."

She turned around to see Drew squatting on his heels behind her, grinning like a Cheshire cat. The sight of him in light blue swimming trunks took her breath away as effectively as the ice cubes on her burning skin. The breeze tossed his blond hair, making him look wild and reckless and consummately male.

"Guilty as charged," he said, smiling broadly.

"I thought as much."

"But Matt was all for the idea."

"Like father, like son."

He walked around her to sit on the end of her beach towel. Matt had tottered toward the water and was taking tentative steps into the surf. "I thought I told you to wear something modest. If that's your idea of modest, you need a new dictionary."

Out of contrariness, she had put on the most provocative of her swimsuits. It was of black crocheted cotton yarn lined with flesh-colored material. The top was two triangles held together with braided strings. The bottom was brief and narrowed on the sides of her hips to a single strand of braid.

"I'm not going to let you bully me. Besides, no one has bothered me. Until now," she said pointedly.

"Do I bother you?" The seductive pitch of his voice and the way his eyes took in every erogenous part of her body sent her senses into pandemonium.

Before she could voice a suitable comeback, Drew

was hailed from the low brick wall that separated the hotel's pool area from the beach.

"Drew! Drew, is that you?"

Drew's eyes searched the crowd to see who had called to him, and Arden saw a mixture of vexation and caution when he identified the man. Unenthusiastically, he raised his hand and waved. "I'll be right back. Do you mind watching Matt?"

"Not at all," she said, more concerned about the grim shadow on Drew's face than the active little boy.

Drew cursed mentally as he weaved his way through the sunbathers on the beach to the steps leading up to the patio surrounding the pool. Of all the people to spot him. The last person he wanted to see. Jerry Arnold, manager of the tennis program at Waialee Country Club.

"Hello, Jerry," he said, extending his hand.

"Drew—God, man, it's good to see you." The man pumped his hand. "You're looking great since I last saw you."

Drew smiled grimly. "Well, that's not saying a helluva lot, is it? The last time you saw me, you had me by the shirt collar and you were dragging me out of the locker room, asking me not to come back. I wasn't so drunk that I don't remember."

Jerry Arnold was a head shorter than Drew and much stouter. At one time, he'd played on the pro tour, but he knew before coaches or anyone else kindly told him that he didn't have what it took to play competitive tennis. He'd surrendered his dreams graciously and done the next best thing. He worked with those who did. "I'm sorry, Drew. You gave me no choice."

"I don't blame you, Jerry. You should have revoked my membership and whipped my ass."

"I couldn't," the man said, smiling. He rubbed his jaw in remembrance. "You've got a mean right hook."

Drew chuckled softly. "I was violent and abusive. I'm sorry."

"So was I. I hate to see talent like yours going to waste." His eyes probed Drew's. "I'm hearing terrific things."

"Oh?"

"You're on the way back."

"Yes, I am."

"Prove it."

Drew had been watching Arden and Matt wrestling in the sand. She had beautifully slender thighs and a nicely rounded tush. It took a bold challenge like Jerry's to snap his eyes and his attention away from that. "What did you say?"

"I said prove that you're on the way back up."

"How? By coming back to the club? Bart Samson already asked me this morning. I told him no."

"By coming back to the club…and playing an exhibition match. Tomorrow."

Drew's mouth went dry, and his hands involuntarily knotted into fists that matched the knots forming in his stomach. "I can't," he whispered, terrified.

"You can. I need you to. McEnroe was supposed to be here to play in a match for charity. Muscular dystrophy. Fifty dollars a pop for tickets. He sprained his thumb in—"

"I read about it."

"So his coach says no playing. Not even exhibition. I need you, buddy. And you need this match."

"Like hell I do."

"Like hell you don't. You've got to start sometime,

Drew. Prove to all those who didn't have faith in you that you can climb right back into that number-one seed."

"Not this year. Next, maybe." He hated the way his insides were churning, the way his hands had become slippery with sweat, the acrid taste of fear in his mouth.

"As I said, you've got to start sometime. I talked to Bart. He told me you were here. He said you ran his tail into the ground this morning, said he couldn't return but half your serves."

"What are you, a cheerleader? Are you asking me to play in this match because you need a warm body on the court to save your face, or do you really care about my floundering career and yet-to-be-seen comeback?"

"Both." The man stared up into Drew's taut face, conceding nothing. He was being brutally honest. At least Drew could appreciate that.

Drew was the first to look away. "I don't know, Jerry."

"Look, if I thought you'd get out there and make a fool of yourself, I wouldn't ask. For both our sakes. You've got your head on straight again. I see you've got a new chick. So—"

"She's not a *chick*," Drew said between his teeth.

Jerry's eyebrows expressed his surprise at Drew's rabid defense. He cast a look at the woman on the beach. She was playing with McCasslin's boy. Jerry returned his gaze to Drew, whose anger was still simmering behind glacial eyes. "I'm sorry. I didn't mean to give offense." His face took on an earnestness that couldn't have been faked. "Drew, I don't care if it's a *guy* you're seeing. I'm glad of whoever or whatever is going to bring you back to where you should be. On top."

Drew let the muscles of his body relax. He was surprised at his possessive, protective attitude toward Arden; it had momentarily overruled his better judgment. He'd been almost ready to kill Jerry for slighting her. In that moment, he realized the extent of his feelings for her. It thrilled him. It also imbued him with confidence.

"Who's playing?"

"Teddy Gonzales."

Drew's curse was terse and explicit. "Thanks, Jerry." He sighed heavily, his flicker of optimism extinguishing.

"Yeah, I know, he's your arch rival."

"And eleven years younger. With eleven years' more stamina."

"And you've got eleven years' more experience. He's a hothead, Drew, an egomaniac. Play with strategy, work on his emotions." Jerry eyed him shrewdly. "Scared?"

Drew stated crudely just how scared he was, and Jerry laughed out loud. "Good. That'll make you play better. Say I can count on you, Drew. You need this match more than I do. If I didn't think so, I wouldn't have asked. I swear to God I wouldn't have."

"Thanks, Jerry." For a brief moment, they looked at each other in honesty and friendship. Drew sought out Arden's graceful form. Just then, she turned toward him and smiled. Matt stumbled in the sand. Her arms were there to help him up. "Can I tell you tonight, Jerry?"

"Sure. I'll call around eight." He clamped his hand

on Drew's shoulder and squeezed it tightly. "I hope you'll say yes. Oh, and Drew," he paused to add after he'd taken several steps, "your lady is very pretty."

Drew made his way back to the beach towel and dropped down on it. He tousled Matt's hair and hugged him tightly before the boy toddled off toward the water. Only then did Drew look at Arden. God, she was beautiful. Just looking at her filled him with an assurance that replaced the fear. If he sat and stared at her long enough, would all of it disappear?

"A friend?" she asked softly.

"I wonder." She didn't pry, but he could see the question in her green eyes. "He wants me to play an exhibition match at Waialee for muscular dystrophy. Tomorrow. Against Teddy Gonzales."

"Are you going to play it?"

"Do you think I should?"

"Absolutely."

CHAPTER SEVEN

HE WANTED TO BE talked into it. Arden knew that. He was nervous and keyed up as they left the beach and returned to the suite. He couldn't stand still. While she bathed sand off Matt, Drew paced the bathroom.

"I don't know if I'm ready."

"Maybe you're not." She would play devil's advocate. If she tried to encourage him, he'd only dig in stubbornly and keep refuting every positive thing she said. Then should he be defeated, he'd have her to blame for talking him into playing.

"On the other hand," he contradicted himself, "I'll never know, will I, until I start playing competitively again."

"That's right."

"But *God!* Tomorrow. Why couldn't it be next week?"

"Too bad it's not. Then you'd have all week to stew over it."

He wasn't really listening or he would have caught her caustic tone. Pacing, he was tapping his thumbnail against his front teeth. His brows were creased. "But if I had a week to think about it, I'd probably talk myself out of it."

"Probably," she said, hiding a smile.

"Maybe it's best that I have to make a hasty decision."

"Yes, maybe."

He stalked her as she carried Matt into the bedroom to dress him. "I'll have to call Ham. He's been after me for months to start playing, even in penny-ante tournaments. But he might not think this exhibition match is a good idea."

"No, he might not."

"But I should mention it to him, anyway," Drew said, heading for the phone. "I'll call him right now."

His manager was thrilled and said he'd try to get a plane out of Los Angeles so he'd be there in time for the match the next day.

"It *would* be Gonzales." Drew had ordered a succulent cut of prime rib but had eaten virtually none of it. Arden had ordered for Matt and herself when it became apparent that Drew was too preoccupied to do so. "The last time I played him, he laughed at me. The bastard turned toward the crowd in the bleachers, spread his arms wide in a gesture of dismay and *laughed*."

If Drew was looking for pity, he'd have to look elsewhere. Coddling was the last thing he needed. "It's unfortunate it couldn't have been someone less intimidating than Gonzales. Then people, sports writers and such, could say you were playing it smart and safe, that you weren't biting off more than you could chew."

"They'd say I was a coward," he said, viciously stabbing a piece of meat with his fork and then wagging it in her face as he made his next point. "No, maybe it's a good thing it's Gonzales. At least they can't say I'm afraid to play."

A vengeful light glowed in his eyes, but when he

saw Arden's knowing smile, his face softened, and he lowered the threatening fork to his plate. "What time is your friend calling for your answer?" she asked softly.

"Eight o'clock."

"Then we'd better get back to the suite." She wiped Matt's mouth free of mashed potatoes.

They had eaten early in deference to Matt's bedtime. As soon as they returned to their rooms, his busy day caught up with him, and he was more than ready for bed. Drew's mind was still on his dilemma even as he helped Arden get Matt settled for the night. The telephone was ringing when they walked back into the sitting room after switching off Matt's bedroom light.

Drew froze, staring at the phone for several seconds before purposefully striding across the room and lifting it to his ear. "Hello," he barked. "Oh, hello, Mrs. Laani."

Arden saw his shoulders sag with relief even as she felt her own relax. "That's good to hear. We've missed you, but Arden has a knack for controlling Matt." He glanced over his shoulder and winked at her. "Well, if you're sure you feel well enough. Don't rush back on our account.... No, that will be fine. As a matter of fact, I might be playing a match tomorrow, so it would be convenient if Matt were taken care of.... Okay... Rest tonight and we'll see you then."

He hung up. "She says she can come back tomorrow. She'll be here in the morning to take Matt shopping. Her sister will drive them."

Arden knew a pang of disappointment. She would have loved to be included on the shopping trip. Selecting clothes for her son, as she'd never been able to do before, would have been a joy. But she saw no way she could arrange to go. Besides, if Drew played the match, which she felt sure he would, she wanted to be there.

"I'm going to say good-night, Drew."

He stopped his pacing and looked at her blankly. "Now? It's not even—"

"I know, but you need time alone. To think."

He crossed the room and put his arms around her waist. "I've been acting crazy since I talked to Jerry today. I'm sorry. I haven't meant to ignore you. You're not angry, are you?"

"Of course not! Give me a little credit, Drew. You're trying to make a monumental decision. Your distraction is understandable."

"But I don't want to be distracted from you," he whispered, nuzzling her neck. "I can use your advice and support. Stay with me."

"No. No one can help you make this decision." How well she knew about making pivotal decisions. The night she'd paced her room from dusk until dawn trying to decide whether to go along with Ron's scheme or not had been the loneliest and most frightening night of her life. Responsibility for the decision had rested solely on her shoulders. No one could make Drew's mind up for him. And she wouldn't be his crutch. This time he had to stand alone, or he might never stand again.

"What should I do, Arden?" he asked, pressing his face into her hair.

She pushed him away. "Do you want to play tennis professionally again?"

"Yes, until I can retire on top and not because I can't hack it anymore. Life spans on the professional circuit are short. There is always going to be someone younger and better. I'm resigned to that. But I wanted to finish in a top seed, not in the shadow of ridicule."

"Then I think you know what you should do."

"I should play." A grin broke across his mouth. "I'll play."

The telephone rang again, and this time there was little doubt who was calling. "Good night," Arden said, slipping into the bedroom and closing the door behind her.

She couldn't hear Drew's conversation, but she could detect the assertiveness in his voice. She was smiling as she picked up her tablet and pen and began making notes on the article she was going to do for the food section of the *Los Angeles Times* about simple Polynesian recipes.

WHEN SHE AWOKE, Matt's crib was empty. She sat up and blinked rapidly, trying to orient herself in the strange room. Flinging off the covers, she went to the window and peeped through the crack in the draperies. It was before sunrise. The calm ocean was a pink-and-violet reflection of the sky.

The bedroom door was open. She tiptoed through the sitting room to the other side where another bedroom door stood ajar. The room she peered into was rose tinted with the encroaching dawn. Unlike the bedroom she had shared with Matt, this one didn't have two double beds but a king-size one. Matt had curled up beside his father. Both were sleeping soundly.

Compelled by something stronger than common sense or prudence, Arden crept farther into the room toward the bed. Matt was on the far side of it. His rump, looking plump and out of proportion because of the overnight diaper under his pajama bottoms, was nestled against his father's chest. He was snoring softly through slightly parted lips.

Drew's arm was draped over his son's body. The hand that dangled in front of Matt's chest was lean and slender, with long tapering fingers. The faint morning light picked up the fine golden body hair dusting his arm. Even in repose, that arm looked sinewy and capable of tremendous power.

Arden's eyes misted over with high emotion as they traveled up the length of that arm to a set of wide shoulders. He was facing away from her, but she feasted on the beauty of his back. It was a smooth expanse of tanned skin and contoured muscles that she longed to touch with her fingertips...her lips?

His spine curved downward, and she followed its course to the shallow dip of his waist. She could see only a suggestion of his buttocks above the covering sheet. Below his waist, his tan was only a slight shade lighter than over the rest of his body. A ribbon of sensation spiraled up through her center at the thought of the nude sunbathing he must have done to acquire that tan.

His hair was a tumbled mass of blond strands on the butter-colored pillowcase. Moving around the bed to view his face, she admired the well-fashioned length of his nose, the mouth that declared his sensuous nature and the chin that proclaimed masculine authority. His lashes were spiky and thick, lighter on the ends than at the base, where they were almost black. It was a face that made women sit up and take notice whether they knew him by reputation or not.

Each time they went out, Arden could feel the envious stares of other women. Covetous eyes would take in the man, the woman close by his side and the child between them. Arden knew that most guessed they were a family. Biologically, yes, they were a family. But in truth…

Reminded once again that she was an interloper, she turned away silently. She took two steps before she was pulled up short by a swift tug on her floor-length nightgown. Twisting around in alarm, she saw that Drew was awake. He had rolled away from Matt and was facing the edge of the bed, the hem of her nightgown wrapped in his fist.

His eyes were slumberous, lazy, as were his movements as he slowly wound the fabric around and around his fist, reeling her in, shortening the distance between them until her knees bumped into the mattress. His hold on her nightgown was unbreakable. But not nearly as unbreakable as the hold his eyes had on hers. It rendered her motionless while his free hand slowly peeled back the sheet.

Her breath started coming in shallow pants. The sound of her heartbeat, loud and irregular, thundered against her eardrums. A lassitude as heavy and binding as chains claimed her limbs, yet she felt infused with energy.

In one lithe motion, Drew rolled to a sitting position on the edge of the bed, careless of his nakedness. His eyes were still fixed on Arden's, and neither seemed capable of turning away.

He positioned her between his spread knees. His thighs, hard and warm, pressed against the outside of hers. Giving in to an impulse she'd had since she first met him, she raised one hand and let her fingers sift through his sleep-tousled hair. He indulged her for a few moments before catching her hand and bringing it to his mouth.

His kiss was tentative at first, a mere brushing of his lips against the cushion of her palm. Then his tongue tickled the sensitized skin, and she broke out in gooseflesh. Soon his mouth was searing her palm and setting off a chain reaction of startling sensations. Like heat-seeking devices, sensual impulses found the hidden target of her sex, and it exploded under the onslaught.

He nipped and kissed each fingertip, her wrists, sending a wave of heat up her arms and into her breasts. They ached with sexual excitement. They filled and overflowed the ecru lace cups of her nightgown.

After appreciating them with his eyes, Drew let his hands drift across her breasts. His flesh touched hers through the dainty lace, and a wildfire of longing swept Arden's body. His fingers caressed her lightly until her nipples flushed and pouted. Leaning forward, he grazed her breasts with his lips, then rested his head against the lush curves, nuzzling her, breathing in her sleepy, warm scent. His head dropped lower, burrowing into her svelte stomach.

One of his hands went to her back and gathered up a fistful of cloth. He added to it until her nightgown was a tight, revealing nylon sheath that encased her body and made her feel more exposed than nakedness could have made her feel. His eyes flickered over her like tongues of flame. He spotted the indentation of her navel and kissed it, outlining the small crater with an impetuous tongue. She watched the damp spot on her gown grow as he kissed her there again and again. Her knees trembled. Her hands had long since found their way to his shoulders. Now they tangled in his hair as his head moved lower along her sleek feminine form.

She held her breath against a whimper of passion when his index finger traced the diagonal groove above her thigh. Her head fell back, and she instinctively arched into him when he treated the other side of the triangle to the same torturous caress. Then he kissed the spot where they met, and the foundations of her world crumbled and fell away and left her suspended without a foothold. Clutching his hair, she sobbed his name.

The hand at her back released the material of her gown and tunneled through her hair as he stood up. His mouth fell on hers, hot and hungry. But with surprising temperance, his tongue made exquisite love to her mouth.

In one sweeping motion, she was being carried in his arms, through the sitting room toward the other bedroom. She felt his desire against her hips. She had seen it, rooted in a nest of dark gold. Like the rest of him, his sex was splendid.

And she knew the act would be. And just as surely, she knew she couldn't afford it.

She wanted him. Every cell in her body was crying out for surcease from this fever that afflicted her. She ached for him to fill that void that yawned wider each time they touched. Her breasts yearned for the sweet suckling of his lips and the indulgence of his tongue. But this wasn't the time. If they made love now, it could spell disaster for them both.

Unaware of her hesitation, Drew stood her next to the bed and began to caress her anew. His hands closed over her buttocks and urged her forward. Her instinct was to grind herself against him, but she resisted.

There were so many reasons why this couldn't happen now. Would their lovemaking affect the way he played his all-important match that afternoon? What if the act reminded him of Ellie? If making love with her wasn't as good as making love with his wife had been, would he feel only disgust afterward? Or if it were better, would he feel guilty? Either way, he'd be thinking about that and not his game.

Afterward, when she told him who she was, he'd never believe that she hadn't merely bartered her body for the sake of being with her son. No, she couldn't make love to him until he knew everything about her.

Once she had made love to Drew, what then? Supposing he won that afternoon after having had sex with her? He might thank her for helping him get back on his feet and bid her a cheerful farewell. Or if he lost, he might blame her for distracting him. In either case, she'd lose him. She'd lose Matt.

No. No. No. She couldn't gamble everything away, even though she wanted him desperately.

"Beautiful," he was murmuring against her throat as he slid the straps of her nightgown down. "I was dreaming of you, woke up wanting you. Then to see you bending over me, watching while I slept. Oh, God, Arden…"

"Drew…no…ah…" His lips had found her breasts, and his tongue was sponging them. "No, please." Her hands went to his shoulders and pushed. He didn't budge.

"So pretty," he whispered, folding his hand around a breast and lifting it to his mouth. His lips moved back and forth across the nipple. "I knew you'd be beautiful. Let me see all of you," he rasped, trying to peel the nightgown the rest of the way down.

"No," she grated, and pushed herself away from him. Grappling with the slippery nylon, she tried to replace the straps of her nightgown on her shoulders. "No," she said more softly, eyeing him warily. She could tell by his swaying stance and glassy eyes that her negative message hadn't quite registered yet.

"No? What do you mean 'no'?"

She wet her lips and twisted her hands together in front of her. She'd thwarted him once, and the repercussions hadn't been pleasant. "I don't think we…you should…before a match. I've heard it's bad for athletes to…uh, you know…before…"

He laughed and took a step toward her. His finger charted the curve of her cheek. "If that were the case, there would be a helluva lot fewer athletes. Arden—"

"No, Drew, please don't," she said, moving away from the caressing hand he'd placed on her hip.

"What's the matter with you?" For the first time, she noted a touch of asperity in his voice. It sounded tight with rising impatience. "Don't tell me you're not in the mood. I know better." He glanced down at her nipples, and she felt her blush start there and stain the rest of her chest and neck like spilling ink. "Why did you come creeping into my bedroom if you didn't want to make love to me?"

She found the arrogant tilt of his chin and the lordly tone of his voice infuriating. "I was checking on Matt. I was worried when I woke up and he wasn't in his crib."

"You know he can climb out of his crib. Besides, one quick look would have let you know he was in bed with me. You didn't have to stand there at my bedside breathing heavy for five full minutes to confirm that Matt was with me."

"Breathing… You… I…" she sputtered.

"That's right. Admit it. Believe me, if I'd found you naked in bed, I'd have been breathing heavy, too. I don't think we've made any secret of the fact that we find each other sexually attractive. So what's the problem?"

"I've already told you. I don't think it's a good idea when you have that match to play today."

"Why? Are you afraid to commit yourself before you know if you're sleeping with a winner or a loser?"

Rage swept over her in a fiery tide that made the hair on the back of her neck stand on end. She caught him on the cheek with her palm in a cracking slap. The resultant silence reverberated in the room until she regained control of herself enough to say, "That was unfair to me, Drew. Cruel, selfish and unfair."

"Well, you don't exactly play fair, either, Ms. Gentry," he hissed. "Coming on like a nymphomaniac one minute and freezing up like an offended vestal virgin the next—twice, I might add—is not my idea of fair play."

She shook with fury. "Well, then, obviously you're not enjoying this game, and neither am I."

"I'm beginning to think that's all this is to you. A game. What's behind this charade you've been putting on?"

He was so close to the truth that she was seized by panic. She stared at him, genuinely frightened that he might somehow, freakishly, stumble onto the truth. It took her a moment to realize that the knocking that echoed through the suite wasn't her heart but some-one at the door.

Drew turned away from her, tearing a towel from the rack in the bathroom and wrapping it around his waist before he went to answer the door. It was Mrs. Laani. Arden rushed into the bathroom and locked her-self in before the housekeeper could see her.

In five minutes, she had gathered up those of her belongings that were in Matt's room. Mrs. Laani was alone in the sitting room, watching television until Matt woke up. Arden could hear the shower running in Drew's bathroom.

"I'm glad you're feeling better," Arden said, a plastic smile on her face as she edged toward the door. Mrs. Laani could be gregarious and was usually endearing, but Arden didn't think she could stand the chatter that morning. "Tell Drew I said good luck on his match."

"But Ms. Gentry, he—"

"I'll see you later."

She ducked into the relative safety of her room, showered and dressed quickly in a sundress, took up her straw hat and sunglasses and was on her way in less than fifteen minutes. All morning she poured her energy into the article she was writing, interviewing chefs in several noted restaurants. And all the while she was checking her wristwatch.

Drew had been right. She hadn't played fair that morning. She shouldn't have upset him before his match. What he didn't know was that she hadn't played fair all along. After their first meeting, she should have confided in him, told him who she was. Instead, she had insinuated herself into his life, his personal *and* professional life. She belonged in neither.

But she had fallen so deeply in love with him. That was the factor she hadn't counted on.

Oh, God, what am I going to do about it? she asked herself.

She took a noon break, stopping at a coffee shop and ordering an egg salad sandwich, which she didn't touch, and a glass of iced tea that was becoming watery with melted ice cubes.

There was no solution but to leave. Leave Drew. Leave her son. What good was she doing them? Drew wanted her in his bed but still loved his wife. Arden couldn't settle for that. She'd lived for years with a man who didn't love her. If she ever lived with another, it wouldn't be a one-sided affair. Never that again.

Matt was a happy, well-adjusted, healthy boy who had a mother figure in Mrs. Laani. Drew was dragging himself out of his self-imposed exile and back into the world of championship tennis. He was a good father to her son. She could only cause strife in their lives.

She had what she'd originally set out for. She knew who her son was. Maybe she could call Drew periodically, as a friend, and check up on Matt. He might even come to see her on the mainland and bring Matt with him.

Drew would think she had left over their "lovers'" quarrel. So much the better. If he pursued it, that could be her explanation. Things hadn't worked out. *I'm sorry, Drew, but these things happen all the time. You understand. But I'd still like to be your friend, keep track of you and Matt.* Yes, better to leave now before he learned the truth.

She left the coffee shop with her mind made up. She'd go back to Maui. With only one more article to write, she could return to California within a week. She glanced at her wristwatch, and acting on impulse, hailed a cab. There was one more thing she had to do.

"Waialee Country Club," she said briskly as she slid into the taxi.

THE CROWD WAS SILENT. Collectively they held their breath. The pent-up tension and anxiety were almost palpable. The sun was hot, but no one seemed to notice. Everyone's attention was focused on the tennis court.

The two players were as oblivious to the heat and their soggy clothes as they were to the crowd. They, too, were intent only on the match. It was the third and final set, each having taken one. It was five games to four, and Gonzales was in the lead. It was his serve. If he won the game, he'd take the match.

He had sauntered onto the court to a cheering crowd. His dark, Latin good looks contrasted with the whiteness of a broad, flashy smile. He was a champion and comported himself as one. His attitude toward his opponent as they shook hands at the net was one of cocky self-assurance. He'd swiftly changed his attitude when he'd barely won the first set six to four and then lost the second seven to five.

He was no longer concentrating so much on pleasing the crowd and posing for the sports photographers. He was trying to win the match, and it was requiring all he had to give.

He went up on his toes and fired a stinging serve into the box. The ball came whizzing back. A heated volley ensued. He slammed the ball into the far corner of his opponent's court and took the point.

"Fifteen, love," the umpire intoned.

Arden swallowed hard and dried her hands on the already limp skirt of her sundress. It was full and loose, and she was grateful that she hadn't worn anything more confining. Perspiration rolled in rivulets down her stomach and thighs, and only a portion of it could be attributed to the heat. It was literally a nervous sweat.

Jerry Arnold had hailed her the moment she stepped out of the cab. He had been sent by Drew to take her to the seat reserved for her. "His manager's with him," Jerry informed her excitedly, though she hadn't inquired. "It's like old times. He's calm but angry, you know? That's good. Anyway, he wanted to make sure you were here. If you need anything, ask one of the staff to fetch me."

"Thank you," Arden had said, a trifle confused. Had Drew expected her even after their argument that morning? And who was he angry with? Her?

He had walked onto the court looking breathtakingly handsome in his tennis whites with that familiar logo on the breast pocket and shorts. His trademark bandanna was rolled and tied around his forehead. Blond hair fell over it.

The tennis enthusiasts weren't impressed. He had received desultory applause. The spectators were carefully reserving judgment. They had paid their fifty dollars to see McEnroe and were disappointed. Would this be just another bloodbath for Drew McCasslin?

Drew hadn't seemed affected by the lack of enthusiasm. His eyes had scanned the crowd until he spotted Arden. He had nodded coolly. He hadn't looked at her since.

Drew took the next point, and Arden closed her

eyes. *Just two more, Drew, and you've held him. Just two more.* Gonzales aced him on the next serve. "Thirty, fifteen."

Gonzales got overconfident. He didn't expect the next return to come from Drew's lethal backhand. He lunged one way, the ball went the other.

"Thirty all."

The crowd shifted nervously and began to applaud. Arden heard supportive shouts directed to Drew, and her heart swelled with pride. He had been spectacular throughout the match. Even if he lost, he'd played excellent tennis.

Gonzales won the next point. "Forty, thirty. Match point."

An exhausting volley won Drew another point. Gonzales cursed viciously in Spanish. "Deuce."

Arden's knuckles were white, her bottom lip chapped from raking it with her teeth. Gonzales's serve was but a blur. Arden thanked God when Drew found it with the sweet spot of his racket. But he overshot his mark. The ball hit past the baseline.

"Advantage Gonzales. Match point."

Leaning over, Drew braced his hands on his knees. His dripping hair fell over his forehead as he hung his head and breathed deeply. Then he positioned himself for his opponent's next serve. Gonzales put all he had into it. Drew returned it with miraculous precision. They whacked the ball back and forth until the spectators were dizzy with watching. Neither made a mistake. Each outguessed the other, dodging to the far side of the court, then racing to the other. Then a ball caught Gonzales in the corner of the court. His perfect fore-hand landed on the ball squarely and sent it jetting to the opposite corner.

Drew reacted immediately. With the speed of a cheetah, he propelled himself toward the ball. When he saw he couldn't beat it, he took one final lunge. His body was like a neat arrow slicing horizontally through the air, his racket extended as far as he could reach. That photograph would later win one sports photographer a journalistic prize.

Drew's racket touched the ball, without the necessary momentum. It had enough impetus to reach the net, but touched it and fell back into Drew's court. Landing, he skidded across the court leaving a trail of blood on his elbow and forearm.

No one moved. No one made a sound. With memorable courage, Drew picked himself up and heaved a deep breath. Then, slowly, with dignity, he walked toward the net, his right hand extended for a congratulatory handshake.

Bedlam broke out. Cheers went up, a roar of approval. Not for the victor but for the vanquished. Photographers and tennis enthusiasts of all ages poured onto the court…and they were all headed for Drew!

Arden's eyes filled with tears as she watched while hundreds of people surged around him in celebration. He was back. He was on top again. That last desperate effort proved that he was willing to give whatever it took to be a champion again.

She could leave him now. He'd be all right.

She pushed her way through the crowd, got a cab and had it wait for her at the hotel long enough for her to retrieve her bag before going on to the airport. She caught the same commuter airline that the McCasslin party had flown over on. Tears bathed her cheeks when she remembered the heavy pressure of Matt's head on her breasts and Drew's drugging kiss after they'd landed. She'd always remember that moment when she'd had father and son together.

The concierge's desk at the resort was peculiarly quiet. Then she remembered it was the dinner hour. A young woman greeted her warmly. "Good evening. May I help you?"

"I'm Ms. Gentry. I have a room, though I've been on Oahu for the last couple of days. I'd like my key now. Room 317."

The girl tapped something into a computer terminal. "Room 317?" she asked.

"Yes," Arden responded, feeling all the emotional turmoil of the day like a bag of bricks on her back.

"Just a moment, please."

There was a whispered conference between the girl and the desk manager. They kept glancing over their shoulders at Arden, who was becoming more and more vexed with each passing minute.

"Ms. Gentry?" The man with whom the desk clerk had conferred came up to her.

They were extremely sorry, but there had been some kind of miscommunication. They were under the impression that she had hastily checked out of the resort. She'd paid with her credit card. The things she'd left in the room had been stored at her request in the resort's offices.

"But I didn't check out!" she argued. "I told the man I was coming back. I only paid for my room so you wouldn't think I'd skipped out."

This mistake was entirely their own. They had given

that room to another guest who was planning on a two-week stay.

"I liked that room, but if you've already given it to someone else, there's not much I can do about it. I'll take another. I'm very tired—"

There was another unfortunate problem. The resort was full.

"Are you telling me that you don't have one single room to give me after booting me out of the other one?"

They regretted that that seemed to be the case. What they would be happy to do was to call the other hotels and resorts to see if they could find lodging for Ms. Gentry. They would be happy to drive her there in their van.

"Thanks," she said tersely. "I'll wait over there," she said, pointing to a group of chairs that was so visible from the desk that they couldn't pretend to forget her.

A half hour went by, and the reports were becoming repetitive and discouraging. "Every place we've called is full. But we're still trying."

She was resting her head on the back cushion of one of the chairs, going over her options, when her head snapped up. Drew was stalking through the door of the resort with grim determination thinning his mouth. He was dressed in shorts as usual and a windbreaker, unzipped halfway down as usual. His hair had been shampooed since the grueling match, but it had been mussed by the wind. There was a nasty-looking fresh scab on his arm and elbow. He did a double take when he saw Arden sitting in the lobby chair.

He stopped in front of her, put his hands on his hips and glared down at her. "I've been looking all over two islands for you. Where the hell did you go after the match?"

"The answer's obvious, isn't it?"

"Don't play cute with me. Why did you run out?"

"Why? Because we had a fight this morning." She came to her feet and put as much strength behind her glare as he had in his. "I want out from under your bullying ways and bad temper."

His mouth crooked into a smile. "You ought to get mad more often. It does great things for your eyes."

She was ready with another angry outburst but was interrupted. "Ms. Gentry!" The desk manager came trotting up to her waving a piece of paper. "We found you a room—"

"Keep it," Drew snapped, swiveling around to face the luckless man and virtually nailing him to the floor with a blue stare.

The hotel man looked up at Drew cautiously, then glanced inquiringly toward Arden. "But Ms. Gentry said she needed a room and—"

"I said to keep it." Drew turned to face her again. "She's coming home with me." His eyes softened as they looked into hers. Then he added quietly, "Please."

CHAPTER EIGHT

HE TOOK HER stunned silence as consent. Before she knew what was happening, Drew was issuing orders that all her belongings be taken out of storage and put in the trunk of his Seville, which was parked outside. He picked up the shoulder bag she'd taken with her to Oahu, and curving his hand around her arm, escorted her out the door. The staff couldn't have been more accommodating, fetching and carrying for him, repeatedly apologizing for having inconvenienced his friend.

She let herself be settled into the front seat of his car but sat with stiff dignity until they had driven away from the resort's entrance gates and onto the dark highway.

"Drew, I won't argue about this. I'm not going home with you. Please drive me to another hotel. I'll find a room."

"I won't argue about it, either. It's crazy for you to go chasing through the night trying to find a place to sleep when I've got three or four empty bedrooms. Besides, I'll let you have one free."

"Free?" she asked archly, leaving no doubt of her meaning.

He brought the Seville onto the narrow shoulder of the highway with a shower of gravel and a screech of tires.

He braked jarringly. The momentum pitched her forward. On her way back, she was caught up against him.

"No. Not free. It's gonna cost you." His hand trapped her jaw, holding her head still. For ponderous moments, his lips hovered over hers. She expected a punishing, brutal kiss. Instead, it was excruciatingly tender. His tongue applied delicate pressure to her lips until they parted. He practiced that evocative thrusting rhythm that splintered her with shards of desire. She felt her body melting along the strength of his, her resolve to leave him dissolving just as surely.

When he lifted his head, he lovingly brushed back silky strands of dark hair from her cheek. "Consider your rent paid for as long as you want to stay."

"No other compensation will be required?"

His eyes coasted over her face, down her throat, back to her mouth. "Not unless you want to give me a gift, a gift you know I want but which I'd never take from you or bargain with you for."

She touched his hair, ran her finger along the brushy bar of his brows. "You played…" Emotion choked back her words as she remembered his brilliant last effort to save the match. "You played stupendously. I was so very proud. I ached with pride."

"Then why did you run away from me, Arden? Didn't you know I'd want to see you more than any person in the world when that match was over?"

"No, I didn't know that. You were so angry after…" She lowered her eyes. It was a gesture that was unconsciously seductive and made his senses reel. "After what happened this morning," she mumbled, "I thought whatever friendship was developing between us was over. I couldn't bear not being at the match, but I didn't think you'd want to see me anymore."

He lifted her hand to his mouth, and pressing it to his lips, spoke against her fingers. "I was mad as hell. But you must concede that when a man is as…uh… ready to make love as I was and then it's called off, he can't be expected to be in the best of moods." He delighted in the shy smile that curved her mouth upward. "And I wasn't in the best frame of mind to begin with. Hell, why mince words? I was scared, scared to death, to face Gonzales in that match."

"By the end of it, Gonzales was afraid of you."

His grin was spontaneous and wide. "Thanks, but that's not the point right now. The point is, I'm sorry for flying off the handle this morning. You certainly had every right to say no."

"I shouldn't have let things go so far before I did."

His eyelids drooped alluringly. "Think about that next time. I can't say what would have happened if Mrs. Laani hadn't knocked on the door." His lips took hers once again. This time, there wasn't even a heartbeat of hesitation in her response. Her mouth moved against his in generous reciprocation.

"What will she think about having a houseguest? And I'm only staying tonight. Tomorrow, I'll have to look for another room."

"I've got twelve or fourteen hours to convince you otherwise," he said breezily as he slid back under the steering wheel and turned on the ignition. "As for Mrs. Laani, she's been throwing daggers at me all day with those beady eyes of hers, grunting instead of speaking and in every way possible showing her displeasure with me for making you run away."

"Did she and Matt have a successful day of shopping?"

"By the number of boxes we brought home, I'd say so," he said, laughing. "Which brings up another point. This afternoon, Matt went to the door of the room you'd occupied and began pounding on it shouting, 'Ah-den. Ah-den.' That's when Mrs. Laani started sniffing with indignation every time she looked in my direction."

If there had been any remaining doubts in Arden's mind, they vanished when she heard that her son missed her. How could she turn down this opportunity to live with him for even a brief span of time?

Could she be blamed later? She hadn't manipulated Drew into the invitation; only a martyr would say no to it. Hadn't she earned the privilege of having her son for a little while? Didn't all those months of mental anguish, of wondering who he was and where he was, of having no image of him, entitle her to *something?*

And Drew. She loved him, in a way she'd never imagined loving a man, intellectually, spiritually and physically. Her love encompassed all that Arden Gentry was. It was a love without hope for a future, but that made it no less genuine, no less fierce. The next few days—she didn't really think she'd leave in the morning—would have to last her a lifetime. She'd not refuse them. She deserved a little selfishness.

They entered his estate from the back, since the front of it faced the Pacific Ocean on the western shore of Maui. They drove through iron gates that swung open when he pushed a transmitter and automatically closed and locked behind them.

The sweeping lawn gently sloped downhill several hundred feet toward the beach. It was well past twilight, but Arden could see vast shadows of the banyan trees that mushroomed over the yard like giant umbrellas, their ropelike roots draping from stout limbs. Plumeria trees, with their yellow, pink or white blossoms, perfumed the evening air. Ti plants, wood rose cloaked with yellow blooms, orchid trees and other flowering shrubs banked lush beds of flowers. Giant oleanders provided hedges and lent the estate total privacy.

The house itself—what could be seen of it behind its veil of blooming vines—appeared to be alternating walls of sand-colored brick and glass. Wide verandas led into rooms left open to the evening air and cooled by the ocean breeze.

"It's gorgeous," Arden said, stepping out of the car without waiting for Drew to come around and open her door. The wind flirted with her hair and filled her nostrils with the scent of flowers and sea.

"I bought it on sight. Come on in. I'll send Mo after your bags."

He led her around to the ocean side where they entered the living room through an opening in the glass wall. Tall, stained-wood shutters, which had been pulled open and stacked together, could be used to close off the glass to provide privacy or protection from the weather. Quarry-tile floors were polished to mirror perfection and dotted with oriental rugs.

The furniture emphasized comfort, not formality. The upholstered pieces were done in a nubby, oatmeal-colored fabric. Brightly colored pillows in varied prints and stripes provided splashes of color. Fresh flowers filled vases and bowls strategically placed around the room. An ebony grand piano stood in stately dignity in one corner; a stone fireplace filled another. Tables were of glass or wood and trimmed in brass. It was one of the most gorgeous rooms Arden had ever seen, and it set the tone for the entire house.

"Formal dining room, breakfast room and kitchen through there," Drew said, pointing. "My office is on the other side. Powder room behind the stairs."

The open staircase had solid-oak steps and a banister inlaid with strips of brass. Drew led her up to the second floor.

"I'm going to put myself back in favor with my housekeeper and my son by bringing you home to them."

They went down a wide second-story hallway, and Drew pushed open a door. Mrs. Laani had somehow wriggled her bulk into a rocking chair and was singing softly to a sleepy Matt.

He sat up instantly when they entered the room. The moment he saw his father and Arden, he flung himself out of Mrs. Laani's arms and hurled himself across the room. He all but tackled Arden, wrapping his chubby arms around her calves. Drew, smiling, lent her support as she knelt down to embrace the boy.

"Hello, Matt," she said, combing her fingers through his halo of blond curls. "Have you been a good boy today? Hmm?" Earlier today she'd planned to leave him. Now she had been granted a few more precious hours. She gathered him to her and hugged him hard. Her eyes grew cloudy with tears when she felt his arms going around her neck and returning her hug.

Pushing her away, his stubby finger found a button on his pajamas, and he declared proudly, "But-n."

"Oh, how clever you are," Arden cried, hugging him again. She searched her own bodice, then realized that her sundress didn't have any buttons. "Well, sometimes I have buttons, too," she said, laughing.

"He's been a terror, so don't you dare compliment him," Mrs. Laani said. "Trying clothes on him is like trying to dress an octopus." She was attempting to maintain a demeanor of solid authority, but she was beaming at Drew and Arden. "You two must be hungry. Mr. McCasslin wouldn't stop to eat before he had us pack up everything and hustled us out to the airport to catch the last flight for the evening. I swear I never saw him in such a hurry." Drew glared at her and cleared his throat threateningly, but she only smiled back, her round dark eyes flashing merrily.

"Don't you have something you could be doing?" he growled.

"As I was about to suggest," she said huffily as she squeezed herself out of the chair, "if the two of you will bed down Matt—and you're welcome to him—I'll fix you a light supper." She folded her arms over her massive bosom and eyed Drew. "I take it you offered the young lady dinner."

He caught her less-than-subtle rebuke. "Arden will be our houseguest for…as long as I can talk her into staying. Will you please ask Mo to get her bags out of the car?"

Mrs. Laani waddled to the door of the nursery. "And which room shall I tell him to put them in?" Her indifference was far too overdone to be authentic.

"In the guest room you think most appropriate," Drew said.

Arden hid her confusion and flaming cheeks by carrying Matt to the rocking chair and continuing where Mrs. Laani had left off. When the housekeeper had left the room, Drew squatted down in front of the chair and rested his hands on Arden's knees. Their eyes met, and an electrical spark arced between them.

"I think Mrs. Laani knows I have the hots for you."

"Drew!" Arden exclaimed.

"And I think she knows you have the hots for me."

"Hot," Matt said, wrinkling up his brows and blowing on his hands. The two adults laughed.

"I'm glad he can't interpret that in the context you said it," Arden said chastisingly.

"But you do, don't you?"

"Do what?" She pretended interest in the design on Matt's pajamas.

"Never mind," Drew said in a voice rife with promise. "We'll continue this discussion later." He slapped Matt lightly on the thigh. "Well, son, are you glad to have your favorite girl back?"

Unaware that he was answering his father's question, Matt laid his head against Arden's chest and yawned broadly.

"He's had quite a day," Arden said, feathering his cheek with the back of her finger.

"Don't spend all your sympathy on him. Save some for me. I've had a helluva day, too."

She looked at him and smiled gently, a Madonna's smile. "You certainly have. This is the first of many tremendous days for you, Drew. I'm sure of it. What happened after the match?"

"I was a captive of the press for about an hour. Everyone wanted to know the gory details of my life this past year—why I became a recluse. They wanted to know if I was on the wagon."

"And what did you tell them?"

"Yes. I told them that the drinking had been the result of my wife's death. That I had come to my senses about six months ago and since then had been working like hell until I felt ready for a day like today."

"You were more than ready. When will you play again?"

He outlined the schedule of tournaments Ham was lining up. "I'm still going to take it slow for a while. I can't catch up this year, but next year I think I can make an impressive showing."

"How many years did you win the Grand Slam?" The research she'd done before coming to Hawaii had taught her that the Grand Slam referred to winning the Australian Open, the U.S. Open, Wimbledon and the Paris Open.

"Twice. With two years in between. I'll never do that again, but it won't matter, Arden. As long as I know I'm playing the best that I can, the winning's not so important anymore. I've won the really important battle."

She reached out to touch his hard, sun-tanned cheek. She could almost feel the new strength and confidence he'd found within himself. Just as her fingers brushed the line of his jaw, she jumped in surprise and uttered a sharp cry.

Matt had curiously slipped his hand into the wrapped bodice of her sundress to investigate something he'd never seen before. He had found her breast and its coral nipple an intriguing formation. He was lightly pinching it between his fingers.

"But-n, but-n," he said in proud discovery.

"Matthew!" Arden gasped, taking his hand away from her and refolding her dress.

Drew fell backward on the floor laughing. "He hasn't been around very many women."

"He's been around Mrs. Laani," Arden said, not daring to meet Drew's dancing eyes.

"Come now, Arden. You and Mrs. Laani are hardly built alike. Matt saw something new and wonderful and had to check it out."

"Well, perhaps before he does too many things like that, you ought to have a man-to-man talk with him."

Drew rolled to his feet and scooped the boy into his arms, carrying him toward the crib. "Yes. I believe I should." He placed his mouth directly over Matt's ear and said loud enough for Arden to hear, "Son, you've got excellent taste in women."

MRS. LAANI HAD set a table in the "casual" dining room. Drew looked at his housekeeper from under reproving brows when he noted the candlelit table. She bustled around busily, ignoring his glower.

"I thought this would be cozy and restful after such a long, tedious day. I hope you like salmon, Ms. Gentry."

"Yes. That sounds wonderful."

Indeed, the cold salmon with cucumber and dill sauce, the vegetable casserole that Mrs. Laani served with it and the rich custard dessert were delicious. But part of Arden's satisfaction over the meal didn't come from the food but from the man who stared at her as intently as she at him.

Drew's eyes sparkled in the candlelight as he discussed the match at her urging. He seemed reluctant to talk about it, self-conscious, humble, but she coaxed him to tell his impressions of it. He seemed pleased that she had watched so closely and knew each stroke he referred to.

"You didn't mind losing it?"

"I always mind losing, Arden. I told you once, I like to win. But if I must lose, I want to lose with dignity in a fair fight. Today was a victory in spite of the score."

"Yes, it was."

His eyes looked into hers across the candlelit table. "I was afraid you weren't going to be at the club after you sneaked out of the hotel."

"I didn't *sneak,*" she said evasively.

"I guess it was just a coincidence that I was in the shower when you returned to your room and an oversight that you didn't leave a message with either Mrs. Laani or the desk as to where you'd be."

She ran her thumb and forefinger up and down the slender taper in the candlestick. "That was inconsiderate of me, I suppose, since I was your guest. Jerry Arnold told me you were angry before the match." There was an unspoken question dangling at the end of the statement.

"I was. When I got to the club and he didn't have a ticket for you, I raised hell. I told him he'd better find a choice seat or else. As you know, he got hospitable real quick." His grin was just short of devilish.

She leaned across the table. "You know something? I think you like to shake people up, throw your weight around, be a bully."

He chuckled. "I do. Especially when something means a great deal to me." He was all seriousness when he said, "Your being at that match meant more than you'll ever know. I could feel your support and encouragement."

Her eyes went round with disbelief. "But you didn't even look at me."

"I didn't have to, to know you were there," he said in a tone that stirred her blood.

Mrs. Laani interrupted the intimate mood. "If you don't mind, I'm going to bed, Mr. McCasslin," she said from the doorway. "I'll clear these dishes in the morning. Ms. Gentry is in the room next to yours. Will that be satisfactory?"

"That will be fine. Thank you, Mrs. Laani. Good night."

"Good night." Arden's voice sounded like corn husks shifting against each other.

"Let's walk on the beach," Drew said, helping her out of her chair. He dropped a light kiss on her shoulder. "But you'd better change into something warmer. The wind can get cool after sundown."

He was waiting for her at the bottom of the stairs when she descended five minutes later wearing an apricot-colored velour warm-up suit. The pants were banded at her ankles, and she was barefoot. She had beautiful feet, with well-pedicured toes. He noticed the tantalizingly free swaying of her breasts beneath the sweatshirt and knew she didn't have a bra on. He had a strong desire to close his hands over her breasts, to feel their full softness under the velvety cloth. The pulses inside his head began to pound and were echoed in the lower part of his body.

"Sure you won't be too cold?" he asked as evenly as his unstable senses would let him. She nodded. He settled his arm over her shoulders and led her out into a moon-bathed night.

It seemed that speaking had become difficult for her,

too, and he appreciated the fact that she didn't force conversation. He could see the emotion, the anticipation of what was about to happen, in her eyes. Words would be superfluous to what their bodies were communicating to each other.

They walked in silence down the gradual slope of the well-kept lawn, stepped over a low brick wall and onto the sand that led to the shore. Drew's beach was in a small semicircular cove. Waves rolled in to spend their force on the lava rocks before gently continuing forward to foam over the sand. The moon shone on the ocean in a silver band that stretched from the shore to the horizon. Its light shimmered in the curling crests of the waves. Wind soughed through the broad fronds of the palms. It was an enchanting setting.

As many times as he had sat on this beach alone and thought it a magical place, Drew now knew this scene would forever lack something if it didn't have Arden in it. She made the magic real, tangible, touchable. The moonlight paled her skin, but made her hair as dark as ebony. The stars had no brilliance compared to the emeralds of her eyes.

He seated himself on the firmly packed sand and pulled her down with him. He sat with one knee raised behind her, the other leg tucked firmly against her derriere, her back against his chest. For a moment, he didn't make any move to touch her or to speak. After all, he didn't know how she would respond when he told her what he felt compelled to say. If he'd known fear that day as he faced Gonzales across the net, he was terrified now. The outcome of the tennis match wasn't nearly as important to him as the result of the conversation to follow.

"I love you, Arden."

There. A simple confession. A bold truth plainly stated.

Her hair swept his face when she turned her head. The moist lips he wanted to claim forever were parted in surprise. "What did you say?"

"I love you."

He looked out at the ocean and felt a kinship with it. It seemed so placid on the surface, yet was roiling beneath, just as he was. "I never thought I'd say that to another woman. I loved Ellie very much. I didn't think I'd ever love that way again. And I don't. I love you more."

All the air left Arden's body. She could feel her chest contracting and it was painful. He was going to kill her with softly spoken words. She couldn't let him. "You have me in residence. You don't have to say that."

He ran his finger down to her cheek, smiling gently. "Don't say something ridiculous and get me mad all over again." His lips caressed her temple, but barely. "I'm not saying it for any reason except that it's true. I've given you ample reason not to trust me. I've behaved badly on occasion. But don't you see, Arden, that I was responding defensively? I felt guilty because I was coming to love you more than I ever loved Ellie. I couldn't cope with that. Today, when I thought you'd left me for good, I nearly went crazy."

"But during the match—"

"Not then, later. After the match, when you couldn't be found anywhere." He laughed. "Actually, during the match, I was still angry over the scene this morning. I don't think I would have played with such energy if you hadn't made me so furious."

She ducked her head in embarrassment. His fingers threaded through her wind-tossed hair. He loved the satiny feel of it as it slipped coolly along his skin. "You played it just right. You didn't coddle me. Nor did you try to talk me into or out of playing. You realized the decision had to be mine even though you knew I had no choice but to play."

"That's right. I knew you had to play. I knew you wanted to. But I couldn't tell you that. You had to figure it out for yourself."

"That's my point, Arden. You didn't tell me what I wanted to hear. As Ellie used to do."

"Drew, please don't."

"I want you to know."

"But I don't need to know."

"Yes, you do. I agreed that when we made love, it would be with no ghosts, no secrets between us."

She looked away quickly, but not for the reason he thought. She still harbored a secret, a secret that might cost her his love.

"Ellie backed anything I said or did even when she must have known I was wrong. She wouldn't come to watch me play because she was afraid I might suffer a defeat and she couldn't stand to see me down."

Arden did look at him then, in amazement. "Strange, isn't it?" Drew asked, seeing her incredulous expression. "When she traveled with me, she stayed away from the courts. And she couldn't be objective when I lost. If she had been alive today, she'd have made excuses, apologies, and commiserated with me over the loss. I'm not sure she would have understood that it was a personal triumph. You did."

He cupped the back of Arden's head and pressed it

down to the hollow between his throat and shoulder. "Ellie could share victory with me. But I don't think she could have ever shared defeat. Even after all we went through to get Matt, I worried about what she'd do if our bubble burst one day."

Arden closed her eyes at the mention of Matt. What would have happened had he not been born perfect and healthy? Would Ellie have rejected him? Ron would never have reared another man's child. He might have even had the infant terminated. The thought made Arden shiver, and Drew's arms tightened around her.

"I was almost more afraid of the future when I was playing well and living with Ellie than I have been recently. I don't think she could have faced a tragedy and survived." His lips found her ear, and his breath filled it warmly. "Arden, I feel that we could face anything together. You make me feel strong and confident, at peace with myself but always trying to be better. When someone thinks you are perfect, as Ellie did me, there isn't much to strive toward."

He captured her face between his hands and looked down into her swimming eyes. "Do you realize what I'm telling you?"

"Comparisons are unfair, Drew. To everyone."

"I know. I just wanted you to know that I wasn't substituting you for her in my life. You're different. Better for me."

"Drew," she whispered, and laid her forehead against his chin, rolling it back and forth. She wasn't prepared for this. God, the last thing she'd ever expected was to have him fall in love with her. It was even more unheard of than her loving him. It was too much.

She couldn't take that much goodness in her life. It frightened her. What price would she have to pay for it?

But with his hands warm and soothing, his words of love drifting into her ear, his heart pounding in tempo with hers, she didn't want to think of the future. She only wanted to revel in the fact that he was loving her. She should tell him about Matt now, while the mood was mellow and he was being honest with her. But...

"Arden, Arden." He uttered her name, only a heartbeat before his tongue filled her mouth. It plundered sweetly, rediscovering her taste, a miracle that happened each time he kissed her.

His hand slipped under the velour top. Her skin was warm velvet; he could feel her heart pulsing against his hand as he held her breast.

She sighed his name and moved against him in unspoken but undeniable need. "I don't want to usurp anyone's place in your heart, Drew."

He kissed her throat as he continued to fondle her breast. "You aren't. You're too rare. You hold a place uniquely your own because no one else has ever been able to fill it." His hands spoke as eloquently as his words as they touched her reverently. Then he withdrew them from her sweatshirt and wrapped his arms around her with unquestionable possession. Her head fell back against his raised knee as he kissed her.

Tongues swirled together in an erotic ballet. His lips clung to hers as though they never intended to let go. "I love tasting you," he said as his mouth moved back and forth over hers. His tongue flicked at the corners of her mouth maddeningly, until her hands came up to imprison his head.

She arched upward, flattening her breasts against

the wall of his chest. Bravely, her tongue pushed past his, and she kissed him in a way she'd never dared kiss anyone before. Former inhibitions fell aside. Again and again, she kissed him, declaring her desire.

"My God," he rasped, when at last they fell apart, groping for oxygen. He clasped her head between his hands as he stared down into her eyes. "Inside?"

She nodded her consent, and they rose together. The house was quiet. Only night-lights along the hallways had been left on. At the door to her room, he settled his hands on her shoulders.

"I've crowded you, Arden. Ever since I first met you, I've had things my way. I won't bully you again. I've told you I love you, and I do. But it's unconditional. It doesn't require anything of you. If you come to me, I'll show you how much I love you. If not, I'll understand."

He faded into the shadows of the hall and disappeared into the room next to hers. Moving automatically and purposefully, she went into the room where her things had already been unpacked. She didn't even notice the blue, avocado and beige décor that was somehow both elegant and informal. The adjoining bathroom was equally well decorated.

She peeled off the sweat suit and turned on the taps of the shower until it was steamy. Meticulously, she showered and shampooed, still caught in that trance that would not let her think beyond her senses, beyond her instincts. Certainly it wouldn't let her conscience become involved in her thoughts.

She dried her hair, splashed herself with a perfume too expensive for such lavish usage and glossed her mouth with peachy gel. With an economy of movement, she wrapped herself in a silk kimono and left the room.

Her soft knock was answered immediately. He stood with a terry-cloth towel around his middle. His hair was only partially dry. The hair blanketing his chest curled damply. His eyes gleamed like sapphires in the dim light.

"Arden?" he questioned softly.

"I want you," she admitted huskily.

"In bed?"

"Yes."

"Naked?"

In answer, she stepped close to him and placed her hands flat on his chest. The springy hair teased her palms, her fingertips. She feathered it; she combed through it down the length of his torso. It became silky just above his navel and narrowed to a fine strip of gold. Her hands fumbled with the tuck he'd made in the towel; then it fell away.

The drumming of her heart drowned out every other sound, even that of her uneven breathing as her fingers drifted downward. They stirred in the thicker, coarser hair. Then courage deserted her, and she raised imploring eyes to him.

"I…can't… I'm…"

"Shh," he said, pulling her against him. "You've come more than halfway. That wasn't a test. You'll never have to do anything just because you think I want it or expect it. Let's learn to love each other together."

His lips were suppliant as they met hers. They moved over her mouth with gentle persuasion until her momentary shyness vanished and she responded with the true sensuality that had lain dormant all her life. Her mouth flowered open beneath his. His tongue dipped repeatedly into it, giving, taking, enriching, ravishing.

His hands trembled with eagerness as he slipped them inside the kimono. He curbed an impulse to tear it from her body and crush her against him. She wasn't one of his fleeting, meaningless nighttime toys. They were in the past. Arden was his present and future. And she was precious, so precious. He wanted to go slow, to appreciate every nuance of her and their lovemaking. He let his hands rest at her waist, caressing softly. Only when he heard her soft whine of longing did his hands lift the garment from her body and let it float to the floor.

He stepped away from her and treated himself to the sight of her perfect nakedness. His hands touched her lightly, following the track of his eyes. Arden was dismayed to feel tears of gratitude flooding her eyes. Drew's slow savoring of her body endeared him to her.

"I've never been worshiped before. Only devoured," she whispered.

His face looked incredibly sad, then incredibly happy. "You're so beautiful," he said hoarsely. He swept her into his arms and carried her to the bed. The spread had already been folded down. He laid her on soft, fragrant linens and followed her down, nestling himself close to her. They smiled in pure enjoyment of the rough texture of his body against the satiny texture of hers.

He caught her wrists in one gentle fist and raised them above her head. His other hand massaged her breasts. "You don't look like you ever had a baby." She caught herself just in time from correcting him that she'd had two children, not one. "Your breasts are firm and round." He circled them with a talented finger. "Your nipples are light and delicate." He touched them in turn, and they responded. "You have no stretch marks."

She arched her back when his finger trailed down the straight column of her stomach and into the dark shadow at the top of her thighs. "You're perfect," he whispered a second before his mouth covered hers. When she had been thoroughly kissed, his lips trailed down her throat. His caresses had prepared her breasts for his mouth, and he suckled them with infinite care. His tongue rolled over her nipples, lubricating them deliciously.

"Let go of my hands." When he complied, she tangled her fingers in his hair and pressed his head closer. "Oh, God, Drew. I've never been loved like this."

"I hope not. I want to be the only man you ever remember having touched you."

"No one has. Not like this."

His mouth practiced merciless torture on her navel, deflowering it with a nimble tongue, loving it with sipping lips. She twisted and writhed beneath him, a stranger to herself. A shudder rippled through her when his mouth nuzzled the dark delta of her femininity. She called his name half in panic, half in joy, when she felt his lips nibbling the inside of her thighs. Then he parted them gently, and the artistry of his touch told her she'd known nothing of intimacy before.

"Please, please, Drew."

He honored her hoarse request and the urgent clawing of her hands and climbed her body until he was poised over her. His eyes locked with hers as he introduced himself into her body. He didn't pause or hesitate but pressed deeply and slowly until she knew all of him. Then he did something her husband had never done during lovemaking; he smiled down into her face. When he began to move, he was still watching her, cataloging her pleasure, memorizing her rapture, noting what movement made her eyes grow smoky with passion.

"You feel so good inside, Arden."

"I do?"

"Oh, God, yes," he ground out. "Move with me."

Conversation? Unheard of during lovemaking. The only sounds she'd ever heard in Ron's bed were meaningless grunts and groans.

"L-like that. Again," she stuttered when he stroked the portal, then sank into her completely. "Yes, yes, yes."

When the crisis came, it wrapped them both in a velvet glove of ecstasy, shook them, squeezed the breath from them and spun them about, lifted them, tossed them to the mercy of the heavens, then let them fall into a realm of glory to which each was alien.

Long minutes later, Drew raised his head from her shoulder and with his little finger lifted damp bangs from her eyes. When they opened in sleepy contentment, he dropped a kiss on her mouth and said, "Thank you, Arden, for making me new."

CHAPTER NINE

THE SHEER DRAPES at the wall of windows overlooking the ocean billowed into the room. Arden's eyes opened languorously, and she sighed with the deepest pleasure she ever remembered feeling. The room, bathed with the ethereal lavender of dawn, encapsulated her like a sensuous cocoon of love. In it she had learned the meaning of life in its most splendored dimension.

Drew's breathing was deep and even. She could feel it on her naked back as he held her close to him, sharing the pillow, his arm lying along her thigh. She turned her head slightly, careful not to awaken him, as she looked about the room she had been too entranced to observe in detail the night before.

It was as tastefully decorated as the rest of the house. The walls were covered with grass cloth that contrasted in texture to the lambskin covering the bed. The thick carpet was ivory colored. Against that neutral background, there were accents of pumpkin and chocolate in two easy chairs arranged close to a small table near the windows, in numerous pillows that had been heedlessly tossed off the bed onto the floor, in subtle prints that hung in brass frames on the walls. The furniture had clean, uncluttered lines. The fireplace, in the wall opposite the windows, was a luxury that she found delicious in a tropical climate. It was bricked in the same ivory color and had a fan-shaped brass screen. She liked the room.

She loved the man.

A sliver of sunlight beamed across the carpet like a miniature spotlight. She ought to return to her room before anyone else began to stir. It was about time for Matt to wake up, and after that, no one slept, Arden thought, smiling.

She eased Drew's leaden arm off her thigh and inched to the edge of the bed. Gaining the floor, she pulled on her jade silk kimono and tiptoed over the carpet, which was lush and seductive against her bare feet. The doorknob was under her hand, and she was twisting it slowly when Drew's arms flattened against the door on either side of her.

She stifled a soft scream and collapsed against the wood.

"Where do you think you're going?" he growled into her neck. He pressed forward, trapping her against the door and his hard frame.

"To my room."

"Guess again." He kissed her neck, parting his lips and letting his tongue moisten a vulnerable spot. "You're not going anywhere except back to bed. With me."

She shivered as his mouth made a damp, treacherous path to the back of her ear. Playfully, his tongue batted at her earlobe. "Ah... Drew...don't... I have to go back to my own room."

His hands slid down the smooth surface of the door to her waist. With a tiny yank, the tie of her kimono, which she'd carelessly looped but hadn't bothered to knot, fell away beneath his deft fingers. "Give me one good reason why."

"Uh…" He separated the folds of her kimono and ran his fingertips over her ribs. Moving closer, he settled his middle against her derriere. She knew he had come to her as he had slept—naked. And she couldn't think of one good reason why she had to leave him at that moment.

His arms crisscrossed her chest, and he closed a hand over each breast. "Your breasts are so pretty," he murmured as his hands formed gentle cones around them. "I like that line that marks your tan about here," he said, letting his index finger trace it. "Of course, if you'd sunbathe on my beach, you wouldn't have a line. I could rub you with oil, and you could tan evenly all over while I watched."

His hands and provocative suggestions were lulling her into that same enchanted sphere she'd known the night before. Through no conscious thought, her body became malleable, conforming to the curves and bulges of his.

The tender caresses on her nipples had made them bead with desire. He whispered his praise of them in her ear, making her both exult and blush with the boldness of his language. "I love the feel of your skin against my tongue. You taste like all things maternal and all things erotic. Your taste epitomizes womanhood."

Drained of all energy and will to resist now, she laid her head against his shoulder. Moving slightly, she rubbed against him and felt his fierce passion nudging her hip.

His breath was like a storm in her ear as one hand

surveyed the smooth plain of her stomach and abdomen. He paused not at all in finding his final destination. His palm settled over the gently swelling mound, while his fingers curved inward to seek the mysteries chastely hidden between her thighs. His thumb roved through the dusky nest.

"I love you here." Even as he spoke, he was moving his thumb in that lazy, hypnotic way that stole her breath, her reason. "Dark. And silky. So silky."

His exploring fingers discovered her dewy and ready for his love, but he prolonged the rapture. Tenderly and carefully, he adored her with his fingertips, giving her untold pleasure and asking nothing in return. He stroked her to unbearable, mindless passion, finding and kneading the magic key that unlocked all that made her woman.

She shuddered against him, soundlessly and breathlessly and incoherently chanting his name. He turned her, and with his hands beneath her hips, lifted her and let her find his accommodating maleness. She sank upon him fully.

She sobbed her love as again and again he arched his back, driving himself higher and higher. The world fell away in one swift, sudden explosion. Her thighs clamped his, and her arms closed around his neck. Her breasts muffled his own ecstatic cries.

When Arden's consciousness returned, modesty prevented her from lifting her head to look at him. Sensing her shyness and knowing the reason for it, Drew carried her back to the bed and laid her down like a child. Still, she wouldn't look at him. He smiled in faint amusement and love, stroking her back.

"Arden," he whispered. "Was it so terrible?"

She rolled over to look up at him. Shaking her head, she closed her eyes. "It was beautiful."

"Then why can't you look at me?" He brought her hand to his lips and kissed the backs of her fingers. There was a tentative smile on her delicious lips.

"I'm embarrassed." The words were spoken so softly, he could barely hear them.

"I didn't mean to embarrass you."

"No!" Her eyes flew wide. "Not you. You don't embarrass me. I embarrass myself. I've never…been like this before." Her eyes stared at the forest of golden hair on his muscular chest. She longed to touch it, but was still timid, half-afraid of the changes taking place in her personality. "I've never done…well, things like this. I don't know myself when I behave with so little self-control."

She rested her cheek against his arms, speaking aloud the thoughts that went through her mind. "It's like there's another woman inside me that I didn't know of before I met you. But that's not right, either, because it's not another woman—it's *me*. I didn't know that part of me existed. And I'm having a hard time getting acquainted with it."

"In other words," he said quietly, "you didn't know until you met me that you were a lusty wanton with an insatiable sex drive." Startled, she looked up at him, but laughed in relief when she saw the teasing light in his blue eyes. "Frankly, I'm delighted."

He clasped her to him, and they laughed softly, rolling together on the bed. His heart was soaring because they took such pleasure in each other and were able to laugh and love in the same minute. Since Ellie died, there had been no joy after sex for him, only a kind of frantic despair.

He couldn't stand the thought of that now, of how empty his life had been. He didn't want to even imagine a life without Arden in it. His arms held her prisoner as he kissed her, not with passion but with a telling need, a message of how vital she had become to him.

"Let's go wash," he said with a huskiness that came from a tangle of emotions.

The bathroom was hedonistically opulent. The sunken bath was enormous and had whirlpool jets placed at intervals along its deep sides. A picture window provided a view of the ocean. The oversize shower had a clear glass door. It was into this that Drew led Arden.

Whatever modesty she had left was swept down the shower drain, never to be regained. Drew's eyes and hands idolized every part of her. And instead of feeling sullied by his frank sexual interest, she felt purified because she knew it came not from lust but from love.

They kissed, licking droplets of water from each other's faces. Her hands slid down the muscled expanse of his back. The narrowness of his waist was briefly appreciated before her hands smoothed lower over his taut buttocks. Bravely, her eyes locked onto his as her hands familiarized themselves with each curve, each masculine line.

He watched with incredulous pleasure as she soaped her hands slowly, provocatively. His throat tightened, and he swallowed convulsively when she took his sex between her lathered hands. Her touch was timid at first but gained confidence and increased pressure as she watched his eyes grow dark and hot.

"Arden," he gasped, "do you know what you're doing to me?"

"I'm doing something wrong?" she asked in alarm, yanking her hands back.

"No, God, no." He caught her hand and replaced it and at the same time pulled her to him with his other arm. "You're perfect, and so sexually innocent despite having been a wife and mother."

"One had nothing to do with the other." She was thinking not only of her private life with Ron but also of the sterile precision with which she'd conceived Matt.

"I'm a selfish bastard to say this, but I'm glad."

They rinsed and went back into the bedroom. "Lie down on your stomach," he instructed gently. Without a qualm, she obliged him. He stretched out beside her. "We really must do something about these strap lines," he murmured. Her back was marked by several pale stripes, and her bottom was noticeably white against her tan back and legs.

"What do you suggest we do now?" she asked sleepily, her head resting on her folded arms.

"Umm, what do you think?" he said with a lascivious inflection.

"You're incorrigible."

"Where you're concerned, I am."

His hands were massaging her shoulders and rubbing her back with a gifted touch.

"What will we do if Matt comes barging in?" she asked.

His hands slid down her ribs and back up again, lifting the plump sides of her breasts on their ascent. She sighed blissfully. "He won't. I locked the door."

He leaned over her back and spoke directly into her ear. "I didn't want to be disturbed, even by my son."

His hand seesawed in the curve of her waist, then coasted over the slope of her derriere. She uttered a responsive moan when she felt his teeth nipping at her waist. As lifeless as a rag doll, she obeyed the urging of his hands to turn over. His lips continued their trail of kisses over her stomach and then lower.

Agilely, he positioned himself between her thighs and laid his head on her abdomen. His breath stirred the dark down. Idly her fingers trailed through his thick, tousled hair. She was astounded at her own acceptance of this new intimacy, her explicit trust in him, the now-familiar way her body began to warm and liquefy and swell with renewed longing.

Her bones melted beneath the warmth of his mouth when he kissed her stomach. "I want to love you again, Arden." His breath struck her skin in hot puffs that made her insides quiver.

"Then love me."

He levered himself up over her, nestling his sex against hers but not taking possession. "Your breasts are going to be sore," he said miserably, looking at their fullness and the tempting crowns. "Not to mention the rest of you."

She hooked a hand around the back of his head and pulled him down to her breast. "Kiss me here," she whispered. "Make them wet."

He groaned softly as he took her nipple into his mouth. He drew on it gently, ever mindful of hurting her. Lifting his head, he appraised his handiwork before painting the hardened tip again with delicate strokes of his tongue. He continued on each breast until they were glistening in the morning light. Arden writhed beneath him, loving the way he tugged on her so sweetly. She felt each contraction deep inside the heart of her femininity. She moved against his body, begging him to fill the void he had created.

With one sure thrust, he obliged her. He buried himself into her warmth, and she sheathed him tightly.

As before, it wasn't a culmination but a beginning. A rebirth. For as surely as Drew's life showered into her body, she filled him with her own essence. They lay together, breathing in the scent of their loving, feeling not depleted but filled with new life and energy.

"Arden," he said softly as he left her, only to gather her close to him.

"Hmm?"

"This illicit affair must come to an end."

She felt as though her heart plummeted to the floor and shattered into a million pieces. "End?"

"Yes," he said earnestly. "You must marry me."

"YOU HAVEN'T RESPONDED to my proposal, Arden."

It was hours since he'd made it. Arden knew no more now how she was going to respond than she had when he'd first astounded her with his proposal. They were on the beach, playing with Matt. The three of them comprised a family unit, and that as much as anything panicked Arden.

Lightly, she shrugged off his statement. "As I recall, it wasn't so much a proposal as an order."

"What else could you expect from a bully?" His retort was spoken lightheartedly, but she could see the underlying seriousness in his eyes.

He hadn't demanded an answer of her when he had

first mentioned marriage. Instead, he had held her while he slept. She, however, couldn't go back to sleep. Her mind had been turbulent with thoughts of the night just past, the sensual discoveries of the new day and Drew's unheralded marriage proposal.

Her? Marry Drew McCasslin, world-famous tennis pro? Drew McCasslin marry Arden Gentry, a nobody, the hired surrogate mother of his child?

When Drew had awakened, they decided they'd been self-indulgent long enough. Matt was already at breakfast when they came down the stairs. He waved at them gleefully and sputtered cornflakes all over his high-chair tray. Drew had dressed in tennis attire, Arden in a casual pair of shorts. He had tried to talk her into going with him while he practiced.

"Drew, my clothes have been packed in a suitcase in a musty closet for nearly a week. I need to sort them out for laundry and dry cleaning."

"I can do that for you," Mrs. Laani offered as she placed a plate of fresh fruit in front of Arden and poured her a cup of coffee.

"I appreciate that," Arden said, smiling at her. "But I'd feel better putting things away myself so I'll know where everything is."

No one seemed to doubt that she was staying indefinitely. Only Arden herself.

Drew had left for his tennis practice alone. After her clothes had been pressed and hung in the closet of the guest bedroom, Arden helped Mrs. Laani sort through the new clothes that had been bought for Matt in Honolulu.

"Oh, this is precious," Arden exclaimed, holding up a playsuit with two tennis rackets appliquéd on the bib.

Mrs. Laani laughed. "I thought his daddy would appreciate that."

Matt was underfoot and in the way and meddlesome as they unwrapped his new clothes and put them either in the closet or the chest of drawers. Arden didn't mind even when he shredded tissue paper all over his bathroom floor. Periodically, she'd hug him to her, examining his face time and again and marveling over him.

How had Drew's seed, transfused into her body so clinically, without the loving emotion such a miracle warranted, produced this unblemished specimen? She thanked God she had had a part in bringing this life into the world.

Drew had returned just before lunch. He was crackling with excitement. "You should have seen the crowd watching Gary and me work out today. They gave me a standing ovation when I walked out on the court. UPI and the Associated Press picked up news of the match yesterday. The story's gone worldwide. Ham's beside himself. He called the resort while I was there and said phone calls have been pouring in, inviting me to play in tournaments both in the States and abroad. My sponsors called to congratulate him."

He referred to the companies whose clothes and shoes he wore, whose tennis racket he used, whose planes he flew when he traveled, whose toothpaste he hyped. These endorsements comprised as much—if not more—of his income as prize money. When his playing began to slide, so had the offers from these companies.

"I was scared that when my contracts came around for renewal, the sponsors would let them drop. Now they're talking bigger and better things. They're still wary, of course. It was only one match, and I didn't *win* it, but at least they haven't given me up for lost. I need to win one. Now I know I can."

His eyes sparkled as he clutched Arden's hand across the luncheon tabletop. "I only need one thing in my life to make me completely happy."

Arden knew what that something was. It had been haunting her all morning. Her heart was full to bursting with joy that Drew loved her enough to marry her. Why was she hesitating? Why hadn't she flung her arms around him the moment the words were out of his mouth and said, *Yes!* she'd marry him? Because she'd been immediately reminded of what had brought her to this man in the first place.

Matt.

What more could she ask for? She'd have her son, live with him, be his mother in every sense of the word, be able to watch him grow into boyhood, adolescence, manhood. She'd be there, witnessing it all, helping him through the tough spots, loving him. Why couldn't she tell Drew that she wanted to marry him more than anything in the world?

Because he had been honest with her and she hadn't been with him. She couldn't enter into a marriage with that lie of omission between them. She'd been in a marriage like that, and it had bred contempt. Ron had married her for self-serving reasons, and she'd never forgiven him. She'd hated him for it. And he'd come to scorn her for her constant, meek submission.

What would happen if Drew found out who she was and the role she'd played in his past? He would think she'd married him solely because she wanted to be with her son. Would he ever believe that she loved him now as much…no, more…than she did the son she'd conceived of his seed? Knowing his pride, she doubted it.

So tell him now, she commanded herself. *Don't risk his finding out later. You can't have this secret between you, so tell him now. Today.* She shivered with dread. No matter who Matt's mother was, Drew wouldn't be happy to meet her. Each time he mentioned the trouble he and Ellie had had "getting" Matt, his eyes betrayed an uneasiness about it. No, he wouldn't be glad to meet Matt's mother. He certainly wouldn't be glad to learn that she was a woman he'd come to trust, to love, who had kept the secret far too long already.

When they had walked down to the beach after lunch, her mind had still been swirling in ever-changing patterns of indecision.

Now Drew was pinning her down for an answer. But Matt chose that moment to launch himself into her chest, knocking her backward. "Oh, you!" she cried, catching him around the waist. "I think you need to go on a diet."

Matt crowed with laughter as she tossed him down on the beach blanket beside her, wrestling him and tickling his fat stomach. When he'd worn her out, he pushed himself up and went jogging toward the surf. "Be careful," Arden called after him. He stopped, turned and then spontaneously came running back. He flung his arms around her neck and kissed her wetly and enthusiastically on the mouth.

Tears blurred his image as he tripped back toward the tide.

"He loves you, too, Arden." Drew's quiet voice compelled her to look at him. When he saw her tears, he smiled. "You love him, don't you?"

The truth couldn't be withheld. "Yes."

"And me? Am I seeing something that really isn't there?"

The tears rolled down her cheeks. She reached out to caress the wind-tousled strands of hair above his rolled-bandanna sweatband. "I love you, too." Her fingers outlined his bottom lip. "I love you so much it hurts."

He caught her hand and pressed it to his cheek. "Then say you'll marry me. Ham wants me to go on tour in two weeks. I want you and Matt to go with me. I want you to go as my wife." The thought of going without her was too dismal to contemplate. On the other hand, he knew he had to go. The timing was right.

"Two weeks," she said mournfully.

"I know I'm not giving you much time. But why wait? If you love me—"

"I do."

"And you know I love you. Marry me now, Arden." He looked toward the boy who was chasing a shallow wave to shore. "I never thought I'd blackmail a woman into marrying me, but I'm going to play every ace." He sighed grimly and said, "Matt needs a mother, Arden."

"He has Mrs. Laani." It was a weak protest. Her heart seemed anchored to something in the bottom of her soul, and it was pulling her down, down, down, into a situation from which there was no easy escape. *Please don't use my son to talk me into doing something I know I shouldn't do.*

"I don't know what I would have done without her," Drew said of his housekeeper and friend. "She put up with my drunken abuse and my dark moods when a less charitable woman would have packed her bags and left. She's great with Matt. I consider her more family than employee, but she could never be a mother to him. She's too old, for one thing."

He took Arden's hand and pressed it between his. "Arden, in a few years I'll have to move from here. When Matt's older and I'm too old to play the circuit, we won't be able to live in this partial isolation. Matt will need a mother, you, when he goes to school and sees that every other kid has one."

He could still see the indecision in her eyes. He had one more shot. It was a mean one, but he was a desperate man. "Be to my son what you couldn't be to Joey."

Her head whipped around, and she jerked her hand from his. "You're being unkind, Drew."

"I know that, dammit, but I can see I might lose you, and I can't let that happen. I'm fighting for my life, and I'm going to use all the ammunition I've got." His eyes were fierce, his jaw hard and stubborn.

"I told you, you weren't merely a replacement for Ellie, and that's the God's truth. Matt can't be a replacement for the son you lost either, but you've said you've grown to love him. Give him what you didn't have a chance to give Joey." He touched her lips with his. "We could even have a child of our own."

"Oh, God," she cried, covering her face with her hands and slumping against him as he pulled her forward. He cradled her in the shelter of his arms, stroking her head and whispering endearments.

"I know I'm bullying you again, but, Arden, I want you in my life. More than tennis. More than anything. Still, I wouldn't ask you if I didn't think you needed Matt and me just as much."

Arden felt a clammy hand on her shoulder and raised her head to see Matt standing beside her. His lower lip was trembling, and his eyes, so like Drew's, were shimmering with silver tears. "Ah-den," he said on the brink of crying. "Ah-den."

"Oh, precious, no, don't cry." She wiped the tears from her eyes and forced a bright smile. "See, nothing's wrong." She remembered that Joey was never so upset as when he saw her crying. It shook a child's world to see an adult so visibly distressed. "I'm fine. See."

He looked doubtfully toward his father, but Drew's eyes remained on Arden. She pulled the boy to her and hugged him, distraught over causing him one moment of insecurity and pain.

"There, see, I'm happy," she said. "Where's your belly button? I see it, I see it," she said, poking it playfully. He giggled, and the tears began to recede.

Mrs. Laani called them from the wall separating the beach from the lawn. "Shame on you, letting that boy run naked like that," she scolded the two adults. "He'll grow up a pagan."

"This is the way God made him, Mrs. Laani," Drew said, casting a conspiratorial grin at Arden.

"Blasphemy," the older woman grumbled as she retrieved the boy and tried to pull bathing trunks up his thrashing, sandy legs. He squirmed and protested until she gave up with a resigned sigh. "See what I mean? He's half-heathen now."

She labored up the hill carrying the boy, who repeated, "No nap," until they were out of sight.

"I didn't know he saw me crying. I shouldn't have upset him."

"If I start crying, will you say you'll marry me?" Drew's expression was so boyishly winning and his eyes so sad that she broke out laughing.

"Oh, Drew," she said, leaning over to kiss him. "I love you, but there are reasons why I shouldn't marry you."

"And so many more why you should."

She rested her head against his breast, letting the crinkly hair tickle her nose. She loved the salty, musky scent of his skin. "There's one profound reason why I shouldn't marry you. Something about me...my past. Something I did that..."

He tilted her head back to peer into her eyes. "Arden, there couldn't have been anything that shameful in your past. And even if there were, when compared to me, you've lived like a saint. I don't *care* about anything in your past. I care only for our future." His fingertips skimmed her cheek. "For that matter, there is something that I've been wavering about telling you, but I honestly can't think of what difference it makes. It doesn't concern or affect the love I have for you."

He kissed the corner of her mouth. "Does this secret have anything to do with me? What you feel for me? Do you love me less because of it?"

She could answer him honestly. "No. It takes nothing away from the love I have for you."

"Then forget it. Our lives started when we met each other. Our pasts we'll keep sacred and private. We'll close the book on them and begin to collect our own sacred and private memories." He kissed her. It was a deep and probing kiss, as though he wanted to erase physically her objections with his mouth. "Marry me, Arden."

"Drew, Drew," she said, meeting his mouth for another long kiss that made everything but the love she had for him seem unimportant.

He ground their mouths together, folding his arms around her possessively and symbolically sealing them off from the rest of the world. "Take off your top," he mumbled against her mouth.

She wriggled free of him in mock exasperation. "Is that the only reason you asked me to marry you? For unlimited carnal use of my body?"

"One of the reasons," he drawled, letting his eyes descend in lecherous approval over the curves that the scant bikini did little to hide.

If he was going to keep Matt's origins from her, was her own secret so much worse? She suddenly felt free of shackles. She wanted to celebrate their love, to be happy, to shed the cloak of worry and guilt. "What if someone moseys by?" Her voice held a hint of mischievous promise.

"Mo and Mrs. Laani are the only ones allowed on the property without my prior approval. They both know that when I'm alone on my beach with a woman, they are to make themselves scarce."

"Oh? And just how many times have you been alone with a woman on your beach?"

"This is the first time. I circulated a memo this morning."

She bit her lip to keep from laughing. "What about boats? What if someone sails by and sees us…me… without any clothes on?"

"We'll see the boat first and duck for cover."

"I see you've thought of everything."

"Everything," he said, looking at her through a screen of thick, sun-gilded lashes. "By the way, did you ever say yes to my proposal? Or am I to assume by your kisses that the answer is yes?" His hands went around her. One untied the string at her neck; the other untied the one across her back.

"I didn't say yes..." The top of her bikini was caught by the wind. It fluttered against her body for a few seconds before being whisked away. "But since I'm going to be cavorting..." Drew stood up and peeled off his trunks. He was a modern rendition of Adam, perfect, golden and strong, a paragon of masculine beauty. The sweatband around his forehead lent him a savage aspect as he slowly lowered himself back to the blanket.

"...cavorting on the beach with you..." As his burning eyes watched, she peeled off her bikini panties. "...naked..." He came to her with sleek grace, and they reclined together on the blanket. "...I guess I'll have to become your wife."

His kisses were hot, almost as hot as the elements—sand, wind, sun—and just as primitive.

CHAPTER TEN

"HELLUVA HONEYMOON," DREW MUTTERED. He was driving toward the picturesque village of Lahaina.

"I think it's wonderful," Arden said, laughing and straightening Matt's shirt under his overalls for the umpteenth time.

"My idea of a honeymoon is having you naked in my bed engaging in all sorts of lewd physical acts."

"We'll get to that," she whispered. Drew's head swiveled around to look at her, branding her with a heated gaze. "But for now, please keep your eyes on the road."

Once she had consented, he'd wasted no time in making arrangements for their marriage, completing everything in a few days' time. The ceremony that morning had been private. They'd flown to Honolulu to be married by a minister Drew knew well. Only Mrs. Laani and the pastor's wife had been in attendance. And Matt. At Arden's request, Drew hadn't notified the press.

"Please, Drew," she had pleaded. "I don't want to be in the limelight. I'll go on tour with you. I'll be there cheering you on at every match, but I don't want to be photographed or interviewed."

She remembered the photographers swarming around him and Ellie as they left the hospital. How had they managed to keep the secret that Ellie wasn't the child's real mother? Arden had her own secret to keep. At least for a while. She had resolved to tell Drew she was Matt's mother, but not until he was secure in her love for him. For now, the fewer people who knew about their marriage, the better. She wanted to maintain a low profile.

"But I'm proud of you," he had objected. "Why would you want to hide the fact that we're married?"

"I don't want to *hide* it. I just don't want it publicized." She groped for a plausible excuse. "Because… because of Ellie. She was so beautiful, so much a part of your life. Until I learn the ropes of the touring life, I don't want people comparing me to her."

"There is no comparison," he had said tenderly, rubbing strands of her dark hair between his fingers.

"Others might think so, and that would make me terribly uncomfortable."

He'd conceded grudgingly, and they'd returned to Maui in the middle of the afternoon to put a cranky Matt down for a nap.

"You need to call Gary for a practice set or two."

"On my wedding day?" Drew had complained.

"Do you want to win on tour or not?"

He'd turned to Mrs. Laani and spread his hands wide. "Married only a few hours and already she's nagging." Beneath his teasing, Arden could tell he was pleased that she understood how demanding his career was. "You'll go with me and watch, won't you?"

"I wouldn't miss it."

Arm in arm, they went upstairs to the master suite. Mrs. Laani had already moved many of Arden's clothes into the spare closet. Her toilet articles and makeup were neatly arranged in the bathroom dressing area. "How'd she manage this so soon?" Arden asked Drew in dismay.

"She was under strict orders to move you in here as soon as possible. You made that ridiculous rule about not sleeping with me again until we were married." He came to her and wrapped his arms around her waist, nuzzling her breasts through the silk blouse she'd worn under her wedding suit. The evidence of his impatience pressed hard against her middle. "I'm hungry for you, Arden," he rasped against her breast, and it swelled with her own desire. "From now on, expect me to be merciless."

Their mouths met urgently, moving together with suppressed longing finally given vent. Keeping his mouth on hers, his hands fumbled with her clothes until she stood in an ivory charmeuse slip. He fondled her breasts, and when her nipples tightened in response, he ducked his head to touch them with his tongue through the shiny, slinky cloth.

She rid him of his shirt and worked feverishly on his belt buckle until he could kick his way free of the trousers. She slid her hands into his tight briefs and over his buttocks. The muscles she kneaded were taut with his forced control.

He caressed her back, her derriere, her thighs, smoothing his hands over the silky slip and her pale panty hose. At the top of her thighs, his thumbs rotated arousingly over her hipbones. When he rubbed the triangular mound of her womanhood with his knuckles, she caught his hair in her fists and pulled his head away from hers.

"You've got to play tennis," she said with heaving breaths.

"To hell with it," he snarled, reaching for her again.

She was adamant. "That's exactly where your game will go if you don't practice."

He muttered a curse but stepped away from her to finish changing his clothes. She puttered with the things that had been left on her dressing table, placing them in drawers and trying not to be distracted by glimpses of Drew's body as he dressed. He wasn't in the least modest about his nakedness as he went back and forth from closet to bureau locating his tennis clothes. She'd never seen a man built finer than he.

He was stepping into a brief-style athletic supporter that he wore under his tennis shorts when he happened to catch her rapt gaze in the mirror. Insolently, he dragged the white stretchy garment up his thighs and adjusted himself within its tight confines. "See anything you like?" he asked, winking at her.

She blushed, rattling the contents of the drawer as she closed it. "I like everything I see," she admitted, risking another glance at him in the mirror. He came up behind her. "I'm glad." He lifted her hair to kiss the back of her neck.

When he had finished dressing and was stuffing a change of clothes into his tennis bag, she was still fiddling with things at the dressing table. "After spurning my romantic overtures for the sake of time, are you going to make me late by dawdling?"

She felt like a schoolgirl as she stood facing him in stocking feet and slip. "Why don't you wait for me downstairs? I...uh... I'll be ready in just a few minutes."

"What's the mat—" He caught himself. Walking to her, he placed understanding hands on her shoulders. "It's been a while since you've shared a room with a man, is that it?" She swallowed hard and nodded her head, feeling like a ninny, a fool. He kissed her cheek and squeezed her shoulders lightly. "I'll be downstairs. Take your time."

Before he was out the door, she halted him. "Drew?" When he turned around, she said, "Thank you."

He smiled and slapped the doorjamb with the palm of his hand. "I'll think of some way for you to repay me." After another hasty wink, he was gone.

Despite his objections to playing tennis on his wedding day, he played well. Another crowd had gathered to watch the practice match, and they applauded enthusiastically whenever Drew executed a particularly difficult return. He was in his element and loving every minute of it. He seemed oblivious to Arden, but she knew he was aware of her supportive presence.

He had planned to take her out for an elaborate celebration dinner, but Matt had set up a howl when they started to leave without him. "Couldn't we take him with us, Drew?" she had asked, clutching the tearful boy to her.

"Arden, since I kissed my bride this morning, I've been sharing her with other people. I want you to myself."

"And I want you, too. But I won't have a good time if we leave Matt crying this way."

Drew appealed to her intelligence. "He's only doing that to get your sympathy."

"I know. And I also know I'll have to start disciplining him. But not tonight."

Several colorful curses later, Drew gave in. "But don't get any ideas about him sleeping with us," he'd warned as he swung the car onto the highway.

"Where are you taking us tonight?" Arden asked now as the traffic on Lahaina's main thoroughfare slowed them down.

"Since you insisted on this family outing," Drew said dryly, "I'm going to let you cook my meal."

"What?" she asked, laughing in surprise.

"Just wait. You'll see."

He took them to the Pioneer Inn, an historic hotel that had accommodated seamen when Lahaina had been an important whaling port. The inn was built around an open-air central courtyard that was lit by lanterns and torches and filled with lush tropical plants.

"I love it," Arden exclaimed as the hostess led them to a table.

"I'm glad. But I wasn't kidding about cooking your own meal. See." He pointed to a large charcoal grill under a protective shed. A clock was mounted on the wall so one could monitor the cooking time according to preference. Condiments and bottled steak sauces lined the grill.

"I happen to be a terrific cook," she boasted. "When I was married and had Joey, I enjoyed planning meals and cooking. Then, after…" A spasm of sadness crossed her face. "I lost interest."

He squeezed her hand. "If you like to cook, you may cook for Matt and me whenever you want to. Starting tonight."

They gathered around the grill after they'd ordered Drew's New York steak, Matt's hamburger and Arden's *mahimahi*. The island fish was filleted and marinated, then wrapped in foil for broiling. There was much joking and advice giving as Arden wielded the long metal spatulas. Matt squealed every time a hissing flame shot up out of the charcoal pit. When the meat dishes were done, they carried them to their table and ate them with hefty salads and bowls of baked beans, the house specialty.

"Delicious," Drew said, rolling his eyes and smacking his lips over his steak. Matt comically imitated him.

Arden's heart was full to overflowing with love for the two men in her life. She cautioned herself about feeling smug. So much happiness terrified her.

MAKING TRAVEL ARRANGEMENTS for them all was an awesome responsibility. Mrs. Laani and Matt would share one room, Drew and Arden another, while Ham occupied a third. Fortunately the manager handled most of the details. With Mrs. Laani's help, Arden learned to pack with economy of space in mind, yet the job seemed endless.

Arden was nervous about meeting Ham Davis. He was a grizzled man well under six feet tall. He chomped a cigar that was foul and fat. His belly poured over pants he was constantly hiking up with hairy, beefy hands. But his charm was undeniable. Arden liked his brusque, candid manner immediately.

He was there to meet them when their plane landed at Los Angeles International. Taking her hands between his, he pressed them hard. His dark eyes probed into hers and apparently liked what they saw. "Whatever you're doing for Drew, keep it up" was all he said, but Arden knew she had earned his unqualified approval.

He was a little put out with Drew for insisting on two things. First, that he honor Arden's request for no publicity about herself. And second, that he leave them a few free days to visit Drew's mother in Oregon.

That was another hurdle Arden dreaded, and she was fidgety and nervous on the flight to Portland. She needn't have worried. Mrs. McCasslin was gracious and warm. After the flurry at the airport and the good-natured confusion of getting them settled into her home for their two-night stay, she and Arden had their first moments alone. They were in her sunny, immaculate and homey kitchen, waiting for the teakettle to come to a boil.

"You're not what I expected," Rose McCasslin said as she reached into the pantry for a tin of flavored tea bags.

"What did you expect?" The blue eyes were a family trait. Rose's were as bright as her son's and grandson's.

"I don't know exactly. Someone stridently efficient. Someone who would have taken over Matt's upbringing and either whipped Drew into shape or browbeaten him into alcoholism. Someone not nearly as beautiful or as…soft."

"Thank you," Arden said, moved. "Drew had whipped himself into shape before he married me."

"That's why I know you're good for him. You let him do it." She cocked her head to one side. "He's very much in love with you, you know."

"I think he is, yes."

"I'm glad. And relieved. I thought when we buried Ellie and he moved to that tiny island, he'd rot there for the rest of his life. He's happy again. I have only one request to make of you."

"What?"

A familiar glint of humor lit the older woman's eyes. "Make him bring you and my grandson to see me more often."

THEY TRAVELED FIRST to Phoenix, then to Dallas, Houston, New Orleans, St. Petersburg. Drew was making an impressive showing, winning steadily in the qualifying rounds but losing in the finals. He wasn't discouraged, and neither was Ham. He was giving the best in the business a run for their money. Then he won in Memphis. And in Atlanta. And in Cincinnati. His ranking began to climb.

Arden was tired of traveling but radiant over Drew's success. Life on the tour was hard, especially with a child as energetic and inquisitive as Matt. She had written all the articles she'd been under contract to do before they left Hawaii. Through long-distance telephone calls, she had been pleased to learn they would all be printed without revisions. For the time being, she had declined requests to do more.

"What do you do all day while I'm working out?" Drew had asked her one night as they lay wrapped together in the aftermath of loving. "Are you getting bored?"

"Bored? With Matt to chase after? Hardly." She snuggled closer, loving the protective feel of him beside her. "I look forward to your matches, and... I daydream...about this." She swept her hand down his stomach to touch him intimately. He gasped softly as her fingers closed around him.

"Good God, Arden, are you trying to kill me for the insurance money? I've played a hard match of tennis today. Five of seven sets and…then made love…. Sweet heaven…"

"You don't feel as though you're on the verge of collapse to me. On the contrary…" she whispered, stroking his hard length.

"When you're not thinking of ways to drive your husband into an early grave, what do you do?" he panted.

"I write."

"Write…? No, don't stop… Yes, like that… Oh, damn… Write what?"

"Things. Notes for a novel. Poetry."

"Poetry? What you're doing to me now is poetry." Rolling her onto her back, he let her guide him into her receptive body. "Write a thousand verses of it."

THEY WERE GLAD to get home. Ham had been argumentative and badgering. He'd even tried to coerce Arden into lending him her support.

"He needs to play in every tournament he can," he said, punctuating each word with stabbing motions of his cigar.

"Drew wants to go home for a few weeks, Ham."

"You can convince him otherwise."

"Perhaps, but I won't."

"I figured that." He shoved the cigar in his mouth, cursed, and then said he'd drive them to the airport.

Mo had the house opened and aired and ready for them. They resumed a reasonably normal routine. Drew played every day with Gary at the club, working on the weak spots that he and Ham had discussed. Arden busied herself with Matt and made plans for their next tour, which would take them to Europe. Just thinking about it exhausted her. How could she convey to non-English-speaking waiters that Matt would prefer a peanut butter and jelly sandwich to anything on their overpriced menus? She hadn't been able to convince English-speaking ones.

One afternoon, she was relaxing in the master suite, curled in one of the chairs beside the wide windows, when Drew came in. He dropped his tennis bag just inside the door. They watched each other from across the room, silently telegraphing the love that had grown between them over the past few weeks.

"You look beautiful sitting there, Arden," he said quietly. "The setting sun's making your hair shine with red streaks."

"Thank you. I planned to be dressed by the time you got back, but I got busy on something." She closed a folder over a tablet and laid it on the table beside the chair.

He closed the door and locked it before proceeding into the room. She was wearing a dressing gown he was partial to. It fell on her shoulders in a wide scoop neckline. It was floor-length, loosely covering her body like a filmy blue cloud. "You've just bathed," he commented.

She smelled of flowery bubble bath and woman. The sheer femininity of her seemed to beckon to his maleness. He knelt beside her chair and placed his fingertips on either side of her neck. He liked to think he felt her pulse accelerate when he touched her.

She symbolized peacefulness, home, love, all the things he'd given up hope of ever having again. Each time he saw her after brief little absences, he was surprised again at how much he loved her, how from the beginning there had been a oneness between them that he couldn't understand or explain.

"What something were you busy on?"

"Nothing really," she said in that offhanded way that he'd learned meant just the opposite. Who had convinced her that her opinion wasn't valuable? The husband she spoke so little of? Almost daily, Drew condemned the man to hell. She had been hurt. Terribly. And by more than Joey's death. The traces of abuse still lingered, though she never talked about her past. If it took a lifetime, Drew planned to teach her how valuable she was.

"You've written something, haven't you?"

Her eyes fluttered away from his. "It's terrible, I know, but it's something I've wanted to put on paper for a long time."

"May I read it?"

"It's not good enough for anyone to read."

"I don't believe that."

She licked her lips. "It's very personal."

"I won't insist if you don't want me to read it."

"I'd like your opinion," she said hurriedly.

He took the initiative of picking up the folder and opening it to the first page of the tablet. "Joey" was written on the top line. He lifted his eyes to hers, but she evaded them. She left the chair and went to stand silhouetted against the window and the vermilion western sky.

Drew read the four-page poem, his throat constricting tighter with each line. It was obvious that the words had seeped out of her soul and that it had been a painful process. They were poignant but not syrupy. They were spiritual but not pompous. They expressed the abysmal, impotent grief of a parent watching a child slowly die. But the last verses were a testimony to the blessings that had been drawn from that child. They expressed an enviable and rare joy.

Drew's eyes were wet when he stood, reverently replacing the folder on the table and going to her. His arms slid under her arms from behind and pulled her tightly against him, laying his forehead against her shoulder.

"It's beautiful, Arden."

"Do you truly think so, or are you just saying that?"

"It's beautiful. Is it too personal for you to share?"

"You mean submit for publication?"

"Yes."

"Is it good enough?"

"God, yes. I think parents, any parent, whether they've suffered the loss of a child or not, would empathize. I know I do. I think you should have it published. It may help someone who's going through what you did."

She turned to him and laid her head on his heart. She loved its steady, solid beat.

"I wish I'd been there when you needed someone. You were here for me to help me out of my crisis, but you had to go through your hell alone. I'm so sorry, my love." His fervently spoken words and the strong hands caressing her back told her of his sincerity. "Come here," he said, taking her hand and leading her to the bed.

He sat down on it and moved her to stand between his thighs. She looked into his loving face and smoothed the bushy slash of his eyebrows with her finger.

"I wish I could love away all that hurt inside you." He leaned forward and rested his head on her midriff.

"I wish I could love away yours, too. But it will always be a part of us. Maybe we love each other better because of past disappointments."

"I only know I love you more than I ever thought it possible to love." His breath, filtering through the gauzy gown onto her skin, was warm and moist. He nuzzled his nose against her breasts, loving their delicious weight on his face. "Arden, you're not using any contraceptives, are you?" He lifted his head and looked up at her.

She shook her head before answering in a strangled voice. "No."

"Good. Let's have a baby." His hands touched her breasts tenderly. He examined their shape, measured their fullness as though touching them for the first time. "Did you breast-feed Joey?"

"Until he got sick."

He nodded. His fingers caressed the nipples, and when they got hard, he rubbed his face against them, back and forth. "I want a baby with you." She clasped his head and pressed it into the softness of her abdomen. "A baby that's exclusively yours and mine. One we make together."

If only he knew what he was saying. She knew why he didn't feel that Matt had been exclusively his and Ellie's. Was this the time to tell him that they had a baby that was theirs, that they had made a beautiful baby together? Could she tell him now? Would his lips continue to ravish her gently? Or would he stop loving her, accuse her of manipulating him unforgivably?

Her lips opened to voice the confession, but she had waited too long. His mood had passed from poignancy to passion. He was kissing the delta between her thighs, paying tribute to her womanhood with his loving mouth and adoring words. His hands gathered up the airy fabric of her dressing gown, raising it up her legs, over her thighs, until it was bunched at her waist. He buried his face in the frothy material, breathing in her scent.

When his lips touched her bare skin, she shivered with anticipation and clutched his shoulders with anxious hands. He pressed ardent kisses into her dark, silky down. "Let me give you a baby, Arden," he whispered. "Let me give you that most wonderful of gifts." His hands went around her, cupped her hips and tilted her forward to meet his mouth.

"Drew," she gasped. "You can't do this." He could. He did. Her whole body was caught up in a conflagration of passion. His seeking mouth sent columns of fire shooting upward, through her loins, through her heart, into her soul.

She responded mindlessly to his directing hands as he laid her down on the bed. He placed her legs over his thighs and knelt before her. "I love you, Arden. Let me heal your pain."

His mouth was masterful. He kissed her again and again with lips that were sure and possessive, yet conversely meek. His tongue was a bold, thrusting, pleasure-giving imp that brought her again and again to crashing climax, then soothed her afterward.

Hovering on the brink of oblivion once again, she tangled his hair around her fingers and drew his head up. "Inside me. Please, now," she gasped as another convulsion shook her.

Somehow he worked free the fastening of his shorts and slipped them over his hips. He was a full, hard, warm pressure that filled her completely. He moved more adventurously than ever before, stroking the walls of her cleft, pausing, stroking again until she was senseless and knew only him and the rhythm of his loving. He plunged deeply time and again, touching her womb, making promises and then fulfilling them with one bursting rush of love so sublime that her fears flowed as freely.

When he withdrew, her body felt leaden, lethargic, yet seemed to defy gravity with a sensation of floating. He removed the rest of his clothing, pulled the twisted dressing gown from her perspiration-sheened body and lay down beside her.

Barely gathering the energy to form the words, she whispered, "Why did you do that?"

He let his finger trail down the center of her body to the dusky shadow of her sex. He followed with his eyes and then brought them back to marvel over her breasts. His eyes shone with the internal light of a fanatic worshiping his idol. "To show you there are no limits to how much I love you."

"I'm weak with love for you."

He smiled tenderly. "And you make me strong." Dipping his head, he plucked at her nipple lightly with his lips, then caressed it with his tongue. "And so very glad that I'm a man."

Her fingers wound through his blond hair. "Do you think we...made a baby?"

He chuckled softly. Laying his head next to hers on

the pillow, he snuggled close. "We'll just keep doing it until it takes."

Then, wearing only the purple twilight for raiment, they slept.

"YOU TWO ARE BONKERS," Arden called to the two tennis professionals.

Drew and Gary were batting the ball back and forth across the net, lobbing it as high as they could. They were clowning to entertain Matt, who was standing beside the court, clapping his hands. When Drew bent over and hit the ball through his legs, Matt yelled happily and jumped up and down.

"Okay, show-off," Arden said, "before you hurt yourself and I have to be the unlucky one to inform Ham you're out of commission, I'm taking your audience home. Maybe then you'll get in some real practice time."

"Party pooper," Gary called congenially before trotting over to confer with his latest conquest, who was waiting for him with a towel and a thermos of cold water.

"Ditto," Drew said, wrapping a towel around his neck. He draped one over Matt, who beamed up at him. "Your mother is a slave driver and a spoilsport," he told the boy before kissing him on the forehead. He straightened up and his voice to a whisper. "Except in bed, and then she's a regular party girl."

"And you're the life of the party," Arden said with a suggestive drawl, rubbing noses with him. "I'd love to kiss you, but I can't find a dry spot."

"Isn't that Bette Davis's line?"

"No, she said, 'I'd love to kiss you, but I just washed my hair.'"

"Oh. I knew it was something like that. Well, owe me a kiss. Do you have to go?"

"You know Matt's a monster if he doesn't get his nap. When you get home, maybe we can take him down to the beach."

"And play *nekkid*."

"Don't you ever think of anything else?"

"Yes," he answered, acting offended. "Sometimes I think about making it with our clothes *on*."

"You're terrible!" she cried, throwing a towel in his face. "Play well and we'll see you at home."

She hoisted Matt onto her hip, and settling her shoulder bag on the other arm, headed toward the parking lot where she'd parked the Seville. She had more or less inherited it after Drew bought himself a Jeep.

They had been in Europe for three months, hopping from country to country, tournament to tournament, and had only returned the week before. Drew was now ranked number five in world tennis. He was hoping that by the same time next year he'd be the number-one seed again.

"Then I'd retire."

"And do what?"

"How does a chain of sporting-goods stores sound? The emphasis would be on family participation. You know, jogging shoes for father and son, matching tennis dresses for mothers and daughters, yard games for the entire family. Things like that."

"It sounds terrific. And I like the concept."

"So do I. We're going to lead the pack."

"We?"

"Ham will retire, too. He says he's too old to start all over again with a cub tennis bum. He wants to go into the business with me. And *you*," he kissed her quickly, "of course."

Her poem "Joey" had been published by a ladies' magazine and then by *Reader's Digest*. The ladies' magazine had asked if she'd think about writing a short story or novelette. She was toying with several ideas.

"Did you enjoy watching daddy play?" she asked Matt, who had celebrated his second birthday in Paris. He was really too heavy for her to carry, but she never passed up an opportunity. He called her "mum," and each time she saw the name on his perpetually damp lips, she wanted to weep with happiness. "Isn't he terrific? But then you're biased in your opinion of him, just as I am."

Arden didn't see the man in the car parked next to hers until he got out. She glanced over her shoulder as she was unlocking the car door. And everything inside her froze. She felt as though the blood were damming up in her veins, her lungs shutting down operation, her heart thudding to a standstill.

He was heavier by twenty pounds. His hair was thinner, grayer and badly cut. His skin looked pallid and contrasted garishly with the capillaries in his nose, which had reddened with too much drink. The jowls on either side of his face looked like empty, oversize pockets. His clothes were less natty and seemed uncomfortably hot and tight. His shoes were scuffed.

But that conniving look still lurked in his eyes. He still wore that familiar smirking grin, the grin that said he had something on someone and couldn't wait to use it to his advantage.

Arden needed very badly to vomit. She swallowed the hot bile that gushed into her throat and instinctively, with the fierce protectiveness of motherhood, clutched Matt to her.

"Hello, Mrs. McCasslin."

He made the name sound like an obscene insult. Revulsion swamped her, and she had an overwhelming impulse to run as far and as fast as she could. Instead, she stared back at him with eyes turned icy with hatred. "Hello, Ron."

CHAPTER ELEVEN

THE BLEARY EYES took a tour down her body that made her feel as though she needed a scalding bath. She didn't want him to know how much he frightened her. That was the only thing that kept her from screaming.

"You're looking well," he said when his thorough appraisal brought his eyes back to hers.

"You look like hell," she said flatly, wondering where her new-found courage came from. But she knew. It was an outgrowth of Drew's love and the happiness she'd found with him.

Ron Lowery blinked, momentarily disconcerted by her uncharacteristic flippancy. When he grinned, it was with an evil curl to his mouth. "True. But then I didn't land on my feet the way you did, Mrs. McCasslin."

She set a squirming Matt down on the parking-lot pavement. He had long since lost interest in the conversation and was much more interested in the yellow metal button that marked the parking space in front of the automobile. Arden saw to it that he was well out of Ron's reach.

"Don't blame me or anyone else for whatever misfortunes have befallen you, Ron. You had all the makings of success handed to you on a silver platter. Or should I say through a golden wedding ring? If you failed to take advantage of those opportunities, then you've no one to blame but yourself."

His fists balled at his sides, and he took a threatening step forward. "Don't get all high and mighty with me. I can topple your little world with one fell swoop, *Mrs. McCasslin.* How'd you find him?"

She decided that her only defense was to admit nothing, to brazen it out. She tilted her chin up haughtily. "I don't know what you're talking about."

Steely fingers bit into her upper arm as Ron hauled her closer to him. "How did you find McCasslin? And don't think I'm stupid enough to believe you're his blushing bride by some wild coincidence."

She swallowed a lump of fear and blinked against waves of pain. She was seeing a side of Ron's nature that she had always known was there but didn't want to acknowledge. He would be ruthless, cruel, violent, if he had to be to get what he wanted.

"Deductive reasoning," she said with relief when his fingers uncurled from around her arm. "I had seen him and his wife the morning they left the hospital."

"Well, congratulations. You pulled off a clever one, didn't you?" He looked down at Matt in a way that made Arden's blood run cold. "He's a cute kid. I did a good job fathering him."

An ocean of nausea washed over Arden, and she thought she might very well faint. It came as a surprise to her to find herself still standing several seconds later. "You?" she wheezed.

He laughed. It was an ugly sound. "What's the matter, Mrs. McCasslin? Do you think you went to all that trouble for nothing? Do you think you're married to the wrong man? Hmm?"

His taunts sickened her further. "Is Matt Drew's child?" she asked desperately.

Ron eyed her slyly, enjoying to the fullest the tidal wave of despair he'd inflicted on her. "He provided the semen, yes. But as you'll recall, I did all the work."

Her relief was so vast that she slumped against the hot metal body of the car. It was several moments before the vertigo passed and the world righted itself. But the brassy taste in her mouth and the sickness in her stomach remained. This man was diabolical, capable of anything.

"Actually, you've done me a great service by marrying McCasslin," he was saying, idly picking his fingernails of imaginary dirt. Or maybe it wasn't imaginary.

She wouldn't humor him by inquiring how that might be. Instead, she met his cunning eyes levelly.

"I've fallen onto hard times, Arden. I know you'll be devastated to learn that the practice your sainted father worked so diligently to establish is no more."

"I divorced myself from it when I divorced myself from you," she said. "It was no longer my father's work but only your plaything. And I wanted nothing of yours."

"Well—" he shrugged "—it's gone, anyway, which brings us to the point of this pleasant visit." He leaned forward and whispered conspiratorially, "You're going to help me recoup some of my losses."

"You're insane. I wouldn't spit on you if you were on fire. And this pleasant little visit, as you call it, has just come to an end. Don't bother me again." She knelt down and picked up Matt, absently dusting off his knees. Yanking open the car door, she shoved him inside, ignoring his protests.

"Just a minute, bitch," Ron said, grabbing her arm before she could climb into the car. "How would you like it if I paid a visit to that new husband of yours?" Arden stopped struggling and held her breath as she stared wordlessly into Ron's feral eyes. "You hold a low opinion of me. But remember he and that insipid wife of his regarded me as just short of the Almighty. He'd be pleased to see me. Shall I go have a chat with him?"

Her panic surged to the surface, and she could only hope it was invisible to her ex-husband. But by the victorious gleam in his eyes, she knew that he'd seen it. "That's what I thought," he crooned. "Mr. McCasslin doesn't know who your former husband was, does he? He doesn't know what a high-priced whore he's married to. Fifty thousand dollars' worth of whoring. He doesn't know all that, does he? Well, isn't that interesting?" He pushed her into the seat of the car, where she landed with a jolt that stunned her. "I'll be in touch."

It was a vow, a threat that left her arms and legs rubbery as she drove home.

"YOU DON'T LIKE the veal scallopini?"

Arden stopped stirring the food around her plate and smiled across the table into her husband's concerned, questioning eyes. "I'm sorry. I guess I wasn't up for a crowd tonight." They were having dinner alone in one of Lahaina's favorite night spots.

"You should have said something. We could have gone somewhere else." He reached for her hand and squeezed it. His look was heart-meltingly intimate. "Or we could have stayed at home, had dinner in our room and had a *really* good time."

The insinuation behind his words, the recollection

of just such evenings, the love so evident in his eyes, made Arden ache with the guilt she lived with.

All afternoon, she'd been as jumpy as a cat, afraid to look over her shoulder for fear of seeing Ron's leering, ominous presence. She loathed him. He was an odious person, and she despised his self-serving motives. Yet was she any better? Hadn't she manipulated Drew McCasslin in the most despicable way? Why hadn't she told him who she was in the beginning? And why was it so hard to tell him now?

The answer to both questions was the same. She loved him too much. The moment she had set eyes on Drew, her objectivity had flown. It had never returned. She could no more tell him now that she was Matt's mother than she could have that first day he'd walked up to her and said hello. But the guilt she lived with was becoming unbearable. It ate at her like a cancer. She didn't like to think of herself in league with someone like Ron Lowery.

"I'm sorry I'm ruining your evening." She sighed, wishing she could climb inside the security of his body and hide from all external dangers.

"No evening I've spent with you has been a ruin," he said softly. A grin slashed across his handsome face. "Well, maybe a few evenings before we married when I wanted to be in your bed and you did everything short of castration to keep me out of it."

She laughed in spite of her mood. "I was only being ladylike," she said with mock demureness.

"A curse on being ladylike. I'll bet you—"

His sentence hung unfinished as he spotted something across the room that rendered him speechless.

"Drew?"

It took a moment for his eyes to drift back to her, and then he seemed unable to focus. "I...what? Oh, I'm sorry. What were you saying?"

"You were saying something, not me." She laughed and turned to see what had captured his attention. Her laugh caught in her throat when she saw Ron Lowery sitting alone at a table across the room, casually studying a menu. His being there was no accident. Of that, Arden was positive.

She whipped her head back toward Drew to see if he had read her dismay, but he was still staring at Ron. "Do you know that man?" she asked hesitantly.

In that moment, she realized she'd chosen to perpetuate her lie. She had been presented with an ideal opportunity to say, "Drew, I believe you know my former husband. You and Ellie went to him about three years ago. He found a surrogate mother for your child. I was the woman." Instead, she had taken the path of least resistance. She couldn't gamble with Drew's love now. It was still too new and fragile. Matt was too precious to her. She couldn't take the risk.

"Uh, yes," Drew said. He was watching Ron as he laughed with a waitress over the wine list. Was there a trace of bitterness in Drew's voice? His lips had narrowed in a way that Arden knew indicated he was displeased with something. Apparently, he didn't hold Ron in the esteem Ron thought.

"He...he... Ellie and I knew him on the mainland. At one time, he was a special friend to us."

"I see," Arden said, gulping at her ice water.

"He's a doctor. He did us a special service for which he was very well paid. Then he tried to wheedle more money out of me."

Arden could feel what little food she'd eaten churning in her stomach. Once she'd borne Matt, Ron had pressed the McCasslins for more money. Was the man totally without principles? "How could he expect you to pay more than he'd asked for?" She hoped the question sounded casual.

"He said he'd run into complications that he hadn't anticipated," Drew said absently, still staring piercingly in Ron's direction. Then, as though realizing he might have said more than he'd intended, he reverted his attention to Arden. His grin was forced. "We came to an understanding. I wonder what's brought him to Maui. Vacation, I suppose."

"No doubt." Arden wondered how her voice could sound so normal when she felt like screaming.

"If you're not going to mutilate that piece of veal anymore, we'll go."

"No. I'm done."

God, how was she going to live through this? she asked herself as she let Drew steer her through the maze of tables toward the door. They would have to pass Ron's table to reach the exit. She knew he'd followed them to the restaurant. It was his way of demonstrating to her just how serious his threats were. He wanted something from her, and he'd hang on with the tenacity of a bulldog until she capitulated. And she knew that to safeguard her life with Drew and Matt, she would.

He played the scene with the aplomb of a Barrymore. He actually let his eyes widen with surprised pleasure when he spotted Drew. Toward her, he exhibited not one sign of recognition. Her heart was hurling itself against her ribs like a caged animal gone mad as she heard him say, "Drew McCasslin! What a treat to see you after all this time."

Drew was coolly polite. "Hello, Dr. Lowery. How are you?"

They shook hands. "You're looking great, Drew," Ron said expansively. "Reports about you on the sports pages have been fantastic lately." His eyes clouded, and his voice lowered sympathetically. "I was sorry to hear about your wife. How is the little boy?"

Arden could feel Drew's muscles contracting with tension, but his voice was composed as he replied. "Thank you for your condolences. Matt is a strapping two-year-old now. He's terrific."

"Ah, that's good to hear."

"And—" Drew pulled her forward "—this is my wife, Arden. Darling, Dr. Ron Lowery."

It occurred to her that playwrights had often created comic scenes out of situations such as this, and she wondered how anyone could ever consider them funny. The irony was too cruel to be humorous. The hysteria that had threatened all day almost erupted. She didn't know if it would have taken the form of a high, deranged laugh or an imbecilic scream. She was able to stop it just in time. "Dr. Lowery," she said. Nothing could have compelled her to extend her hand.

"Mrs. McCasslin," Ron said kindly.

His sincere-looking smile infuriated her. She wanted nothing more than to expose him for the sham he was. But to expose him would be to expose herself.

The two men exchanged pleasantries, Ron saying that he was on the islands for several weeks' vacation and Drew wishing him a good time. Somehow she lived through it without going berserk. The smile on her lips was so brittle, she thought her face might crack like a china plate if she held it much longer.

"It was wonderful to see you again," Ron said silkily as Drew finally escorted her toward the door.

"Same here. Have a good trip," Drew said as they walked away.

Once in the car, he started the motor, but didn't engage the gears. He stared sightlessly over the hood ornament. "Is something wrong?" she asked.

"No, not really. There's just something about…" Drew's voice faded to nothingness while Arden sat stiffly beside him, only her rigid physical control managing to keep her hysteria at bay. "Dr. Lowery was important to Ellie and me. I told you that she had trouble conceiving. He…well, he made Matt possible. I have him to thank for my son. But…hell, I can't explain it, Arden."

He shook his head, as though by doing so, his random thoughts would rearrange themselves logically. "It's more than his demand for additional money. There's something about his mannerisms that bugs me, makes me wary of trusting him too far. I don't know why exactly, but for some reason, it disturbed me to see him tonight. On my turf, so to speak. I haven't seen him since Matt was born, and I didn't plan on seeing him ever again."

He chuckled in self-derision and shifted the car into drive. "I guess you think I'm crazy."

"No," she said, staring entranced at the lighted dials on the dashboard. "I don't think you're crazy. I don't trust him, either."

"NOW THAT THE lights are out, will you tell me what's been troubling you all day?"

Arden had already been in bed for several minutes when Drew snapped off the bedside lamp and joined her. He was naked, as was she. She had dispensed with wearing nightclothes. "Saves time," Drew had said with a sexy grin the first week of their marriage. That night, Arden hadn't put on a nightgown, but she had wanted to. Her impulse had been to hide, to cover herself. She had curled up on her side of the bed, facing the edge, holding herself stiff.

"Nothing's troubling me," she mumbled into the pillow.

"Then you've undergone a personality change since you left the club this afternoon. You've been a bundle of nerves—you didn't eat your dinner, you were silent on the way home, and most unusual of all, you almost forgot to go into Matt's room to kiss him good-night. Now dammit, something's wrong."

All her anxiety surfaced, and she lashed out at the nearest object, Drew. "Just because I don't want to make love tonight, you think something's wrong. Maybe I'm just not in the mood, okay? My God, you expect me to turn on and off like a light bulb. Can't I have one night's peace?" She pulled the covers up higher.

Several seconds of silence elapsed before Drew flung the covers off himself and shot out of bed. "Your memory is playing you false. I don't recall asking you to make love tonight."

He was three lunging strides across the room before she implored him to come back. "Drew!" she cried, sitting up and extending her arms. "I'm sorry, I'm sorry. Please come back. Hold me."

The moonlight filtering through the wide windows revealed the silver streams of tears on her cheeks. He was there instantly, gathering her to him tightly, smoothing her hair with loving hands, pressing her face into the curve of his shoulder. "What is it, Arden? What's wrong? Something I've done? Not done?"

"No, no," she said mournfully, rolling her head from side to side. "I shouldn't have been cross with you. I didn't mean it. I..."

"What? Tell me."

She searched her soul, looking for the courage to tell him about Ron, about Matt. She couldn't find it. At that moment, bravery was as elusive as the moonbeam that glinted on his hair.

She sniffed back her tears. "It's nothing, really. Just... I haven't felt 'with it' today. That's all."

"Lie down," he instructed softly, and reclined with her onto the soft linens. It was warm enough for them to lie uncovered, with the ocean breeze whispering across their flesh. He lay behind her, drawing her to him and wrapping his arms around her protectively. His breath sifted through her hair to caress her ear as he whispered, "I love you, Arden."

"I love you, too," she vowed, nestling her hips against him, feeling his manhood proud and warm.

He moved his hands up and down her front, trailing his fingertips in the shallow valley that divided her torso into left and right. "Are you worried because you haven't become pregnant?"

She had been concerned but hadn't spoken of it. Ever since that day he'd read her poem, they had been hoping she'd become pregnant soon. "It will happen," she said quietly.

"I think so, too. But whether it does or not doesn't matter all that much to me. I love you. *You.* I don't want you to think that if we don't have a child of our own, I'll love you any less."

She brought his hand to her lips and kissed it. "I'm selfish. I want to be everything to you."

"You are. I already feel like you're Matt's mother. To see you two together, no one would guess otherwise."

She stifled a sob and snuggled closer. She didn't deserve this blind trust. This love.

"When I make love to you, Arden, making a baby is the last thing on my mind. You are on my mind. I'm loving you. Exclusively."

Her dwindling sobs mingled with a sigh as his hand closed around her breast. His deep voice murmured a lullaby of love words in her ears.

"I think about your breasts, how perfectly they are shaped. I love their fullness. I like to caress them. Like this." His fingers grazed the dainty peaks and found them already aroused by his heated words. "You're so pretty," he whispered as his fingertips worked their magic on her flesh.

"Your skin is creamy and smooth." His hand stroked down her stomach. "I love kissing it. It feels so good against my face and lips. And this…" His fingers brushed through the tuft at the top of her thighs. "This is what woman should be." The sweet exploration intensified. "I love you here."

Arden moaned in ecstasy at his bold touch and the tender invasion of his fingers. "It feels so good when you hold me here, buried inside you."

"Drew." She turned her head to meet his mouth. He kissed her deeply.

"Nothing you do could make me love you less. You can't win my love, Arden. You already have it. Free and unqualified and unconditionally and eternally."

She twisted in his arms and turned to face him. "I've changed my mind. I want to make love very much."

He smiled in pleasure and surprise when she flattened her hands on his shoulders and pressed him onto his back. She positioned herself over him, and he groaned his ecstasy. Her breasts were a tantalizing display before his eyes. Not believing her own daring, she cupped one in each hand like an offering. "Can you…?"

He levered himself up to replace her hands with his, accepting her gift gladly. He laved her tight, aching nipples with his tongue, rolling it over the dusky beads until she felt the swirling motion deep inside her. He took one breast into his mouth just as she sank onto his sex.

Against her breasts, he ground out curses that might have been prayers as she rocked upon him, sending him deeper into the well of her love to find its very source. "Ah, sweet…" he moaned, collapsing backward onto the pillows.

She rotated her hips, raised them, lowered them, wanting to take all of him inside herself so there could be no doubt of their belonging together, no question of the rightness of their marriage.

His breath was uneven and harsh, but his touch was tender. He fondled her breasts, then let one hand slip into the deep shadow where their bodies were fused. An exquisite thrill rocketed through her body at his knowing touch.

"Oh, Drew. Please, please." Whether she was pleading for him to stop or never to stop, she didn't know. But he knew. He continued that divine torment until he felt her body quaking with the coming tumult. His hands gripped her hips and anchored her to him as they experienced the final sensual assault together.

Exhausted, she collapsed onto him, their stomachs moving in and out together, panting for air. Their bodies were dewy with perspiration, their muscles limp and useless, but their hearts were full.

At last, Drew rolled them to their sides. He brushed damp strands of dark hair from her face as he held her close. "Our love represents all that is pure and good and honest in the world, Arden."

"Yes," she said huskily, smiling up at him. It was after he fell asleep that she began again to weep quietly.

"Is this the lady of the house?"

Arden's fingers gripped the telephone receiver tighter. She recognized the oily voice immediately. For days, she had dreaded hearing it. She had known Ron would call, she just hadn't known when. Now that he had finally contacted her, she could almost feel relieved. At least the suspense was over. Now she only had to dread what he wanted of her. "Yes," she replied curtly.

"The Orchid Lounge. Three o'clock."

The phone went dead in her hand. She replaced it with the care of one who has gone through physical therapy and wants to make sure his actions are precise and correct. Ron hadn't given her much time. It was past two now. Matt was taking his nap. Drew was in his office talking to Ham long-distance on the other line. As soon as Matt awakened, they planned to go down to the beach.

"Mrs. Laani," Arden said, sticking her head around the corner of the kitchen door. "I don't want to disturb Drew while he's on the telephone. Would you tell him I've decided to do some shopping this afternoon. He and Matt should go to the beach without me. Maybe I can join them later."

"I'll be glad to do any household shopping for you tomorrow," the housekeeper offered.

"No, thank you. I need a few things for myself. I shouldn't be long."

She left the house a few minutes later, dressed in a poplin skirt and a polo shirt. She'd be damned before she'd dress up for Ron.

She knew the Orchid Lounge was in a ramshackle row of buildings on the outskirts of Lahaina. She had passed it many times on her way into the town. It was worse than she had expected. It was dim and smoky, the smell of stale beer permeating its gloomy atmosphere.

It took her several minutes to adjust her eyes to the darkness, and when she did, she noted she was the only female in the place. Pairs of leering eyes glowed at her from dark corners. Swallowing her trepidation, she walked straight to the nearest red vinyl booth and slid into the lumpy seat.

"Club soda, please," she said to the bartender, who came scurrying to the booth to serve her. His hair was thick with white grooming cream. The Hawaiian print shirt he wore was loud and baggy and none too clean.

"Yes, ma'am," he said in a lilting voice that made her flesh crawl. She trained her eyes on the neon clock on the opposite wall and left them there, even when the glass of soda was thumped down in front of her without benefit of napkin or coaster. She wouldn't have drunk out of it for all the gold in the world. She ignored the speculative glances thrown in her direction, the whispered comments followed by guffaws of laughter, the sinister stares.

Ron was over fifteen minutes late. *Damn him.* He was doing this on purpose to weaken her, frighten her, humiliate her. It was just the kind of psychological warfare he was capable of. Well, she wasn't going to stay in this sleazy tavern another moment.

Just as she was gathering up her purse to leave, Ron slid into the booth across from her. "Where are you going?" he asked belligerently.

"I don't like your choice of meeting places," she said tightly. The other patrons were smirking at her knowledgeably. She had been there to meet a lover. Or a client? She shivered in revulsion.

"You're not supposed to like it." Ron signaled to the bartender. "Double Scotch. Neat." Then he pinned her with those treacherous eyes that penetrated her wall of defenses like twin battering rams. "I need twenty thousand dollars."

The bartender asked if she wanted another drink when he set Ron's whiskey down on the greasy tabletop. It was a ludicrous question, since she hadn't touched the first. She shook her head, not deigning to look at him. He reminded her of a cockroach, the way he scuttled around in the dark.

Ron tossed down half the drink, winced, swallowed hard, then took a smaller sip. "You're going to get it for me."

"Go to hell. I'll do nothing of the sort."

His eyes slithered down her chest as a nasty curl deformed his heavy mouth. "Yes, you will." He took another pull on the drink. "I've got men after me, Arden. Hard men, butchers. I'm up to my ass in debt to them. They want their money."

"That's your problem, not mine."

"Oh, it's yours all right. I'm making it yours. You're married to a rich tennis player now. VIP. High roller. Big-timer. You wouldn't ever have met him if it weren't for me. You owe me."

She did something she never thought she'd do in Ron Lowery's presence. She laughed. "You fool," she said with unveiled contempt. "After all you did to hurt me, even asking me to have a child for another man, you say that *I* owe *you.*"

He shrugged. "Whatever. You'll do as I say just as you always have. Because you're a spineless coward, Arden."

"I am not!" she retorted.

"No?" he asked with a sneer and another softly sinister laugh. He glanced over his shoulder at the dozen or so men watching them with keen interest. "Weren't you just a teeny-weeny bit afraid before I came in? You didn't like it in here, did you? All these guys were ogling you, thinking about what's under your skirt. Did that scare you a little? Huh? Weren't you just the least bit nervous? I'll bet there's a little river of sweat running between your breasts. Right? Are those nice big tits of yours damp with sweat?"

"Stop it."

"And there's probably a trickle of sweat between

your thighs, too. Hmm? One word from me and I'll bet these guys would check that out."

"Ron, please."

He feigned surprise. "What? Did I actually hear a tremor in your voice? A plea for mercy?" He crossed his arms on the table and leaned forward. "That's where I want you, Arden. Compliant." He sat back after taking another sip of whiskey and signaled for more. "Now, let's get down to business." When he had his fresh drink, he said, "I need five thousand immediately. The other fifteen, we can spread out over a few weeks."

"Ron," she exclaimed, struggling to hang on to her reason. "I don't have that kind of money."

"You have a goddam checking account, and I know it!" he shouted, his fist crashing down on the table.

She jumped in spite of her resolve not to show her fear. "Yes, I have a checking account," she said with forced composure. "But how am I supposed to account to Drew for that kind of spending?"

"That's up to you. If you're resourceful enough to con this guy into marrying you, you can think of a way to get that money."

"I didn't con him into marrying me," she said heatedly.

"But that's what he'd think, wouldn't he, if I went to him and told him who I had impregnated with his semen?" He shook his head pityingly. "No. I don't think he'd be quite the ardent groom if he found that out."

"I could deny it. I could admit that you were my husband, but that doesn't prove that I had Drew's child. I'd claim you were lying for the sake of blackmailing us."

He tsked. "Arden, Arden, are you still so naive? Remember the lawyer, sweetheart? He's a buddy of mine. He's got the records sealed in a safe. All I'd have to do is show them to McCasslin. Besides, I told you he thinks I hung the moon because I got him that boy."

It was her turn to look smug. "Don't count on that, Ron. He told me how you tried to get more money out of him because of the *complications* you ran into. He doesn't think nearly as well of you as you think."

One corner of his mouth tilted. "Be that as it may, he wouldn't want me to tell the press that I know about that kid. It would make him look like a fool, not to mention besmirching the reputation of his dear departed wife." He lowered one calculating eyelid. "Tell me. Isn't it crowded with the three of you in bed? You, your tennis player and his wife's ghost?"

He had intended to hurt her, and he had. Whether he knew it or not, he had touched her one vulnerable point. "It's not that way," she said desperately.

"No? He was crazy in love with that woman. Even someone as jaded as I on the topic of love could see that. Do you expect me to believe you've replaced her? Remember, I was married to you, too, Arden. And you may be a helluva of a housekeeper, cook and mother, but as a lover, you're pathetic."

Hatred, undiluted and pure, coursed through her. She wanted to flaunt her sex life with Drew, to tell this buffoon every glorious detail of their life together. Her fists were tightly clenched as she said, "He loves me. I love him. We want to have a baby. We—"

His rude laughter interrupted her. "Baby?" He laughed harder. "*You* have another baby? Where did you get the mistaken idea you could still have children?"

CHAPTER TWELVE

"WHA...WHAT DO you mean?" Her lungs were squeezing closed. She had no air. She was going to die in the Orchid Lounge.

"I mean, Mrs. McCasslin, that when you had your baby, you were fixed. Spayed. Sterilized."

"That's impossible," she whispered. "That's impossible."

"You were anesthetized, remember?"

"But...but there was no incision. For a tubal ligation—"

He waved off her arguments. "There are always new methods to try. Who is a better guinea pig than a gynecologist's wife? I was afraid you might regret giving up the baby later on, especially in light of Joey's health. Should your maternal instincts surface, I didn't want you to be able to have another child. I certainly didn't want another one. Joey cost me a fortune in medical expenses."

She uttered an anguished cry, as if he'd dealt her a mortal blow. How could he speak that way of Joey, his own son? And now all hope of her having another child was banished by the base cruelty of this man. Feeling utterly defeated, she groped blindly for her purse. "How much do you need? Five thousand?" She wanted him out of her life. If buying him off would achieve that, she would give him any amount.

"For starters, yes. I need it tomorrow."

"Tomorrow?" How could she come up with that kind of money in that length of time? "I don't think I can get it that soon, but I'll try," she said as she stood. Dizzily, she swayed.

He caught her arm. "You'll deliver it tomorrow, or I'll pay a visit to that good-looking husband of yours. He and I have a lot to chat about."

Arden, still feeling poleaxed, worked her arm free and stumbled toward the door. The sunlight blinded her. Or was it her tears?

"TOMORROW?" ARDEN REPEATED. Drew had dropped his bomb just as she was bringing a bite of food to her mouth. Her fork was held suspended in midair. She lowered it to her plate. "We're leaving for California tomorrow?" Tomorrow, tomorrow, tomorrow. The word rolled around inside her head like a roulette ball. It seemed that she had echoed that word all day.

"I know it's a nuisance, but I only found out myself a few minutes ago." He had joined them in the dining room late. He'd been talking on the telephone to Ham again. Matt, as usual, was restless and eager for his dinner, so Arden had begun to feed him. "Mrs. Laani can pack for Matt tonight. We're catching a one o'clock plane to Honolulu tomorrow afternoon, then an overnighter to L.A."

"But why the rush?" Arden was dismayed. How was she going to pay off Ron? Ever since she'd left him, she had been trying to come up with an excuse to give Drew when she asked him for the five thousand dollars.

"Use your napkin like daddy, Matt," Drew said, demonstrating for his son. He smiled when the child did as instructed. "There are several reasons. First, there are three tournaments that Ham thinks I should play in. Few of the top seeds are going to play, so I might be able to rack up some wins. One's in San Diego, one's in Vegas and the other is in San Francisco, so the travel won't be extensive. There are only a few days between them. And Ham and I have other business to take care of."

She stared into her plate. It had been increasingly difficult to meet Drew's eyes ever since she had returned from her meeting with Ron. Now she had two secrets to hide—that she was Matt's mother and that she was barren. Should he find out either one, he'd have more than ample reason to despise her. Now she was trying to come up with a way to con him out of money to pay off her blackmailer. God, what had she sunk to?

Contrary to what Ron believed, she didn't have a limitless bank account. Drew had opened up an account in her name and kept a generous reserve in it. Into that account, too, went her checks for the articles or stories she sold. "It's yours to do with as you see fit," Drew had said when he made the initial deposit. "Just don't spend it on the household. There's another account for that. This is yours to play with."

She had checked the balance of it that day, and it was a far cry from twenty thousand. Currently, it was even short of five thousand. She knew Ron wouldn't hesitate to tell Drew about her should she not come up with the money. By tomorrow. And tomorrow they were leaving for the mainland.

She only nodded absently when Mrs. Laani came in to carry Matt upstairs so she and Drew could finish their dinner alone. She kissed the boy's cheek but later didn't even remember it. She felt like a mummy, swathed tightly in her problem, restricted and immobile, separated from life.

"You see," Drew went on once they were alone, "Ham and I have a chance to buy into an existing chain of sporting-goods stores right now. It's a nationwide operation. We figure that in a few years we can buy out the other partners and then do with it as we want."

"That's wonderful, Drew."

"I've arranged a line of credit with a Honolulu bank. Cash may be tight for a few months until I chalk up a few wins and some of those renewed contracts start paying off. Can you stand living on a budget?"

His eyes were sparkling teasingly, but she could barely manufacture a smile. Even if she came up with a believable lie, Drew couldn't give her any money now. He would be using all the cash he had to buy into the sporting-goods business so that their future would be sure. Arden could feel her spirit suffocating, could see her dreams leaking out of her heart, to be swallowed up by a black oppression.

Drew was startled by Arden's anxiety over their imminent departure. But then he'd been worried sick about her for days. He didn't know what to think of her sudden reversal of temperament. She'd never been nervous or high-strung before, but lately the slightest provocation set off either a crying jag or a fit of temper.

If he wasn't talking to her directly, she was gazing into space, totally unaware of what was going on around her. Even when they were engaged in conversation, her eyes would often glaze, and he knew that though she made the proper responses, she wasn't really listening to him. Even Matt, for whom she always had unlimited patience, had felt the brunt of her temper.

At first, he'd thought it was her monthly cycle throwing her off balance, but it had lasted too long. Then he'd thought with a surge of hope that she might be pregnant, but when he suggested that possibility with a teasing smile, she'd burst into tears and accused him of wanting her only as a brood mare. He'd stymied the impulse to curse and stamp from the room. Instead, he'd gone to her, taken her into his arms and comforted her with words that declared his boundless love. She'd cried all the harder.

Damned if he knew what was troubling her, but something was. Why wouldn't she open up to him, confide in him? He could help. He knew it. If only she'd tell him what was bothering her. He wanted his wife back, the one who laughed and loved as generously and as spontaneously as a young girl.

Her distress had been compounded by the news of their trip. Why? Was she dreading tour life? He had thought she'd adjusted to it so well. Nothing had seemed to ruffle her. *Dammit, what was wrong?* Was it him? Was she unhappy with their marriage? The thought brought an excruciating pain to his chest.

"I… I don't really have to go, do I?" He saw her tongue flash out to wet her lips nervously. "I mean, it sounds to me as though you'd get along better without me…without all of us tagging along after you. Meetings and all…"

He studied her for a moment, his dinner forgotten. "I never think of you and Matt as 'tagging along.' I want you with me. As for the other, I was hoping that you'd attend the business meetings, too. I want you to be a visible and integral partner in any endeavor of my life. Since this venture is vital to our future, I would have thought you'd want to get involved."

His eyes bored into hers incisively. "There's another reason why you must go. More important than all the others. I want you to see a doctor."

To keep her hands from trembling, she clasped the seat of her chair until her knuckles turned white. "B-but that's ridiculous. A doctor? Why?"

"Because I think you need a thorough checkup. You insist that nothing is wrong, but I want a professional opinion."

"What kind of doctor?" she asked testily. "A psychiatrist?"

"I think we'll start with a medical doctor." His gaze softened appreciably. "Arden, you're not Wonder Woman. You've taken on a new husband, child and climate. It's understandable if your psyche and your body are going through a period of readjustment. I think we'd both feel better once you see a doctor."

No doubt she'd feel very good when the doctor told her husband, "Your wife is in perfect health, but she's barren. I'm sorry, Mr. McCasslin. I hear you wanted another child."

What could she do? *What?* She really didn't have to do anything. Because when Ron didn't get his money the next day, he'd tell Drew about her, and then it would all be over, anyway. There would never be a doctor's appointment to worry about. For the time being, she wouldn't fight it. It was too energy consuming. The heartache and guilt plaguing her had depleted her strength. "All right, I'll see a doctor."

"Super. Ham's making an appointment for you."

Drew didn't make love to her that night. Instead, he showed his love by kissing her thoroughly and tucking her against his warmth. Even so, she shivered through the long hours of the night.

"WHAT DO YOU mean you can't get it?" Ron's voice was both threatening and desperate.

"Just what I told you," she whispered, fearing she'd wake the rest of the household. It was just past dawn. She'd slipped out of Drew's arms, wrapped a robe around her and crept downstairs to call the number Ron had given her. She didn't know where the telephone was. She didn't want to know. But he answered on the second ring. "I can give you a little over three thousand today. That's all I've got, and I can't get any more."

"That's no good!" he shouted. "I've got to have five."

"I haven't got it," she snapped back.

"Get it."

"I can't. Ron, you gave me less than twenty-four hours. Be reasonable."

"The guys after me won't be reasonable."

"You should have thought of that before getting mixed up with them." She tried to push down the panic in her voice. "We're leaving for the mainland. Perhaps when we get back—"

"And when will that be?"

"About three weeks."

"Forget that, I'll be dead by then."

She couldn't say that that would be a relief, but that was what she was thinking. He sensed it. "Don't think my sudden demise would get you off the hook. Before I let them blow my brains out, I'd tell them where they could collect their money and give them the scoop on you and your new husband. If you think I'm a nuisance, honey, you haven't seen anything like these guys. You're far better off dealing with me."

"I'll get you the money," she said firmly. "You'll just have to put your creditors off for a while."

"No sale, Arden. You be at that bar at noon today with five thousand cash, or I'll make a lovely scene at the airport." He hung up.

She sat staring at the ocean for a long while before she climbed the stairs. It seemed as though she had a ball and chain around her ankles, making each step a dragging effort. Drew was right. Her mental anguish was like a physical ailment.

She heard sounds of laughter and scuffling coming from her bedroom the moment she reached the landing. Pushing the door open, she saw that Matt had joined his father in bed. They were wrestling, one as naked as the other. Matt was shrieking with laughter as Drew tickled him, making growling sounds.

Arden went to the bed and sat down on the edge. Love flooded her heart, as tears did her eyes. These two were all she had in the world. They loved her. Until that afternoon. Then she would be exposed to them as a fraud. But her love wasn't fraudulent. She should tell Drew now, but she feared his wrath and misunderstanding. She had waited too long. And there was an outside chance she might be able to put Ron off. Perhaps if she went to the bar with what cash she had in hand, she could buy time. Each day with Drew and her son was valuable. She would collect as many as she could.

Drew winked at her as he stood Matt on his flat, hard stomach. "He's quite a boy, isn't he?"

"Yes." Her voice was husky with emotion.

Matt was toasty brown, but against his father's bronzed body, he was several shades lighter. His little buttocks were round and dimpled. Rolls of baby fat scalloped his thighs. Stubby, fat toes dug into his father's flesh. With unabashed vanity, he submitted to their adoring inspection. Taking his small penis in his hand, he declared, "Pee-pee."

Drew hooted with laughter. "Yeah, you know all the terminology, you just haven't learned the practical applications." He turned to Arden, smiling with paternal pride. When he saw her tear-clouded eyes, his smile faded. "Arden?"

She smiled a watery smile. "I love you both so much. So very much. You're my world, my life, everything."

Drew's own eyes became embarrassingly misty. "God, I've waited days for you to tell me that again. I was beginning to wonder if you felt you had made a bad bargain."

She reached out and touched his chest, combing her fingers through the luxuriant golden hair. "No. I got far more than I bargained for."

"More than two can join this orgy of the flesh," he suggested gruffly.

It wasn't fair to him for her to make love with lies weighing heavily on her heart, but it might be the last time she would ever know his touch, his kiss, his earth-moving lovemaking. Demurely, she lowered her lashes, drawing her fingernails over his flat brown nipples. "I've always thought more than two at an orgy was too many."

"You're absolutely right. One of us has to go." He sprung upright as though hinged at the waist and came nose to nose with his son. "Guess who, pal." He carried the boy to the door, set him on his feet, smacked him on the seat and said, "Go find Mrs. Laani. I think you're a fugitive from bathtime, anyway."

Matt took off down the hall shouting, "Yawni, Yawni."

Drew locked the door behind him and hastened back to the bed. He wasted no time. He fell upon Arden, feasting hungrily on her mouth while his hands rid her of her robe and daringly explored.

Her fingers wound through his thick hair, holding his head still as she twisted her mouth under his for a better vantage point. She arched and writhed against his body, touching him in the places she'd learned he loved being touched, stroked, scratched. Her nipples beaded against his chest in their own caress. Her thighs parted to cradle his, and she strained toward him. He was full and throbbing with his need.

"God, I've missed you," he said frantically, as though she'd been away and had just come home. "I've wanted you like this, unbound by whatever it was that was upsetting you. Don't ever withdraw from me that way again, Arden. It scares the hell out of me. I can't lose you. I can't."

He rubbed her neck with his mouth, letting his teeth nip the delicate flesh. She moaned her consent to this gentle abuse, and when his lips closed over one flushed nipple, she told him in panted, disjointed phrases what heaven that was.

Her fingers glided down the ridges of his ribs, over his lean pelvic bones and into the dark golden thatch at the juncture of his thighs. She brushed him timidly, examined him, then ringed him with massaging fingers. She let him know her readiness, rubbing him against her body, moistening him.

"Sweet, sweet Arden." His sighs were music, love songs composed exclusively for her.

With one surging thrust, she arched up to drive him home. Hearts and bodies pulsed together. He stroked her long and leisurely, then quick and furiously, and she matched the pace he set, answering with responsive movements.

Despair was vanquished. He exorcised all of her devils and gave her his blessing, his love. This was her celebration of life before death, her swan song, the last wish granted to one doomed. She chanted his name and cried it softly when she felt his life stream bathing her womb.

She clung to him long after it was over, folding her legs across his back. She filed every sensation away in her mind for the time when she'd be without him. Greedy for his touch on her damp skin, his intoxicating smell in her nostrils, his hard fullness within her, she trapped him tighter in her velvet warmth.

His groan was one of pure animal pleasure. "Guess what?"

"What?"

He began to move again. "We're not finished yet."

"But… Drew…ahh…the time…?"

"We'll make… Oh, my love, yes…we'll make time."

"I NEED TO run a few errands," Arden said uneasily once she was showered and dressed and downstairs. Drew and Matt were eating a breakfast of Mrs. Laani's macadamia-nut muffins.

"Now?" Drew asked, brushing crumbs from Matt's mouth. "Don't you want to eat something?"

"No, no," she said hastily. "There are a few things I need to pick up before the trip."

"Well, don't get too carried away shopping. Remember our flight time. Are you already packed?"

"Yes, except for last-minute things."

She was almost out of the room when Drew called her back. "I almost forgot. You have mail." Drew got up and left the informal dining room.

Arden sat down beside Matt and ate the bite of muffin he offered her even though she didn't think she could swallow anything. Drew's lovemaking had been the sweetest, most fervent, most dear, she'd ever known. In her silent way, she'd said her goodbye to him. Now she scanned Matt's face, loving everything about him. Her fingers treasured each curl on his head. She touched him lovingly, wondering how she'd survive giving him up again.

"Here," Drew said, resuming his chair and pushing an envelope toward her. It was from the magazine that had published her first short story. Inside was a check for two thousand dollars.

"Oh!" she exclaimed, tears springing into her eyes. "I'd forgotten all about this." Unconsciously, she clutched the check to her breasts. Drew laughed.

"You sure look relieved to see it. Do you think I can't support you?"

"No, no," she stammered. Her heart was racing with exhilaration, but she couldn't let on too much. "Of course, I know you can support me. But last night you said...your business..."

His smile was the wide, brilliant one she loved.

"Darling, just because I said we'd be on a budget for a while, that doesn't mean you have to start living the life of a pauper. Did I give you that impression?" He patted her hand. "You spend that money in whatever way you see fit. It's yours. I'll handle the family finances."

On a sudden inspiration, she sat down and called for Mrs. Laani to bring her a cup of coffee. "I think I'll wait and do my shopping in L.A. or maybe San Francisco. I want to have breakfast with my husband and son."

Matt clapped his hands when his father leaned across the table and wrapped his mother in a warm embrace, sealing her mouth with a blazing kiss.

ARDEN LEFT THE house long enough to cash the check and make a withdrawal from her account. She sealed the five thousand dollars in a manila envelope and stopped at a pay telephone to call the Orchid Lounge. She asked to speak to Ron Lowery, purposefully leaving off any form of address.

"Where the hell are you? You're thirty minutes late."

"I'm not coming." She let him digest that for a moment before she continued. "The money will be in our mailbox when we leave. It's on the road that fronts the house and is plainly marked."

"What are you trying to pull? I said—"

"If you want your money, that's where you can find it. We're leaving for the airport about two-thirty. Goodbye, Ron."

"Wait a minute!" he shouted. "When do I get the next installment?"

"When we get back from our trip." She hung up the phone before he could say anything more. She had no doubt that he'd be there to take the money out of the mailbox. He was more terrified of the loan sharks he owed money to than she was of him.

As she sped home, she was glad that she'd been able to pay him off with her own money instead of having to ask Drew for it under false pretenses. That would mean one less lie. How she'd get the next five thousand, she didn't know. But she had bought another month of happiness.

DREW WATCHED FROM the bed as his wife fumbled with the clasp on her strand of pearls. The slender, well-manicured fingers, usually so deft, were trembling. The body that he loved, the lithe form that became so malleable to his loving touch in bed, was drawn as tight as a piano wire. It seemed that all one had to do was touch her and she'd snap in two.

Mrs. Laani had left their suite of rooms earlier with Matt. Drew had instructed her to keep him entertained for several hours. Now Drew came up off the bed where he'd been lounging with the morning newspaper and crossed to Arden.

He extricated the delicate gold clasp from her fingers and latched it easily. He watched her in the mirror. He saw that hated wariness, that fear, clouding her green eyes just as he had dreaded he would. It had bewildered him several weeks before. It bewildered him more so now. For the last few weeks, they had been happier than ever before.

He'd won all three tournaments. He was now seeded third in world tennis. Few remembered and even fewer remarked on the months he'd been off the circuit or the reasons for his temporary retirement. He'd proved

he could come back. He was a champion again. And
Arden had been there to celebrate each victory with
him. Now he could feel her withdrawing into that shell
he couldn't penetrate.

By God, he wasn't going to let her slip back into it
without a fight!

He caught her shoulders so she couldn't evade him.
"You're making far too much fuss over a medical examination, Arden."

"*You* are making too much of it," she snapped back.

"That's the prerogative of a worried husband. If the
shoe were on the other foot, you'd feel the same."

"I wouldn't badger you."

"Yes, you would."

Yes, she would, Arden admitted. But there was
nothing wrong with her! Nothing except that in a few
hours Drew would learn they could never have another child.

She put on her earrings. "I'm fine, Drew. Have I
seemed sick to you?"

"No," he answered honestly. Since the day they left
Hawaii, she'd been all a man could hope for in a wife,
a woman, a lover. Only in the last few days, when he'd
insisted that she see the doctor—two appointments
in Los Angeles had already been canceled—had she
started behaving in that guarded way again. And each
mention of home dropped a veil of discontent over her
features. Drew felt a sudden wrenching in his gut. Did
she suspect that something terrible was wrong with
her? Lumps? Pains? *My God, no.* Was there something she hadn't told him to keep him from worrying?

"Arden," he said, turning her to face him. His blue
eyes searched hers as though looking for signs of suf-

fering. "You're not… I mean, you don't hurt anywhere or anything, do you? Darling, if you suspect something is wrong, it's better to have it seen to. It's what you don't—"

She covered his mouth with her fingertips. "Shh." Her heart turned over when she realized the unnecessary worry she had caused him. "No. No, darling, no. I'm in perfect health."

His relief was visible. One arm slid around her waist and pulled her close. The other hand smoothed the glossy length of her hair. "You like our home on Maui, don't you, Arden?"

"Of course," she said earnestly, seeing the concerned furrow between his thick brows and hating herself for etching it there.

"Because each time we mention going home, you seem upset by the idea. If you don't like it there, we can leave. I bought that place as a refuge. I don't need it anymore. All I need is you. And Matt. With the two of you, I can live anywhere. It's difficult for some people to live in so remote a place—"

"But I'm not one of them. I loved your home the first time you took me there, and now it's *my* home. I could live there forever with you and Matt."

He crushed her to him, loving the feel of her compact body against his. He knew each curve, each hollow, each dainty bone intimately. He loved them all. Every time he touched her, naked or clothed, he was filled with strength. She had made him happier than he'd had any right to expect, and he couldn't bear to think that she wasn't completely happy with him.

"I love you, Arden. Have I told you that today?"

"I can't remember," she mumbled into his shirtfront.

Oh, God, he would feel so betrayed if he ever found out about Matt. It would kill him. "Just in case, tell me again."

His lips said it all as they came down on hers tenderly. His tongue roamed her mouth lazily as the pressure of his lips increased. The knuckles of his right hand lightly rubbed her nipple until he felt it flower beneath the ecru georgette blouse. The tip of his tongue touched hers suggestively, and he smiled when he heard her throaty purr. His other hand found the firm curve of her derriere and squeezed it gently, urging her forward and upward.

She pulled back in alarm. "Drew, you're getting—"

"Um-huh." He grinned wolfishly and started to pull her back.

"We can't. I'm not supposed to right before going to the doctor."

"Oh, hell," he ground out, burying his face in the fragrant hollow of her neck. "I forgot about that."

Then a brilliant idea occurred to her. She pressed close again and let her hand trail down his stomach to the fly of his trousers. "It probably wouldn't matter," she cooed, outlining his shape with a bold caress.

"No, you don't," he said, pushing her away. "I know what you're thinking, and it won't work." He made an agonized face as he turned away from her to pick up his sport jacket. "Get your purse. Let's go before I change my mind. Or lose it."

"ARE YOU SURE?" Arden stared at the doctor with wide, disbelieving eyes. Thank God Drew had agreed to let her see this doctor in San Francisco. The one Ham had made an appointment with would have known her as the ex-Mrs. Ron Lowery. This doctor was a stranger to her, but after what he'd just told her, she thought she might forever think of him as a friend. "Are you absolutely positive?"

The doctor chuckled. "I'm absolutely positive that there's no medical or physical reason why you can't have another baby. If you're asking me for a guarantee that you'll get pregnant, I'm afraid that's something I can't give you." He noted Arden's astonishment. "Where did you ever get the idea that you'd been sterilized?"

She licked her lips, trying at one and the same time to absorb the fact that she wasn't sterile and to tamp down a killing rage at Ron Lowery. This had been just another of his psychopathically cruel tricks. "I... I... uh...had an infection, and the doctor I was seeing at the time thought it had made me infertile."

The doctor looked puzzled. "I saw no remnants of any infection. You're a wonderfully healthy woman with a normal set of reproductive organs." Linking his fingers together on his desktop, he leaned toward her. "Are you happy with your husband? Do you love him?"

"Yes," she said fervently. She could actually feel the burden she had carried with her for over a month being lifted from her shoulders. "Yes," she repeated, breaking out in laughter.

"Then let's go tell him that you're as fine as a fiddle." At the door, he caught her arm. "Relax, Mrs. McCasslin. You'll have that other baby."

Arden was as impulsive and playful as a child as they drove the rented Lincoln back to the hotel. She virtually sat in Drew's lap, her left arm around his neck. Every chance she got, she stole a kiss from his lips.

While he negotiated the hilly streets of San Francisco, she contented herself with nibbling his neck, his ear.

"For God's sake, Arden, did that doctor give you a tonic, an aphrodisiac? You're driving me crazy."

"How crazy?" she breathed as her hand slid between his thighs. There she felt a good indication of how near he was to losing control.

"What did you and that doctor do to turn you on like this?"

"That's crude." She punished him with a gentle squeeze that almost made him swerve the car into another lane. "I'm turned on because I have the handsomest, smartest, sexiest..." She placed her lips against his ear. "And hardest husband in the whole world."

His curse testified to his agitation. "Okay, two can play this lusty game. Did you know that every time I look at your breasts, I'm ready to make love right then? Remember that cocktail party in San Diego after the tournament? You were wearing that yellow halter dress, and I knew you didn't have a bra under it. All the time I was making small talk to everyone, I was thinking about how I'd love to slide my hand inside your dress and touch your breasts."

"Drew," she groaned. Moving slightly closer, she pressed her breast against his arm. His sensual monologue was producing the desired effect.

"The other day when we met Ham for lunch on Fisherman's Wharf, you wore that peasant skirt with sandals and no stockings. I had watched you dress that morning. All you had on under your skirt was that pair of lilac panties with the lace panel in front. I couldn't think about anything else but the last time you'd worn them and I kissed you through that lace—"

"Stop," she cried, laying her head on his shoulder. "This is insane. We won't be able to walk through the lobby."

That was close to the truth. They were breathless with excitement by the time Drew latched the hotel door behind them with a *DO NOT DISTURB* sign dangling from the knob. He had already stripped off his coat and tie, his shoes and socks, before Arden stopped him.

"Wait. I want to." First, she eased out of her own clothes with the practiced, sinuous moves of a courtesan. The georgette blouse had an interminable number of tiny pearl buttons, and Drew's eyes were glazed with passion by the time she peeled it off her shoulders and down her arms. Her breasts thrust proudly beneath the lacy confinement of her brassiere. It came off with deliberate slowness. His eyes ravaged the warm mounds and coral nipples. She peeled off her half-slip and panty hose with one graceful movement, then stood before him wearing the panties he'd mentioned earlier.

His mouth curved with humor as he reached for his top shirt button. Staying his hand, she led him to the bed. She sat down on its edge and ran her fingers up his chest to the top button. Each one was released with meticulous precision. Her fingers took leisurely detours over the crinkly mat of hair, the firm bunched muscles, the smooth flesh, the masculine nipples.

"Arden, please," he begged on a shuddering breath. She took off his shirt, then met the fiery gaze he turned on her upraised face. "Let me love you."

"Let me love *you*." She worked free his belt buckle, the snap of his trousers, the zippered fly. Her eyes were still locked with his as she slid her hands beneath the tight briefs and cupped his taut buttocks. She smoothed her hands down, taking the garments with them. When he was free of them, she laid her cheek on him.

"I love you," she vowed in a soft whisper. Then her lips took him beyond paradise.

CHAPTER THIRTEEN

THE ORCHID LOUNGE was as murky, the clientele as unsavory, as before. A dozen or so men were grouped in pairs and trios. Their conversations were low and indistinct to the only woman in the place. The air was thick with the odor of beer and tobacco smoke.

Arden had never been more composed in her life.

The trip home from San Francisco had been nothing short of a party for them all. Drew was still euphoric over his success at the tournaments. He was no less glad over Arden's frame of mind since her visit to the doctor. Whatever had been worrying her seemed to have been resolved in that hour. His heart still flip-flopped, and his breath grew short each time he remembered the unselfish way she had loved him afterward. That whole afternoon had been given over to sexual indulgence. He would recommend such an afternoon to any married couple.

Arden, after having dreaded it, was now anxious to return home. She was basking in the glow of Drew's success and his love. During the long flight over the Pacific, she could barely keep her hands off him. She took advantage of every occasion to touch him and he responded in kind.

Matt sensed their lightheartedness and was at his most good-natured. He charmed all the flight attendants until Mrs. Laani pulled him into her lap and he fell asleep on her generous bosom. Arden could have been jealous, but Drew pulled her into his own arms for a little "nap." Numerous times, she had to covertly swat his hand when it crept into compromising territory.

The morning after their return, Ron telephoned.

"It's about time you answered. The first two times I called, I got your housekeeper and had to hang up."

"I'm sorry to have inconvenienced you."

"Cocky all of a sudden, aren't you?" He chuckled unpleasantly. "Don't forget your bills are due."

"Where and when?"

"The same place. Two o'clock."

She had hung up without another word. Now she was sitting in the same booth, and he was as late as before. She had disdained the bartender's ingratiating invitation to have a drink on the house. Instead, she sat with her back straight, her hands folded in her lap. And rather than ignore the stares this time, she met them with enough condescension to turn them away.

"Glad to be back?" Ron asked as he slid into the booth opposite her. "Good trip?"

"Yes, on both accounts."

"Your husband's making a name for himself. Does it make you proud to have such a famous hubby?"

"I'd be proud of him whether he was famous or not."

He placed his hand over his heart. "Such wifely devotion makes me thirsty." He called his order to the bartender, then turned back to her. "Wonder how proud he'd be of you if he knew you'd sold your body for fifty thousand dollars?"

"I don't know. But I intend to find out. I'm going to tell him everything."

Ron's eyes glittered in reptilian fashion as he stared at her. Even when his drink was set before him, he didn't move.

"You bastard," Arden said in a calm, emotionless voice. That tone conveyed her contempt more than shouting at him would have. He wasn't worth wasting the energy shouting would require. "I didn't know that any man, even one as low as you, could play a trick as dirty as the one you played on me."

His grin was insolent and obnoxious. "You found out I'd lied about sterilizing you." He began to laugh a low, rumbling laugh that could have passed for the devil's. "Scared you, didn't I?"

"Why did you tell me that?"

"Because you were getting too self-assured. You seemed to think you could shake me off like a bad dream. I wanted you to know that I meant business. I still do."

"Well, I'm terribly sorry to disappoint you, Ron, but our *business* dealings are over. Your threats are empty ones. If they weren't, you wouldn't be skulking around in dives like this and hanging up when I don't answer the telephone. You accused me of being a coward, but you are the coward. It takes a man to make it in the real world. And you never could. Even when you had all the advantages handed to you, you couldn't hack it as a doctor, as a husband, as a father, as a man."

She stood up with proud dignity. "You don't frighten me anymore. You've browbeaten and used me for the last time. There's nothing you can do to hurt me any longer. Go to hell."

She turned on her heel and walked out. Her knees were weak and her mouth dry by the time she reached the car. But she had done it! She had rid herself of Dr. Ron Lowery forever. That night, she'd tell Drew the entire story. She was no longer afraid that their love couldn't withstand the truth. Their lives were grafted together too securely to be torn apart now. She would make the setting perfect. She'd tell him everything. And then, at last, she'd be free.

THE BOTTLE OF wine almost slipped from under her arm as she maneuvered her way through the wide front door. "Mrs. Laani," she called, laughing. She clutched the bouquet of flowers, trying to keep them from being crushed against the box that contained her new negligee.

Mrs. Laani came rushing out from the back of the house, but the moment Arden saw her, she knew it wasn't her call that had brought the housekeeper running. "Mrs. McCasslin, I'm so glad you're home."

"Is something wrong?"

The housekeeper darted her eyes toward Drew's office. The door was closed. "Mr. McCasslin wants to see you right away. He said the moment you got back." The normally self-contained woman was wringing her hands.

"Why? What's—" Arden gripped Mrs. Laani's arm. "Matt? Has something happened to Matt?"

"No, he's with me in the kitchen. You'd better go to your husband." She wouldn't meet Arden's questioning eyes.

Arden's reflexes took over. She operated mechanically, acting as though nothing were wrong when indeed she knew something was terribly wrong. Mrs. Laani wasn't the kind to panic. "Chill the wine and arrange the flowers in a vase for our bedroom, please. We'll eat the steaks tonight. Please see that Matt's dinner is ready beforehand. And put this box in my closet."

"Yes, Mrs. McCasslin," Mrs. Laani said, relieving Arden of her packages and backing away from her. Arden was alarmed by the commiserating look on the woman's face.

She smoothed her hands over her skirt and was amazed to note that the palms were damp. Stifling her panic, she turned the knob and pushed her way through the door into Drew's office.

"Darling, I'm—" The first thing that caught her eye was the bottle of Scotch on the polished surface of Drew's desk. She stared at it for several seconds before her eyes wandered to the highball glass next to it. A white-knuckled hand was wrapped around the glass. Drew's hand. It wasn't until then that the incongruity of that struck her.

Her eyes flew up to meet his, and she flinched at the hatred she saw smoldering there. His hair was a wild blond tangle, and it wasn't simply windblown. It had been torn at with maniacal hands. The muscles of his jaw were working as he ground his teeth, and in his temple beat a furious pulse.

"Come in, Mrs. McCasslin," he said in a voice Arden had never heard. It dripped with sarcasm and repugnance. "I believe you know our guest."

For the first time, Arden noticed the man ensconced in the deep easy chair facing Drew's desk. He turned, and she met Ronald Lowery's mocking face. Her knees collapsing, she slumped against the door, clutching at it for support.

Drew laughed harshly. "You act surprised to see

your ex-husband when in fact Ron's told me that the two of you have been seeing a great deal of each other."

Bile rose into her throat, but she forced it back down. She must make Drew see the true situation. "Drew," she said, reaching out a beseeching hand. "Drew, what has he told you?"

"Quite a tale, quite a tale," he said with that same sneering laugh. "I thought I was the king of sinners. I certainly didn't think any form of human treachery would surprise me. I congratulate you on your ingeniousness."

"Drew, please," Arden said, advancing into the room. "Listen to me. I don't know what he's told you, but—"

"*Did* you let your husband impregnate you with my sperm, and *did* you carry my child for nine months, and then *did* you give him…or should I say *sell* him…for half the one hundred thousand dollars your husband charged me? *Did* you do all that?"

Tears streamed down her face. "Yes, but—"

"And then *did* you have a change of heart and come to Hawaii to worm your way into my confidence, into my life? *Did* you?"

"It wasn't—"

"Godammit, what a fool I've been." The chair went flying backward when he lunged out of it. He drained the glass of Scotch and then slammed it back onto the desktop. He turned his back on them as if they were too disgusting to look at.

"It wasn't like that," Arden said. "It *wasn't*."

Ignoring her pleas for understanding, he whirled around. "How much were you planning to bleed me for, huh?"

He was demanding that of her, not Ron. "Nothing."

"Nothing! Nothing? My money, my son? When was it going to be enough? You already had my life sewn up with your deceit."

She swallowed, trying to capture the thoughts that were darting through her head. She couldn't think with Drew scowling at her, his eyes as hard and cold as diamonds. "He contacted me several weeks ago. He said he'd tell you who I was if…" She quailed at his snarl but doggedly continued. "If I didn't give him twenty thousand dollars. He's a gambler and indebted to loan sharks. That's why he needed the money before, the money you paid him for Matt. I needed that money too, for Joey. And I wanted to be free of Ron." Distressed, she rubbed her forehead when Drew righted the chair and dropped down into it. His whole being reflected indifference to her dilemma. She must make him understand!

"I paid him five thousand dollars before we went to the mainland. It was my money, Drew, not yours. Mine. And I would have given him twice that to spare you this scene."

"So you would have gone on giving this scum money indefinitely to keep me from finding out what a deceitful bitch I'm married to. Your concern for my welfare overwhelms me."

She sobbed and shook her head. "No, Drew, no. I was going to tell you myself."

"When? When, Arden? I'd be interested to know. When Matt went off to grade school? When he graduated from college? Or when he was marching down the aisle with his bride, were you planning to tap me on the arm and say, 'Oh, by the way, I'm the woman who gave him birth.' Is that when you planned to tell me?"

The scornful words pounded against her skull like tiny mallets. "I couldn't live with the secret any longer. I love you and Matt. I was going to tell you…tonight."

He bellowed with laughter then, ugly, ridiculing laughter. "*Tonight!* Isn't that touching?" He stared up at her from under glowering brows. "Do you really think I'll believe that now, when you've lied to me from the very beginning?"

"I didn't lie!"

"This whole goddamned affair has been a lie!" he roared. Once again, he came out of the chair like a bullet. "When I think of how you duped me." He shook his head, laughing mirthlessly. "So prim and proper, so polite, so sympathetic, so—" He waved a hand toward her and then dropped it at his side in a gesture that stated how pathetic a creature he found her.

His attention returned to Ron, who was sitting like a vulture anticipating the bleeding carcass that would be left for him to finish off. "Get out," Drew said succinctly. The gloating smirk on Ron's face disappeared.

"Wait a minute. We haven't talked about how we're going to handle this."

"If you think I'll give you one goddamn cent, you're crazy as well as criminal. And if you don't get out of here now, I'm going to beat the bloody hell out of you, and then I'm going to turn you over to the police."

Ron stood, trembling with rage. "You'll sing a different tune when I tell the newspapers my titillating story about you and your pale wife and how you came to me asking to find a mother for your baby. That would make the son you hold so dear little more than a freak in a sideshow. To top that off, you're now married to the natural mother. Maybe I won't tell them that I artificially inseminated Arden. Maybe I'll let them think Matt came about in the natural way. That would make the kid a bastard."

Arden shivered, but Drew shrugged theatrically. "Who do you think is going to believe such a farfetched story? Especially from a doctor who has lost his practice, the respect of his peers, who is in debt to everyone in the world, including the Mafia, and is now living the life of a bum. Who do you think they'll believe? Me or you? Celebrities of my status are constantly the victims of crackpots out to make a quick buck, and the press knows that. They'll laugh in your face, Lowery."

Arden could see the confidence leaking out of Ron as freely as his sweat. "That lawyer. He's got papers. He'll back me up."

"Will he? If you were him, who would you back up? A world-famous tennis player who's on the rise or a derelict out for revenge on the wife who left him? Even your caliber of friend wouldn't be that stupid. If he were, I could pay him more to keep quiet than you could to talk."

Ron's face had gone the color of putty. Drew came around the desk. "I say once again, get out. And if you so much as show your face to any member of my family or household again, I'll have you locked up so tight that only your Mafia buddies can get to you. And you know what they'll do when they find you."

"You can't get rid of me so easy, McCasslin."

"Yes, I can, and you know it. That's why you stink of fear."

Ron looked at Arden, his gaze filled with hate. "At

least I ruined you, too. He despises you, just as I always did." He left the room. Moments later, she heard the front door opening and closing.

Minutes passed. There was no movement in the study. A deathlike pall hung over them. Drew stared out the window at the incessant motion of the ocean. Arden stared at his back, wondering how she could ever make him understand enough to forgive her. Why hadn't she told him? *Why?* If only she had it all to live over, she would tell him everything. She could imagine him taking her in his arms and whispering his understanding. "You did what you had to do at the time," he would say. "I can't fault you for that. I know you married me because you love me, not because you wanted to be with Matt. I know. I understand."

Instead, he was brittle with fury and wounded pride. She didn't recognize the face that turned to her now. "Are you still here? I thought maybe you would leave with your first husband to see what new adventure the two of you could embark upon."

She bowed her head. "It was never an adventure. I did it for Joey."

"So there really was a Joey? I was beginning to wonder."

Her head snapped up a moment before she lurched toward him angrily. "I did it to prolong his life. I did it because it was the only way I had to get out of an intolerable marriage with a man I loathed more every day. When you stop feeling sorry for yourself, maybe you can see your way clear to understand what it was like for me."

"Feeling sorry for myself!" he shouted. "I feel nothing but contempt for my blind stupidity. Every time I think about the callow way I watched you, how I carefully planned my approach like a jerk asking for his first dance, how I sat there talking to you with my pants near to bursting, I could retch. How did you manage to keep a straight face? I don't know why you didn't collapse with laughter."

"It wasn't like that, Drew," she protested urgently. "Initially, yes, I wanted to meet you because of Matt. *I wanted to see my son!*" she shouted. "Was that so wrong? But once I met you, I wanted you, too. Even more than I wanted Matt." That admission cost her dearly, but she knew it to be the truth.

"You wanted nothing but to seduce me."

"Seduce…" she began incredulously. "Have you lost your memory as well as your reason? If that's all it had taken, I'd have done that the first night."

"Oh, no, not you. You're too smart a schemer. If you'd taken me to bed right away, I might never have come back. No, you baited me with all that well-thought-out resistance. To a man who has women clustered around him all the time, that's the strongest turn-on of all."

"Yes, you could have had your pick of girls. They follow you in packs. So don't make me out as a temptress who snared you into a trap with the promise of sex that couldn't be had anywhere else." Her impatience with his bullheadedness was increasing and with it her volume. "You were a bonus I hadn't counted on. My objective was to become a trusted friend, not a lover. Then I fell in love with you and couldn't find the courage to tell you who I was for fear you'd act exactly as you're acting. Your pride, your fierce temper, makes you unreasonable, Drew."

Her breasts heaved with agitation beneath her silk sweater. He found himself staring at them and tore his eyes away, sending blistering curses toward the ceiling.

Even now, knowing what he did about her, she appealed to him as no other women ever had. She was so damned beautiful. He still wanted her. Vivid in his memory was the first time he'd seen her sitting under the umbrella of that patio table. Her serenity seemed to lure him. He'd wanted to be near her, to absorb that peace she seemed to exude. How could she have fooled him? Why hadn't he been able to see the calculation in her eyes? It must have been there no matter how much she denied it now. She'd plotted the whole thing long before he'd ever seen her. All right, yes, part of his anger was out of pride. But what man likes to find out that he's been manipulated like a puppet into loving and marrying a woman? What man with any pride could tolerate that?

He kept telling himself he hated her. Why then did he want to kiss her mindless, to empty his frustration, which was only a hair away from being desire, into her? Why did he still crave the succor of her body and the joy of her laugh and the balm of her love? He hated her most for the weakness she induced in him.

"I tried to tell you once," she said barely above a whisper. "And you said that any secrets about our pasts were better kept to ourselves. That if they didn't affect the way we loved each other, they were better left unspoken."

"I didn't know your little secret was of such magnitude, Arden." It was his superior tone, that arrogant drawl, that went down her spine like fingernails on a blackboard and brought her own temper to the surface.

"And what about *your* secret, Drew? You never told me that Matt was born not of Ellie, your beloved wife, but of a woman you wouldn't recognize if you met her on the street. You were willing to let me marry you without knowing that, weren't you?"

"What difference did it make?"

"None!" she yelled. "That's my point. I would love you and Matt just the same if I weren't his mother."

"Would you, Arden?"

The question had the impact of an explosion in the room. For seconds after it had been detonated, there was an intense silence.

"Yes, Drew," she said with soft intensity. "Yes."

He impaled her with his startling blue gaze. "But I'll never know for sure, will I? You sold your body to me once for the sake of a son. Isn't that what you've done again?"

She watched in helpless desperation as he went to the desk and picked up the bottle of Scotch. Going to the open window, he leaned forward and shattered the bottle on the outside wall of the house. He tossed the jagged bottle neck into the shrubbery.

"I sure as hell won't let you drive me back to *that*," he said. "I'm a winner again, and I won't let you or anyone take that away from me."

"YOU'RE MAKING A MISTAKE."

Arden turned from folding a blouse into her suitcase to see Mrs. Laani standing in the door of the master suite. She looked comfortingly domestic and normal with a dish towel slung over her shoulder. Arden longed to go to her, to lay her head on that maternal breast and let loose the tears that she thought should have been spent by now. She'd been crying for a week, ever since Drew left.

Without a word of goodbye to her, he'd left his office and packed quietly. The next thing she knew, he was striding across the lawn calling to Mo. "Drive me to the airport, please." He'd called three times since to check on Matt. He spoke with Mrs. Laani, never to her. He was in Los Angeles, ostensibly working with Ham on his serve and closing the final negotiations of their business deal.

"I don't think it's a mistake," Arden now said quietly, and turned back to the suitcase that lay opened on the bed.

She heard Mrs. Laani's shuffling footsteps as she came into the room. "He's a stubborn man, Mrs. McCasslin. Proud. I would have had to be deaf not to hear the argument the two of you had after that horrible man left. You're Matt's mother. I should have guessed."

Arden smiled. "It was easy to slip into the active role. Sometimes I thought my love would be so transparent that you...or Drew...would guess, but..." Her voice trailed off on a tremulous sigh.

"It was a shock to Mr. McCasslin, but when he thinks about it, he'll realize how irrational he's been."

"He's had a week to think about it. I don't know what he plans to do about us, but I can't just sit here like a convict awaiting execution. I'm the intruder. He was already playing competitive tennis before he met me. He and Matt have a close relationship. They don't need me interfering in their lives any more than I already have."

Mrs. Laani pulled herself erect and crossed her arms

over her stomach. "So you're going to play the martyr and sneak away like a coward."

Arden sat down on the bed and looked up at the woman's reproachful expression. "Try to understand this, Mrs. Laani. All my life I've been a coward. I did what my husband wanted me to do even when I knew it was wrong. Before that, my father took care of me, made my decisions for me."

She sighed and fiddled with the lacy hem of a slip she'd been folding. Drew liked its peachy color. He'd remarked on it every time she wore it. Once, jokingly, he'd pretended to take a bite out of her breast, chewing lustily. "The ripest fruit on the tree," he'd said, and they'd laughed together at his clowning. Would memories like that haunt her in the lonely years to come?

"The cowardly thing to do would be to stay and submit to Drew's scorn, to live with it, just like I lived with my former husband's. He actually hated me for the doormat I became. I can see that now. He contrived ways to humiliate me, perhaps in the hope that I'd show some backbone and say no to him just once."

"But Mr. McCasslin would never be like that," Mrs. Laani protested vehemently.

"No, he wouldn't be cruel. But year after year, I'd see his respect dwindling. Because I'd be so afraid of offending him again, I'd want to do everything he asked. I'd be tempted to cater to him for fear he'd throw my one major mistake in my face again and again. I'd feel forced to prove my love by never disagreeing with him. And very soon, he'd hate me. And I'd hate myself worse."

She looked back up at the housekeeper, whom she considered a friend. "I can't live like that again. If

Drew doesn't know by now how much I love him, then no amount of demonstration will convince him. I won't spend my life trying."

"But Matt." Mrs. Laani's eyes were filled with tears.

"Yes, Matt." Arden smiled gently with remembrance of the week they'd had together. She'd spent every waking hour with him. At night, she'd go into his room, sit in the bentwood rocker beside his baby bed and watch him as he slept. Her heart ached for what she must do. "Hopefully, Drew will let me see him periodically. I wouldn't be so unreasonable as to fight him for custody. This is the only life Matt knows. I couldn't uproot him from it." A tear rolled down her cheek. "It's just that he changes every day. Months will go by, and I won't see him, and I'll miss so many of those wonderful changes."

"Please change your mind." Mrs. Laani was weeping unashamedly now. Arden envied her the freedom to do so. "You love them both too much to leave."

"I love them too much not to," Arden responded quietly.

She explained the same thing to Matt later that night. He had long since fallen into the innocent sleep of a child.

"I don't know what your daddy will tell you about me. I hope someday you'll know who I am and that you'll forgive me for giving you up. I was trying to save your brother's life, Matt." A poignant smile flickered over her lips. "I wish you had known Joey. You would have liked each other." She wiped her cheeks of flowing tears.

"Your father is a competitor, Matt. He can't bear to lose without having fought an honest fight." She re-

membered the match against Gonzales. It had been a
defeat, but a defeat Drew hadn't minded because he'd
played hard and fair. Arden hadn't allowed him to play
fair. She'd cheated him of an honest game, because the
victory had been certain. He'd been a pawn and not a
participant. That was what he couldn't forgive.

"I love your father, Matt. And I don't want to leave
either of you. But it would be an unhealthy family environment for you to grow up in with him holding me
in contempt and me hating him for his intolerance.
Someday you may learn that love can't exist if one's
self-esteem is sacrificed to it. I can't be an object for
any man again, something that goes with the house,
something with no will, no opinion worth considering.
Please understand why I must leave."

She fingered the soft, butter-colored curls. She
traced his pudgy cheek to the drooling mouth. She
touched the dimpled knuckles of his fist.

"I had to give you up before, Matt. Then as now, it
wasn't because I didn't love you." She stood, groped
her way to the door and fumbled for the light switch.
She didn't look back before she plunged the room into
darkness, a darkness not nearly as absolute as the one
in her soul.

CHAPTER FOURTEEN

THE MOTEL ROOM was like an efficiency apartment. It was on the wrong side of Kalakaua Avenue if one wanted a view of Waikiki. The complex had seen better days. Now it was only an insignificant, inexpensive motel dwarfed and humbled by progress and modern architecture. It suited Arden's budget and needs, as good a place as any to idle away the long, lonely days.

She wasn't completely without occupation. She took long walks along the beach. She thought about Matt, wondered what he was doing, if he was missing her. And she thought about Drew, what he was doing, if he was missing her. She wrote. Thoughts and impressions that had no form filled tablet after tablet. She was seized by a compulsion to put her feelings on paper.

She was doing just that on the fourth day after leaving Maui. The muses had taken leave, for she had stared at the blank page for fifteen minutes. A shadow crossed the sheet of paper, and she looked up at the window to see Drew standing there.

For a small eternity, they stared at each other through the smudged window screen. Her mental faculties failed her. Stunned fingers let go of the pen. It dropped to the tabletop and rolled onto the cheaply carpeted floor. He didn't speak before he moved toward the door.

She had to persuade her muscles to move. Wobbly knees brought her to her feet. Self-consciously, she smoothed her hair and ran her palms over the old jeans covering her thighs. It was ridiculous, but she wished she had put on a bra that morning under the T-shirt she wore. Unreasonably, she felt vulnerable, unprotected; she would have felt more confident behind the lacy armor. She stepped to the door. He hadn't knocked, but she pulled it open.

His face looked so ravaged that at first she feared he'd been drinking abusively again. But despite the lines around them, his eyes were clear, and his marvelous athletic body was agile and lithe as he walked into the room. His hair was longer and shaggier than usual. He had on a pair of white shorts and a yellow polo shirt. To her, he'd never looked better. She ached with the need to touch him.

After one cursory glance around the stark room, he turned to her. "Hi."

"Hi."

"Are you all right?"

She looked down at the floor, then as quickly back up into his eyes, unable to keep from looking at him. "Yes." She could sense a tension about him as powerful as that which gripped her. He seemed to radiate a heat that her body responded to. Her breast filled with emotion. "You? Are you well? Matt?"

"I only returned to Maui this morning."

"Oh."

"I wasn't home long, but Matt seemed fine. Health-wise, that is. Mrs. Laani said he's been crying a lot lately." He seemed to find the palm tree outside the screened window captivating. He stared at it as he said, "He misses you."

She ducked her head. "I miss him, too." A pain like a laser beam shot through her heart. *And I miss you!*

"I...uh... I didn't know you had left until I got home." He coughed unnecessarily and cleared his throat. It sounded loud in the cramped room. "I flew back to Honolulu immediately."

She turned toward the window and gazed out. Her pulse was pounding so hard she could count each beat, and her hand trembled as she toyed with the draw cord of the tacky drapes. "How did you find me?"

"With a bag of quarters."

She turned her head. "Pardon?"

"I got a bag of quarters from the bank, found a pay phone and started dialing."

"Oh." She turned back to the window before allowing herself to smile. "I decided to stay in Hawaii until arrangements were made in Los Angeles. Since...since my trip over here was left deliberately open-ended, I gave up my apartment before I left. I'm waiting to hear from a friend. She's looking for a place for me."

"You're going back, then? Back to L.A., I mean?"

Was there anxiety underlying the question? She didn't dare look at him. What if that tremor in his voice indicated relief? "I suppose so, yes," she mumbled.

She heard him coming nearer. He stood in front of the table where she'd been working. The sheets of paper she'd discarded rustled under his hand. "You're writing?"

"Yes," she said huskily. He wasn't going to argue with her about the separation. He was going to let her go. He was condemning her to a sterile existence without color, without life. "I write when the mood strikes me," she said with forced casualness.

She heard more paper crackling in the brief pause that followed. "What mood were you in when you wrote this?"

In her peripheral vision, she saw a wrinkled piece of paper floating to the tabletop. Turning slowly, puzzled, she looked first at Drew. His eyes seared into hers, and she rapidly shifted her gaze to the sheet of paper he referred to.

She recognized her handwriting instantly. After reading the first line, she realized it was a poem she'd penned more than a month before. Like everything she wrote, she had dated it at the top of the page. They'd been in San Francisco. Mrs. Laani had taken Matt downstairs to the hotel's restaurant for his breakfast. They'd ordered theirs up from room service. After a leisurely breakfast in bed, they'd made even more leisurely love. When Drew left for his practice session, Arden had reached for a tablet and pen and, still languorous from their sweet lovemaking, she'd composed the poem.

It was a tribute to him, to what he meant to her. The last two lines were, "Where once your life transformed my body, / Your love now shapes my soul."

Tears blinded her and made the edited lines bleed together. "I think the mood is self-explanatory." She hazarded a glance up at him to find his own eyes shiny and wet.

"I found it crumpled in the corner of the suitcase yesterday."

"I'd forgotten what I did with it."

"I had decided days ago that I was the biggest heel

in history. You had every right to hate me for the things I'd said, not to mention my goddamned stubborn pride and short temper. I was going to beg you for your forgiveness, promise that I'd never consider you an opponent again. Finding this gave me the courage to come home and face you. I figured that if you felt this for me once, you might find it in your heart to feel it again."

"*You* were going to ask *my* forgiveness?"

"Yes. For behaving like a moron, a sore loser, a spoiled brat."

"But darling, your anger was justified. I tricked you into marrying me."

They had been inclining toward each other. Now he pulled her into his arms and crushed her against his body. He buried his face in the glossy mass of her hair. "You did no such thing. I married you because I love you. I wanted you for my wife. I still do. God, I almost died when Mrs. Laani told me you had left. Don't leave me, Arden."

"I didn't want to," she cried. "I only left because I thought you couldn't bear the sight of me." She pushed him away and peered up into his eyes. "But I can't live with judgment every day. I have to know you understand why I did what I did. Given the same set of circumstances, I'd make the same choice, Drew. I won't live the rest of my life being censured for it."

"Come here," he said gently, leading her to the bed. They sat down on the faded spread, and he took both her hands in his. "What you did wasn't wrong, Arden. Unorthodox, maybe, but not wrong. When Lowery told Ellie and me he had found a healthy young woman who was willing to have our child, in our minds, we placed her on a pedestal. The day Matt was born, we thought she was the most wonderful woman on the face of the earth."

Lovingly, he touched her face, her hair, as he talked. "Why I acted the way I did when I learned you were that woman, I can't explain. I guess I felt betrayed because you hadn't told me in the beginning that you were Matt's mother. It hurt that you hadn't trusted my love enough to tell me. What I should have done when I found out was what I'd felt like doing the first time I saw my son. I should have dropped to my knees and thanked you from the bottom of my heart."

"You don't think less of me because I sold my baby?"

He lifted tears from her cheeks with his fingertip. "I didn't think badly of you before I knew who you were. Why would I now? I know you did it to try to save Joey's life. If I thought I could save Matt such a fate, I'd make a bargain with the devil."

"I did."

He smiled wryly. "Having come to know your former husband better, I couldn't agree with you more. I can't believe that at one time I actually considered him a miracle worker."

"You're not afraid he'll make more trouble?"

"I don't think he will. He's a gutless bastard running scared."

"I should have realized that the first time he approached me on Maui. I was so afraid of what he might do. Kidnap Matt. Anything was possible."

"He's got more than us to worry about. But if he does bring on a crisis, I know I can face anything as long as I have you and Matt with me." He planted a tender kiss in her palm. "You will come home with me, won't you? And never leave?"

"Is that what you want?"

"It's what I wanted from the first time I saw you, touched you, kissed you." His mouth blended with hers as they fell back onto the bed. It was a sweet kiss, but rife with hunger. He sampled the texture and taste of her lips before breaching them with his tongue. He reclaimed her mouth with the gentle thrusts and lazy strokes that characterized his kisses. They sent desire curling around her breasts and weaving between her thighs. But the time wasn't right for them to give way to their physical needs, and Arden was gratified that Drew was sensitive enough to realize it, too.

Pushing her away gently, he sat up. His eyes darted around the room. "God, this is a depressing place. Let's go home."

MATT WAS ELATED over having such an appreciative audience. His parents sat on the living-room floor on the oriental rug and applauded his playful antics, which became wilder by the minute. He somersaulted and jigged and ran in circles until he toppled over backward and bumped his head on the leg of the grand piano and set up a howl.

"You'd better put him to bed before he gets any more wound up," Mrs. Laani cautioned. She'd been dabbing copious tears of happiness out of her eyes ever since Drew and Arden came through the front door, arm in arm, looking grubby but radiant.

"Okay, Bozo, you heard the voice of authority." To quell Matt's tears, Drew lifted him up to straddle his neck. His hands caught in his father's thick blond hair.

Arden placed her arm around Drew's waist as they ascended the stairs.

Arden decided that they had waited too late to calm Matt down. He was uncontrollable, bucking their attempts to snap him into pajamas. "Pee-pee," he kept repeating.

"Maybe it's not a false alarm," she said. Drew looked highly skeptical. He was wondering how many more delays were going to keep Arden and him from their own bed. His body was raging. He made his decision quickly.

Off came the pajamas, off came the bulky overnight diaper. Matt was carried into his bathroom and placed in front of the training potty. He did the deed, to his mother's overwhelming praise and his father's astonishment. Matt beamed up at them and submitted to their hugs and kisses of congratulations. Even Mrs. Laani was summoned to join the celebration. Such adoration was tiring. As soon as he was redressed for bed, Matt curled up into a ball and fell asleep, one chubby arm strangling Pooh Bear.

"We made a great kid," Drew whispered, his arm keeping Arden close.

"We certainly did," she concurred, snuggling against him. "Before I gave Ron the five thousand dollars, he told me he had sterilized me after I had Matt."

Drew's curse was vivid. "No wonder you walked around here like a zombie during those weeks."

She shivered, and he placed his other arm around her, as well. "That's why I protested so much over seeing a doctor. I didn't want you to find that out. I was already keeping one secret from you."

"It doesn't matter, Arden. We don't need any other child—"

"No," she cried softly, not wanting to disturb their sleeping son. "He was lying. He only told me that to terrorize me."

"That son of a bitch," he said viciously.

"That's why I was so relieved and happy after we left the doctor's office. Remember?"

His hand found her breast and fondled it lovingly. "I remember," he rasped.

"The doctor said there was no reason why I couldn't have as many children as we want."

He branded a kiss on her forehead. "I'll love them if we do. But it won't bother me if we don't. I'm going to be the top-seeded professional tennis player next year." She squeezed his waist to show him she fully agreed. "Then I can gracefully retire. I have a wonderful son. And I have a wife whom I love with all that I am. What more could I ask for?"

They gave the sleeping boy one final good-night kiss and left the room. The hallway yawned before them, and they were both suddenly self-conscious and nervous.

Drew looked down at her. "I can't help wanting to rush you into my bed again, but I know you like to be courted."

Her eyes took on a dreamy glow. "That was before I was married."

"And now?"

"Now I want to make love with my husband."

"I need to clean up."

"So do I."

"I'll use the bathroom downstairs. Fifteen minutes?"

She smiled, glad that he was going to leave her alone to prepare for him. "Or less."

She bathed and shampooed quickly, blew her hair dry, scented herself with perfume and moisturized her skin with lotion. The negligee she had brought home the day her world fell apart was still in its long, flat box. She shook out the transparent violet folds and slipped into it. Its sheer covering only enhanced her nakedness beneath.

She was reclining against the pillows when he came in, wearing only a terry-cloth wrapper around his loins. It rode low, just below his navel with its whorl of dark golden hair. She tracked the intriguing pattern of hair up a silky narrow strip to the spot where it fanned out over the broad expanse of his chest.

Locking his eyes with hers, he walked to the bed, unsnapped the wrapper and let it fall. Unashamed, she looked at him.

"That's pretty," he said of the new nightgown. His eyes traveled down the slender column of her throat to the curves of her breasts. Beneath the gossamer fabric, he could see her nipples. The material clung to her thighs and legs, outlining their shape. Her slender, high-arched feet were chastely crossed.

"Thank you," she answered.

"I like you in that color."

"I'll remember that. I like you in that color, too."

He flashed her a wide grin. "I need to work on my tan. It has paled in the last week." Leaning down, he slipped one finger into the V at her bosom and peeped inside. "Yours needs work, too."

The tantalizing touch of his finger near her nipple made her breath falter. Her breasts rose and fell against his finger, and her eyes took on that slumberous quality that made desire concentrate in his loins.

"Arden," he whispered. He lay down beside her facing the opposite way, resting his head on her thigh. "I love you. I've hated being separated from you. Let's never be apart again."

"Never," she vowed, running her fingers through his hair.

He parted the folds of her nightgown and laid his hard cheek against her silky skin. "You smell so good," he murmured. His kissed her navel, consummating his love for it with his tongue. "You had my son. Carried him...here." His lips glided over her abdomen as he flicked the responsive flesh with his tongue.

"Yes," she breathed. She turned her head into his warmth, pulled his scent into her body by taking deep breaths of it. His body hair felt good against her face, her lips. Her mouth encountered the deep dimple of his navel and explored it inquisitively.

"Oh, God, Arden." His fingers dug into her hair, pressing her head nearer.

"Each time I felt the baby move, I'd think about you." Her arm slid around his hip. "I wondered what you looked like, prayed that you'd be a good father to my child, imagined what I'd say to you if we ever met."

"I thought about you, too. I knew you were healthy, so I couldn't see you as overweight or too thin. But I was curious about what you looked like, your personality, your motivation for having a stranger's child. I wondered if you ever thought about me."

She smiled against the golden nest that surrounded his manhood. "Yes. I did." His whole body convulsed when first her lips, then the tip of her tongue, touched him. "Drew," she murmured, "when you…collected the…the…" She couldn't bring herself to ask, and she didn't want to speak of Ellie now. Not now. Not when his hand was closing over the curve of her derriere and drawing her toward his mouth.

"I was alone," he said, divining her thought. His breath stirred the dark down that sheltered her feminine mystery. "And had I met you before then, seen you, thoughts of you might have conflicted with thoughts of my wife." He planted an ardent, intimate kiss at the point of the triangle, using all his mouth.

The love play went on and on until desire was flowing through them like warm, thick honey. He turned to her, kneeling between her thighs and parting them lovingly and slowly. Just as tenderly, he draped her thighs over his and slid his hands under her hips, lifting her to him. His gaze fused with hers just as he sheathed himself in her.

Working his hands up her back in a sensuous massage, he brought her upward to face him. He sealed her mouth with his in a kiss that declared his eternal need for her. His hands stroked up her rib cage to her breasts. Touching them, he marveled over their lushness, their womanly heaviness. Then his thumbs lightly circled the love-swollen nipples.

"Drew, do what I never felt Matt do."

He understood. Lowering his head, he lifted her breast to his mouth. Her nipple was drawn between his lips with sweet tugging pressure. He suckled her gently, but with an urgency that continued to build. Responding to it, her body milked him, contracting and releasing him until their passions reached a summit. When the crisis was imminent, he gently lowered her to her back and followed her down. With one final surge, he imbedded himself deep within her and gave her all his love.

The earth swirled around them, timelessly, directionless, in uncharted chaos. They didn't mind. They had created their own private universe in each other. Jealously, they guarded it. It was a long time before they returned to a world more mundane and less splendored.

"Arden, I love you." He braced himself above her and gazed down at her replete body with unqualified love.

"I love you. From the first. Irrevocably."

"Tell me everything. From the beginning. Fill me in on all the details I don't know, no matter how insignificant. I want to know how you felt when you learned you had conceived. What did you think and feel when you discovered I was the man who had fathered your child? How did you find out about me? Let me experience it all with you."

Painstakingly, she began, leaving out nothing, neither the heartache nor the joy. Her quiet voice drifted on the cool ocean breeze that wafted through the open windows and caressed their entwined naked bodies.

Loving lips frequently got in the way and promised that the best chapters of their life together were yet to unfold.

* * * * *

her to her back and followed her down. With one final
surge, he unleashed himself deep within her and gave
her all his love.

The earth revolved around them, timeless, direc-